ON THE ROAD

Jack Kerouac was the descendant of Breton Cana-
dians who married with Mohawk and Caughnawaga
Indians. He was born in Lowell, Massachusetts, where,
he said, he 'roamed fields and riverbanks by day and
night, wrote little novels in my room, first novel
written at age eleven, also kept extensive diaries and
"newspapers" covering my own-invented horseracing
and baseball and football worlds (as recorded in novel
Doctor Sax)'. He was educated by Jesuit brothers in
Lowell. He said that he 'decided to become a writer at
age seventeen under influence of Sebastian Sampas,
local young poet, who later died on Anzio beach head;
read the life of Jack London at eighteen and decided
to also be a lonesome traveller; early literary influences
Saroyan and Hemingway; later Wolfe (after I had
broken leg in Freshman football at Columbia read Tom
Wolfe and roamed his New York on crutches)'.

Kerouac wished, however, to develop his own new
prose style, which he called 'spontaneous prose'. In it
he recorded the life of the American 'traveller', and the
experience of the beat generation of the 1950s. This
may clearly be seen in his most famous novel, *On the
Road*, and also in *The Subterraneans* and *The Dharma
Bums*. Other works include *Big Sur*, *Desolation Angels*,
Lonesome Traveller, *Visions of Gerard*, *Tristessa*, and
a book of poetry called *Mexican City Blues*. His first
more orthodox published novel was *The Town and
the City*. Jack Kerouac, who described himself as a
'strange solitary crazy Catholic mystic', was working
on his longest novel, a surrealistic study of the last
ten years of his life, when he died in 1969, aged
forty-seven.

'. . . that is the meaning of *On The Road*. What does its narrator, Sal Paradise, say? ". . . The only people for me are the mad ones, the ones who are mad to live, mad to talk, mad to be saved, desirous of everything at the same time, the ones who never yawn or say a commonplace thing, but burn, burn, burn like fabulous yellow roman candles . . ."

'And what does Dean Moriarty, Sal's American hero-saint say? "And of course no one can tell us that there is no God. We've passed through all forms. . . . Everything is fine, God exists without qualms. As we roll along this way I am positive beyond doubt that everything will be taken care of for us – that even you, as you drive, fearful of the wheel . . . the thing will go along of itself and you won't go off the road and I can sleep."

'This search for affirmation takes Sal on the road to Denver and San Francisco; Los Angeles and Texas and Mexico; sometimes with Dean, sometimes without; sometimes in the company of other beat individuals whose tics vary, but whose search is very much the same (not infrequently ending in death or derangement; the search for belief is very likely the most violent known to man).

'There are sections of *On The Road* in which the writing is of a beauty almost breathtaking. There is a description of a cross-country automobile ride fully the equal, for example, of the train ride told by Thomas Wolfe in *Of Time and the River*. There are details of a trip to Mexico (and an interlude in a Mexican bordello) that are, by turns, awesome, tender and funny. And, finally, there is some writing on jazz that has never been equalled in American fiction, either for insight, style, or technical virtuosity. *On The Road* is a major novel!'

New York Times

JACK KEROUAC

ON THE ROAD

PENGUIN BOOKS

Penguin Books Ltd, Harmondsworth, Middlesex, England
Penguin Books Australia Ltd, Ringwood, Victoria, Australia

—

First published in the U.S.A. 1957
Published in Great Britain by André Deutsch 1958
Published in Penguin Books 1972
Reprinted 1972 (twice)
Copyright © Jack Kerouac 1955, 1957

—

Made and printed in Great Britain
by Hazell Watson & Viney Ltd
Aylesbury, Bucks
Set in Linotype Pilgrim

PART ONE

I

I FIRST met Dean not long after my wife and I split up. I had just gotten over a serious illness that I won't bother to talk about, except that it had something to do with the miserably weary split-up and my feeling that everything was dead. With the coming of Dean Moriarty began the part of my life you could call my life on the road. Before that I'd often dreamed of going West to see the country, always vaguely planning and never taking off. Dean is the perfect guy for the road because he actually was born on the road, when his parents were passing through Salt Lake City in 1926, in a jalopy, on their way to Los Angeles. First reports of him came to me through Chad King, who'd shown me a few letters from him written in a New Mexico reform school. I was tremendously interested in the letters because they so naïvely and sweetly asked Chad to teach him all about Nietzsche and all the wonderfully intellectual things that Chad knew. At one point Carlo and I talked about the letters and wondered if we would ever meet the strange Dean Moriarty. This is all far back, when Dean was not the way he is today, when he was a young jailkid shrouded in mystery. Then news came that Dean was out of reform school and was coming to New York for the first time; also there was talk that he had just married a girl called Marylou.

One day I was hanging around the campus and Chad and Tim Gray told me Dean was staying in a cold-water pad in East Harlem, the Spanish Harlem. Dean had arrived the night before, the first time in New York, with his beautiful little sharp chick Marylou; they got off the Greyhound bus at 50th Street and cut around the corner looking for a place to eat and went right in Hector's, and since then Hector's cafeteria has always been a

7

big symbol of New York for Dean. They spent money on beautiful big glazed cakes and creampuffs.

All this time Dean was telling Marylou things like this : 'Now, darling, here we are in New York and although I haven't quite told you everything that I was thinking about when we crossed Missouri and especially at the point when we passed the Booneville reformatory which reminded me of my jail problem, it is absolutely necessary now to postpone all those leftover things concerning our personal lovethings and at once begin thinking of specific worklife plans ...' and so on in the way that he had in those early days.

I went to the cold-water flat with the boys, and Dean came to the door in his shorts. Marylou was jumping off the couch; Dean had dispatched the occupant of the apartment to the kitchen, probably to make coffee, while he proceeded with his loveproblems, for to him sex was the one and only holy and important thing in life, although he had to sweat and curse to make a living and so on. You saw that in the way he stood bobbing his head, always looking down, nodding, like a young boxer to instructions, to make you think he was listening to every word, throwing in a thousand 'Yeses' and 'That's rights'. My first impression of Dean was of a young Gene Autry – trim, thin-hipped, blue-eyed, with a real Oklahoma accent – a sideburned hero of the snowy West. In fact he'd just been working on a ranch, Ed Wall's in Colorado, before marrying Marylou and coming East. Marylou was a pretty blonde with immense ringlets of hair like a sea of golden tresses; she sat there on the edge of the couch with her hands hanging in her lap and her smoky blue country eyes fixed in a wide stare because she was in an evil grey New York pad that she'd heard about back West, and waiting like a longbodied emaciated Modigliani surrealist woman in a serious room. But, outside of being a sweet little girl, she was awfully dumb and capable of doing horrible things. That night we all drank beer and pulled wrists and talked till dawn, and in the morning, while we sat around dumbly smoking butts from ashtrays in the grey light of a gloomy day, Dean got up nervously, paced around, thinking, and decided the thing to do was to have Marylou make breakfast and sweep the floor. 'In other words we've got to get on the ball, darling,

8

what I'm saying, otherwise it'll be fluctuating and lack of true knowledge or crysallization of our plans.' Then I went away.

During the following week he confided in Chad King that he absolutely had to learn how to write from him; Chad said I was a writer and he should come to me for advice. Meanwhile Dean had gotten a job in a parking lot, had a fight with Marylou in their Hoboken apartment – God knows why they went there – and she was so mad and so down deep vindictive that she reported to the police some false trumped-up hysterical crazy charge, and Dean had to lam from Hoboken. So he had no place to live. He came right out to Paterson, New Jersey, where I was living with my aunt, and one night while I was studying there was a knock on the door, and there was Dean, bowing, shuffling obsequiously in the dark of the hall, and saying, 'Hel-lo, you remember me – Dean Moriarty? I've come to ask you to show me how to write.'

'And where's Marylou?' I asked, and Dean said she'd apparently whored a few dollars together and gone back to Denver – 'the whore!' So we went out to have a few beers because we couldn't talk like we wanted to talk in front of my aunt, who sat in the living room reading her paper. She took one look at Dean and decided that he was a madman.

In the bar I told Dean, 'Hell, man, I know very well you didn't come to me only to want to become a writer, and after all what do I really know about it except you've got to stick to it with the energy of a benny addict.' And he said, 'Yes, of course, I know exactly what you mean and in fact all those problems have occurred to me, but the thing that I want is the realization of those factors that should one depend on Schopenhauer's dichotomy for any inwardly realized ...' and so on in that way, things I understood not a bit and he himself didn't. In those days he really didn't know what he was talking about; that is to say, he was a young jailkid all hung-up on the wonderful possibilities of becoming a real intellectual, and he liked to talk in the tone and using the words, but in a jumbled way, that he had heard from 'real intellectuals' – although, mind you, he wasn't so naïve as that in all other things, and it took him just a few months with Carlo Marx to become completely *in there* with all the terms and jargon. Nonetheless we understood each other on other levels of madness, and I agreed that he could stay at my house till he found a job and furthermore we agreed to go out West sometime. That was the winter of 1947.

One night when Dean ate supper at my house – he already had the parking-lot job in New York – he leaned over my shoulder as I typed rapidly away and said, 'Come on, man, those girls won't wait, make it fast.'

I said, 'Hold on just a minute, I'll be right with you as soon as I finish this chapter', and it was one of the best chapters in the book. Then I dressed and off we flew to New York to meet some girls. As we rode in the bus in the weird phosphorescent void of the Lincoln Tunnel we leaned on each other with fingers waving and yelled and talked excitedly, and I was beginning to get the bug like Dean. He was simply a youth tremendously excited with life, and though he was a con-man, he was only conning because he wanted so much to live and to get involved with people who would otherwise pay no attention to him. He was conning me and I knew it (for room and board and 'how-to write', etc.), and he knew I knew (this has been the basis of our relationship), but I didn't care and we got along fine – no pestering, no catering; we tiptoed around each other like heart-breaking new friends. I began to learn from him as much as he probably learned from me. As far as my work was concerned he said, 'Go ahead, everything you do is great.' He watched over my shoulder as I wrote stories, yelling, 'Yes! That's right! Wow! Man!' and 'Phew!' and wiped his face with his hand-kerchief. 'Man, wow, there's so many things to do, so many things to write! How to even *begin* to get it all down and without modified restraints and all hung-up on like literary inhibitions and grammatical fears ...'

'That's right, man, now you're talking.' And a kind of holy lightning I saw flashing from his excitement and his visions, which he described so torrentially that people in buses looked around to see the 'overexcited nut'. In the West he'd spent a third of his time in the poolhall, a third in jail, and a third in the public library. They'd seen him rushing eagerly down the winter streets, bareheaded, carrying books to the poolhall, or climbing trees to get into the attics of buddies where he spent days reading or hiding from the law.

We went to New York – I forget what the situation was, two coloured girls – there were no girls there; they were supposed to meet him in a diner and didn't show up. We went to his parking lot where he had a few things to do – change his clothes in the shack in back and spruce up a bit in front of a cracked mirror and so on, and then we took off. And that was the night Dean met Carlo Marx. A tremendous thing happened when Dean met Carlo Marx. Two keen minds that they are, they took to each other at the drop of a hat. Two piercing eyes glanced into two piercing eyes – the holy con-man with the shining mind, and the sorrowful poetic con-man with the dark mind that is Carlo Marx. From that moment on I saw very little of Dean, and I was a little sorry too. Their energies met head-on, I was a lout compared, I couldn't keep up with them. The whole mad swirl of everything that was to come began then; it would mix up all my friends and all I had left of my family in a big dust cloud over the American Night. Carlo told him of Old Bull Lee, Elmer Hassel, Jane: Lee in Texas growing weed, Hassel on Riker's Island, Jane wandering on Times Square in a benzedrine hallucination, with her baby girl in her arms and ending up in Bellevue. And Dean told Carlo of unknown people in the West like Tommy Snark, the clubfooted poolhall rotation shark and cardplayer and queer saint. He told him of Roy Johnson, Big Ed Dunkel, his boyhood buddies, his street buddies, his innumerable girls and sex-parties and pornographic pictures, his heroes, heroines, adventures. They rushed down the street together, digging everything in the early way they had, which later became so much sadder and perceptive and blank. But then they danced down the streets like dingledodies, and I shambled after as I've been doing all my life after people who interest me, because the only people for me are the mad ones, the ones who are mad to live, mad to talk, mad to be saved, desirous of everything at the same time, the ones who never yawn or say a commonplace thing, but burn, burn, burn like fabulous yellow roman candles exploding like spiders across the stars and in the middle you see the blue centrelight pop and everybody goes 'Awww!' What did they call such young people in Goethe's Germany? Wanting dearly to learn how to write like Carlo, the first thing you know, Dean was attacking him with a great amorous soul such as only a con-man can have. 'Now, Carlo, let *me* speak – here's what *I'm* saying . . .' I didn't see them for about two weeks, during which time they cemented their relationship to fiendish allday-allnight-talk proportions.

Then came spring, the great time of travelling, and everybody in the scattered gang was getting ready to take one trip or another. I was busily at work on my novel and when I came to the halfway mark, after a trip down South with my aunt to visit my brother Rocco, I got ready to travel West for the very first time.

Dean had already left. Carlo and I saw him off at the 34th Street Greyhound station. Upstairs they had a place where you could make pictures for a quarter. Carlo took off his glasses and looked sinister. Dean made a profile shot and looked coyly around. I took a straight picture that made me look like a thirty-year-old Italian who'd kill anybody who said anything against his mother. This picture Carlo and Dean neatly cut down the middle with a razor and saved a half each in their wallets. Dean was wearing a real Western business suit for his big trip back to Denver; he'd finished his first fling in New York. I say fling, but he only worked like a dog in parking lots. The most fantastic parking-lot attendant in the world, he can back a car forty miles an hour into a tight squeeze and stop at the wall, jump out, race among fenders, leap into another car, circle it fifty miles an hour in a narrow space, back swiftly into tight spot, *hump*, snap the car with the emergency so that you see it bounce as he flies out; then clear to the ticket shack, sprinting like a track star, hand a ticket, leap into a newly arrived car before the owner's half out, leap literally under him as he steps out, start the car with the door flapping, and roar off to the next available spot, arc, pop in, brake, out, run; working like that without pause eight hours a night, evening rush hours and after-theatre rush hours, in greasy wino pants with a frayed fur-lined jacket and beat shoes that flap. Now he'd bought a new suit to go back in; blue with pencil stripes, vest and all – eleven dollars on Third Avenue, with a watch and watch chain, and a portable typewriter with which he was going to start writing in a Denver rooming house as soon as he got a job there. We had a farewell meal of franks and beans in a Seventh Avenue

Riker's, and then Dean got on the bus that said Chicago and roared off into the night. There went our wrangler. I promised myself to go the same way when spring really bloomed and opened up the land.

And this was really the way that my whole road experience began, and the things that were to come are too fantastic not to tell.

Yes, and it wasn't only because I was a writer and needed new experiences that I wanted to know Dean more, and because my life hanging around the campus had reached the completion of its cycle and was stultified, but because, somehow, in spite of our difference in character, he reminded me of some long-lost brother; the sight of his suffering bony face with the long side-burns and his straining muscular sweating neck made me re-member my boyhood in those dye-dumps and swim-holes and riversides of Paterson and the Passaic. His dirty workclothes clung to him so gracefully, as though you couldn't buy a better fit from a custom tailor but only earn it from the Natural Tailor of Natural Joy, as Dean had, in his stresses. And in his excited way of speaking I heard again the voices of old companions and brothers under the bridge, among the motorcycles, along the wash-lined neighbourhood and drowsy doorsteps of afternoon where boys played guitars while their older brothers worked in the mills. All my other current friends were 'intellectuals' – Chad the Nietzschean anthropologist, Carlo Marx and his nutty surrealist low-voiced serious staring talk, Old Bull Lee and his critical anti-everything drawl – or else they were slinking criminals like Elmer Hassel, with that hip sneer; Jane Lee the same, sprawled on the Oriental cover of her couch, sniffing at the *New Yorker*. But Dean's intelligence was every bit as formal and shining and complete, without the tedious intellectualness. And his 'criminality' was not something that sulked and sneered; it was a wild yea-saying overburst of American joy; it was Western, the west wind, an ode from the Plains, something new, long prophesied, long a-coming (he only stole cars for joy rides). Besides, all my New York friends were in the negative, nightmare position of putting down society and giving their tired bookish or political or psychoanalytical reasons, but Dean just raced in society, eager for bread and love; he didn't care one way or the other, 'so long's I can get that lil ole gal with that lil sumpin down there tween her legs, boy', and 'so long's we can *eat*, son, y'ear me? I'm *hungry*, I'm *starving*, yet's *eat right now!*' – and off we'd rush to *eat*, whereof, as saith Ecclesiastes, 'It is your portion under the sun.'

A western kinsman of the sun, Dean. Although my aunt warned me that he would get me in trouble, I could hear a new call and see a new horizon, and believe it at my young age; and a little bit of trouble or even Dean's eventual rejection of me as a buddy, putting me down, as he would later, on starving sidewalks and sickbeds – what did it matter? I was a young writer and I wanted to take off.

Somewhere along the line I knew there'd be girls, visions, everything; somewhere along the line the pearl would be handed to me.

2

IN the month of July 1947, having saved about fifty dollars from old veteran benefits, I was ready to go to the West Coast. My friend Remi Boncœur had written me a letter from San Francisco, saying I should come and ship out with him on an around-the-world liner. He swore he could get me into the engine room. I wrote back and said I'd be satisfied with any old freighter so long as I could take a few long Pacific trips and come back with enough money to support myself in my aunt's house while I finished my book. He said he had a shack in Mill City and I would have all the time in the world to write there while we went through the rigmarole of getting the ship. He was living with a girl called Lee Ann; he said she was a marvellous cook and everything would jump. Remi was an old prepschool friend, a Frenchman brought up in Paris and a really mad guy – I didn't know how mad at this time. So he expected me to arrive in ten days. My aunt was all in accord with my trip to the West; she said it would do me good, I'd been working so hard all winter and staying in too much; she even didn't complain when I told her I'd have to hitchike some. All she wanted was for me to come back in one piece. So, leaving my big half-manuscript sitting on top of my desk, and folding back my comfortable home sheets for the last time one morning, I left with my canvas bag in which a few fundamental things were packed and took off for the Pacific Ocean with the fifty dollars in my pocket.

I'd been poring over maps of the United States in Paterson for months, even reading books about the pioneers and savouring names like Platte and Cimarron and so on, and on the road-map was one long red line called Route 6 that led from the tip of Cape Cod clear to Ely, Nevada, and there dipped down to Los Angeles. I'll just stay on 6 all the way to Ely, I said to myself and confidently started. To get to 6 I had to go up to Bear Mountain. Filled with dreams of what I'd do in Chicago, in Denver, and then finally in San Fran, I took the Seventh Avenue subway to the end of the line at 242nd Street, and there took a trolley into Yonkers; in downtown Yonkers I transferred to an outgoing trolley and went to the city limits on the east bank of the Hudson River. If you drop a rose in the Hudson River at its mysterious source in the Adirondacks, think of all the places it journeys by as it goes out to sea forever – think of that wonderful Hudson Valley. I started hitching up the thing. Five scattered rides took me to the desired Bear Mountain Bridge, where Route 6 arched in from New England. It began to rain in torrents when I was let off there. It was mountainous. Route 6 came over the river, wound around a traffic circle, and disappeared into the wilderness. Not only was there no traffic but the rain came down in buckets and I had no shelter. I had to run under some pines to take cover; this did no good; I began crying and swearing and socking myself on the head for being such a damn fool. I was forty miles north of New York; all the way up I'd been worried about the fact that on this, my big opening day, I was only moving north instead of the so-longed-for west. Now I was stuck on my northernmost hangup. I ran a quarter-mile to an abandoned cute English-style filling station and stood under the dripping eaves. High up over my head the great hairy Bear Mountain sent down thunderclaps that put the fear of God in me. All I could see were smoky trees and dismal wilderness rising to the skies. 'What the hell am I doing up here?' I cursed, I cried for Chicago. 'Even now they're all having a big time, they're doing this, I'm not there, when will I get there!' – and so on. Finally a car stopped at the empty filling station; the man and the two women in it wanted to study a map. I stepped right up and gestured in the rain; they consulted; I looked like a maniac, of course, with my hair all wet, my shoes sopping. My shoes, damn fool that I am, were Mexican huaraches, plantlike sieves not fit for the rainy night of America and the raw road night. But the people let me in and rode me *back* to Newburgh, which I accepted as a better alternative than being trapped in the Bear Mountain wilderness all night. 'Besides,' said the man, 'there's no traffic passes through 6. If you want to go to Chicago you'd do better going across the Holland Tunnel in New York and head for Pittsburgh', and I knew he was right. It was my dream that screwed up, the stupid hearthside idea that it would be wonderful to follow one great red line across America instead of trying various roads and routes.

In Newburgh it had stopped raining. I walked down to the river, and I had to ride back to New York in a bus with a delegation of schoolteachers coming back from a weekend in the mountains – chatter-chatter blah-blah, and me swearing for all the time and the money I'd wasted, and telling myself, I wanted to go west and here I've been all day and into the night going up and down, north and south, like something that can't get started. And I swore I'd be in Chicago tomorrow, and made sure of that, taking a bus to Chicago, spending most of my money, and didn't give a damn, just as long as I'd be in Chicago tomorrow.

3

IT WAS an ordinary bus trip with crying babies and hot sun, and countryfolk getting on at one Penn town after another, till we got on the plain of Ohio and really rolled, up by Ashtabula and straight across Indiana in the night. I arrived in Chi quite early in the morning, got a room in the Y, and went to bed with a very few dollars in my pocket. I dug Chicago after a good day's sleep.

The wind from Lake Michigan, bop at the Loop, long walks around South Halsted and North Clark, and one long walk after midnight into the jungles, where a cruising car followed me as a suspicious character. At this time, 1947, bop was going like mad all over America. The fellows at the Loop blew, but with a tired air, because bop was somewhere between its Charlie Parker Ornithology period and another period that began with Miles Davis. And as I sat there listening to that sound of the night which bop has come to represent for all of us, I thought of all my friends from one end of the country to the other and how they were really all in the same vast backyard doing something so frantic and rushing-about. And for the first time in my life, the following afternoon, I went into the West. It was a warm and beautiful day for hitchhiking. To get out of the impossible complexities of Chicago traffic I took a bus to Joliet, Illinois, went by the Joliet pen, stationed myself just outside town after a walk through its leafy rickety streets behind, and pointed my way. All the way from New York to Joliet by bus, and I had spent more than half my money.

My first ride was a dynamite truck with a red flag, about thirty miles into great green Illinois, the truckdriver pointing out the place where Route 6, which we were on, intersects Route 66 before they both shoot west for incredible distances. Along about three in the afternoon, after an apple pie and ice cream in a roadside stand, a woman stopped for me in a little coupe. I had a twinge of hard joy as I ran after the car. But she was a middle-aged woman, actually the mother of sons my age, and wanted somebody to help her drive to Iowa. I was all for it. Iowa! Not so far from Denver, and once I got to Denver I could relax. She drove the first few hours, at one point insisted on visiting an old church somewhere, as if we were tourists, and then I took over the wheel and, though I'm not much of a driver, drove clear through the rest of Illinois to Davenport, Iowa, via Rock Island. And here for the first time in my life I saw my beloved Mississippi River, dry in the summer haze, low water, with its big rank smell that smells like the raw body of

America itself because it washes it up. Rock Island – railroad tracks, shacks, small downtown section; and over the bridge to Davenport, same kind of town, all smelling of sawdust in the warm midwest sun. Here the lady had to go on to her Iowa hometown by another route, and I got out.

The sun was going down. I walked, after a few cold beers, to the edge of town, and it was a long walk. All the men were driving home from work, wearing railroad hats, baseball hats, all kinds of hats, just like after work in any town anywhere. One of them gave me a ride up the hill and left me at a lonely crossroads on the edge of the prairie. It was beautiful there. The only cars that came by were farmer-cars; they gave me suspicious looks, they clanked along, the cows were coming home. Not a truck. A few cars zipped by. A hotrod kid came by with his scarf flying. The sun went all the way down and I was standing in the purple darkness. Now I was scared. There weren't even any lights in the Iowa countryside; in a minute nobody would be able to see me. Luckily a man going back to Davenport gave me a lift downtown. But I was right where I started from.

I went to sit in the bus station and think this over. I ate another apple pie and ice cream; that's practically all I ate all the way across the country, I knew it was nutritious and it was delicious, of course. I decided to gamble. I took a bus in downtown Davenport, after spending a half-hour watching a waitress in the bus-station café, and rode to the city limits, but this time near the gas stations. Here the big trucks roared, wham, and inside two minutes one of them cranked to a stop for me. I ran for it with my soul whoopeeing. And what a driver – a great big tough truckdriver with popping eyes and a hoarse raspy voice who just slammed and kicked at everything and got his rig under way and paid hardly any attention to me. So I could rest my tired soul a little, for one of the biggest troubles hitchhiking is having to talk to innumerable people, make them feel that they didn't make a mistake picking you up, even entertain them almost, all of which is a great strain when you're going all the way and don't plan to sleep in hotels. The guy just yelled above the roar, and all I had to do was yell back, and we relaxed. And he balled that thing clear to Iowa City and yelled me the funniest stories about how he got around the law in every town that had an unfair speed limit, saying over and over again, 'Them goddam cops can't put no flies on *my* ass!' Just as we rolled into Iowa City he saw another truck coming behind us, and because he had to turn off at Iowa City he blinked his tail lights at the other guy and slowed down for me to jump out, which I did with my bag, and the other truck, acknowledging this exchange, stopped for me, and once again, in the twink of nothing, I was in another big high cab, all set to go hundreds of miles across the night, and was I happy! And the new truck-driver was as crazy as the other and yelled just as much, and all I had to do was lean back and roll on. Now I could see Denver looming ahead of me like the Promised Land, way out there beneath the stars, across the prairie of Iowa and the plains of Nebraska, and I could see the greater vision of San Francisco beyond, like jewels in the night. He balled the jack and told stories for a couple of hours, then, at a town in Iowa where years later Dean and I were stopped on suspicion in what looked like a stolen Cadillac, he slept a few hours in the seat. I slept too, and took one little walk along the lonely brick walls illuminated by one lamp, with the prairie brooding at the end of each little street and the smell of the corn like dew in the night.

He woke up with a start at dawn. Off we roared, and an hour later the smoke of Des Moines appeared ahead over the green cornfields. He had to eat his breakfast now and wanted to take it easy, so I went right on into Des Moines, about four miles, hitching a ride with two boys from the University of Iowa; and it was strange sitting in the brand-new comfortable car and hearing them talk of exams as we zoomed smoothly into town. Now I wanted to sleep a whole day. So I went to the Y to get a room; they didn't have any, and by instinct I wandered down to the railroad tracks – and there're a lot of them in Des Moines – and wound up in a gloomy old Plains inn of a hotel by the locomotive roundhouse, and spent a long day sleeping on a big clean hard white bed with dirty remarks carved in the wall beside my pillow and the beat yellow windowshades pulled over the smoky scene of the railyards. I woke up as the sun was reddening; and that was the one distinct time in my life, the strangest moment of all, when I didn't know who I was

– I was far away from home, haunted and tired with travel, in a cheap hotel room I'd never seen, hearing the hiss of steam outside, and the creak of the old wood of the hotel, and footsteps upstairs, and all the sad sounds, and I looked at the cracked high ceiling and really didn't know who I was for about fifteen strange seconds. I wasn't scared; I was just somebody else, some stranger, and my whole life was a haunted life, the life of a ghost. I was halfway across America, at the dividing line between the East of my youth and the West of my future, and maybe that's why it happened right there and then, that strange red afternoon.

But I had to get going and stop moaning, so I picked up my bag, said so long to the old hotelkeeper sitting by his spittoon, and went to eat. I ate apple pie and ice cream – it was getting better as I got deeper into Iowa, the pie bigger, the ice cream richer. There were the most beautiful bevies of girls everywhere I looked in Des Moines that afternoon – they were coming home from high school – but I had no time now for thoughts like that and promised myself a ball in Denver. Carlo Marx was already in Denver; Dean was there; Chad King and Tim Gray were there, it was their hometown; Marylou was there; and there was mention of a mighty gang including Ray Rawlins and his beautiful blonde sister Babe Rawlins; two waitresses Dean knew, the Bettencourt sisters; and even Roland Major, my old college writing buddy, was there. I looked forward to all of them with joy and anticipation. So I rushed past the pretty girls, and the prettiest girls in the world live in Des Moines.

A guy with a kind of toolshack on wheels, a truck full of tools that he drove standing up like a modern milkman, gave me a ride up the long hill, where I immediately got a ride from a farmer and his son heading out for Adel in Iowa. In this town, under a big elm tree near a gas station, I made the acquaintance of another hitchhiker, a typical New Yorker, an Irishman who'd been driving a truck for the post office most of his work years and was now headed for a girl in Denver and a new life. I think he was running away from something in New York, the law most likely. He was a real red-nosed young drunk of thirty and would have bored me ordinarily, except that my senses were sharp for any kind of human friendship. He wore a beat sweater and baggy pants and had nothing with him in the way of a bag – just a toothbrush and handkerchiefs. He said we ought to hitch together. I should have said no, because he looked pretty awful on the road. But we stuck together and got a ride with a taciturn man to Stuart, Iowa, a town in which we were really stranded. We stood in front of the railroad-ticket shack in Stuart, waiting for the westbound traffic till the sun went down, a good five hours, dawdling away the time, at first telling about ourselves, then he told dirty stories, then we just kicked pebbles and made goofy noises of one kind and another. We got bored. I decided to spend a buck on beer; we went to an old saloon in Stuart and had a few. There he got as drunk as he ever did in his Ninth Avenue night back home, and yelled joyously in my ear all the sordid dreams of his life. I kind of liked him; not because he was a good sort, as he later proved to be, but because he was enthusiastic about things. We got back on the road in the darkness, and of course nobody stopped and nobody came by much. That went on till three o'clock in the morning. We spent some time trying to sleep on the bench at the railroad ticket office, but the telegraph clicked all night and we couldn't sleep, and big freights were slamming around outside. We didn't know how to hop a proper chain gang; we'd never done it before; we didn't know whether they were going east or west or how to find out or what box-cars and flats and de-iced reefers to pick, and so on. So when the Omaha bus came through just before dawn we hopped on it and joined the sleeping passengers – I paid for his fare as well as mine. His name was Eddie. He reminded me of my cousin-in-law from the Bronx. That was why I stuck with him. It was like having an old friend along, a smiling good-natured sort to goof along with.

We arrived at Council Bluffs at dawn; I looked out. All winter I'd been reading of the great wagon parties that held council there before hitting the Oregon and Santa Fe trails; and of course now it was only cute suburban cottages of one damn kind and another, all laid out in the dismal grey dawn. Then Omaha, and, by God, the first cowboy I saw, walking along the bleak walls of the wholesale meat warehouses in a ten-gallon hat and Texas boots, looked like any beat character of the brick-wall dawns of the East except for the getup. We got off the bus and walked clear up the hill, the long hill formed over the millenniums by the mighty Missouri, alongside of which Omaha is built, and got out to the country and stuck our thumbs out. We got a brief ride from a wealthy rancher in a ten-gallon hat, who said the valley of the Platte was as great as the Nile Valley of Egypt, and as he said so I saw the great trees in the distance that snaked with the river-bed and the great verdant fields around it, and almost agreed with him. Then as we were standing at another crossroads and it was starting to get cloudy another cowboy, this one six feet tall in a modest half-gallon hat, called us over and wanted to know if either one of us could drive. Of course Eddie could drive, and he had a licence and I didn't. Cowboy had two cars with him that he was driving back to Montana. His wife was at Grand Island, and he wanted us to drive one of the cars there, where she'd take over. At that point he was going north, and that would be the limit of our ride with him. But it was a good hundred miles into Nebraska, and of course we jumped for it. Eddie drove alone, the cowboy and myself following, and no sooner were we out of town than Eddie started to ball that jack ninety miles an hour out of sheer exuberance. 'Damn me, what's that boy doing!' the cowboy shouted, and took off after him. It began to be like a race. For a minute I thought Eddie was trying to get away with the car – and for all I know that's what he meant to do. But the cowboy stuck to him and caught up with him and tooted the horn. Eddie slowed down. The cowboy tooted to stop. 'Damn, boy, you're liable to get a flat going that speed. Can't you drive a little slower?'

'Well, I'll be damned, was I really going ninety?' said Eddie. 'I didn't realize it on this smooth road.'

'Just take it a little easy and we'll all get to Grand Island in one piece.'

'Sure thing.' And we resumed our journey. Eddie had calmed down and probably even got sleepy. So we drove a hundred miles across Nebraska, following the winding Platte with its verdant fields.

'During the depression,' said the cowboy to me, 'I used to hop freights at least once a month. In those days you'd see hundreds

22

of men riding a flatcar or in a boxcar, and they weren't just bums, they were all kinds of men out of work and going from one place to another and some of them just wandering. It was like that all over the West. Brakemen never bothered you in those days. I don't know about today. Nebraska I ain't got no use for. Why in the middle nineteen thirties this place wasn't nothing but a big dustcloud as far as the eye could see. You couldn't breathe. The ground was black. I was here in those days. They can give Nebraska back to the Indians far as I'm concerned. I hate this damn place more than any place in the world. Montana's my home now – Missoula. You come up there sometime and see God's country.' Later in the afternoon I slept when he got tired talking – he was an interesting talker.

We stopped along the road for a bit to eat. The cowboy went off to have a spare tyre patched, and Eddie and I sat down in a kind of homemade diner. I heard a great laugh, the greatest laugh in the world, and here came this rawhide old-timer Nebraska farmer with a bunch of other boys into the diner; you could hear his raspy cries clear across the plains, across the whole grey world of them that day. Everybody else laughed with him. He didn't have a care in the world and had the hugest regard for everybody. I said to myself, Wham, listen to that man laugh. That's the West, here I am in the West. He came booming into the diner, calling Maw's name, and she made the sweetest cherry pie in Nebraska, and I had some with a mountainous scoop of ice cream on top. 'Maw, rustle me up some grub afore I have to start eatin myself raw or some damn silly idee like that.' And he threw himself on a stool and went hyaw hyaw hyaw hyaw. 'And thow some beans in it.' It was the spirit of the West sitting right next to me. I wished I knew his whole raw life and what the hell he'd been doing all these years besides laughing and yelling like that. Whooee, I told my soul, and the cowboy came back and off we went to Grand Island.

We got there in no time flat. He went to fetch his wife and off to whatever fate awaited him, and Eddie and I resumed on the road. We got a ride from a couple of young fellows – wranglers, teenagers, country boys in a put-together jalopy – and were left off somewhere up the line in a thin drizzle of rain. Then an old man who said nothing – and God knows why he picked us up – took us to Shelton. Here Eddie stood forlornly in the road in front of a staring bunch of short, squat Omaha Indians who had nowhere to go and nothing to do. Across the road was the railroad track and the watertank saying SHELTON. 'Damn me,' said Eddie with amazement, 'I've been in this town before. It was years ago, during the war, at night, late at night when everybody was sleeping. I went out on the platform to smoke, and there we was in the middle of nowhere and black as hell, and I look up and see that name Shelton written on the watertank. Bound for the Pacific, everybody snoring, every damn sucker, and we only stayed a few minutes, stoking up or something, and off we went. Damn me, this Shelton! I hated this place ever since!' And we were stuck in Shelton. As in Davenport, Iowa, somehow all the cars were farmer-cars, and once in a while a tourist car, which is worse, with old men driving and their wives pointing out the sights or poring over maps, and sitting back looking at everything with suspicious faces.

The drizzle increased and Eddie got cold; he had very little clothing. I fished a wool plaid shirt from my canvas bag and he put it on. He felt a little better. I had a cold. I bought cough drops in a rickety Indian store of some kind. I went to the little two-by-four post office and wrote my aunt a penny postcard. We went back to the grey road. There she was in front of us, Shelton, written on the watertank. The Rock Island balled by. We saw the faces of Pullman passengers go by in a blur. The train howled off across the plains in the direction of our desires. It started to rain harder.

A tall, lanky fellow in a gallon hat stopped his car on the wrong side of the road and came over to us; he looked like a sheriff. We prepared our stories secretly. He took his time coming over. 'You boys going to get somewhere, or just going?' We didn't understand his question, and it was a damned good question.

'Why?' we said.

'Well, I own a little carnival that's pitched a few mile down the road and I'm looking for some old boys willing to work and make a buck for themselves. I've got a roulette concession and a wooden-ring concession, you know, the kind you throw around dolls and take your luck. You boys want to work for me, you can get thirty per cent of the take.'

'Room and board?'

'You can get a bed but no food. You'll have to eat in town. We travel some.' We thought it over. 'It's a good opportunity,' he said, and waited patiently for us to make up our minds. We felt silly and didn't know what to say, and I for one didn't want to get hung-up with a carnival. I was in such a bloody hurry to get to the gang in Denver.

I said, 'I don't know, I'm going as fast as I can and I don't think I have the time.' Eddie said the same thing, and the old man waved his hand and casually sauntered back to his car and drove off. And that was that. We laughed about it awhile and speculated about what it would have been like. I had visions of a dark and dusty night on the plains, and the faces of Nebraska families wandering by, with their rosy children looking at everything with awe, and I know I would have felt like the devil himself rooking them with all those cheap carnival tricks. And the Ferris wheel revolving in the flatlands darkness, and, Godalmighty, the sad music of the merry-go-round and me wanting to get on to my goal – and sleeping in some gilt wagon on a bed of burlap.

Eddie turned out to be a pretty absent-minded pal of the road. A funny old contraption rolled by, driven by an old man; it was made of some kind of aluminium, square as a box – a trailer, no doubt, but a weird, crazy Nebraska homemade trailer. He was going very slow and stopped. We rushed up; he said he could only take one; without a word Eddie jumped in and slowly rattled from my sight, and wearing my wool plaid shirt. Well, alackaday, I kissed the shirt good-bye; it had only sentimental value in any case. I waited in our personal godawful Shelton for a long, long time, several hours, and I kept thinking it was getting night; actually it was only early afternoon, but dark. Denver, Denver, how would I ever get to Denver? I was just about giving up and planning to sit over coffee when a fairly new car stopped, driven by a young guy. I ran like mad.

'Where you going?'

'Denver.'

'Well, I can take you a hundred miles up the line.'

'Grand, grand, you saved my life.'

'I used to hitchhike myself, that's why I always pick up a fellow.'

'I would too if I had a car.' And so we talked, and he told me about his life, which wasn't very interesting, and I started to sleep some and woke up right outside the town of Gothenburg, where he let me off.

4

THE greatest ride in my life was about to come up, a truck, with a flatboard at the back, with about six or seven boys sprawled out on it, and the drivers, two young blond farmers from Minnesota, were picking up every single soul they found on that road – the most smiling, cheerful couple of handsome bumpkins you could ever wish to see, both wearing cotton shirts and overalls, nothing else; both thick-wristed and earnest, with broad howareyou smiles for anybody and anything that came across their path. I ran up, said 'Is there room?' They said, 'Sure, hop on, 'sroom for everybody.'

I wasn't on the flatboard before the truck roared off; I lurched, a rider grabbed me, and I sat down. Somebody passed a bottle of rotgut, the bottom of it. I took a big swig in the wild, lyrical, drizzling air of Nebraska. 'Whooee, here we go!' yelled a kid in a baseball cap, and they gunned up the truck to seventy and passed everybody on the road. 'We been riding this sonofabitch since Des Moines. These guys never stop. Every now and then you have to yell for pisscall, otherwise you have to piss off the air, and hang on, brother, hang on.'

I looked at the company. There were two young farmer boys from North Dakota in red baseball caps, which is the standard North Dakota farmer-boy hat, and they were headed for the harvests; their old men had given them leave to hit the road for a summer. There were two young city boys from Columbus, Ohio, high-school football players, chewing gum, winking, singing in the breeze, and said they were hitchhiking around the United States for the summer. 'We're going to LA!' they yelled.

'What are you going to do there?'

'Hell, we don't know. Who cares?'

26

Then there was a tall slim fellow who had a sneaky look. 'Where you from?' I asked. I was lying next to him on the platform; you couldn't sit without bouncing off, it had no rails. And he turned slowly to me, opened his mouth, and said, 'Mon-ta-na.'

Finally there were Mississippi Gene and his charge. Mississippi Gene was a little dark guy who rode freight trains around the country, a thirty-year-old hobo but with a youthful look so you couldn't tell exactly what age he was. And he sat on the boards crosslegged, looking out over the fields without saying anything for hundreds of miles, and finally at one point he turned to me and said, 'Where *you* headed?' ...

I said Denver.

'I got a sister there but I ain't seed her for several couple years.' His language was melodious and slow. He was patient. His charge was a sixteen-year-old tall blond kid, also in hobo rags; that is to say, they wore old clothes that had been turned black by the soot of railroads and the dirt of boxcars and sleeping on the ground. The blond kid was also quiet and he seemed to be running away from something, and it figured to be the law the way he looked straight ahead and wet his lips in worried thought. Montana Slim spoke to them occasionally with a sardonic and insinuating smile. They paid no attention to him. Slim was all insinuation. I was afraid of his long goofy grin that he opened up straight in your face and held there half-moronically.

'You got any money?' he said to me.

'Hell no, maybe enough for a pint of whisky till I get to Denver. What about you?'

'I know where I can get some.'

'Where?'

'Anywhere. You can always folly a man down an alley, can't you?'

'Yeah, I guess you can.'

'I ain't beyond doing it when I really need some dough. Headed up to Montana to see my father. I'll have to get off this rig at Cheyenne and move up some other way. These crazy boys are going to Los Angeles.'

'Straight?'

'All the way – if you want to go to LA you got a ride.'

I mulled this over; the thought of zooming all night across Nebraska, Wyoming, and the Utah desert in the morning, and then most likely the Nevada desert in the afternoon, and actually arriving in Los Angeles within a foreseeable space of time almost made me change my plans. But I had to go to Denver. I'd have to get off at Cheyenne too, and hitch south ninety miles to Denver.

I was glad when the two Minnesota farmboys who owned the truck decided to stop in North Platte and eat; I wanted to have a look at them. They came out of the cab and smiled at all of us. 'Pisscall!' said one. 'Time to eat!' said the other. But they were the only ones in the party who had money to buy food. We all shambled after them to a restaurant run by a bunch of women, and sat around over hamburgers and coffee while they wrapped away enormous meals just as if they were back in their mother's kitchen. They were brothers; they were transporting farm machinery from Los Angeles to Minnesota and making good money at it. So on their trip to the Coast empty they picked up everybody on the road. They'd done this about five times now; they were having a hell of a time. They liked everything. They never stopped smiling. I tried to talk to them – a kind of dumb attempt on my part to befriend the captains of our ship – and the only responses I got were two sunny smiles and large white corn-fed teeth.

Everybody had joined them in the restaurant except the two hobo kids, Gene and his boy. When we all got back they were still sitting in the truck, forlorn and disconsolate. Now the darkness was falling. The drivers had a smoke; I jumped at the chance to go buy a bottle of whisky to keep warm in the rushing cold air of night. They smiled when I told them. 'Go ahead, hurry up.'

'You can have a couple of shots!' I reassured them.

'Oh no, we never drink, go ahead.'

Montana Slim and the two high-school boys wandered the streets of North Platte with me till I found a whisky store. They chipped in some, and Slim some, and I bought a fifth. Tall, sullen men watched us go by from false-front buildings; the main street was lined with square box-houses. There were immense vistas of the plains beyond every sad street. I felt something different in the air in North Platte, I didn't know what it was. In five minutes I did. We got back on the truck and roared off. It got dark quickly. We all had a shot, and suddenly I looked, and the verdant farmfields of the Platte began to disappear and in their stead, so far you couldn't see to the end, appeared long flat wastelands of sand and sage-brush. I was astounded.

'What in the hell is this?' I cried out to Slim.

'This is the beginning of the rangelands, boy. Hand me an-other drink.'

'Whoopee!' yelled the high-school boys. 'Columbus, so long! What would Sparkie and the boys say if they was here. Yow!'

The drivers had switched up front; the fresh brother was gunning the truck to the limit. The road changed too: humpy in the middle, with soft shoulders and a ditch on both sides about four feet deep, so that the truck bounced and teetered from one side of the road to the other – miraculously only when there were no cars coming the opposite way – and I thought we'd all take a somersault. But they were tremendous drivers. How that truck disposed of the Nebraska nub – the nub that sticks out over Colorado! And soon I realized I was actually at last over Colorado, though not officially in it, but looking southwest towards Denver itself a few hundred miles away. I yelled for joy. We passed the bottle. The great blaz-ing stars came out, the far-receding sand hills got dim. I felt like an arrow that could shoot out all the way.

And suddenly Mississippi Gene turned to me from his cross-legged, patient reverie, and opened his mouth, and leaned close, and said, 'These plains put me in the mind of Texas.'

'Are you from Texas?'

'No sir, I'm from Green-vell Muzz-sippy.' And that was the way he said it.

'Where's that kid from?'

'He got into some kind of trouble back in Mississippi, so I offered to help him out. Boy's never been out on his own. I take care of him best as I can, he's only a child.' Although Gene was white there was something of the wise and tired old Negro in him, and something very much like Elmer Hassel, the New

York dope addict, in him, but a railroad Hassel, a travelling epic Hassel, crossing and recrossing the country every year, south in the winter and north in the summer, and only because he had no place he could stay in without getting tired of it and because there was nowhere to go but everywhere, keep rolling under the stars, generally the Western stars.

'I been to Og-den a couple of times. If you want to ride on to Og-den I got some friends there we could hole up with.'

'I'm going to Denver from Cheyenne.'

'Hell, go right straight thu, you don't get a ride like this every day.'

This too was a tempting offer. What was in Ogden? 'What's Ogden?' I said.

'It's the place where most of the boys pass thu and always meet there; you're liable to see anybody there.'

In my earlier days I'd been to sea with a tall rawboned fellow from Louisiana called Big Slim Hazard, William Holmes Hazard, who was hobo by choice. As a little boy he'd seen a hobo come up to ask his mother for a piece of pie, and she had given it to him, and when the hobo went off down the road the little boy had said, 'Ma, what is that fellow?' 'Why, that's a ho-bo.' 'Ma, I want to be a ho-bo someday.' 'Shet your mouth, that's not for the like of the Hazards.' But he never forgot that day, and when he grew up, after a short spell playing football at LSU, he did become a hobo. Big Slim and I spent many nights telling stories and spitting tobacco juice in paper containers. There was something so indubitably reminiscent of Big Slim Hazard in Mississippi Gene's demeanour that I said, 'Do you happen to have met a fellow called Big Slim Hazard somewhere?'

And he said, 'You mean the tall fellow with the big laugh?'

'Well, that sounds like him. He came from Ruston, Louisiana.'

'That's right. Louisiana Slim he's sometimes called. Yes-sir, I shore have met Big Slim.'

'And he used to work in the East Texas oil fields?'

'East Texas is right. And now he's punching cows.'

And that was exactly right; and still I couldn't believe Gene could have really known Slim, whom I'd been looking for, more or less, for years. 'And he used to work in tugboats in New York?'

'Well now, I don't know about that.'

'I guess you only knew him in the West.'

'I reckon. I ain't never been to New York.'

'Well, damn me, I'm amazed you know him. This is a big country. Yet I knew you must have known him.'

'Yessir, I know Big Slim pretty well. Always generous with his money when he's got some. Mean, tough fellow, too; I seen him flatten a policeman in the yards at Cheyenne, one punch.' That sounded like Big Slim; he was always practising that one punch in the air; he looked like Jack Dempsey, but a young Jack Dempsey who drank.

'Damn!' I yelled into the wind, and I had another shot, and by now I was feeling pretty good. Every shot was wiped away by the rushing wind of the open truck, wiped away of its bad effects, and the good effect sank in my stomach. 'Cheyenne, here I come!' I sang. 'Denver, look out for your boy.'

Montana Slim turned to me, pointed at my shoes, and commented, 'You reckon if you put them things in the ground something'll grow up?' – without cracking a smile, of course, and the other boys heard him and laughed. And they were the silliest shoes in America; I brought them along specifically because I didn't want my feet to sweat in the hot road, and except for the rain in Bear Mountain they proved to be the best possible shoes for my journey. So I laughed with them. And the shoes were pretty ragged by now, the bits of coloured leather sticking up like pieces of a fresh pineapple and my toes showing through. Well, we had another shot and laughed. As in a dream we zoomed through small crossroads towns smack out of the darkness, and passed long lines of lounging harvest hands and cowboys in the night. They watched us pass in one motion of the head, and we saw them slap their thighs from the continuing dark the other side of town – we were a funny-looking crew.

A lot of men were in this country at that time of the year; it was harvest time. The Dakota boys were fidgeting. 'I think we'll get off at the next pisscall; seems like there's a lot of work around here.'

'All you got to do is move north when it's over here,' counselled Montana Slim, 'and jes follow the harvest till you get to Canada.' The boys nodded vaguely; they didn't take much stock in his advice.

Meanwhile the blond young fugitive sat the same way; every now and then Gene leaned out of his Buddhistic trance over the rushing dark plains and said something tenderly in the boy's ear. The boy nodded. Gene was taking care of him, of his moods and his fears. I wondered where the hell they would go and what they would do. They had no cigarettes. I squandered my pack on them, I loved them so. They were grateful and gracious. They never asked, I kept offering. Montana Slim had his own but never passed the pack. We zoomed through another crossroads town, passed another line of tall lanky men in jeans clustered in the dim light like moths on the desert, and returned to the tremendous darkness, and the stars overhead were pure and bright because of the increasingly thin air as we mounted the high hill of the western plateau, about a foot a mile, so they say, and no trees obstructing any low-levelled stars anywhere. And once I saw a moody whitefaced cow in the sage by the road as we flitted by. It was like riding a railroad train, just as steady and just as straight.

By and by we came to a town, slowed down, and Montana Slim said, 'Ah, pisscall', but the Minnesotans didn't stop and went right on through. 'Damn, I gotta go,' said Slim.

'Go over the side,' said somebody.

'Well, I *will*,' he said, and slowly, as we all watched, he inched to the back of the platform on his haunch, holding on as best he could, till his legs dangled over. Somebody knocked on the window of the cab to bring this to the attention of the brothers. Their great smiles broke as they turned. And just as Slim was ready to proceed, precarious as it was already, they began zigzagging the truck at seventy miles an hour. He fell back a moment; we saw a whale's spout in the air; he struggled back to a sitting position. They swung the truck. Wham, over he went on his side, watering all over himself. In the roar we could hear him faintly cursing, like the whine of a man far across the hills. 'Damn ... damn ...' He never knew we were doing this deliberately; he just struggled, as grim as Job. When he was finished, as such, he was wringing wet, and now he had to edge and shimmy his way back, and with a most woebegone look, and everybody laughing, except the sad blond boy, and the Minnesotans roaring in the cab. I handed him the bottle to make up for it.

'What the hail,' he said, 'was they doing that on purpose?'

'They sure were.'

'Well, damn me, I didn't know that. I know I tried it back in Nebraska and didn't have half so much trouble.'

We came suddenly into the town of Ogallala, and here the fellows in the cab called out, *'Pisscall!'* and with great good delight. Slim stood sullenly by the truck, rueing a lost opportunity. The two Dakota boys said good-bye to everybody and figured they'd start harvesting here. We watched them disappear in the night towards the shacks at the end of town where lights were burning, where a watcher of the night in jeans said the employment men would be. I had to buy more cigarettes. Gene and the blond boy followed me to stretch their legs. I walked into the least likely place in the world, a kind of lonely Plains soda fountain for the local teenage girls and boys. They were dancing, a few of them, to the music on the jukebox. There was a lull when we came in. Gene and Blondey just stood there, looking at nobody; all they wanted was cigarettes. There were some pretty girls, too. And one of them made eyes at Blondey and he never saw it, and if he had he wouldn't have cared, he was so sad and gone.

I bought a pack each for them; they thanked me. The truck was ready to go. It was getting on midnight now, and cold. Gene, who'd been around the country more times than he could count on his fingers and toes, said the best thing to do now was for all of us to bundle up under the big tarpaulin or we'd freeze. In this manner, and with the rest of the bottle, we kept warm as the air grew ice-cold and pinged our ears. The stars seemed to get brighter the more we climbed the High Plains. We were in Wyoming now. Flat on my back, I stared straight up at the magnificent firmament, glorying in the time I was making, in how far I had come from sad Bear Mountain after all, and tingling with kicks at the thought of what lay ahead of me in Denver – whatever, whatever it would be. And

Mississippi Gene began to sing a song. He sang it in a melodious, quiet voice, with a river accent, and it was simple, just 'I got a purty little girl, she's sweet six-teen, she's the purti-est thing you ever seen', repeating it with other lines thrown in, all concerning how far he'd been and how he wished he could go back to her but he done lost her.

I said, 'Gene, that's the prettiest song.'

'It's the sweetest I know,' he said with a smile.

'I hope you get where you're going, and be happy when you do.'

'I always make out and move along one way or the other.'

Montana Slim was asleep. He woke up and said to me, 'Hey, Blackie, how about you and me investigatin' Cheyenne together tonight before you go to Denver?'

'Sure thing.' I was drunk enough to go for anything.

As the truck reached the outskirts of Cheyenne, we saw the high red lights of the local radio station, and suddenly we were bucking through a great crowd of people that poured along both sidewalks. 'Hell's bells, it's Wild West Week,' said Slim. Big crowds of businessmen, fat businessmen in boots and ten-gallon hats, with their hefty wives in cowgirl attire, bustled and whooped on the wooden sidewalks of old Cheyenne; farther down were the long stringy boulevard lights of new down-town Cheyenne, but the celebration was focusing on Oldtown. Blank guns went off. The saloons were crowded to the sidewalk. I was amazed, and at the same time I felt it was ridiculous: in my first shot at the West I was seeing to what absurd devices it had fallen to keep its proud tradition. We had to jump off the truck and say good-bye; the Minnesotans weren't interested in hanging around. It was sad to see them go, and I realized that I would never see any of them again, but that's the way it was. 'You'll freeze your ass tonight,' I warned. 'Then you'll burn 'em in the desert tomorrow afternoon.'

'That's all right with me long's as we get out of this cold night,' said Gene. And the truck left, threading its way through the crowds, and nobody paying attention to the strangeness of the kids inside the tarpaulin, staring at the town like babes from a coverlet. I watched it disappear into the night.

5

I WAS with Montana Slim and we started hitting the bars. I had about seven dollars, five of which I foolishly squandered that night. First we milled with all the cowboy-dudded tourists and oilmen and ranchers, at bars, in doorways, on the sidewalk; then for a while I shook Slim, who was wandering a little slaphappy in the street from all the whisky and beer : he was that kind of drinker; his eyes got glazed, and in a minute he'd be telling an absolute stranger about things. I went into a chili joint and the waitress was Mexican and beautiful. I ate, and then I wrote her a little love note on the back of the bill. The chili joint was deserted; everybody was somewhere else, drinking. I told her to turn the bill over. She read it and laughed. It was a little poem about how I wanted her to come and see the night with me.

'I'd love to, Chiquito, but I have a date with my boy friend.'

'Can't you shake him?'

'No, no, I don't,' she said sadly, and I loved the way she said it.

'Some other time I'll come by here,' I said, and she said, 'Any time, kid.' Still I hung around, just to look at her, and had another cup of coffee. Her boy friend came in sullenly and wanted to know when she was off. She bustled around to close the place quick. I had to get out. I gave her a smile when I left. Things were going on as wild as ever outside, except that the fat burpers were getting drunker and whooping up louder. It was funny. There were Indian chiefs wandering around in big headdresses and really solemn among the flushed drunken faces. I saw Slim tottering along and joined him.

He said, 'I just wrote a postcard to my Paw in Montana. You reckon you can find a mailbox and put it in?' It was a strange request; he gave me the postcard and tottered through the swinging doors of a saloon. I took the card, went to the box, and took a quick look at it. 'Dear Paw, I'll be home Wednesday. Everything's all right with me and I hope the same is with you. Richard.' It gave me a different idea of him; how tenderly polite he was with his father. I went in the bar and joined him. We picked up two girls, a pretty young blonde and a fat brunette. They were dumb and sullen, but we wanted to make them. We took them to a rickety nightclub that was already closing, and there I spent all but two dollars on Scotches for them and beer for us. I was getting drunk and didn't care; everything was fine. My whole being and purpose was pointed at the little blonde. I wanted to go in there with all my strength. I hugged her and wanted to tell her. The nightclub closed and we all wandered out in the rickety dusty streets. I looked up at the sky; the pure, wonderful stars were still there, burning. The girls wanted to go to the bus station, so we all went, but they apparently wanted to meet some sailor who was there waiting for them, a cousin of the fat girl's, and the sailor had friends with him. I said to the blonde, 'What's up?' She said she wanted to go home, in Colorado just over the line south of Cheyenne. 'I'll take you in a bus,' I said.

'No, the bus stops on the highway and I have to walk across that damn prairie all by myself. I spend all afternoon looking at the damn thing and I don't aim to walk over it tonight.'

'Ah, listen, we'll take a nice walk in the prairie flowers.'

'There ain't no flowers there,' she said. 'I want to go to New York. I'm sick and tired of this. Ain't no place to go but Cheyenne and ain't nothin in Cheyenne.'

'Ain't nothin in New York.'

'Hell there ain't,' she said with a curl of her lips.

The bus station was crowded to the doors. All kinds of people were waiting for buses or just standing around; there were a lot of Indians, who watched everything with their stony eyes. The girl disengaged herself from my talk and joined the sailor and the others. Slim was dozing on a bench. I sat down. The floors of bus stations are the same all over the country, always covered with butts and spit and they give a feeling of sadness that only bus stations have. For a moment it was no different from being in Newark, except for the great hugeness outside that I loved so much. I rued the way I had broken up the purity of my entire trip, not saving every dime, and dawdling and not really making time, fooling around with this sullen girl and spending all my money. It made me sick. I hadn't slept in so long I got too tired to curse and fuss and went off to sleep; I curled up on the seat with my canvas bag for a pillow, and slept till eight o'clock in the morning among the dreamy murmurs and noises of the station and of hundreds of people passing.

I woke up with a big headache. Slim was gone – to Montana, I guess. I went outside. And there in the blue air I saw for the first time, far off, the great snowy tops of the Rocky Mountains. I took a deep breath. I had to get to Denver at once. First I ate a breakfast, a modest one of toast and coffee and one egg, and then I cut out of town to the highway. The Wild West festival was still going on; there was a rodeo, and the whooping and jumping were about to start all over again. I left it behind me. I wanted to see my gang in Denver. I crossed a railroad overpass and reached a bunch of shacks where two highways forked off, both for Denver. I took the one nearest the mountains so I could look at them, and pointed myself that way. I got a ride right off from a young fellow from Connecticut who was driving around the country in his jalopy, painting; he was the son of an editor in the East. He talked and talked; I was sick from drinking and from the altitude. At one point I almost had to stick my head out the window. But by the time he let me off at Longmont, Colorado, I was feeling normal again and had even started telling him about the state of my own travels. He wished me luck.

It was beautiful in Longmont. Under a tremendous old tree was a bed of green lawn-grass belonging to a gas station. I asked the attendant if I could sleep there, and he said sure; so I stretched out a wool shirt, laid my face flat on it, with an elbow out, and with one eye cocked at the snowy Rockies in the hot sun for just a moment. I fell asleep for two delicious hours, the only discomfort being an occasional Colorado ant. And here I am in Colorado! I kept thinking gleefully. Damn! damn! damn! I'm making it! And after a refreshing sleep filled with cobwebby dreams of my past life in the East I got up, washed in the station men's room, and strode off, fit and slick as a fiddle, and got me a rich thick milkshake at the roadhouse to put some freeze in my hot, tormented stomach.

Incidentally, a very beautiful Colorado gal shook me that cream. she was all smiles too; I was grateful, it made up for last night. I said to myself, Wow! What'll *Denver* be like! I got on that hot road, and off I went in a brand-new car driven by a Denver businessman of about thirty-five. He went seventy. I tingled all over; I counted minutes and subtracted miles. Just ahead, over the rolling wheatfields all golden beneath the distant snows of Estes, I'd be seeing old Denver at last. I pictured myself in a Denver bar that night, with all the gang, and in their eyes I would be strange and ragged and like the Prophet who has walked across the land to bring the dark Word, and the only Word I had was 'Wow!' The man and I had a long, warm conversation about our respective schemes in life, and before I knew it we were going over the wholesale fruitmarkets outside Denver; there were smokestacks, smoke, railyards, redbrick buildings, and the distant downtown greystone buildings, and here I was in Denver. He let me off at Larimer Street. I stumbled along with the most wicked grin of joy in the world, among the old bums and beat cowboys of Larimer Street.

6

IN THOSE days I didn't know Dean as well as I do now, and the first thing I wanted to do was look up Chad King, which I did. I called up his house, talked to his mother – she said, 'Why, Sal, what are you doing in Denver?' Chad is a slim blond boy with a strange witch-doctor face that goes with his interest in anthropology and prehistory Indians. His nose beaks softly and almost creamily under a golden flare of hair; he has the beauty and grace of a Western hotshot who's danced in roadhouses and played a little football. A quavering twang comes out when he speaks. 'The thing I always liked, Sal, about the Plains Indians was the way they always got s'danged embarrassed after they boasted the number of scalps they got. In Ruxton's *Life in the Far West* there's an Indian who gets red all over blushing because he got so many scalps and he runs like hell into the plains to glory over his deeds in hiding. Damn, that tickled *me!*'

Chad's mother located him, in the drowsy Denver afternoon, working over his Indian basket-making at the local museum. I called him there; he came and picked me up in his old Ford coupe that he used to take trips in the mountains, to dig for Indian objects. He came into the bus station wearing jeans and a big smile. I was sitting on my bag on the floor talking to the very same sailor who'd been in the Cheyenne bus station with me, asking him what happened to the blonde. He was so bored he didn't answer. Chad and I got in his little coupe and the first thing he had to do was get maps at the State building. Then he had to see an old schoolteacher, and so on, and all I wanted to do was drink beer. And in the back of my mind was the wild thought, Where is Dean and what is he doing right now? Chad had decided not to be Dean's friend any more, for some odd reason, and he didn't even know where he lived.

'Is Carlo Marx in town?'

'Yes.' But he wasn't talking to him any more either. This was the beginning of Chad King's withdrawal from our general gang. I was to take a nap in his house that afternoon. The word was that Tim Gray had an apartment waiting for me up Colfax Avenue, that Roland Major was already living in it and was waiting for me to join him. I sensed some kind of conspiracy in the air, and this conspiracy lined up two groups in the gang: it was Chad King and Tim Gray and Roland Major, together with the Rawlinses, generally agreeing to ignore Dean Moriarty and Carlo Marx. I was smack in the middle of this interesting war.

It was a war with social overtones. Dean was the son of a wino, one of the most tottering bums of Larimer Street, and Dean had in fact been brought up generally on Larimer Street and thereabouts. He used to plead in court at the age of six to have his father set free. He used to beg in front of Larimer alleys and sneak the money back to his father, who waited among the broken bottles with an old buddy. Then when Dean grew up he began hanging around the Glenarm poolhalls; he set a Denver record for stealing cars and went to the reformatory. From the age of eleven to seventeen he was usually in reform school. His specialty was stealing cars, gunning for girls coming out of high school in the afternoon, driving them out to the mountains, making them, and coming back to sleep in any available hotel bathtub in town. His father, once a respectable and hardworking tinsmith, had become a wine alcoholic, which is worse than a whisky alcoholic, and was reduced to riding freights to Texas in the winter and back to Denver in the summer. Dean had brothers on his dead mother's side – she died when he was small – but they disliked him. Dean's only buddies were the poolhall boys. Dean, who had the tremendous energy of a new kind of American saint, and Carlo were the underground monsters of that season in Denver, together with the poolhall gang, and, symbolizing this most beautifully, Carlo had a basement apartment on Grant Street and we all met there many a night that went to dawn – Carlo, Dean, myself, Tom Snark, Ed Dunkel, and Roy Johnson. More of these others later.

My first afternoon in Denver I slept in Chad King's room while his mother went on with her housework downstairs and Chad worked at the library. It was a hot high-plains afternoon in July. I would not have slept if it hadn't been for Chad King's father's invention. Chad King's father, a fine kind man, was in his seventies, old and feeble, thin and drawn-out, and telling stories with a slow, slow relish; good stories, too, about his boyhood on the North Dakota plains in the eighties, when for diversion he rode ponies bareback and chased after coyotes with a club. Later he became a country schoolteacher in the Oklahoma panhandle, and finally a businessman of many devices in Denver. He still had his old office over a garage down the street – the rolltop desk was still there, together with countless dusty papers of past excitement and moneymaking. He had invented a special air-conditioner. He put an ordinary fan in a window frame and somehow conducted cool water through coils in front of the whirring blades. The result was perfect – within four feet of the fan – and then the water apparently turned into steam in the hot day and the downstairs part of the house was just as hot as usual. But I was sleeping right under the fan on Chad's bed, with a big bust of Goethe staring at me, and I comfortably went to sleep, only to wake up in twenty minutes freezing to death. I put a blanket on and still I was cold. Finally it was so cold I couldn't sleep, and I went downstairs. The old man asked me how his invention worked. I said it worked damned good, and I meant it within bounds. I liked the man. He was lean with memories. 'I once made a spot remover that has since been copied by big firms in the East. I've been trying to collect on that for some years now. If I only had enough money to raise a decent lawyer ...' But it was too late to raise a decent lawyer; and he sat in his house dejectedly. In the evening we had a wonderful dinner his mother cooked, venison steak that Chad's uncle had shot in the mountains. But where was Dean?

7

THE following ten days were, as W. C. Fields said, 'fraught with eminent peril' – and mad. I moved in with Roland Major in the really swank apartment that belonged to Tim Gray's folks. We each had a bedroom, and there was a kitchenette with food in the icebox, and a huge living room where Major sat in his silk dressing gown composing his latest Hemingwayan short story – a choleric, red-faced, pudgy hater of everything, who could turn on the warmest and most charming smile in the world when real life confronted him sweetly in the night. He sat like that at his desk, and I jumped around over the thick soft rug, wearing only my chino pants. He'd just written a story about a guy who comes to Denver for the first time. His name is Phil. His travelling companion is a mysterious and quiet fellow called Sam. Phil goes out to dig Denver and gets hung-up with arty types. He comes back to the hotel room. Lugubriously he says, 'Sam, they're here too.' And Sam is just looking out the window sadly. 'Yes,' says Sam, 'I know.' And the point was that Sam didn't have to go and look to know this. The arty types were all over America, sucking up its blood. Major and I were great pals; he thought I was the farthest thing from an arty type. Major liked good wines, just like Hemingway. He reminisced about his recent trip to France. 'Ah, Sal, if you could sit with me high in the Basque country with a cool bottle of Poignon Dix-neuf, then you'd know there are other things besides boxcars.'

'I know that. It's just that I love boxcars and I love to read the names on them like Missouri Pacific, Great Northern, Rock Island Line. By Gad, Major, if I could tell you everything that happened to me hitching here.'

The Rawlinses lived a few blocks away. This was a delightful family – a youngish mother, part owner of a decrepit, ghost-town hotel, with five sons and two daughters. The wild son was Ray Rawlins, Tim Gray's boyhood buddy. Ray came roaring in to get me and we took to each other right away. We went off and drank in the Colfax bars. One of Ray's sisters was a beautiful blonde called Babe – a tennis-playing, surf-riding doll of the West. She was Tim Gray's girl. And Major, who was only passing through Denver and doing so in real style in the apartment, was going out with Tim Gray's sister Betty. I was the only guy without a girl. I asked everybody, 'Where's Dean?' They made smiling negative answers.

Then finally it happened. The phone rang, and it was Carlo Marx. He gave me the address of his basement apartment. I said, 'What are you doing in Denver? I mean what are you *doing*? What's going on?'

'Oh, wait till I tell you.'

I rushed over to meet him. He was working in May's department store nights; crazy Ray Rawlins called him up there from a bar, getting janitors to run after Carlo with a story that somebody had died. Carlo immediately thought it was me who had died. And Rawlins said over the phone, 'Sal's in Denver,' and gave him my address and phone.

'And where is Dean?'

'Dean is in Denver. Let me tell you.' And he told me that Dean was making love to two girls at the same time, they being Marylou, his first wife, who waited for him in a hotel room, and Camille, a new girl, who waited for him in a hotel room. 'Between the two of them he rushes to me for our own unfinished business.'

'And what business is that?'

'Dean and I are embarked on a tremendous season together

42

We're trying to communicate with absolute honesty and absolute completeness everything on our minds. We've had to take benzedrine. We sit on the bed, crosslegged, facing each other. I have finally taught Dean that he can do anything he wants, become mayor of Denver, marry a millionairess, or become the greatest poet since Rimbaud. But he keeps rushing out to see the midget auto races. I go with him. He jumps and yells, excited. You know, Sal, Dean is really hung-up on things like that.' Marx said 'Hmm' in his soul and thought about this.

'What's the schedule?' I said. There was always a schedule in Dean's life.

'The schedule is this: I came off work a half-hour ago. In that time Dean is balling Marylou at the hotel and gives me time to change and dress. At one sharp he rushes from Marylou to Camille – of course neither one of them knows what's going on – and bangs her once, giving me time to arrive at one-thirty. Then he comes out with me – first he has to beg with Camille, who's already started hating me – and we come here to talk till six in the morning. We usually spend more time than that, but it's getting awfully complicated and he's pressed for time. Then at six he goes back to Marylou – and he's going to spend all day tomorrow running around to get the necessary papers for their divorce. Marylou's all for it, but she insists on banging in the interim. She says she loves him – so does Camille.'

Then he told me how Dean had met Camille. Roy Johnson, the poolhall boy, had found her in a bar and took her to a hotel; pride taking over his sense, he invited the whole gang to come up and see her. Everybody sat around talking with Camille. Dean did nothing but look out the window. Then when everybody left, Dean merely looked at Camille, pointed at his wrist, made the sign 'four' (meaning he'd be back at four), and went out. At three the door was locked to Roy Johnson. At four it was opened to Dean. I wanted to go right out and see the madman. Also he had promised to fix me up; he knew all the girls in Denver.

Carlo and I went through rickety streets in the Denver night. The air was soft, the stars so fine, the promise of every cobbled alley so great, that I thought I was in a dream. We came to the rooming house where Dean haggled with Camille. It was an old red-brick building surrounded by wooden garages and old trees that stuck up from behind fences. We went up carpeted stairs. Carlo knocked; then he darted to the back to hide; he didn't want Camille to see him. I stood in the door. Dean opened it stark naked. I saw a brunette on the bed, one beautiful creamy thigh covered with black lace, look up with mild wonder.

'Why, Sa-a-al!' said Dean. 'Well now – ah – ahem – yes, of course, you've arrived – you old sonumbitch you finally got on that old road. Well, now, look here – we must – yes, yes, at once – we must, we really must! Now Camille –' And he swirled on her. 'Sal is here, this is my old buddy from New Yor-r-k, this is his first night in Denver and it's absolutely necessary for me to take him out and fix him up with a girl.'

'But what time will you be back?'

'It is now' (looking at his watch) 'exactly one-fourteen. I shall be back at exactly *three*-fourteen, for our hour of reverie together, real sweet reverie, darling, and then, as you know, as I told you and as we agreed, I have to go and see the one-legged lawyer about those papers – in the middle of the night, strange as it seems and as I tho-ro-ly explained.' (This was a coverup for his rendezvous with Carlo, who was still hiding.) 'So now in this exact minute I must dress, put on my pants, go back to life, that is to outside life, streets and what not, as we agreed, it is now one-*fifteen* and time's running, running –'

'Well, all right, Dean, but please be sure and be back at three.'

'Just as I said, darling, and remember not three but three-fourteen. Are we straight in the deepest and most wonderful depths of our souls, dear darling?' And he went over and kissed her several times. On the wall was a nude drawing of Dean, enormous dangle and all, done by Camille. I was amazed. Everything was so crazy.

Off we rushed into the night; Carlo joined us in an alley. And we proceeded down the narrowest, strangest, and most croooked little city street I've ever seen, deep in the heart of Denver Mexican-town. We talked in loud voices in the sleeping stillness. 'Sal,' said Dean, 'I have just the girl waiting for you at this very minute – if she's off duty' (looking at his watch). 'A waitress, Rita Bettencourt, fine chick, slightly hung-up on a few sexual difficulties which I've tried to straighten up and I think you can manage, you fine gone daddy you. So we'll go there at once – we must bring beer, no, they have some themselves, and damn!' he said socking his palm. 'I've just got to get into her sister Mary tonight.'

'What?' said Carlo. 'I thought we were going to talk.'

'Yes, yes, after.'

'Oh, these Denver doldrums!' yelled Carlo to the sky.

'Isn't he the finest sweetest fel-low in the world?' said Dean, punching me in the ribs. 'Look at him. *Look* at him!' And Carlo began his monkey dance in the streets of life as I'd seen him do so many times everywhere in New York.

And all I could say was, 'Well, what the hell are we doing in Denver?'

'Tomorrow, Sal, I know where I can find you a job,' said Dean, reverting to businesslike tones. 'So I'll call on you, soon as I have an hour off from Marylou, and cut right into that apartment of yours, say hello to Major, and take you on a trolley (damn, I've no car) to the Camargo markets, where you can begin working at once and collect a paycheck come Friday. We're really all of us bottomly broke. I haven't had time to work in weeks. Friday night beyond all doubt the three of us – the old threesome of Carlo, Dean, and Sal – must go to the midget auto races, and for that I can get us a ride from a guy downtown I know . . .' And on and on into the night.

We got to the house where the waitress sisters lived. The one for me was still working; the sister that Dean wanted was in. We sat down on her couch. I was scheduled at this time to call Ray Rawlins. I did. He came over at once. Coming into the door, he took off his shirt and undershirt and began hugging the absolute stranger, Mary Bettencourt. Bottles rolled on the floor. Three o'clock came. Dean rushed off for his hour of reverie with Camille. He was back on time. The other sister showed up. We all needed a car now, and we were making too much noise. Ray Rawlins called up a buddy with a car. He came. We all piled in; Carlo was trying to conduct his scheduled talk with Dean in the back seat, but there was too much confusion. 'Let's all go to my apartment!' I shouted. We did; the moment the car stopped there I jumped out and stood on my head in the grass. All my keys fell out; I never found them. We ran, shouting, into the building. Roland Major stood barring our way in his silk dressing gown.

'I'll have no goings-on like this in Tim Gray's apartment!'

'What?' we all shouted. There was confusion. Rawlins was rolling in the grass with one of the waitresses. Major wouldn't let us in. We swore to call Tim Gray and confirm the party and also invite him. Instead we all rushed back to the Denver downtown hangouts. I suddenly found myself alone in the street with no money. My last dollar was gone.

I walked five miles up Colfax to my comfortable bed in the apartment. Major had to let me in. I wondered if Dean and Carlo were having their heart-to-heart. I would find out later. The nights in Denver are cool, and I slept like a log.

8

THEN everybody began planning a tremendous trek to the mountains. This started in the morning, together with a phone call that complicated matters – my old road friend Eddie, who took a blind chance and called; he remembered some of the names I had mentioned. Now I had the opportunity to get my shirt back. Eddie was with his girl in a house off Colfax. He wanted to know if I knew where to find work, and I told him to come over, figuring Dean would know. Dean arrived, hurrying, while Major and I were having a hasty breakfast. Dean wouldn't even sit down. 'I have a thousand things to do, in fact hardly any time to take you down Camargo, but let's go, man.'

'Wait for my road buddy Eddie.'

Major found our hurrying troubles amusing. He'd come to Denver to write leisurely. He treated Dean with extreme deference. Dean paid no attention. Major talked to Dean like this: 'Moriarty, what's this I hear about you sleeping with three girls at the same time?' And Dean shuffled on the rug and said, 'Oh yes, oh yes, that's the way it goes,' and looked at his watch, and Major snuffed down his nose. I felt sheepish rushing off with Dean – Major insisted he was a moron and a fool. Of course he wasn't, and I wanted to prove it to everybody somehow.

We met Eddie. Dean paid no attention to him either, and off we went in a trolley across the hot Denver noon to find the jobs. I hated the thought of it. Eddie talked and talked the way he always did. We found a man in the markets who agreed to hire both of us; work started at four o'clock in the morning and went till six p.m. The man said, 'I like boys who like to work.'

'You've got your man,' said Eddie, but I wasn't so sure about myself. 'I just won't sleep,' I decided. There were so many other interesting things to do.

Eddie showed up the next morning; I didn't. I had a bed, and Major bought food for the icebox, and in exchange for that I cooked and washed the dishes. Meantime I got all involved in everything. A big party took place at the Rawlinses' one night. The Rawlins mother was gone on a trip. Ray Rawlins called everybody he knew and told them to bring whisky; then he went through his address book for girls. He made me do most of the talking. A whole bunch of girls showed up. I phoned Carlo to find out what Dean was doing now. Dean was coming to Carlo's at three in the morning. I went there after the party.

Carlo's basement apartment was on Grant Street in an old red-brick rooming house near a church. You went down an alley, down some stone steps, opened an old raw door, and went through a kind of cellar till you came to his board door. It was like the room of a Russian saint : one bed, a candle burning, stone walls that oozed moisture, and a crazy makeshift ikon of some kind that he had made. He read me his poetry. It was called 'Denver Doldrums'. Carlo woke up in the morning and heard the 'vulgar pigeons' yakking in the street outside his cell; he saw the 'sad nightingales' nodding on the branches and they reminded him of his mother. A grey shroud fell over the city. The mountains, the magnificent Rockies that you can see to the west from any part of town, were 'papier-mâché'. The whole universe was crazy and cock-eyed and extremely strange. He wrote of Dean as a 'child of the rainbow' who bore his torment in his agonized priapus. He referred to him as 'Oedipus Eddie' who had to 'scrape bubble gum off windowpanes'. He brooded in his basement over a huge journal in which he was keeping track of everything that happened every day – everything Dean did and said.

Dean came on schedule. 'Everything's straight,' he announced. 'I'm going to divorce Marylou and marry Camille and go live with her in San Francisco. But this is only after you and I, dear Carlo, go to Texas, dig Old Bull Lee, that gone cat I've never met and both of you've told me so much about, and then I'll go to San Fran.'

Then they got down to business. They sat on the bed cross-legged and looked straight at each other. I slouched in a near-by chair and saw all of it. They began with an abstract thought, discussed it; reminded each other of another abstract point forgotten in the rush of events; Dean apologized but promised he could get back to it and manage it fine, bringing up illustrations.

Carlo said, 'And just as we were crossing Wazee I wanted to tell you about how I felt of your frenzy with the midgets and it was just then, remember, you pointed out that old bum with the baggy pants and said he looked just like your father?'

'Yes, yes, of course I remember; and not only that, but it started a train of my own, something real wild that I had to tell you, I'd forgotten it, now you just reminded me of it ...' and two new points were born. They hashed these over. Then Carlo asked Dean if he was honest and specifically if he was being honest with *him* in the bottom of his soul.

'Why do you bring that up again?'

'There's one last thing I want to know –'

'But, dear Sal, you're listening, you're sitting there, we'll ask Sal. What would he say?'

And I said, 'That last thing is what you can't get, Carlo. Nobody can get to that last thing. We keep on living in hopes of catching it once for all.'

'No, no, no, you're talking absolute bullshit and Wolfean romantic posh!' said Carlo.

And Dean said, 'I didn't mean that at all, but we'll let Sal have his own mind, and in fact, don't you think, Carlo, there's a kind of a dignity in the way he's sitting there and digging us, crazy cat came all the way across the country – old Sal won't tell, old Sal won't tell.'

'It isn't that I won't tell,' I protested. 'I just don't know what you're both driving at or trying to get at. I know it's too much for anybody.'

'Everything you say is negative.'

'Then what is it you're trying to do?'

'Tell him.'

'No, you tell him.'

'There's nothing to tell,' I said and laughed. I had on Carlo's hat. I pulled it down over my eyes. 'I want to sleep,' I said.

'Poor Sal always wants to sleep.' I kept quiet. They started in again. 'When you borrowed that nickel to make up the check for the chicken-fried steaks –'

'No, man, the chili! Remember, the Texas Star?'

'I was mixing it with Tuesday. When you borrowed that nickel you said, now listen, you said, "Carlo, this is the last time I'll impose on you," as if, and really, you meant that I had agreed with you about no more imposing.'

'No, no, no, I didn't mean that – you harken back now if you will, my dear fellow, to the night Marylou was crying in the room, and when, turning to you and indicating by my extra added sincerity of tone which we both knew was contrived but had its intention, that is, by my play-acting I showed that – But wait, that isn't it.'

'Of course that isn't it! Because you forget that – But I'll stop accusing you. Yes is what I said ...' And on, on into the night they talked like this. At dawn I looked up. They were tying up the last of the morning's matters. 'When I said to you that I had to sleep *because* of Marylou, that is, seeing her this morning at ten, I didn't bring my peremptory tone to bear in regard to what you'd just said about the unnecessariness of sleep but only, *only*, mind you, because of the fact that I absolutely, simply, purely and without any whatevers have to sleep now, I mean, man, my eyes are closing, they're redhot, sore, tired, beat ...'

49

'Ah, child,' said Carlo.

'We'll just have to sleep now. Let's stop the machine.'

'You can't stop the machine!' yelled Carlo at the top of his voice. The first birds sang.

'Now, when I raise my hand,' said Dean, 'we'll stop talking, we'll both understand purely and without any hassle that we are simply stopping talking, and we'll just sleep.'

'You can't stop the machine like that.'

'Stop the machine,' I said. They looked at me.

'He's been awake all this time, listening. What were you thinking, Sal?' I told them that I was thinking they were very amazing maniacs and that I had spent the whole night listening to them like a man watching the mechanism of a watch that reached clear to the top of Berthoud Pass and yet was made with the smallest works of the most delicate watch in the world. They smiled. I pointed my finger at them and said, 'If you keep this up you'll both go crazy, but let me know what happens as you go along.'

I walked out and took a trolley to my apartment, and Carlo Marx's papier-mâché mountains grew red as the great sun rose from the eastward plains.

9

IN the evening I was involved in that trek to the mountains and didn't see Dean or Carlo for five days. Babe Rawlins had the use of her employer's car for the weekend. We brought suits and hung them on the car windows and took off for Central City, Ray Rawlins driving, Tim Gray lounging in the back, and Babe up front. It was my first view of the interior of the Rockies. Central City is an old mining town that was once called the Richest Square Mile in the World, where a veritable shelf of silver had been found by the old buzzards who roamed the hills. They grew wealthy overnight and had a beautiful little opera house built in the midst of their shacks on the steep slope. Lillian Russell had come there, and opera stars from Europe. Then Central City became a ghost town, till the energetic

Chamber of Commerce types of the new West decided to re-
vive the place. They polished up the opera house, and every
summer stars from the Metropolitan came out and performed.
It was a big vacation for everybody. Tourists came from everywhere, even Hollywood stars. We drove up the mountain and
found the narrow streets chock full of chichi tourists. I thought
of Major's Sam, and Major was right. Major himself was there,
turning on his big social smile to everybody and ooh-ing and
aah-ing most sincerely over everything. 'Sal,' he cried, clutching my arm, 'just look at this old town. Think how it was a
hundred – what the hell, only eighty, sixty years ago; they had
opera!'

'Yeah,' I said, imitating one of his characters, 'but *they're*
here.'

'The bastards,' he cursed. But he went off to enjoy himself,
Betty Gray on his arm.

Babe Rawlins was an enterprising blonde. She knew of an
old miner's house at the edge of town where we boys could
sleep for the weekend; all we had to do was clean it out. We
could also throw vast parties there. It was an old shack of a
thing covered with an inch of dust inside; it had a porch and
a well in back. Tim Gray and Ray Rawlins rolled up their
sleeves and started in cleaning it, a major job that took them
all afternoon and part of the night. But they had a bucket of
beer bottles and everything was fine.

As for me, I was scheduled to be a guest at the opera that
afternoon, escorting Babe on my arm. I wore a suit of Tim's.
Only a few days ago I'd come into Denver like a bum; now
I was all racked up sharp in a suit, with a beautiful well-dressed
blonde on my arm, bowing to dignitaries and chatting in the
lobby under chandeliers. I wondered what Mississippi Gene
would say if he could see me.

The opera was *Fidelio*. 'What gloom!' cried the baritone,
rising out of the dungeon under a groaning stone. I cried for
it. That's how I see life too. I was so interested in the opera
that for a while I forgot the circumstances of my crazy life
and got lost in the great mournful sounds of Beethoven and
the rich Rembrandt tones of his story.

'Well, Sal, how did you like the production for this year?'

asked Denver D. Doll proudly in the street outside. He was connected with the opera association.

'What gloom, what gloom,' I said. 'It's absolutely great.'

'The next thing you'll have to do is meet the members of the cast,' he went on in his official tones, but luckily he forgot this in the rush of other things, and vanished.

Babe and I went back to the miner's shack. I took off my duds and joined the boys in the cleaning. It was an enormous job. Roland Major sat in the middle of the front room that had already been cleaned and refused to help. On a little table in front of him he had his bottle of beer and his glass. As we rushed around with buckets of water and brooms he reminisced. 'Ah, if you could just come with me sometime and drink Cinzano and hear the musicians of Bandol, then you'd be living. Then there's Normandy in the summers, the sabots, the fine old Calvados. Come on, Sam,' he said to his invisible pal. 'Take the wine out of the water and let's see if it got cold enough while we fished.' Straight out of Hemingway, it was.

We called out to girls who went by in the street. 'Come on help us clean up the joint. Everybody's invited to our party tonight.' They joined us. We had a huge crew working for us. Finally the singers in the opera chorus, mostly young kids, came over and pitched in. The sun went down.

Our day's work over, Tim, Rawlins, and I decided to sharp up for the big night. We went across town to the rooming house where the opera stars were living. Across the night we heard the beginning of the evening performance. 'Just right,' said Rawlins. 'Latch on to some of these razors and towels and we'll spruce up a bit.' We also took hairbrushes, colognes, shaving lotions, and went laden into the bathroom. We all took baths and sang. 'Isn't this great?' Tim Gray kept saying. 'Using the opera stars' bathroom and towels and shaving lotion and electric razors.'

It was a wonderful night. Central City is two miles high; at first you get drunk on the altitude, then you get tired, and there's a fever in your soul. We approached the lights around the opera house down the narrow dark street; then we took a sharp right and hit some old saloons with swinging doors. Most of the tourists were in the opera. We started off with a few extra-size beers. There was a player piano. Beyond the back door was a view of mountainsides in the moonlight. I let out a yahoo. The night was on.

We hurried back to our miner's shack. Everything was in preparation for the big party. The girls, Babe and Betty, cooked up a snack of beans and franks, and then we danced and started on the beer for fair. The opera over, great crowds of young girls came piling into our place. Rawlins and Tim and I licked our lips. We grabbed them and danced. There was no music, just dancing. The place filled up. People began to bring bottles. We rushed out to hit the bars and rushed back. The night was getting more and more frantic. I wished Dean and Carlo were there – then I realized they'd be out of place and unhappy. They were like the man with the dungeon stone and the gloom, rising from the underground, the sordid hipsters of America, a new beat generation that I was slowly joining.

The boys from the chorus showed up. They began singing 'Sweet Adeline'. They also sang phrases such as 'Pass me the beer' and 'What are you doing with your face hanging out?' and great long baritone howls of 'Fi-de-lio!' 'Ah me, what gloom!' I sang. The girls were terrific. They went out in the backyard and necked with us. There were beds in the other rooms, the uncleaned dusty ones, and I had a girl sitting on one and was talking with her when suddenly there was a great in-rush of young ushers from the opera, who just grabbed girls and kissed them without proper come-ons. Teenagers, drunk, dishevelled, excited – they ruined our party. Inside of five minutes every single girl was gone and a great big fraternity-type party got under way with banging of beerbottles and roars.

Ray and Tim and I decided to hit the bars. Major was gone, Babe and Betty were gone. We tottered into the night. The opera crowd was jamming the bars from bar to wall. Major was shouting above heads. The eager, bespectacled Denver D. Doll was shaking hands with everybody and saying, 'Good afternoon, how are you?' and when midnight came he was saying, 'Good afternoon, how are you?' At one point I saw him going off somewhere with a dignitary. Then he came back with a middle-aged woman; next minute he was talking to a couple of young ushers in the street. The next minute he was shaking my hand without recognizing me and saying, 'Happy New Year, m'boy.' He wasn't drunk on liquor, just drunk on what he liked – crowds of people milling. Everybody knew him. 'Happy New Year,' he called, and sometimes 'Merry Christmas.' He said this all the time. At Christmas he said Happy Halloween.

There was a tenor in the bar who was highly respected by everyone; Denver Doll had insisted that I meet him and I was trying to avoid it; his name was D'Annunzio or some such thing. His wife was with him. They sat sourly at a table. There was also some kind of Argentinian tourist at the bar. Rawlins gave him a shove to make room; he turned and snarled. Rawlins handed me his glass and knocked him down on the brass rail with one punch. The man was momentarily out. There were screams; Tim and I scooted Rawlins out. There was so much confusion the sheriff couldn't even thread his way through the crowd to find the victim. Nobody could identify Rawlins. We went to other bars. Major staggered up a dark street. 'What the hell's the matter? Any fights? Just call on me.' Great laughter rang from all sides. I wondered what the Spirit of the Mountain was thinking, and looked up and saw jackpines in the moon, and saw ghosts of old miners, and wondered about it. In the whole eastern dark wall of the Divide this night there was silence and the whisper of the wind, except in the ravine where we roared; and on the other side of the Divide was the great Western Slope, and the big plateau that went to Steamboat Springs, and dropped, and led you to the Eastern Colorado desert and the Utah desert; all in darkness now as we fumed and screamed in our mountain nook, mad drunken Americans in the mighty land. We were on the roof of America and all we could do was yell, I guess – across the night, eastward over the Plains, where somewhere an old man with white hair was probably walking toward us with the Word, and would arrive any minute and make us silent.

Rawlins insisted on going back to the bar where he'd fought. Tim and I didn't like it but stuck to him. He went up to D'Annunzio, the tenor, and threw a highball in his face. We dragged him out. A baritone singer from the chorus joined us and we went to a regular Central City bar. Here Ray called the waitress a whore. A group of sullen men were ranged along the bar; they hated tourists. One of them said, 'You boys better be out of here by the count of ten.' We were. We staggered back to the shack and went to sleep.

In the morning I woke up and turned over; a big cloud of dust rose from the mattress. I yanked at the window; it was nailed. Tim Gray was in the bed too. We coughed and sneezed. Our breakfast consisted of stale beer. Babe came back from her hotel and we got our things together to leave.

Everything seemed to be collapsing. As we were going out to the car Babe slipped and fell flat on her face. Poor girl was over-wrought. Her brother and Tim and I helped her up. We got in the car; Major and Betty joined us. The sad ride back to Denver began.

Suddenly we came down from the mountain and overlooked the great sea-plain of Denver; heat rose as from an oven. We began to sing songs. I was itching to get on to San Francisco.

10

THAT night I found Carlo and to my amazement he told me he'd been in Central City with Dean.

'What did you do?'

'Oh, we ran around the bars and then Dean stole a car and we drove back down the mountain curves ninety miles an hour.'

'I didn't see you.'

'We didn't know you were there.'

'Well, man, I'm going to San Francisco.'

'Dean has Rita lined up for you tonight.'

'Well, then, I'll put it off.' I had no money. I sent my aunt an airmail letter asking her for fifty dollars and said it would be the last money I'd ask; after that she would be getting money back from me, as soon as I got that ship.

Then I went to meet Rita Bettencourt and took her back to the apartment. I got her in my bedroom after a long talk in the dark of the front room. She was a nice little girl, simple and true, and tremendously frightened of sex. I told her it was beautiful. I wanted to prove this to her. She let me prove it, but I was too impatient and proved nothing. She sighed in the dark. 'What do you want out of life?' I asked, and I used to ask that all the time of girls.

'I don't know,' she said. 'Just wait on tables and try to get along.' She yawned. I put my hand over her mouth and told her not to yawn. I tried to tell her how excited I was about life and the things we could do together; saying that, and planning to leave Denver in two days. She turned away wearily. We lay on our backs, looking at the ceiling and wondering what God had wrought when He made life so sad. We made vague plans to meet in Frisco.

My moments in Denver were coming to an end, I could feel it when I walked her home, on the way back I stretched out on the grass of an old church with a bunch of hobos, and their talk made me want to get back on that road. Every now and then one would get up and hit a passer-by for a dime. They talked of harvests moving north. It was warm and soft. I wanted to go and get Rita again and tell her a lot more things, and really make love to her this time, and calm her fears about men. Boys and girls in America have such a sad time together; sophistication demands that they submit to sex immediately without proper preliminary talk. Not courting talk – real straight talk about souls, for life is holy and every moment is precious. I heard the Denver and Rio Grande locomotive howling off to the mountains. I wanted to pursue my star further.

Major and I sat sadly talking in the midnight hours. 'Have you ever read *Green Hills of Africa*? It's Hemingway's best.' We wished each other luck. We would meet in Frisco. I saw Rawlins under a dark tree in the street. 'Good-bye, Ray. When do we meet again?' I went to look for Carlo and Dean – nowhere to be found. Tim Gray shot his hand up in the air and said, 'So you're leaving, Yo.' We called each other Yo. 'Yep,' I said. The next few days I wandered around Denver. It seemed to me every bum on Larimer Street maybe was Dean Moriarty's father; Old Dean Moriarty they called him, the Tinsmith. I went in the Windsor Hotel, where father and son had lived and where one night Dean was frightfully waked up by the legless man on the rollerboard who shared the room with them; he came thundering across the floor on his terrible wheels to touch the boy. I saw the little midget newspaper-selling woman with the short legs, on the corner of Curtis and 15th. I walked around the sad honkytonks of Curtis Street; young kids in jeans and red shirts; peanut shells, movie marquees, shooting parlours. Beyond the glittering street was darkness, and beyond the darkness the West. I had to go.

At dawn I found Carlo. I read some of his enormous journal, slept there, and in the morning, drizzly and grey, tall, six-foot Ed Dunkel came in with Roy Johnson, a handsome kid, and Tom Snark, the clubfooted poolshark. They sat around and listened with abashed smiles as Carlo Marx read them his apocalyptic, mad poetry. I slumped in my chair, finished. 'Oh ye Denver birds!' cried Carlo. We all filed out and went up a typical cobbled Denver alley between incinerators smoking slowly. 'I used to roll my hoop up this alley,' Chad King had told me. I wanted to see him do it; I wanted to see Denver ten years ago when they were all children, and in the sunny cherry blossom morning of springtime in the Rockies rolling their hoops up the joyous alleys full of promise – the whole gang. And Dean, ragged and dirty, prowling by himself in his pre-occupied frenzy.

Roy Johnson and I walked in the drizzle; I went to Eddie's girl's house to get back my wool plaid shirt, the shirt of Shelton, Nebraska. It was there, all tied up, the whole enormous sadness of a shirt. Roy Johnson said he'd meet me in Frisco. Everybody was going to Frisco. I went and found my money had arrived. The sun came out, and Tim Gray rode a trolley with me to the bus station. I bought my ticket to San Fran, spending half of the fifty, and got on at two o'clock in the afternoon. Tim Gray waved good-bye. The bus rolled out of the storied, eager Denver streets. 'By God, I gotta come back and see what else will happen!' I promised. In a last-minute phone call Dean said he and Carlo might join me on the Coast; I pondered this, and realized I hadn't talked to Dean for more than five minutes in the whole time.

11

I WAS two weeks late meeting Remi Boncœur. The bus trip from
Denver to Frisco was uneventful except that my whole soul
leaped to it the nearer we got to Frisco. Cheyenne again, in
the afternoon this time, and then west over the range; crossing
the Divide at midnight at Creston, arriving at Salt Lake City at
dawn – a city of sprinklers, the least likely place for Dean to
have been born; then out to Nevada in the hot sun, Reno by
nightfall, its twinkling Chinese streets; then up the Sierra Nevada, pines, stars, mountain lodges signifying Frisco romances –
a little girl in the back seat, crying to her mother, 'Mama when
do we get home to Truckee?' And Truckee itself, homey
Truckee, and then down the hill to the flats of Sacramento. I
suddenly realized I was in California. Warm, palmy air – air
you can kiss – and palms. Along the storied Sacramento River
on a superhighway; into the hills again; up, down; and suddenly the vast expanse of bay (it was just before dawn) with
the sleepy lights of Frisco festooned across. Over the Oakland
Bay Bridge I slept soundly for the first time since Denver; so
that I was rudely jolted in the bus station at Market and Fourth
into the memory of the fact that I was three thousand two
hundred miles from my aunt's house in Paterson, New Jersey. I
wandered out like a haggard ghost, and there she was, Frisco –
long, bleak streets with trolley wires all shrouded in fog and
whiteness. I stumbled around a few blocks. Weird bums (Mission and Third) asked me for dimes in the dawn. I heard music
somewhere. 'Boy, am I going to dig all this later! But now I've
got to find Remi Boncœur.'

Mill City, where Remi lived, was a collection of shacks in a
valley, housing-project shacks built for Navy Yard workers during the war; it was in a canyon, and a deep one, treed pro-
fusedly on all slopes. There were special stores and barber shops
and tailor shops for the people of the project. It was, so they
say, the only community in America where whites and Negroes
lived together voluntarily; and that was so, and so wild and

joyous a place I've never seen since. On the door of Remi's shack was the note he had pinned up there three weeks ago.

Sal Paradise! [in huge letters, printed] If nobody's home climb in through the window.

Signed,
Remi Boncœur.

The note was weatherbeaten and grey by now.

I climbed in and there he was, sleeping with his girl, Lee Ann – on a bed he stole from a merchant ship, as he told me later; imagine the deck engineer of a merchant ship sneaking over the side in the middle of the night with a bed, and heaving and straining at the oars to shore. This barely explains Remi Boncœur.

The reason I'm going into everything that happened in San Fran is because it ties up with everything else all the way down the line. Remi Boncœur and I met at prep school years ago; but the thing that really linked us together was my former wife. Remi found her first. He came into my dorm room one night and said, 'Paradise, get up, the old maestro has come to see you.' I got up and dropped some pennies on the floor when I put my pants on. It was four in the afternoon; I used to sleep all the time in college. 'All right, all right, don't drop your gold all over the place. I have found the gonest little girl in the world and I am going straight to the Lion's Den with her tonight.' And he dragged me to meet her. A week later she was going with me. Remi was a tall, dark, handsome Frenchman (he looked like a kind of Marseille black-marketeer of twenty); because he was French he had to talk in jazz American; his English was perfect, his French was perfect. He liked to dress sharp, slightly on the collegiate side, and go out with fancy blondes and spend a lot of money. It's not that he ever blamed me for taking off with his girl; it was only a point that always tied us together; that guy was loyal to me and had real affection for me, and God knows why.

When I found him in Mill City that morning he had fallen on the beat and evil days that come to young guys in their middle twenties. He was hanging around waiting for a ship, and to earn his living he had a job as a special guard in the barracks across the canyon. His girl Lee Ann had a bad tongue and gave him a calldown every day. They spent all week saving pennies and went out Saturdays to spend fifty bucks in three hours. Remi wore shorts around the shack, with a crazy Army cap on his head. Lee Ann went around with her hair up in pincurls. Thus attired, they yelled at each other all week. I never saw so many snarls in all my born days. But on Saturday night, smiling graciously at each other, they took off like a pair of successful Hollywood characters and went on the town.

Remi woke up and saw me come in the window. His great laugh, one of the greatest laughs in the world, dinned in my ear. 'Aaaaah Paradise, he comes in through the window, he follows instructions to a T. Where have you been, you're two weeks late!' He slapped me on the back, he punched Lee Ann in the ribs, he leaned on the wall and laughed and cried, he pounded the table so you could hear it everywhere in Mill City, and that great long 'Aaaaah' resounded around the canyon. 'Paradise!' he screamed. 'The one and only indispensable Paradise.'

I had just come through the little fishing village of Sausalito, and the first thing I said was, 'There must be a lot of Italians in Sausalito.'

'There must be a lot of Italians in Sausalito!' he shouted at the top of his lungs. 'Aaaaah!' He pounded himself, he fell on the bed, he almost rolled on the floor. 'Did you hear what Paradise said? There must be a lot of Italians in Sausalito? Aaaah-haaa! Hoo! Wow! Whee!' He got red as a beet, laughing. 'Oh, you slay me, Paradise, you're the funniest man in the world, and here you are, you finally got here, he came in through the window, you saw him, Lee Ann, he followed instructions and came in through the window. Aaah! Hooo!'

The strange thing was that next door to Remi lived a Negro called Mr Snow whose laugh, I swear on the Bible, was positively and finally the one greatest laugh in all this world. This Mr Snow began his laugh from the supper table when his old wife said something casual; he got up, apparently choking, leaned on the wall, looked up to heaven, and started; he staggered through the door, leaning on neighbours' walls; he was drunk with it, he reeled throughout Mill City in the shadows, raising his whooping triumphant call to the demon god that must have prodded him to do it. I don't know if he ever finished supper. There's a possibility that Remi, without knowing it, was picking up from this amazing man, Mr Snow. And though Remi was having worklife problems and bad lovelife with a sharp-tongued woman, he at least had learned to laugh almost better than anyone in the world, and I saw all the fun we were going to have in Frisco.

The pitch was this : Remi slept with Lee Ann in the bed across the room, and I slept in the cot by the window. I was not to touch Lee Ann. Remi at once made a speech concerning this. 'I don't want to find you two playing around when you think I'm not looking. You can't teach the old maestro a new tune. This is an original saying of mine.' I looked at Lee Ann. She was a fetching hunk, a honey-coloured creature, but there was hate in her eyes for both of us. Her ambition was to marry a rich man. She came from a small town in Oregon. She rued the day she ever took up with Remi. On one of his big showoff week-ends he spent a hundred dollars on her and she thought she'd found an heir. Instead she was hung-up in this shack, and for lack of anything else she had to stay there. She had a job in Frisco; she had to take the Greyhound bus at the crossroads and go in every day. She never forgave Remi for it.

I was to stay in the shack and write a shining original story for a Hollywood studio. Remi was going to fly down in a strato-sphere liner with this harp under his arm and make us all rich; Lee Ann was to go with him; he was going to introduce her to his buddy's father, who was a famous director and an intimate of W. C. Fields. So the first week I stayed in the shack in Mill City, writing furiously at some gloomy tale about New York that I thought would satisfy a Hollywood director, and the trouble with it was that it was too sad. Remi could barely read it, and so he just carried it down to Hollywood a few weeks later. Lee Ann was too bored and hated us too much to bother reading it. I spent countless rainy hours drinking coffee and scribbling. Finally I told Remi it wouldn't do; I wanted a job; I had to depend on them for cigarettes. A shadow of disappoint-ment crossed Remi's brow – he was always being disappointed about the funniest things. He had a heart of gold.

He arranged to get me the same kind of job he had, as a guard in the barracks. I went through the necessary routine, and to my surprise the bastards hired me. I was sworn in by the local police chief, given a badge, a club, and now I was a special policeman. I wondered what Dean and Carlo and Old Bull Lee would say about this. I had to have navy-blue trousers to go with my black jacket and cop cap; for the first two weeks I had to wear Remi's trousers; since he was so tall, and had a potbelly from eating voracious meals out of boredom, I went flapping around like Charlie Chaplin to my first night of work. Remi gave me a flashlight and his ·32 automatic.

'Where'd you get this gun?' I asked.

'On my way to the Coast last summer I jumped off the train at North Platte, Nebraska, to stretch my legs, and what did I see in the window but this unique little gun, which I promptly bought and barely made the train.'

And I tried to tell him what North Platte meant to me, buying the whisky with the boys, and he slapped me on the back and said I was the funniest man in the world.

With the flashlight to illuminate my way, I climbed the steep walls of the south canyon, got up on the highway streaming with cars Frisco-bound in the night, scrambled down the other side, almost falling, and came to the bottom of a ravine where a little farmhouse stood near a creek and where every blessed night the same dog barked at me. Then it was a fast walk along a silvery, dusty road beneath inky trees of California – a road like in *The Mark of Zorro* and a road like all the roads you see in Western B movies. I used to take out my gun and play cowboys in the dark. Then I climbed another hill and there were the barracks. These barracks were for the temporary quartering of overseas construction workers. The men who came through stayed there, waiting for their ship. Most of them were bound for Okinawa. Most of them were running away from something – usually the law. There were tough groups from Alabama, shifty men from New York, all kinds from all over. And, knowing full well how horrible it would be to work a full year in Okinawa, they drank. The job of the special guard was to see that they didn't tear the barracks down. We had our headquarters in the main building, just a wooden contraption with panel-walled offices. Here at a roll-top desk we sat around, shifting our guns off our hips and yawning, and the old cops told stories.

It was a horrible crew of men, men with cop-souls, all except Remi and myself. Remi was only trying to make a living, and so was I, but these men wanted to make arrests and get compliments from the chief of police in town. They even said that if you didn't make at least one a month you'd be fired. I gulped at the prospect of making an arrest. What actually happened was that I was as drunk as anybody in the barracks the night all hell broke loose.

This was a night when the schedule was so arranged that I was all alone for six hours – the only cop on the grounds; and everybody in the barracks seemed to have gotten drunk that night. It was because their ship was leaving in the morning. They drank like seamen the night before the anchor goes up. I sat in the office with my feet on the desk, reading *Blue Book* adventures about Oregon and the north country, when suddenly I realized there was a great hum of activity in the usually quiet night. I went out. Lights were burning in practically every damned shack on the grounds. Men were shouting, bottles were breaking. It was do or die for me. I took my flashlight and went to the noisiest door and knocked. Someone opened it about six inches.

'What do *you* want?'

I said, 'I'm guarding these barracks tonight and you boys are supposed to keep quiet as much as you can' – or some such silly remark. They slammed the door in my face. I stood looking at the wood of it against my nose. It was like a Western movie; the time had come for me to assert myself. I knocked again. They opened up wide this time. 'Listen,' I said, 'I don't want to come around bothering you fellows, but I'll lose my job if you make too much noise.'

'Who are you?'

'I'm a guard here.'

'Never seen you before.'

'Well, here's my badge.'

'What are you doing with that pistolcracker on your ass?'

'It isn't mine,' I apologized. 'I borrowed it.'

'Have a drink, fer krissakes.' I didn't mind if I did. I took two.

63

I said, 'Okay, boys? You'll keep quiet, boys? I'll get hell, you know.'

'It's all right, kid,' they said. 'Go make your rounds. Come back for another drink if you want one.'

And I went to all the doors in this manner, and pretty soon I was as drunk as anybody else. Come dawn, it was my duty to put up the American flag on a sixty-foot pole, and this morning I put it up upside down and went home to bed. When I came back in the evening the regular cops were sitting around grimly in the office.

'Say, bo, what was all the noise around here last night? We've had complaints from people who live in those houses across the canyon.'

'I don't know,' I said. 'It sounds pretty quiet right now.'

'The whole contingent's gone. You was supposed to keep order around here last night – the chief is yelling at you. And another thing – do you know you can go to jail for putting the American flag upside down on a government pole?'

'Upside down?' I was horrified; of course I hadn't realized it. I did it every morning mechanically.

'Yessir,' said a fat cop who'd spent twenty-two years as a guard in Alcatraz. 'You could go to jail for doing something like that.' The others nodded grimly. They were always sitting around on their asses; they were proud of their jobs. They handled their guns and talked about them. They were itching to shoot somebody. Remi and me.

The cop who had been an Alcatraz guard was potbellied and about sixty, retired but unable to keep away from the atmospheres that had nourished his dry soul all his life. Every night he drove to work in his '35 Ford, punched the clock exactly on time, and sat down at the rolltop desk. He laboured painfully over the simple form we all had to fill out every night – rounds, time, what happened, and so on. Then he leaned back and told stories. 'You should have been here about two months ago when me and Sledge' (that was another cop, a youngster who wanted to be a Texas Ranger and had to be satisfied with his present lot) 'arrested a drunk in Barrack G. Boy, you should have seen the blood fly. I'll take you over there tonight and show you the stains on the wall. We had him bouncing from one wall to another. First Sledge hit him, and then me, and then he subsided and went quietly. That fellow swore to kill us when he got out of jail – got thirty days. Here it is *sixty* days and he ain't showed up.' And this was the big point of the story. They'd put such a fear in him that he was too yellow to come back and try to kill them.

The old cop went on, sweetly reminiscing about the horrors of Alcatraz. 'We used to march 'em like an Army platoon to breakfast. Wasn't one man out of step. Everything went like clockwork. You should have seen it. I was a guard there for twenty-two years. Never had any trouble. Those boys knew we meant business. A lot of fellows get soft guarding prisoners, and they're the ones that usually get in trouble. Now you take you – from what I've been observing about you, you seem to me a little bit too *leenent* with the men.' He raised his pipe and looked at me sharp. 'They take advantage of that, you know.'

I knew that. I told him I wasn't cut out to be a cop.

'Yes, but that's the job that you *applied for.* Now you got to make up your mind one way or the other, or you'll never get anywhere. It's your duty. You're sworn in. You can't compromise with things like this. Law and order's got to be kept.'

I didn't know what to say; he was right; but all I wanted to do was sneak out into the night and disappear somewhere, and go and find out what everybody was doing all over the country.

The other cop, Sledge, was tall, muscular, with a black-haired crew-cut and a nervous twitch in his neck – like a boxer who's always punching one fist into another. He rigged himself out like a Texas Ranger of old. He wore a revolver down low, with ammunition belt, and carried a small quirt of some kind, and pieces of leather hanging everywhere, like a walking torture chamber : shiny shoes, low-hanging jacket, cocky hat, everything but boots. He was always showing me holds – reaching down under my crotch and lifting me up nimbly. In point of strength I could have thrown him clear to the ceiling with the same hold, and I knew it well; but I never let him know for fear he'd want a wrestling match. A wrestling match with a guy like that would end up in shooting. I'm sure he was a better shot; I'd never had a gun in my life. It scared me even to load one. He desperately wanted to make arrests. One night we were alone on duty and he came back red-faced mad.

'I told some boys in there to keep quiet and they're still making noise. I told them twice. I always give a man two chances. Not three. You come with me and I'm going back there and arrest them.'

'Well, let *me* give them a third chance,' I said. 'I'll talk to them.'

'No, sir, I never gave a man more than two chances.' I sighed. Here we go. We went to the offending room, and Sledge opened the door and told everybody to file out. It was embarrassing. Every single one of us was blushing. This is the story of America. Everybody's doing what they think they're supposed to do. So what if a bunch of men talk in loud voices and drink the night? But Sledge wanted to prove something. He made sure to bring me along in case they jumped him. They might have. They were all brothers, all from Alabama. We strolled back to the station, Sledge in front and me in back.

One of the boys said to me, 'Tell that crotch-eared mean-ass to take it easy on us. We might get fired for this and never get to Okinawa.'

'I'll talk to him.'

In the station I told Sledge to forget it. He said, for everybody to hear, and blushing, 'I don't give anybody no more than two chances.'

'What the hail,' said the Alabaman, 'what difference does it make? We might lose our jobs.' Sledge said nothing and filled out the arrest forms. He arrested only one of them; he called the prowl car in town. They came and took him away. The other brothers walked off sullenly. 'What's Ma going to say?' they said. One of them came back to me. 'You tell that Texass son-ofabitch if my brother ain't out of jail tomorrow night he's going to get his ass fixed.' I told Sledge, in a neutral way, and he said nothing. The brother was let off easy and nothing happened. The contingent shipped out; a new wild bunch came in. If it hadn't been for Remi Boncœur I wouldn't have stayed at this job two hours.

But Remi Boncœur and I were on duty alone many a night, and that's when everything jumped. We made our first round of the evening in a leisurely way, Remi trying all the doors to see if they were locked and hoping to find one unlocked. He'd say, 'For years I've an idea to develop a dog into a superthief who'd go into these guys' rooms and take dollars out of their pockets. I'd train him to take nothing but green money; I'd make him smell it all day long. If there was any humanly possible way, I'd train him to take only twenties.' Remi was full of mad schemes; he talked about that dog for weeks. Only once he found an unlocked door. I didn't like the idea, so I sauntered on down the hall. Remi stealthily opened it up. He came face to face with the barracks supervisor. Remi hated that man's face. He asked me, 'What's the name of that Russian author you're always talking about – the one who put the newspapers in his shoe and walked around in a stovepipe hat he found in a garbage pail?' This was an exaggeration of what I'd told Remi of Dostoevski. 'Ah, that's it – that's *it* – Dostioffski. A man with a face like that supervisor can only have one name – it's Dostioffski. The only unlocked door he ever found belonged to Dostioffski. D. was asleep when he heard someone fiddling with his doorknob. He got up in his pyjamas. He came to the door looking twice as ugly as usual. When Remi opened it he saw a haggard face suppurated with hatred and dull fury.

'What is the meaning of this?'

'I was only trying this door. I thought this was the – ah – mop room. I was looking for a mop.'

'What do you *mean* you were looking for a mop?'

'Well – ah.'

And I stepped up and said, 'One of the men puked in the hall upstairs. We have to mop it up.'

'This is *not* the mop room. This is *my* room. Another incident like this and I'll have you fellows investigated and thrown out! Do you understand me clearly?'

'A fellow puked upstairs,' I said again.

'The mop room is down the hall. Down there.' And he pointed, and waited for us to go and get a mop, which we did, and foolishly carried it upstairs.

I said, 'Goddammit, Remi, you're always getting us into trouble. Why don't you lay off? Why do you have to steal all the time?'

'The world owes me a few things, that's all. You can't teach the old maestro a new tune. You go on talking like that and I'm going to start calling you Dostioffski.'

Remi was just like a little boy. Somewhere in his past, in his lonely schooldays in France, they'd taken everything from him; his step-parents just stuck him in schools and left him there; he was browbeaten and thrown out of one school after another; he walked the French roads at night devising curses out of his innocent stock of words. He was out to get back everything he'd lost; there was no end to his loss; this thing would drag on forever.

The barracks cafeteria was our meat. We looked around to make sure nobody was watching, and especially to see if any of our cop friends were lurking about to check on us; then I squatted down, and Remi put a foot on each shoulder and up he went. He opened the window, which was never locked since he saw to it in the evenings, scrambled through, and came down on the flour table. I was a little more agile and just jumped and crawled in. Then we went to the soda fountain. Here, realizing a dream of mine from infancy, I took the cover off the chocolate ice cream and stuck my hand in wrist-deep and hauled me up a skewer of ice cream and licked at it. Then we got ice-cream boxes and stuffed them, poured chocolate syrup over and sometimes strawberries too, then walked around in the kitchens, opened iceboxes, to see what we could take home in our pockets. I often tore a piece of roast beef and wrapped it in a napkin. 'You must know what President Truman said,' Remi would say. 'We must cut down on the cost of living.'

One night I waited a long time as he filled a huge box full of groceries. Then we couldn't get it through the window. Remi had to unpack everything and put it back. Later in the night, when he went off duty and I was all alone on the base, a strange thing happened. I was taking a walk along the old canyon trail, hoping to meet a deer (Remi had seen deer around, that country being wild even in 1947), when I heard a frightening noise in the dark. It was a huffing and puffing. I thought it was a rhinoceros coming for me in the dark. I grabbed my gun. A tall figure appeared in the canyon gloom; it had an enormous head. Suddenly I realized it was Remi with a huge box of groceries on his shoulder. He was moaning and groaning from the enormous weight of it. He'd found the key to the cafeteria somewhere and had got his groceries out the front door. I said, 'Remi, I thought you were home; what the hell are you doing?'

And he said, 'Paradise, I have told you several times what President Truman said, *we must cut down on the cost of living.*' And I heard him huff and puff into the darkness. I've already described that awful trail back to our shack, up hill and down dale. He hid the groceries in the tall grass and came back to me. 'Sal, I just can't make it alone. I'm going to divide it into two boxes and you're going to help me.'

'But I'm on duty.'

'I'll watch the place while you're gone. Things are getting rough all around. We've just got to make it the best way we can, and that's all there is to it.' He wiped his face. 'Whoo! I've told you time and time again, Sal, that we're buddies, and we're in this thing together. There's just no two ways about it. The Dostioffskis, the cops, the Lee Anns, all the evil skulls of this world, are out for our skin. It's up to us to see that nobody pulls any schemes on us. They've got a lot more up their sleeves besides a dirty arm. Remember that. You can't teach the old maestro a new tune.'

I finally asked, 'Whatever are we going to do about shipping out?' We'd been doing these things for ten weeks. I was making fifty-five bucks a week and sending my aunt an average of forty. I'd spent only one evening in San Francisco in all that time. My life was wrapped in the shack, in Remi's battles with Lee Ann, and in the middle of the night at the barracks.

Remi was gone off in the dark to get another box. I struggled with him on that old Zorro road. We piled up the groceries a mile high on Lee Ann's kitchen table. She woke up and rubbed her eyes.

'You know what President Truman said?' She was delighted. I suddenly began to realize that everybody in America is a natural-born thief. I was getting the bug myself. I even began to try to see if doors were locked. The other cops were getting suspicious of us; they saw it in our eyes; they understood with unfailing instinct what was on our minds. Years of experience had taught them the likes of Remi and me.

In the daytime Remi and I went out with the gun and tried to shoot quail in the hills. Remi sneaked up to within three feet of the clucking birds and let go a blast of the ·32. He missed. His tremendous laugh roared over the California woods and over America. 'The time has come for you and me to go and see the Banana King.'

It was Saturday; we got all spruced up and went down to the bus station on the crossroads. We rode into San Francisco and strolled through the streets. Remi's huge laugh resounded everywhere we went. 'You must write a story about the Banana King,' he warned me. 'Don't pull any tricks on the old maestro and write about something else. The Banana King is your meat. There stands the Banana King.' The Banana King was an old man selling bananas on the corner. I was completely bored. But Remi kept punching me in the ribs and even dragging me along by the collar. 'When you write about the Banana King you write about the human-interest things of life.' I told him I didn't give a damn about the Banana King. 'Until you learn to realize the importance of the Banana King you will know absolutely nothing about the human-interest things of the world,' said Remi emphatically.

There was an old rusty freighter out in the bay that was used as a buoy. Remi was all for rowing out to it, so one afternoon Lee Ann packed a lunch and we hired a boat and went out there. Remi brought some tools. Lee Ann took all her clothes off and lay down to sun herself on the flying bridge. I watched her from the poop. Remi went clear down to the boiler rooms below, where rats scurried around, and began hammering and banging away for copper lining that wasn't there. I sat in the dilapidated officer's mess. It was an old, old ship and had been beautifully appointed, with scroll-work in the wood, and built-in sea-chests. This was the ghost of the San Francisco of Jack London. I dreamed at the sunny messboard. Rats ran in the pantry. Once upon a time there'd been a blue-eyed sea captain dining in here.

I joined Remi in the bowels below. He yanked at everything loose. 'Not a thing. I thought there'd be copper, I thought there'd be at least an old wrench or two. This ship's been stripped by a bunch of thieves.' It had been standing in the bay for years. The copper had been stolen by a hand that was a hand no more.

I said to Remi, 'I'd love to sleep in this old ship some night when the fog comes in and the thing creaks and you hear the big B-O of the buoys.'

Remi was astounded; his admiration for me doubled. 'Sal, I'll pay you five dollars if you have the nerve to do that. Don't you realize this thing may be haunted by the ghosts of old sea captains? I'll not only pay you five, I'll row you out and pack you a lunch and lend you blankets and candle.'

'Agreed!' I said. Remi ran to tell Lee Ann. I wanted to jump down from a mast and land right in her, but I kept my promise to Remi. I averted my eyes from her.

Meanwhile I began going to Frisco more often; I tried everything in the books to make a girl. I even spent a whole night with a girl on a park bench, till dawn, without success. She was a blonde from Minnesota. There were plenty of queers. Several times I went to San Fran with my gun and when a queer approached me in a bar john I took out the gun and said, 'Eh? Eh? What's that you say?' He bolted. I've never understood why I did that; I knew queers all over the country. It was just the loneliness of San Francisco and the fact that I had a gun. I had to show it to someone. I walked by a jewelry store and had the sudden impulse to shoot up the window, take out the finest rings and bracelets, and run to give them to Lee Ann. Then we could flee to Nevada together. The time was coming for me to leave Frisco or I'd go crazy.

I wrote long letters to Dean and Carlo, who were now at Old Bull's shack in the Texas bayou. They said they were ready to come join me in San Fran as soon as this-and-that was ready. Meanwhile everything began to collapse with Remi and Lee Ann and me. The September rains came, and with them harangues. Remi had flown down to Hollywood with her, taking my sad silly movie original, and nothing had happened. The famous director was drunk and paid no attention to them; they hung around his Malibu Beach cottage; they started fighting in front of other guests; and they flew back.

The final topper was the racetrack. Remi saved all his money, about a hundred dollars, spruced me up in some of his clothes, put Lee Ann on his arm, and off we went to Golden Gate race-track near Richmond across the bay. To show you what a heart that guy had, he put half of our stolen groceries in a tremendous brown paper bag and took them to a poor widow he knew in Richmond in a housing project much like our own, wash flapping in the California sun. We went with him. There were sad ragged children. The woman thanked Remi. She was the sister of some seaman he vaguely knew. 'Think nothing of it, Mrs Carter,' said Remi in his most elegant and polite tones. 'There's plenty more where that came from.'

We proceeded to the racetrack. He made incredible twenty-dollar bets to win, and before the seventh race he was broke. With our last two food dollars he placed still another bet and lost. We had to hitchhike back to San Francisco. I was on the road again. A gentleman gave us a ride in his snazzy car. I sat up front with him. Remi was trying to put a story down that he'd lost his wallet in back of the grandstand at the track. 'The truth is,' I said, 'we lost all our money on the races, and to forestall any more hitching from racetracks, from now on we go to a bookie, hey, Remi?' Remi blushed all over. The man finally admitted he was an official of the Golden Gate track. He let us off at the elegant Palace Hotel; we watched him disappear among the chandeliers, his pockets full of money, his head held high.

'Wagh! Whoo!' howled Remi in the evening streets of Frisco. 'Paradise rides with the man who runs the racetrack and swears he's switching to bookies. Lee Ann, Lee Ann!' He punched and mauled her. 'Positively the funniest man in the world! There must be a lot of Italians in Sausalito. Aaah-how!' He wrapped himself around a pole to laugh.

That night it started raining as Lee Ann gave dirty looks to both of us. Not a cent left in the house. The rain drummed on the roof. 'It's going to last for a week,' said Remi. He had taken off his beautiful suit; he was back in his miserable shorts and Army cap and T-shirt. His great brown sad eyes stared at the planks of the floor. The gun lay on the table. We could hear Mr Snow laughing his head off across the rainy night somewhere.

'I get so sick and tired of that sonofabitch,' snapped Lee Ann.

She was on the go to start trouble. She began needling Remi. He was busy going through his little black book, in which were names of people, mostly seamen, who owed him money. Beside their names he wrote curses in red ink. I dreaded the day I'd ever find my way into that book. Lately I'd been sending so much money to my aunt that I only bought four or five dollars' worth of groceries a week. In keeping with what President Truman said, I added a few more dollars' worth. But Remi felt it wasn't my proper share; so he'd taken to hanging the grocery slips, the long ribbon slips with itemized prices, on the wall of the bathroom for me to see and understand. Lee Ann was convinced Remi was hiding money from her, and that I was too, for that matter. She threatened to leave him.

Remi curled his lip. 'Where do you think you'll go?'

'Jimmy.'

'*Jimmy*? A cashier at the racetrack? Do you hear that, Sal, Lee Ann is going to go and put the latch on a cashier at the racetrack. Be sure and bring your broom, dear, the horses are going to eat a lot of oats this week with my hundred-dollar bill.'

Things grew to worse proportions; the rain roared. Lee Ann originally lived in the place first, so she told Remi to pack up and get out. He started packing. I pictured myself all alone in this rainy shack with that untamed shrew. I tried to intervene. Remi pushed Lee Ann. She made a jump for the gun. Remi gave me the gun and told me to hide it; there was a clip of eight shells in it. Lee Ann began screaming, and finally she put on her raincoat and went out in the mud to find a cop, and what a cop – if it wasn't our old friend Alcatraz. Luckily he wasn't home. She came back all wet. I hid in my corner with my head between my knees. Gad, what was I doing three thousand miles from home? Why had I come here? Where was my slow boat to China?

'And another thing, you dirty man,' yelled Lee Ann. 'Tonight was the last time I'll ever make you your filthy brains and eggs, and your filthy lamb curry, so you can fill your filthy belly and get fat and sassy right before my eyes.'

'It's all right,' Remi just said quietly. 'It's perfectly all right. When I took up with you I didn't expect roses and moonshine and I'm not surprised this day. I tried to do a few things for you – I tried my best for both of you; you've both let me down. I'm terribly, terribly disappointed in both of you,' he continued in absolute sincerity. 'I thought something would come of us together, something fine and lasting, I tried, I flew to Hollywood, I got Sal a job, I bought you beautiful dresses, I tried to introduce you to the finest people in San Francisco. You refused, you both refused to follow the slightest wish I had. I asked for nothing in return. Now I ask for one last favour and then I'll never ask a favour again. My stepfather is coming to San Francisco next Saturday night. All I ask is that you come with me and try to look as though everything is the way I've written him. In other words, you, Lee Ann, you are my girl, and you, Sal, you are my friend. I've arranged to borrow a hundred dollars for Saturday night. I'm going to see that my father has a good time and go away without any reason in the world to worry about me.'

This surprised me. Remi's stepfather was a distinguished doctor who had practised in Vienna, Paris, and London. I said, 'You mean to tell me you're going to spend a hundred dollars on your stepfather? He's got more money than you'll ever have! You'll be in debt, man!'

'That's all right,' said Remi quietly and with defeat in his voice. 'I ask only one last thing of you – that you *try* at least to make things look all right and *try* to make a good impression. I love my stepfather and I respect him. He's coming with his young wife. We must show him every courtesy.' There were times when Remi was really the most gentlemanly person in the world. Lee Ann was impressed, and looked forward to meeting his stepfather; she thought he might be a catch, if his son wasn't.

Saturday night rolled around. I had already quit my job with the cops, just before being fired for not making enough arrests, and this was going to be my last Saturday night. Remi and Lee Ann went to meet his stepfather at the hotel room first; I had travelling money and got crocked in the bar downstairs. Then I went up to join them all, late as hell. His father opened the door, a distinguished tall man in pince-nez. 'Ah,' I said on seeing him. 'Monsieur Boncœur, how are you? *Je suis haut!*' I cried, which was intended to mean in French, 'I am high, I have been drinking', but means absolutely nothing in French. The doctor was perplexed. I had already screwed up Remi. He blushed at me.

We all went to a swank restaurant to eat – Alfred's, in North Beach, where poor Remi spent a good fifty dollars for the five of us, drinks and all. And now came the worst thing. Who should be sitting at the bar in Alfred's but my old friend Roland Major! He had just arrived from Denver and got a job on a San Francisco paper. He was crocked. He wasn't even shaved. He rushed over and slapped me on the back as I lifted a highball to my lips. He threw himself down on the booth beside Dr Bon-cœur and leaned over the man's soup to talk to me. Remi was red as a beet.

'Won't you introduce your friend, Sal?' he said with a weak smile.

'Roland Major of the San Francisco *Argus*,' I tried to say with a straight face. Lee Ann was furious at me.

Major began chatting in the monsieur's ear. 'How do you like teaching high-school French?' he yelled.

'Pardon me, but I don't teach high-school French.'

'Oh, I thought you taught high-school French.' He was being deliberately rude. I remembered the night he wouldn't let us have our party in Denver; but I forgave him.

I forgave everybody, I gave up, I got drunk. I began talking moonshine and roses to the doctor's young wife. I drank so much I had to go to the men's room every two minutes, and to do so I had to hop over Dr Boncœur's lap. Everything was falling apart. My stay in San Francisco was coming to an end. Remi would never talk to me again. It was horrible because I really loved Remi and I was one of the very few people in the world who knew what a genuine and grand fellow he was. It would take years for him to get over it. How disastrous all this was compared to what I'd written him from Paterson, planning my red line Route 6 across America. Here I was at the end of America – no more land – and now there was nowhere to go but back. I determined at least to make my trip a circular one: I decided then and there to go to Hollywood and back through Texas to see my bayou gang; then the rest be damned.

Major was thrown out of Alfred's. Dinner was over anyway, so I joined him; that is to say, Remi suggested it, and I went off with Major to drink. We sat at a table in the Iron Pot and Major said, 'Sam, I don't like that fairy at the bar,' in a loud voice.

'Yeah, Jake?' I said.

'Sam,' he said, 'I think I'll get up and conk him.'

'No, Jake,' I said, carrying on with the Hemingway imitation. 'Just aim from here and see what happens.' We ended up swaying on a street corner.

In the morning, as Remi and Lee Ann slept, and as I looked with some sadness at the big pile of wash Remi and I were scheduled to do in the Bendix machine in the shack in the back (which had always been such a joyous sunny operation among the coloured women and with Mr Snow laughing his head off), I decided to leave. I went out on the porch. 'No, dammit,' I said to myself, 'I promised I wouldn't leave till I climbed that mountain.' That was the big side of the canyon that led mysteriously to the Pacific Ocean.

So I stayed another day. It was Sunday. A great heat wave descended; it was a beautiful day, the sun turned red at three. I started up the mountain and got to the top at four. All those lovely California cottonwoods and eucalypti brooded on all sides. Near the peak there were no more trees, just rocks and grass. Cattle were grazing on the top of the coast. There was the Pacific, a few more foothills away, blue and vast and with a great wall of white advancing from the legendary potato patch where Frisco fogs are born. Another hour and it would come streaming through the Golden Gate to shroud the romantic city in white, and a young man would hold his girl by the hand and climb slowly up a long white sidewalk with a bottle of Tokay in his pocket. That was Frisco; and beautiful women standing in white doorways, waiting for their men; and Coit Tower, and the Embarcadero, and Market Street, and the eleven teeming hills.

I spun around till I was dizzy; I thought I'd fall down as in a dream, clear off the precipice. Oh where is the girl I love? I thought, and looked everywhere, as I had looked everywhere in the little world below. And before me was the great raw bulge and bulk of my American continent; somewhere far across, gloomy, crazy New York was throwing up its cloud of dust and brown steam. There is something brown and holy about the East; and California is white like washlines and emptyheaded — at least that's what I thought then.

12

IN THE morning Remi and Lee Ann were asleep as I quietly packed and slipped out the window the same way I'd come in, and left Mill City with my canvas bag. And I never spent that night on the old ghost ship – the *Admiral Freebee*, it was called – and Remi and I were lost to each other.

In Oakland I had a beer among the bums of a saloon with a wagon wheel in front of it, and I was on the road again. I walked clear across Oakland to get on the Fresno road. Two rides took me to Bakersfield, four hundred miles south. The first was the mad one, with a burly blond kid in a souped-up rod. 'See that toe?' he said as he gunned the heap to eighty and passed everybody on the road. 'Look at it.' It was swathed in bandages. 'I just had it amputated this morning. The bastards wanted me to stay in the hospital. I packed my bag and left. What's a toe?' Yes, indeed, I said to myself, look out now, and I hung on. You never saw a driving fool like that. He made Tracy in no time. Tracy is a railroad town; brakemen eat surly meals in diners by the tracks. Trains howl away across the valley. The sun goes down long and red. All the magic names of the valley unrolled – Manteca, Madera, all the rest. Soon it got dusk, a grapy dusk, a purple dusk over tangerine groves and long melon fields; the sun the colour of pressed grapes, slashed with burgundy red, the fields the colour of love and Spanish mysteries. I stuck my head out of the window and took deep breaths of the fragrant air. It was the most beautiful of all moments. The madman was a brakeman with the Southern Pacific and he lived in Fresno; his father was also a brakeman. He lost his toe in the Oakland yards, switching, I didn't quite understand how. He drove me into buzzing Fresno and let me off by the south side of town. I went for a quick Coke in a little grocery by the tracks, and here came a melancholy Armenian youth along the red box-cars, and just at that moment a locomotive howled, and I said to myself, Yes, yes, Saroyan's town.

I had to go south; I got on the road. A man in a brand-new pick-up truck picked me up. He was from Lubbock, Texas, and was in the trailer business. 'You want to buy a trailer?' he asked me. 'Any time, look me up.' He told stories about his father in Lubbock. 'One night my old man left the day's receipts settin on top of the safe, plumb forgot. What happened – thief came in the night, acetylene torch and all, broke open the safe, riffled up the papers, kicked over a few chairs, and left. And that thousand dollars was settin right there on top of the safe, what do you know about that?'

He let me off south of Bakersfield, and then my adventure began. It grew cold. I put on the flimsy Army raincoat I'd bought in Oakland for three dollars and shuddered in the road. I was standing in front of an ornate Spanish-style motel that was lit like a jewel. The cars rushed by, LA-bound. I gestured frantically. It was too cold. I stood there till midnight, two hours straight, and cursed and cursed. It was just like Stuart, Iowa, again. There was nothing to do but spend a little over two dollars for a bus the remaining miles to Los Angeles. I walked back along the highway to Bakersfield and into the station, and sat down on a bench.

I had bought my ticket and was waiting for the LA bus when all of a sudden I saw the cutest little Mexican girl in slacks come cutting across my sight. She was in one of the buses that had just pulled in with a big sigh of airbrakes; it was discharging passengers for a rest stop. Her breasts stuck out straight and true; her little flanks looked delicious; her hair was long and lustrous black; and her eyes were great big blue things with timidities inside. I wished I was on her bus. A pain stabbed my heart, as it did every time I saw a girl I loved who was going the opposite direction in this too-big world. The announcer called the LA bus. I picked up my bag and got on, and who should be sitting there alone but the Mexican girl. I dropped right opposite her and began scheming right off. I was so lonely, so sad, so tired, so quivering, so broken, so beat, that I got up my courage, the courage necessary to approach a strange girl, and acted. Even then I spent five minutes beating my thighs in the dark as the bus rolled down the road.

You gotta, you gotta or you'll die! Damn fool, talk to her! What's wrong with you? Aren't you tired enough of yourself by now? And before I knew what I was doing I leaned across the aisle to her (she was trying to sleep on the seat) and said, 'Miss, would you like to use my raincoat for a pillow?'

She looked up with a smile and said, 'No, thank you very much.'

I sat back, trembling; I lit a butt. I waited till she looked at me, with a sad little sidelook of love, and I got right up and leaned over her. 'May I sit with you, miss?'

'If you wish.'

And this I did. 'Where going?'

'LA.' I loved the way she said 'LA'; I love the way everybody says 'LA' on the Coast; it's their one and only golden town when all is said and done.

'That's where I'm going too!' I cried. 'I'm very glad you let me sit with you, I was very lonely and I've been travelling a hell of a lot.' And we settled down to telling our stories. Her story was this: She had a husband and child. The husband beat her, so she left him, back at Sabinal, south of Fresno, and was going to LA to live with her sister awhile. She left her little son with her family, who were grape-pickers and lived in a shack in the vineyards. She had nothing to do but brood and get mad. I felt like putting my arms around her right away. We talked and talked. She said she loved to talk with me. Pretty soon she was saying she wished she could go to New York too. 'Maybe we could!' I laughed. The bus groaned up Grapevine Pass and then we were coming down into the great sprawls of light. Without coming to any particular agreement we began holding hands, and in the same way it was mutely and beautifully and purely decided that when I got my hotel room in LA she would be beside me. I ached all over for her; I leaned my head in her beautiful hair. Her little shoulders drove me mad; I hugged her and hugged her. And she loved it.

'I love love,' she said, closing her eyes. I promised her beautiful love. I gloated over her. Our stories were told; we subsided into silence and sweet anticipatory thoughts. It was as simple as that. You could have all your Peaches and Bettys and Marylous and Ritas and Camilles and Inezes in this world; this was my girl and my kind of girlsoul, and I told her that. She confessed she saw me watching her in the bus station. 'I thought you was a nice college boy.'

'Oh, I'm a college boy!' I assured her. The bus arrived in Hollywood. In the grey, dirty dawn, like the dawn when Joel McCrea met Veronica Lake in a diner, in the picture *Sullivan's Travels*, she slept in my lap. I looked greedily out the window : stucco houses and palms and drive-ins, the whole mad thing, the ragged promised land, the fantastic end of America. We got off the bus at Main Street, which was no different from where you get off a bus in Kansas City or Chicago or Boston – red brick, dirty, characters drifting by, trolleys grating in the hopeless dawn, the whorey smell of a big city.

And here my mind went haywire, I don't know why, I began getting the foolish paranoiac visions that Teresa, or Terry – her name – was a common little hustler who worked the buses for a guy's bucks by making appointments like ours in LA where she brought the sucker first to a breakfast place, where her pimp waited, and then to a certain hotel to which he had access with his gun or his whatever. I never confessed this to her. We ate breakfast and a pimp kept watching us; I fancied Terry was making secret eyes at him. I was tired and felt strange and lost in a faraway, disgusting place. The goof of terror took over my thoughts and made me act petty and cheap. 'Do you know that guy?' I said.

'What guy you mean, ho-ney?' I let it drop. She was slow and hung-up about everything she did; it took her a long time to eat; she chewed slowly and stared into space, and smoked a cigarette, and kept talking, and I was like a haggard ghost suspicioning every move she made, thinking she was stalling for time. This was all a fit of sickness. I was sweating as we went down the street hand in hand. The first hotel we hit had a room, and before I knew it I was locking the door behind me and she was sitting on the bed taking off her shoes. I kissed her meekly. Better she'd never know. To relax our nerves I knew we needed whisky, especially me. I ran out and fiddled all over twelve blocks, hurrying till I found a pint of whisky for sale at a news-stand. I ran back, all energy. Terry was in the bathroom, fixing her face. I poured one big drink in a water glass, and we had slugs. Oh, it was sweet and delicious and worth my whole lugubrious voyage. I stood behind her at the mirror, and we danced in the bathroom that way. I began talking about my friends back east.

I said, 'You ought to meet a great girl I know called Dorie. She's a six-foot redhead. If you came to New York she'd show you where to get work.'

'Who is this six-foot redhead?' she demanded suspiciously. 'Why do you tell me about her?' In her simple soul she couldn't fathom my kind of glad, nervous talk. I let it drop. She began to get drunk in the bathroom.

'Come on to bed!' I kept saying.

'Six-foot redhead, hey? And I thought you was a nice college boy, I saw you in your lovely sweater and I said to myself, Hmm, ain't he nice? No! And no! And no! You have to be a goddam pimp like all of them!'

'What on earth are you talking about?'

'Don't stand there and tell me that six-foot redhead ain't a madame, 'cause I know a madame when I hear about one, and you, you're just a pimp like all the rest I meet, everybody's a pimp.'

'Listen, Terry, I am not a pimp. I swear to you on the Bible I am not a pimp. Why should I be a pimp? My only interest is you.'

'All the time I thought I met a nice boy. I was so glad, I hugged myself and said, Hmm, a real nice boy instead of a pimp.'

'Terry,' I pleaded with all my soul. 'Please listen to me and understand, I'm not a pimp.' An hour ago I'd thought *she* was a hustler. How sad it was. Our minds, with their store of madness, had diverged. O gruesome life, how I moaned and pleaded, and then I got mad and realized I was pleading with a dumb little Mexican wench and I told her so; and before I knew it I picked up her red pumps and hurled them at the bathroom door and told her to get out. 'Go on, beat it!' I'd sleep and forget it; I had my own life, my own sad and ragged life forever. There was a dead silence in the bathroom. I took my clothes off and went to bed.

Terry came out with tears of sorriness in her eyes. In her simple and funny little mind had been decided the fact that a pimp does not throw a woman's shoes against the door and does not tell her to get out. In reverent and sweet little silence she took all her clothes off and slipped her tiny body into the sheets with me. It was brown as grapes. I saw her poor belly where there was a Caesarian scar; her hips were so narrow she couldn't bear a child without getting gashed open. Her legs were like little sticks. She was only four foot ten. I made love to her in the sweetness of the weary morning. Then, two tired angels of some kind, hung-up forlornly in an LA shelf, having found the closest and most delicious thing in life together, we fell asleep till late afternoon.

13

FOR THE next fifteen days we were together for better or for worse. When we woke up we decided to hitch-hike to New York together; she was going to be my girl in town. I envisioned wild complexities with Dean and Marylou and everybody — a season, a new season. First we had to work to earn enough money for the trip. Terry was all for starting at once with the twenty dollars I had left. I didn't like it. And, like a damn fool, I considered the problem for two days, as we read the want ads of wild LA papers I'd never seen before in my life, in cafeterias and bars, until my twenty dwindled to just over ten. We were very happy in our little hotel room. In the middle of the night I got up because I couldn't sleep, pulled the cover over baby's bare brown shoulder, and examined the LA night. What brutal, hot, siren-whining nights they are! Right across the street there was trouble. An old rickety rundown rooming house was the scene of some kind of tragedy. The cruiser was pulled up below and the cops were questioning an old man with grey hair. Sobbings came from within. I could hear everything, together with the hum of my hotel neon. I never felt sadder in my life. LA is the loneliest and most brutal of American cities; New York gets god-awful cold in the winter but there's a feeling of wacky comradeship somewhere in some streets. LA is a jungle.

South Main Street, where Terry and I took strolls with hot dogs, was a fantastic carnival of lights and wildness. Booted cops frisked people on practically every corner. The beatest characters in the country swarmed on the sidewalks – all of it under those soft Southern California stars that are lost in the brown halo of the huge desert encampment LA really is. You could smell tea, weed, I mean marijuana, floating in the air, together with the chili beans and beer. That grand wild sound of bop floated from beer parlours; it mixed medleys with every kind of cowboy and boogie-woogie in the American night. Everybody looked like Hassel. Wild Negroes with bop caps and goatees came laughing by; then long-haired brokendown hipsters straight off Route 66 from New York; then old desert rats, carrying packs and heading for a park bench at the Plaza; then Methodist ministers with ravelled sleeves, and an occasional Nature Boy saint in beard and sandals. I wanted to meet them all, talk to everybody, but Terry and I were too busy trying to get a buck together.

We went to Hollywood to try to work in the drugstore at Sunset and Vine. Now there was a corner! Great families off jalopies from the hinterlands stood around the sidewalk gaping for sight of some movie star, and the movie star never showed up. When a limousine passed they rushed eagerly to the kerb and ducked to look: some character in dark glasses sat inside with a bejewelled blonde. 'Don Ameche! Don Ameche!' 'No, George Murphy! George Murphy!' They milled around, looking at one another. Handsome queer boys who had come to Hollywood to be cowboys walked around, wetting their eyebrows with hincty fingertip. The most beautiful little gone gals in the world cut by in slacks; they came to be starlets; they ended up in drive-ins. Terry and I tried to find work at the drive-ins. It was no soap anywhere. Hollywood Boulevard was a great, screaming frenzy of cars; there were minor accidents at least once a minute; everybody was rushing off towards the farthest palm – and beyond that was the desert and nothingness. Hollywood Sams stood in front of swank restaurants, arguing exactly the same way Broadway Sams argue at Jacobs Beach, New York, only here they wore light-weight suits and their talk was cornier. Tall, cadaverous preachers shuddered by. Fat screaming women ran across the boulevard to get in line for the quiz shows. I saw Jerry Colonna buying a car at Buick Motors; he was inside the vast plate-glass window, fingering his mustachio. Terry and I ate in a cafeteria downtown which was decorated to look like a grotto, with metal tits spurting everywhere and great impersonal stone but-tockses belonging to deities and soapy Neptune. People ate lugubrious meals around the waterfalls, their faces green with marine sorrow. All the cops in LA looked like handsome gigolos; obviously they'd come to LA to make the movies. Everybody had come to make the movies, even me. Terry and I were finally reduced to trying to get jobs on South Main Street among the beat countermen and dishgirls who made no bones about their beatness, and even there it was no go. We still had ten dollars.

'Man, I'm going to get my clothes from Sis and we'll hitch-hike to New York,' said Terry. 'Come on, man. Let's do it. "If you can't boogie I know I'll show you how." ' That last part was a song of hers she kept singing. We hurried to her sister's house in the sliverous Mexican shacks somewhere be-yond Alameda Avenue. I waited in a dark alley behind Mexican kitchens because her sister wasn't supposed to see me. Dogs ran by. There were little lamps illuminating the little rat alleys. I could hear Terry and her sister arguing in the soft, warm night. I was ready for anything.

Terry came out and led me by the hand to Central Avenue, which is the coloured main drag of LA. And what a wild place it is, with chickenshacks barely big enough to house a jukebox, and the jukebox blowing nothing but blues, bop, and jump. We went up dirty tenement stairs and came to the room of Terry's friend Margarina, who owed Terry a skirt and a pair of shoes. Margarina was a lovely mulatto; her husband was black as spades and kindly. He went right out and bought a pint of whisky to host me proper. I tried to pay part of it, but he said no. They had two little children. The kids bounced on the bed; it was their play-place. They put their arms around me and looked at me with wonder. The wild humming night of Central Avenue – the night of Hamp's 'Central Avenue Breakdown' – howled and boomed along outside. They were singing in the halls, singing from their windows, just hell be damned and look out. Terry got her clothes and we said good-bye. We went down to a chickenshack and played records on the jukebox. A couple of Negro characters whispered in my ear about tea. A buck. I said okay, bring it. The connection came in and motioned me to the cellar toilet, where I stood dumbly as he said, 'Pick up, man, pick up.'

'Pick up what?' I said.

He had my dollar already. He was afraid to point at the floor. It was no floor, just basement. There lay something that looked like a little brown turd. He was absurdly cautious. 'Got to look out for myself, things ain't cool this past week.' I picked up the turd, which was a brown-paper cigarette, and went back to Terry, and off we went to the hotel room to get high. Nothing happened. It was Bull Durham tobacco. I wished I was wiser with my money.

Terry and I had to decide absolutely and once and for all what to do. We decided to hitch to New York with our remaining money. She picked up five dollars from her sister that night. We had about thirteen or less. So before the daily room rent was due again we packed up and took off on a red car to Arcadia, California, where Santa Anita racetrack is located under snow-capped mountains. It was night. We were pointed towards the American continent. Holding hands, we walked several miles down the road to get out of the populated district. It was a Saturday night. We stood under a roadlamp, thumbing, when suddenly cars full of young kids roared by with streamers flying. 'Yaah! Yaah! we won! we won!' They all shouted. Then they yoohooed us and got great glee out of seeing a guy and a girl on the road. Dozens of such cars passed, full of young faces and 'throaty young voices', as the saying goes. I hated every one of them. Who did they think they were, yaahing at somebody on the road just because they were little high-school punks and their parents carved the roast beef on Sunday afternoons? Who did they think they were, making fun of a girl reduced to poor circumstances with a man who wanted to belove? We were minding our own business.

And we didn't get a blessed ride. We had to walk back to town, and worst of all we needed coffee and had the misfortune of going into the only place open, which was a high-school soda fountain, and all the kids were there and remembered us. Now they saw that Terry was Mexican, a Pachuco wildcat; and that her boy was worse than that.

With her pretty nose in the air she cut out of there and we wandered together in the dark up along the ditches of the highways. I carried the bags. We were breathing fogs in the cold night air. I finally decided to hide from the world one more night with her, and the morning be damned. We went into a motel court and bought a comfortable little suite for about four dollars – shower, bathtowel, wall radio, and all. We held each other tight. We had long, serious talks and took baths and discussed things with the light on and then with the light out. Something was being proved, I was convincing her of something, which she accepted, and we concluded the pact in the dark, breathless, then pleased, like little lambs.

In the morning we boldly struck out on our new plan. We were going to take a bus to Bakersfield and work picking grapes. After a few weeks of that we were headed for New York in the proper way, by bus. It was a wonderful afternoon, riding up to Bakersfield with Terry: we sat back, relaxed, talked, saw the countryside roll by, and didn't worry about a thing. We arrived in Bakersfield in late afternoon. The plan was to hit every fruit wholesaler in town. Terry said we could live in tents on the job. The thought of living in a tent and picking grapes in the cool California mornings hit me right. But there were no jobs to be had, and much confusion, with everybody giving us innumerable tips, and no job materialized. Nevertheless we ate a Chinese dinner and set out with reinforced bodies. We went across the SP tracks to Mexican town. Terry jabbered with her brethren, asking for jobs. It was night now, and the little Mextown street was one blazing bulb of lights : movie marquees, fruit stands, penny arcades, five-and-tens, and hundreds of rickety trucks and mud-spattered jalopies, parked. Whole Mexican fruit-picking families wandered around eating popcorn. Terry talked to everybody. I was beginning to despair. What I needed – what Terry needed, too – was a drink, so we bought a quart of California port for thirty-five cents and went to the railroad yards to drink. We found a place where hobos had drawn up crates to sit over fires. We sat there and drank the wine. On our left were the freight cars, sad and sooty red beneath the moon; straight ahead the lights and airport pokers of Bakersfield proper; to our right a tremendous aluminium Quonset warehouse. Ah, it was a fine night, a warm night, a wine-drinking night, a moony night, and a night to hug your girl and talk and spit and be heavengoing. This we did. She was a drinking little fool and kept up with me and passed me and went right on talking till midnight. We never budged from those crates. Occasionally bums passed, Mexican mothers passed with children, and the prowl car came by and the cop got out to leak, but most of the time we were alone and mixing up our souls ever more and ever more till it would be terribly hard to say good-bye. At midnight we got up and goofed towards the highway.

Terry had a new idea. We would hitchhike to Sabinal, her hometown, and live in her brother's garage. Anything was all right with me. On the road I made Terry sit down on my bag to make her look like a woman in distress, and right off a truck stopped and we ran for it, all glee-giggles. The man was a good man; his truck was poor. He roared and crawled on up the valley. We got to Sabinal in the wee hours before dawn. I had finished the wine while Terry slept, and I was proper stoned. We got out and roamed the quiet leafy square of the little California town – a whistle stop on the SP. We went to find her brother's buddy, who would tell us where he was. Nobody home. As dawn began to break I lay flat on my back in the lawn of the town square and kept saying over and over again, 'You won't tell what he done up in Weed, will you? What'd he do up in Weed? You won't tell, will you? What'd he do up in Weed?' This was from the picture *Of Mice and Men*, with Burgess Meredith talking to the foreman of the ranch. Terry giggled. Anything I did was all right with her. I could lie there and go on doing that till the ladies came out for church and she wouldn't care. But finally I decided we'd be all set soon because of her brother, and I took her to an old hotel by the tracks and we went to bed comfortably.

In the bright, sunny morning Terry got up early and went to find her brother. I slept till noon; when I looked out the window I suddenly saw an SP freight going by with hundreds of hobos reclining on the flatcars and rolling merrily along with packs for pillows and funny papers before their noses, and some munching on good California grapes picked up by the siding. 'Damn!' I yelled. 'Hooee! It *is* the promised land.' They were all coming from Frisco; in a week they'd all be going back in the same grand style.

Terry arrived with her brother, his buddy, and her child. Her brother was a wild-buck Mexican hotcat with a hunger for booze, a great good kid. His buddy was a big flabby Mexican who spoke English without much accent and was loud and overanxious to please. I could see he had eyes for Terry. Her little boy was Johnny, seven years old, dark-eyed and sweet. Well, there we were, and another wild day began.

Her brother's name was Rickey. He had a '38 Chevy. We piled into that and took off for parts unknown. 'Where we going?' I asked. The buddy did the explaining – his name was Ponzo, that's what everybody called him. He stank. I found out why. His business was selling manure to farmers; he had a truck. Rickey always had three or four dollars in his pocket and was happy-go-lucky about things. He always said, 'That's right, man, there you go – dah you go, dah you go!' And he went. He drove seventy miles an hour in the old heap, and we went to Madera beyond Fresno to see some farmers about manure.

Rickey had a bottle. 'Today we drink, tomorrow we work. Dah you go, man – take a shot!' Terry sat in back with her baby; I looked back at her and saw the flush of homecoming joy on her face. The beautiful green countryside of October in California reeled by madly. I was guts and juice again and ready to go.

'Where do we go now, man?'

'We go find a farmer with some manure laying around. Tomorrow we drive back in the truck and pick it up. Man, we'll make a lot of money. Don't worry about nothing.'

'We're all in this together!' yelled Ponzo. I saw that was so – everywhere I went, everybody was in it together. We raced through the crazy streets of Fresno and on up the valley to some farmers in back roads. Ponzo got out of the car and conducted confused conversations with old Mexican farmers; nothing, of course, came of it.

'What we need is a drink!' yelled Rickey, and off we went to a crossroads saloon. Americans are always drinking in crossroads saloons on Sunday afternoon; they bring their kids; they gabble and brawl over brews; everything's fine. Come nightfall the kids start crying and the parents are drunk. They go weaving back to the house. Everywhere in America I've been in crossroads saloons drinking with whole families. The kids eat popcorn and chips and play in back. This we did. Rickey and I and Ponzo and Terry sat drinking and shouting with the music; little baby Johnny goofed with other children around the jukebox. The sun began to get red. Nothing had been accomplished. What was there to accomplish? '*Mañana*,' said Rickey. '*Mañana*, man, we make it; have another beer, man, dah you go, *dah you go!*'

We staggered out and got in the car; off we went to a highway bar. Ponzo was a big, loud, vociferous type who knew everybody in San Joaquin Valley. From the highway bar I went with him alone in the car to find a farmer; instead we wound up in Madera Mextown, digging the girls and trying to pick up a few for him and Rickey. And then, as purple dusk descended over the grape country, I found myself sitting dumbly in the car as he argued with some old Mexican at the kitchen door about the price of a watermelon the old man grew in the back yard. We got the watermelon; we ate it on the spot and threw the rinds on the old man's dirt sidewalk. All kinds of pretty little girls were cutting down the darkening street. I said, 'Where in the hell are we?'

'Don't worry, man,' said big Ponzo. 'Tomorrow we make a lot of money; tonight we don't worry.' We went back and picked up Terry and her brother and the kid and drove to Fresno in the highway lights of night. We were all raving hungry. We bounced over the railroad tracks in Fresno and hit the wild streets of Fresno Mextown. Strange Chinese hung out of windows, digging the Sunday night streets; groups of Mex chicks swaggered around in slacks; mambo blasted from jukeboxes; the lights were festooned around like Halloween. We went into a Mexican restaurant and had tacos and mashed pinto beans rolled in tortillas; it was delicious. I whipped out my last shining five-dollar bill which stood between me and the New Jersey shore and paid for Terry and me. Now I had four bucks. Terry and I looked at each other.

'Where we going to sleep tonight, baby?'

'I don't know.'

Rickey was drunk; now all he was saying was, 'Dah you go, man – dah you go, man,' in a tender and tired voice. It had been a long day. None of us knew what was going on, or what the Good Lord appointed. Poor little Johnny fell asleep on my arm. We drove back to Sabinal. On the way we pulled up sharp at a roadhouse on Highway 99. Rickey wanted one last beer. In back of the roadhouse were trailers and tents and a few rickety motel-style rooms. I inquired about the price and it was two bucks. I asked Terry how about it, and she said fine because we had the kid on our hands now and had to make him comfortable. So after a few beers in the saloon, where sullen Okies reeled to the music of a cowboy band, Terry and I and Johnny went into a motel room and got ready to hit the sack. Ponzo kept hanging around; he had no place to sleep. Rickey slept at his father's house in the vineyard shack.

'Where do you live, Ponzo?' I asked.

'Nowhere, man. I'm supposed to live with Big Rosey but she threw me out last night. I'm gonna get my truck and sleep in it tonight.'

Guitars tinkled. Terry and I gazed at the stars together and kissed. '*Mañana*,' she said. 'Everything'll be all right tomorrow, don't you think, Sal-honey, man?'

'Sure, baby, *mañana*.' It was always *mañana*. For the next week that was all I heard – *mañana*, a lovely word and one that probably means heaven.

Little Johnny jumped in bed, clothes and all, and went to sleep; sand spilled out of his shoes, Madera sand. Terry and I got up in the middle of the night and brushed the sand off the sheets. In the morning I got up, washed, and took a walk around the place. We were five miles out of Sabinal in the cotton fields and grape vineyards. I asked the big fat woman who owned the camp if any of the tents were vacant. The cheapest one, a dollar a day, was vacant. I fished up a dollar and moved into it. There were a bed, a stove, and a cracked mirror hanging from a pole; it was delightful. I had to stoop to get in, and when I did there was my baby and my baby boy. We waited for Rickey and Ponzo to arrive with the truck. They arrived with beer bottles and started to get drunk in the tent.

'How about the manure?'

'Too late today. Tomorrow, man, we make a lot of money; today we have a few beers. What do you say, beer?' I didn't have to be prodded. 'Dah you go – *dah you go!*' yelled Rickey. I began to see that our plans for making money with the manure truck would never materialize. The truck was parked outside the tent. It smelled like Ponzo.

That night Terry and I went to bed in the sweet night air beneath our dewy tent. I was just getting ready to go to sleep when she said, 'You want to love me now?'

I said, 'What about Johnny?'

'He don't mind. He's asleep.' But Johnny wasn't asleep and he said nothing.

The boys came back the next day with the manure truck and drove off to find whisky; they came back and had a big time in the tent. That night Ponzo said it was too cold and slept on the ground in our tent, wrapped in a big tarpaulin smelling of cowflaps. Terry hated him; she said he hung around with her brother in order to get close to her.

Nothing was going to happen except starvation for Terry and me, so in the morning I walked around the countryside asking for cotton-picking work. Everybody told me to go to the farm across the highway from the camp. I went, and the farmer was in the kitchen with his women. He came out, listened to my story, and warned me he was paying only three dollars per hundred pounds of picked cotton. I pictured myself picking at least three hundred pounds a day and took the job. He fished out some long canvas bags from the barn and told me the picking started at dawn. I rushed back to Terry, all glee. On the way a grape truck went over a bump in the road and threw off great bunches of grapes on the hot tar. I picked them up and took them home. Terry was glad. 'Johnny and me'll come with you and help.'

'Pshaw!' I said. 'No such thing!'

'You see, you see, it's very hard picking cotton. I show you how.'

We ate the grapes, and in the evening Rickey showed up with a loaf of bread and a pound of hamburg and we had a picnic. In a larger tent next to ours lived a whole family of Okie cotton-pickers; the grandfather sat in a chair all day long, he was too old to work; the son and daughter, and their children, filed every dawn across the highway to my farmer's field and went to work. At dawn the next day I went with them. They said the cotton was heavier at dawn because of the dew and you could make more money than in the afternoon. Nevertheless they worked all day from dawn to sundown. The grandfather had come from Nebraska during the great plague of the thirties – that selfsame dustcloud my Montana cowboy had told me about – with the entire family in a jalopy truck. They had been in California ever since. They loved to work. In the ten years the old man's son had increased his children to the number of four, some of whom were old enough now to pick cotton. And in that time they had progressed from ragged poverty in Simon Legree fields to a kind of smiling respectability in better tents, and that was all. They were extremely proud of their tent.

'Ever going back to Nebraska?'

'Pshaw, there's nothing back there. What we want to do is buy a trailer.'

We bent down and began picking cotton. It was beautiful. Across the field were the tents, and beyond them the sere brown cottonfields that stretched out of sight to the brown arroyo foothills and then the snow-capped Sierras in the blue morning air. This was so much better than washing dishes on South Main Street. But I knew nothing about picking cotton. I spent too much time disengaging the white ball from its crackly bed; the others did it in one flick. Moreover, my fingertips began to bleed; I needed gloves, or more experience. There was an old Negro couple in the field with us. They picked cotton with the same God-blessed patience their grandfathers

92

had practised in ante-bellum Alabama; they moved right along their rows, bent and blue, and their bags increased. My back began to ache. But it was beautiful kneeling and hiding in that earth. If I felt like resting I did, with my face on the pillow of brown moist earth. Birds sang an accompaniment. I thought I had found my life's work. Johnny and Terry came waving at me across the field in the hot lullal noon and pitched in with me. Be damned if little Johnny wasn't faster than I was! — and of course Terry was twice as fast. They worked ahead of me and left me piles of clean cotton to add to my bag — Terry workmanlike piles, Johnny little childly piles. I stuck them in with sorrow. What kind of old man was I that couldn't support his own ass, let alone theirs? They spent all afternoon with me. When the sun got red we trudged back together. At the end of the field I unloaded my burden on a scale; it weighed fifty pounds, and I got a buck fifty. Then I borrowed a bicycle from one of the Okie boys and rode down 99 to a crossroads grocery store where I bought cans of cooked spaghetti and meatballs, bread, butter, coffee, and cake, and came back with the bag on the handlebars. LA-bound traffic zoomed by; Frisco-bound harassed my tail. I swore and swore. I looked up at the dark sky and prayed to God for a better break in life and a better chance to do something for the little people I loved. Nobody was paying any attention to me up there. I should have known better. It was Terry who brought my soul back; on the tent stove she warmed up the food, and it was one of the greatest meals of my life, I was so hungry and tired. Sighing like an old Negro cotton-picker, I reclined on the bed and smoked a cigarette. Dogs barked in the cool night. Rickey and Ponzo had given up calling in the evenings. I was satisfied with that. Terry curled up beside me, Johnny sat on my chest, and they drew pictures of animals in my notebook. The light of our tent burned on the frightful plain. The cowboy music twanged in the roadhouse and carried across the fields, all sadness. It was all right with me. I kissed my baby and we put out the lights.

In the morning the dew made the tent sag; I got up with my towel and toothbrush and went to the general motel toilet to wash; then I came back, put on my pants, which were all torn from kneeling in the earth and had been sewed by Terry in the evening, put on my ragged straw hat, which had originally served as Johnny's toy hat, and went across the highway with my canvas cotton-bag.

Every day I earned approximately a dollar and a half. It was just enough to buy groceries in the evening on the bicycle. The days rolled by. I forgot all about the East and all about Dean and Carlo and the bloody road. Johnny and I played all the time; he liked me to throw him up in the air and down in the bed. Terry sat mending clothes. I was a man of the earth, precisely as I had dreamed I would be, in Paterson. There was talk that Terry's husband was back in Sabinal and out for me; I was ready for him. One night the Okies went mad in the road-house and tied a man to a tree and beat him to a pulp with sticks. I was asleep at the time and only heard about it. From then on I carried a big stick with me in the tent in case they got the idea we Mexicans were fouling up their trailer camp. They thought I was a Mexican, of course; and in a way I am.

But now it was October and getting much colder in the nights. The Okie family had a woodstove and planned to stay for the winter. We had nothing, and besides the rent for the tent was due. Terry and I bitterly decided we'd have to leave. 'Go back to your family,' I said. 'For God's sake, you can't be batting around tents with a baby like Johnny; the poor little tyke is cold.' Terry cried because I was criticizing her motherly instincts; I meant no such thing. When Ponzo came in the truck one grey afternoon we decided to see her family about the situation. But I mustn't be seen and would have to hide in the vineyard. We started for Sabinal; the truck broke down, and simultaneously it started to rain wildly. We sat in the old truck, cursing. Ponzo got out and toiled in the rain. He was a good old guy after all. We promised each other one more big bat. Off we went to a rickety bar in Sabinal Mextown and spent an hour sopping up the brew. I was through with my chores in the cottonfield. I could feel the pull of my own life calling me back. I shot my aunt a penny postcard across the land and asked for another fifty.

We drove to Terry's family shack. It was situated on the old road that ran between the vineyards. It was dark when we got there. They left me off a quarter-mile away and drove to the door. Light poured out of the door; Terry's six other brothers were playing their guitars and singing. The old man was drinking wine. I heard shouts and arguments above the singing. They called her a whore because she'd left her no-good husband and gone to LA and left Johnny with them. The old man was yelling. But the sad, fat brown mother prevailed, as she always does among the great fellahin peoples of the world, and Terry was allowed to come back home. The brothers began to sing gay songs, fast. I huddled in the cold, rainy wind and watched everything across the sad vineyards of October in the valley. My mind was filled with that great song 'Lover Man' as Billie Holiday sings it; I had my own concert in the bushes. 'Someday we'll meet, and you'll dry all my tears, and whisper sweet, little things in my ear, hugging and a-kissing, oh what we've been missing, Lover Man, oh where can you be . . .' It's not the words so much as the great harmonic tune and the way Billie sings it, like a woman stroking her man's hair in soft lamplight. The winds howled. I got cold.

Terry and Ponzo came back and we rattled off in the old truck to meet Rickey. Rickey was now living with Ponzo's woman, Big Rosey; we tooted the horn for him in rickety alleys. Big Rosey threw him out. Everything was collapsing. That night we slept in the truck. Terry held me tight, of course, and told me not to leave. She said she'd work picking grapes and make enough money for both of us; meanwhile I could live in Farmer Heffelfinger's barn down the road from her family. I'd have nothing to do but sit in the grass all day and eat grapes. 'You like that?'

In the morning her cousins came to get us in another truck. I suddenly realized thousands of Mexicans all over the countryside knew about Terry and me and that it must have been a juicy, romantic topic for them. The cousins were very polite and in fact charming. I stood on the truck, smiling pleasantries, talking about where we were in the war and what the pitch was. There were five cousins in all, and every one of them was nice. They seemed to belong to the side of Terry's family that didn't fuss off like her brother. But I loved that wild Rickey. He swore he was coming to New York to join me. I pictured him in New York, putting off everything till *mañana*. He was drunk in a field someplace that day.

I got off the truck at the crossroads, and the cousins drove Terry home. They gave me the high sign from the front of the house; the father and mother weren't home, they were off picking grapes. So I had the run of the house for the afternoon. It was a four-room shack; I couldn't imagine how the whole family managed to live in there. Flies flew over the sink. There were no screens, just like in the song, 'The window she is broken and the rain she is coming in.' Terry was at home now and puttering around pots. Her two sisters giggled at me. The little children screamed in the road.

When the sun came out red through the clouds of my last valley afternoon, Terry led me to Farmer Heffelfinger's barn. Farmer Heffelfinger had a prosperous farm up the road. We put crates together, she brought blankets from the house, and I was all set except for a great hairy tarantula that lurked at the pinpoint top of the barn roof. Terry said it wouldn't harm me if I didn't bother it. I lay on my back and stared at it. I went out to the cemetery and climbed a tree. In the tree I sang 'Blue Skies'. Terry and Johnny sat in the grass; we had grapes. In California you chew the juice out of grapes and spit the skin away, a real luxury. Nightfall came. Terry went home for supper and came to the barn at nine o'clock with delicious tortillas and mashed beans. I lit a woodfire on the cement floor of the barn to make light. We made love on the crates. Terry got up and cut right back to the shack. Her father was yelling at her; I could hear him from the barn. She'd left me a cape to keep warm; I threw it over my shoulder and skulked through the moonlit vineyard to see what was going on. I crept to the end of a row and knelt in the warm dirt. Her five brothers were singing melodious songs in Spanish. The stars bent over the little roof; smoke poked from the stovepipe chimney. I smelled mashed beans and chili. The old man growled. The brothers kept right on yodelling. The mother was silent. Johnny and the kids were giggling in the bedroom. A California home; I hid in the grapevines, digging it all. I felt like a million dollars; I was adventuring in the crazy American night.

Terry came out, slamming the door behind her. I accosted her on the dark road. 'What's the matter?'

'Oh, we fight all the time. He wants me to go to work tomorrow. He says he don't want me foolin' around. Sallie, I want to go to New York with you.'

'But how?'

'I don't know, honey. I'll miss you. I love you.'

'But I have to leave.'

'Yes, yes. We lay down one more time, then you leave.' We went back to the barn; I made love to her under the tarantula. What was the tarantula doing? We slept awhile on the crates as the fire died. She went back at midnight; her father was drunk; I could hear him roaring; then there was silence as he fell asleep. The stars folded over the sleeping countryside.

In the morning Farmer Heffelfinger stuck his head through the horse gate and said, 'How you doing, young fella?'

'Fine. I hope it's all right my staying here.'

'Sure thing. You going with that little Mexican floozy?'

'She's a very nice girl.'

'Very pretty too. I think the bull jumped the fence. She's got blue eyes.' We talked about his farm.

Terry brought my breakfast. I had my canvas bag all packed and ready to go to New York, as soon as I picked up my money in Sabinal. I knew it was waiting there for me by now. I told Terry I was leaving. She had been thinking about it all night and was resigned to it. Emotionlessly she kissed me in the vineyard and walked off down the row. We turned at a dozen paces, for love is a duel, and looked at each other for the last time.

'See you in New York, Terry,' I said. She was supposed to drive to New York in a month with her brother. But we both knew she wouldn't make it. At a hundred feet I turned to look at her. She just walked on back to the shack, carrying my breakfast plate in one hand. I bowed my head and watched her. Well, lackadaddy, I was on the road again.

I walked down the highway to Sabinal, eating black walnuts from the walnut tree. I went on the SP tracks and balanced along the rail. I passed a watertower and a factory.

This was the end of something. I went to the telegraph office of the railroad for my money order from New York. It was closed. I swore and sat on the steps to wait. The ticket master got back and invited me in. The money was in; my aunt had saved my lazy butt again. 'Who's going to win the World Series next year?' said the gaunt old ticket master. I suddenly realized it was fall and that I was going back to New York.

I walked along the tracks in the long sad October light of the valley, hoping for an SP freight to come along so I could join the grape-eating hobos and read the funnies with them. It didn't come. I got out on the highway and hitched a ride at once. It was the fastest, whoopingest ride of my life. The driver was a fiddler for a California cowboy band. He had a brand-new car and drove eighty miles an hour. 'I don't drink when I drive,' he said and handed me a pint. I took a drink and offered him one. 'What the hail,' he said and drank. We made Sabinal to LA in the amazing time of four hours flat about 250 miles. He dropped me off right in front of Columbia Pictures in Hollywood; I was just in time to run in and pick up my rejected original. Then I bought my bus ticket to Pittsburgh. I didn't have enough money to go all the way to New York. I figured to worry about that when I got to Pittsburgh.

With the bus leaving at ten, I had four hours to dig Hollywood alone. First I bought a loaf of bread and salami and made myself ten sandwiches to cross the country on. I had a dollar left. I sat on the low cement wall in back of a Hollywood parking lot and made the sandwiches. As I laboured at this absurd task, great Kleig lights of a Hollywood première stabbed in the sky, that humming West Coast sky. All around me were the noises of the crazy gold-coast city. And this was my Hollywood career – this was my last night in Hollywood, and I was spreading mustard on my lap in back of a parking-lot john.

14

AT dawn my bus was zooming across the Arizona desert – Indio, Blythe, Salome (where she danced); the great dry stretches leading to Mexican mountains in the south. Then we swung north to the Arizona mountains, Flagstaff, clifftowns. I had a book with me I stole from a Hollywood stall, *Le Grand Meaulnes* by Alain-Fournier, but I preferred reading the American landscape as we went along. Every bump, rise, and stretch in it mystified my longing. In inky night we crossed New Mexico; at grey dawn it was Dalhart, Texas; in the bleak Sunday afternoon we rode through one Oklahoma flat-town after another; at nightfall it was Kansas. The bus roared on. I was going home in October. Everybody goes home in October.

We arrived in St Louis at noon. I took a walk down by the Mississippi River and watched the logs that came floating from Montana in the north – grand Odyssean logs of our continental dream. Old steamboats with their scrollwork more scrolled and withered by weathers sat in the mud inhabited by rats. Great clouds of afternoon overtopped the Mississippi Valley. The bus roared through Indiana cornfields that night; the moon illuminated the ghostly gathered husks; it was almost Hallowe'en. I made the acquaintance of a girl and we necked all the way to Indianapolis. She was nearsighted. When we got off to eat I had to lead her by the hand to the lunch counter. She bought my meals; my sandwiches were all gone. In exchange I told her long stories. She was coming from Washington State, where she had spent the summer picking apples. Her home was on an upstate New York farm. She invited me to come there. We made a date to meet at a New York hotel anyway. She got off at Columbus, Ohio, and I slept all the way to Pittsburgh. I was wearier than I'd been for years and years. I had three hundred and sixty-five miles yet to hitchhike to New York, and a dime in my pocket. I walked five miles to get out of Pittsburgh, and two rides, an apple truck and a big trailer truck, took me to Harrisburg in the soft Indian-summer rainy night. I cut right along. I wanted to get home.

It was the night of the Ghost of the Susquehanna. The Ghost was a shrivelled little old man with a paper satchel who claimed he was headed for 'Canady'. He walked very fast, commanding me to follow, and said there was a bridge up ahead we could cross. He was about sixty years old; he talked incessantly of the meals he had, how much butter they gave him for pancakes, how many extra slices of bread, how the old men had called him from a porch of a charity home in Maryland and invited him to stay for the weekend, how he took a nice warm bath before he left; how he found a brand-new hat by the side of the road in Virginia and that was it on his head; how he hit every Red Cross in town and showed them his World War I credentials; how the Harrisburg Red Cross was not worthy of the name; how he managed in this hard world. But as far as I could see he was just a semi-respectable walking hobo of some kind who covered the entire Eastern Wilderness on foot, hitting Red Cross offices and sometimes bumming on Main Street corners for a dime. We were bums together. We walked seven miles along the mournful Susquehanna. It is a terrifying river. It has bushy cliffs on both sides that lean like hairy ghosts over the unknown waters. Inky night covers all. Sometime from the railyards across the river rises a great red locomotive flare that illuminates the horrid cliffs. The little man said he had a fine belt in his satchel and we stopped for him to fish it out. 'I got me a fine belt here somewheres – got it in Frederick, Maryland. Damn, now did I leave that thing on the counter at Fredericksburg?'

'You mean Frederick.'

'No, no, Fredericksburg, *Virginia!*' He was always talking about Frederick, Maryland, and Fredericksburg, Virginia. He walked right in the road in the teeth of advancing traffic and almost got hit several times. I plodded along in the ditch. Any minute I expected the poor little madman to go flying in the night, dead. We never found that bridge. I left him at a railroad underpass and, because I was so sweaty from the hike, I changed shirts and put on two sweaters; a roadhouse illuminated my sad endeavours. A whole family came walking down the dark road and wondered what I was doing. Strangest thing of all, a tenorman was blowing very fine blues in this Pennsylvania hick house; I listened and moaned. It began to rain hard. A man gave me a ride back to Harrisburg and told me I was on the wrong road. I suddenly saw the little hobo standing under a sad street lamp with his thumb stuck out – poor forlorn man, poor lost sometimeboy, now broken ghost of the penniless wilds. I told my driver the story and he stopped to tell the old man.

'Look here, fella, you're on your way west, not east.'

'Heh?' said the little ghost. 'Can't tell me I don't know my way around here. Been walkin this country for years. I'm headed for Canady.'

'But this ain't the road to Canada, this is the road to Pittsburgh and Chicago.' The little man got disgusted with us and walked off. The last I saw of him was his bobbing little white bag dissolving in the darkness of the mournful Alleghenies.

I thought all the wilderness of America was in the West till the Ghost of the Susquehanna showed me different. No, there is a wilderness in the East; it's the same wilderness Ben Franklin plodded in the oxcart days when he was postmaster, the same as it was when George Washington was a wild-buck Indian-fighter, when Daniel Boone told stories by Pennsylvania lamps and promised to find the Gap, when Bradford built his road and men whooped her up in log cabins. There were not great Arizona spaces for the little man, just the bushy wilderness of eastern Pennsylvania, Maryland, and Virginia, the backroads, the black-tar roads that curve among the mournful rivers like Susquehanna, Monongahela, old Potomac and Monocacy.

That night in Harrisburg I had to sleep in the railroad station on a bench; at dawn the station masters threw me out. Isn't it true that you start your life a sweet child believing in everything under your father's roof? Then comes the day of the Laodiceans, when you know you are wretched and miserable and poor and blind and naked, and with the visage of a gruesome grieving ghost you go shuddering through nightmare life. I stumbled haggardly out of the station; I had no more control. All I could see of the morning was a whiteness like the whiteness of the tomb. I was starving to death. All I had left in the form of calories were the last of the cough drops I'd bought in Shelton, Nebraska, months ago; these I sucked for their sugar.

I didn't know how to panhandle. I stumbled out of town with barely enough strength to reach the city limits. I knew I'd be arrested if I spent another night in Harrisburg. Cursed city! The ride I proceeded to get was with a skinny, haggard man who believed in controlled starvation for the sake of health. When I told him I was starving to death as we rolled east he said, 'Fine, fine, there's nothing better for you. I myself haven't eaten for three days. I'm going to live to be a hundred and fifty years old.' He was a bag of bones, a floppy doll, a broken stick, a maniac. I might have gotten a ride with an affluent fat man who'd say, 'Let's stop at this restaurant and have some pork chops and beans.' No, I had to get a ride that morning with a maniac who believed in controlled starvation for the sake of health. After a hundred miles he grew lenient and took out bread-and-butter sandwiches from the back of the car. They were hidden among his salesman samples. He was selling plumbing fixtures around Pennsylvania. I devoured the bread and butter. Suddenly I began to laugh. I was all alone in the car, waiting for him as he made business calls in Allentown, and I laughed and laughed. Gad, I was sick and tired of life. But the madman drove me home to New York.

Suddenly I found myself on Times Square. I had travelled eight thousand miles around the American continent and I was back on Times Square; and right in the middle of a rush hour, too, seeing with my innocent road-eyes the absolute madness and fantastic hoorair of New York with its millions and millions hustling for ever for a buck among themselves, the mad dream – grabbing, taking, giving, sighing, dying, just so they could be buried in those awful cemetery cities beyond Long Island City. The high towers of the land – the other end of the land, the place where Paper America is born. I stood in a subway doorway, trying to get enough nerve to pick up a beautiful long butt, and every time I stooped great crowds rushed by and obliterated it from my sight, and finally it was crushed. I had no money to go home in the bus. Paterson is quite a few miles from Times Square. Can you picture me walking those last miles through the Lincoln Tunnel or over the Washington Bridge and into New Jersey? It was dusk. Where was Hassel? I dug the square for Hassel; he wasn't there, he was in Riker's

Island, behind bars. Where Dean? Where everybody? Where life? I had my home to go to, my place to lay my head down and figure the losses and figure the gain that I knew was in there somewhere too. I had to panhandle two bits for the bus. I finally hit a Greek minister who was standing around the corner. He gave me the quarter with a nervous lookaway. I rushed immediately to the bus.

When I got home I ate everything in the icebox. My aunt got up and looked at me. 'Poor little Salvatore,' she said in Italian. 'You're thin, you're thin. Where have you been all this time?' I had on two shirts and two sweaters; my canvas bag had torn cottonfield pants and the tattered remnants of my huarache shoes in it. My aunt and I decided to buy a new electric refrigerator with the money I had sent her from California; it was to be the first one in the family. She went to bed, and late at night I couldn't sleep and just smoked in bed. My half-finished manuscript was on the desk. It was October, home, and work again. The first cold winds rattled the windowpane, and I had made it just in time. Dean had come to my house, slept several nights there, waiting for me; spent afternoons talking to my aunt as she worked on a great rag rug woven of all the clothes in my family for years, which was now finished and spread on my bedroom floor, as complex and as rich as the passage of time itself; and then he had left, two days before I arrived, crossing my path probably somewhere in Pennsylvania or Ohio, to go to San Francisco. He had his own life there; Camille had just gotten an apartment. It had never occurred to me to look her up while I was in Mill City. Now it was too late and I had also missed Dean.

PART TWO

I

IT WAS over a year before I saw Dean again. I stayed home all that time, finished my book and began going to school on the GI Bill of Rights. At Christmas 1948 my aunt and I went down to visit my brother in Virginia, laden with presents. I had been writing to Dean and he said he was coming East again; and I told him if so he would find me in Testament, Virginia, between Christmas and New Year's. One day when all our Southern relatives were sitting around the parlour in Testament, gaunt men and women with the old Southern soil in their eyes, talking in low, whining voices about the weather. the crops, and the general weary recapitulation of who had a baby, who got a new house, and so on, a mud-spattered '49 Hudson drew up in front of the house on the dirt road. I had no idea who it was. A weary young fellow, muscular and ragged in a T-shirt, unshaven, red-eyed, came to the porch and rang the bell. I opened the door and suddenly realized it was Dean. He had come all the way from San Francisco to my brother Rocco's door in Virginia, and in an amazingly short time, because I had just written my last letter, telling where I was. In the car I could see two figures sleeping. 'I'll be goddamned! Dean! Who's in the car?'

'Hel-lo, hel-lo, man, it's Marylou. And Ed Dunkel. We gotta have place to wash up immediately, we're dog-tired.'

'But how did you get here so fast?'

'Ah, man, that Hudson goes!'

'Where did you get it?'

'I bought it with my savings. I've been working on the railroad, making four hundred dollars a month.'

There was utter confusion in the following hour. My Southern relatives had no idea what was going on, or who or what Dean, Marylou, and Ed Dunkel were; they dumbly stared.

My aunt and my brother Rocky went in the kitchen to consult. There were, in all, eleven people in the little Southern house. Not only that, but my brother had just decided to move from that house, and half his furniture was gone; he and his wife and baby were moving closer to the town of Testament. They had bought a new parlour set and their old one was going to my aunt's house in Paterson, though we hadn't yet decided how. When Dean heard this he at once offered his services with the Hudson. He and I would carry the furniture to Paterson in two fast trips and bring my aunt back at the end of the second trip. This was going to save us a lot of money and trouble. It was agreed upon. My sister-in-law made a spread, and the three battered travellers sat down to eat. Marylou had not slept since Denver. I thought she looked older and more beautiful now.

I learned that Dean had lived happily with Camille in San Francisco ever since that fall of 1947; he got a job on the railroad and made a lot of money. He became the father of a cute little girl, Amy Moriarty. Then suddenly he blew his top while walking down the street one day. He saw a '49 Hudson for sale and rushed to the bank for his entire roll. He bought the car on the spot. Ed Dunkel was with him. Now they were broke. Dean calmed Camille's fears and told her he'd be back in a month. 'I'm going to New York and bring Sal back.' She wasn't too pleased at this prospect.

'But what is the purpose of all this? Why are you doing this to me?'

'It's nothing, it's nothing, darling – ah – hem – Sal has pleaded and begged with me to come and get him, it is absolutely necessary for me to – but we won't go into all these explanations – and I'll tell you why ... No, listen, I'll tell you why.' And he told her why, and of course it made no sense.

Big tall Ed Dunkel also worked on the railroad. He and Dean had just been laid off during a seniority lapse because of a drastic reduction of crews. Ed had met a girl called Galatea who was living in San Francisco on her savings. These two mindless cads decided to bring the girl along to the East and have her foot the bill. Ed cajoled and pleaded; she wouldn't go unless he married her. In a whirlwind few days Ed Dunkel married Galatea, with Dean rushing around to get the necessary papers, and a few days before Christmas they rolled out of San Francisco at seventy miles per, headed for LA and the snowless southern road. In LA they picked up a sailor in a travel bureau and took him along for fifteen dollars' worth of gas. He was bound for Indiana. They also picked up a woman with her idiot daughter, for four dollars' gas fare to Arizona. Dean sat the idiot girl with him up front and dug her, as he said, 'All the *way*, man! such a gone sweet little soul. Oh, we talked, we talked of fires and the desert turning to a paradise and her parrot that swore in Spanish.' Dropping off these passengers, they proceeded to Tucson. All along the way Galatea Dunkel, Ed's new wife, kept complaining that she was tired and wanted to sleep in a motel. If this kept up they'd spend all her money long before Virginia. Two nights she forced a stop and blew tens on motels. By the time they got to Tucson she was broke. Dean and Ed gave her the slip in a hotel lobby and resumed the voyage alone, with the sailor, and without a qualm.

Ed Dunkel was a tall, calm, unthinking fellow who was completely ready to do anything Dean asked him; and at this time Dean was too busy for scruples. He was roaring through Las Cruces, New Mexico, when he suddenly had an explosive yen to see his sweet first wife Marylou again. She was up in Denver. He swung the car north, against the feeble protests of the sailor, and zoomed into Denver in the evening. He ran and found Marylou in a hotel. They had ten hours of wild lovemaking. Everything was decided again : they were going to stick. Marylou was the only girl Dean ever really loved. He was sick with regret when he saw her face again, and, as of yore, he pleaded and begged at her knees for the joy of her being. She understood Dean; she stroked his hair; she knew he was mad. To soothe the sailor, Dean fixed him up with a girl in a hotel room over the bar where the old poolhall gang always drank. But the sailor refused the girl and in fact walked off in the night and they never saw him again; he evidently took a bus to Indiana.

Dean, Marylou, and Ed Dunkel roared east along Colfax and out to the Kansas plains. Great snowstorms overtook them. In Missouri, at night, Dean had to drive with his scarf-wrapped head stuck out the window, with snowglasses that made him look like a monk peering into the manuscripts of the snow, because the windshield was covered with an inch of ice. He drove by the birth county of his forebears without a thought. In the morning the car skidded on an icy hill and flapped into a ditch. A farmer offered to help them out. They got hung-up when they picked up a hitchhiker who promised them a dollar if they'd let him ride to Memphis. In Memphis he went into his house, puttered around looking for the dollar, got drunk, and said he couldn't find it. They resumed across Tennessee; the bearings were beat from the accident. Dean had been driving ninety; now he had to stick to a steady seventy or the whole motor would go whirring down the mountainside. They crossed the Great Smoky Mountains in midwinter. When they arrived at my brother's door they had not eaten for thirty hours – except for candy and cheese crackers.

They ate voraciously as Dean, sandwich in hand, stood bowed and jumping before the big phonograph, listening to a wild bop record I had just bought called 'The Hunt', with Dexter Gordon and Wardell Gray blowing their tops before a screaming audience that gave the record fantastic frenzied volume. The Southern folk looked at one another and shook their heads in awe. 'What kind of friends does Sal have, anyway?' they said to my brother. He was stumped for an answer. Southerners don't like madness the least bit, not Dean's kind. He paid absolutely no attention to them. The madness of Dean had bloomed into a weird flower. I didn't realize this till he and I and Marylou and Dunkel left the house for a brief spin-the-Hudson, when for the first time we were alone and could talk about anything we wanted. Dean grabbed the wheel, shifted to second, mused a minute, rolling, suddenly seemed to decide something and shot the car full-jet down the road in a fury of decision.

'All right now, children,' he said, rubbing his nose and bending down to feel the emergency and pulling cigarettes out of the compartment, and swaying back and forth as he did these things and drove. 'The time has come for us to decide what we're going to do for the next week. Crucial, crucial. Ahem!' He dodged a mule wagon; in it sat an old Negro plodding along. 'Yes!' yelled Dean. 'Yes. Dig him! Now consider his soul stop awhile and consider.' And he slowed down the car for all of us to turn and look at the old jazzbo moaning along. 'Oh yes, dig him sweet; now there's thoughts in that mind that I would give my last arm to know; to climb in there and find out just what he's poor-ass pondering about this year's turnip greens and ham. Sal, you don't know it but I once lived with a farmer in Arkansas for a whole year, when I was eleven. I had awful chores, I had to skin a dead horse once. Haven't been to Arkansas since Christmas nineteen-forty-three, five years ago, when Ben Gavin and I were chased by a man with a gun who owned the car we were trying to steal; I say all this to show you that of the South I can speak. I have known – I mean, man, I dig the South, I know it in and out – I've dug your letters to me about it. Oh yes, oh yes,' he said, trailing off and stopping altogether, and suddenly jumping the car back to seventy and hunching over the wheel. He stared doggedly ahead. Marylou was smiling serenely. This was the new and complete Dean, grown to maturity. I said to myself, My God, he's changed. Fury spat out of his eyes when he told of things he hated; great glows of joy replaced this when he suddenly got happy; every muscle twitched to live and go. 'Oh, man, the things I could tell you,' he said, poking me, 'Oh, man, we must absolutely find the time – What has happened to Carlo? We all get to see Carlo, darlings, first thing tomorrow. Now, Marylou, we're getting some bread and meat to make a lunch for New York. How much money do you have, Sal? We'll put everything in the back seat, Mrs P's furniture, and all of us will sit up front cuddly and close and tell stories as we zoom to New York. Marylou, honeythighs, you sit next to me, Sal next, then Ed at the window, big Ed to cut off draughts, whereby he comes into using the robe this time. And then we'll all go off to sweet life, 'cause now is the time and *we all know time!*' He rubbed his jaw furiously, he swung the car and passed three trucks, he roared into downtown Testament, looking in every direction and seeing everything in an arc of 180 degrees around his eyeballs without moving his head. Bang, he found a parking space in no time, and we were parked. He leaped out of the car. Furiously he hustled into the railroad station; we followed sheepishly. He bought cigarettes. He had become absolutely mad in his movements; he seemed to be doing everything at the same time. It was a shaking of the head, up and down, sideways; jerky, vigorous hands; quick walking, sitting, crossing the legs, uncrossing, getting up, rubbing the hands, rubbing his fly, hitching his pants, looking up and saying 'Am', and sudden slitting of the eyes to see everywhere; and all the time he was grabbing me by the ribs and talking, talking.

It was very cold in Testament; they'd had an unseasonable snow. He stood in the long bleak main street that runs along the railroad, clad in nothing but a T-shirt and low-hanging pants with the belt unbuckled, as though he was about to take them off. He came sticking his head in to talk to Marylou; he backed away, fluttering his hands before her. 'Oh, yes, I know! I know *you*, I know *you*, darling!' His laugh was maniacal; it started low and ended high, exactly like the laugh of a radio maniac, only faster and more like a titter. Then he kept reverting to businesslike tones. There was no purpose in our coming downtown, but he found purposes. He made us all hustle, Marylou for the lunch groceries, me for a paper to dig the weather report, Ed for cigars. Dean loved to smoke cigars. He smoked one over the paper and talked. 'Ah, our holy American slop-jaws in Washington are planning fur-ther inconveniences – ah-hem! – aw – hup! hup!' And he leaped off and rushed to see a coloured girl that just then passed outside the station. 'Dig her,' he said standing with limp finger pointed, fingering himself with a goofy smile, 'that little gone black lovely. Ah! Hmm!' We got in the car and flew back to my brother's house.

I had been spending a quiet Christmas in the country, as I realized when we got back into the house and I saw the Christmas tree, the presents, and smelled the roasting turkey and listened to the talk of the relatives, but now the bug was on me again, and the bug's name was Dean Moriarty and I was off on another spurt around the road.

WE packed my brother's furniture in back of the car and took off at dark, promising to be back in thirty hours – thirty hours for a thousand miles north and south. But that's the way Dean wanted it. It was a tough trip, and none of us noticed it; the heater was not working and consequently the windshield developed fog and ice; Dean kept reaching out while driving seventy to wipe it with a rag and make a hole to see the road. 'Ah, holy hole!' In the spacious Hudson we had plenty of room for all four of us to sit up front. A blanket covered our laps. The radio was not working. It was a brand-new car bought five days ago, and already it was broken. There was only one instalment paid on it, too. Off we went, north to Washington, on 301, a straight two-lane highway without much traffic. And Dean talked, no one else talked. He gestured furiously, he leaned as far as me sometimes to make a point, sometimes he had no hands on the wheel and yet the car went as straight as an arrow, not for once deviating from the white line in the middle of the road that unwound, kissing our left front tyre.

It was a completely meaningless set of circumstances that made Dean come, and similarly I went off with him for no reason. In New York I had been attending school and romancing around with a girl called Lucille, a beautiful Italian honey-haired darling that I actually wanted to marry. All these years I was looking for the woman I wanted to marry. I couldn't meet a girl without saying to myself, What kind of wife would she make? I told Dean and Marylou about Lucille. Marylou wanted to know all about Lucille, she wanted to meet her. We zoomed through Richmond, Washington, Baltimore, and up to Philadelphia on a winding country road and talked. 'I want to marry a girl,' I told them, 'so I can rest my soul with her till we both get old. This can't go on all the time – all this franticness and jumping around. We've got to go someplace, find something.'

'Ah, now, man,' said Dean, 'I've been digging you for years about the *home* and marriage and all those fine wonderful things about your soul.' It was a sad night; it was also a merry night. In Philadelphia we went into a lunchcart and ate hamburgers with our last food dollar. The counterman – it was three a.m. – heard us talk about money and offered to give us the hamburgers free, plus more coffee, if we all pitched in and washed dishes in the back because his regular man hadn't shown up. We jumped to it. Ed Dunkel said he was an old pearl-diver from way back and pitched his long arms into the dishes. Dean stood googing around with a towel, so did Marylou. Finally they started necking among the pots and pans; they withdrew to a dark corner in the pantry. The counterman was satisfied as long as Ed and I did the dishes. We finished them in fifteen minutes. When daybreak came we were zooming through New Jersey with the great cloud of Metropolitan New York rising before us in the snowy distance. Dean had a sweater wrapped around his ears to keep warm. He said we were a band of Arabs coming in to blow up New York. We swished through the Lincoln Tunnel and cut over to Times Square; Marylou wanted to see it.

'Oh damn, I wish I could find Hassel. Everybody look sharp, see if they can find him.' We all scoured the sidewalks. 'Good old gone Hassel. Oh you should have *seen* him in Texas.'

So now Dean had come about four thousand miles from Frisco, via Arizona and up to Denver, inside four days, with innumerable adventures sandwiched in, and it was only the beginning.

3

WE went to my house in Paterson and slept. I was the first to wake up, late in the afternoon. Dean and Marylou were sleeping on my bed, Ed and I on my aunt's bed. Dean's battered unhinged trunk lay sprawled on the floor with socks sticking out. A phone call came for me in the drugstore downstairs. I ran down; it was from New Orleans. It was Old Bull Lee, who'd moved to New Orleans. Old Bull Lee in his high, whining voice was making a complaint. It seemed a girl called Galatea

Dunkel had just arrived at his house for a guy Ed Dunkel; Bull had no idea who these people were. Galatea Dunkel was a tenacious loser. I told Bull to reassure her that Dunkel was with Dean and me and that most likely we'd be picking her up in New Orleans on the way to the Coast. Then the girl herself talked on the phone. She wanted to know how Ed was. She was all concerned about his happiness.

'How did you get from Tucson to New Orleans?' I asked. She said she wired home for money and took a bus. She was determined to catch up with Ed because she loved him. I went upstairs and told Big Ed. He sat in the chair with a worried look, an angel of a man, actually.

'All right, now,' said Dean, suddenly waking up and leaping out of bed, 'what we must do is eat, at once. Marylou, rustle around the kitchen see what there is. Sal, you and I go downstairs and call Carlo. Ed, you see what you can do straightening out the house.' I followed Dean, bustling downstairs.

The guy who ran the drugstore said, 'You just got another call – this one from San Francisco – for a guy called Dean Moriarty. I said there wasn't anybody by that name.' It was sweetest Camille, calling Dean. The drugstore man, Sam, a tall, calm friend of mine, looked at me and scratched his head. 'Geez, what are you running, an international whorehouse?'

Dean tittered maniacally. 'I dig you, man!' He leaped into the phone booth and called San Francisco collect. Then we called Carlo at his home in Long Island and told him to come over. Carlo arrived two hours later. Meanwhile Dean and I got ready for our return trip alone to Virginia to pick up the rest of the furniture and bring my aunt back. Carlo Marx came, poetry under his arm, and sat in an easy chair, watching us with beady eyes. For the first half-hour he refused to say anything; at any rate, he refused to commit himself. He had quieted down since the Denver Doldrum days; the Dakar Doldrums had done it. In Dakar, wearing a beard, he had wandered the back streets with little children who led him to a witch-doctor who told him his fortune. He had snapshots of crazy streets with grass huts, the hip back-end of Dakar. He said he almost jumped off the ship like Hart Crane on the way back. Dean sat on the floor with a music box and listened with tremendous

amazement at the little song it played, 'A Fine Romance' –
'Little tinkling whirling doodlebells. Ah! Listen! We'll all bend
down together and look into the centre of the music box till
we learn about the secrets – tinklydoodlebell, whee.' Ed Dunkel
was also sitting on the floor; he had my drumsticks; he suddenly began beating a tiny beat to go with the music box, that
we barely could hear. Everybody held his breath to listen. 'Tick
... tack ... tick-tick ... tack-tack.' Dean cupped a hand over his
ear; his mouth hung open; he said, 'Ah! Whee!'

Carlo watched this silly madness with slitted eyes. Finally
he slapped his knee and said, 'I have an announcement to make.'

'Yes? Yes?'

'What is the meaning of this voyage to New York? What
kind of sordid business are you on now? I mean, man, whither
goest thou? Whither goest thou, America, in thy shiny car in
the night?'

'Whither goest thou?' echoed Dean with his mouth open.
We sat and didn't know what to say; there was nothing to talk
about any more. The only thing to do was go. Dean leaped up
and said we were ready to go back to Virginia. He took a
shower, I cooked up a big platter of rice with all that was left
in the house, Marylou sewed his socks, and we were ready to
go. Dean and Carlo and I zoomed into New York. We promised
to see Carlo in thirty hours, in time for New Year's Eve. It was
night. We left him at Times Square and went back through the
expensive tunnel and into New Jersey and on the road. Taking
turns at the wheel, Dean and I made Virginia in ten hours.

'Now this is the first time we've been alone and in a position
to talk for years,' said Dean. And he talked all night. As in a
dream, we were zooming back through sleeping Washington
and back in the Virginia wilds, crossing the Appomattox River
at daybreak, pulling up at my brother's door at eight a.m.
And all this time Dean was tremendously excited about everything he saw, everything he talked about, every detail of every
moment that passed. He was out of his mind with real belief.
'And of course now no one can tell us that there is no God.
We've passed through all forms. You remember, Sal, when I
first came to New York and I wanted Chad King to teach me
about Nietzsche. You see how long ago? Everything is fine,

God exists, we know time. Everything since the Greeks has been predicated wrong. You can't make it with geometry and geometrical systems of thinking. It's all *this!*' He wrapped his finger in his fist; the car hugged the line straight and true. 'And not only that but we both understand that I could have time to explain why I know and you know God exists.' At one point I moaned about life's troubles – how poor my family was, how much I wanted to help Lucille, who was also poor and had a daughter. 'Troubles, you see, is the generalization-word for what God exists in. The thing is not to get hung-up. My head rings!' he cried, clasping his head. He rushed out of the car like Groucho Marx to get cigarettes – that furious, ground-hugging walk with the coattails flying, except that he had no coat-tails. 'Since Denver, Sal, a lot of things – Oh, the things – I've thought and thought. I used to be in reform school all the time, I was a young punk, asserting myself – stealing cars a psychological expression of my position, hincty to show. All my jail-problems are pretty straight now. As far as I know I shall never be in jail again. The rest is not my fault.' We passed a little kid who was throwing stones at the cars in the road. 'Think of it,' said Dean. 'One day he'll put a stone through a man's wind-shield and the man will crash and die – all on account of that little kid. You see what I mean? God exists without qualms. As we roll along this way I am positive beyond doubt that everything will be taken care of for us – that even you, as you drive, fearful of the wheel' (I hated to drive and drove carefully) – 'the thing will go along of itself and you won't go off the road and I can sleep. Furthermore we know America, we're at home; I can go anywhere in America and get what I want because it's the same in every corner, I know the people, I know what they do. We give and take and go in the incredibly complicated sweetness zigzagging every side.' There was nothing clear about the things he said, but what he meant to say was somehow made pure and clear. He used the word 'pure' a great deal. I had never dreamed Dean would become a mystic. These were the first days of his mysticism, which would lead to the strange, ragged W. C. Fields saintliness of his later days.

Even my aunt listened to him with a curious half-ear as we roared back north to New York that same night with the furniture in the back. Now that my aunt was in the car, Dean settled down to talking about his worklife in San Francisco. We went over every single detail of what a brakeman has to do, demonstrating every time we passed yards, and at one point he even jumped out of the car to show me how a brakeman gives a highball at a meet at a siding. My aunt retired to the back seat and went to sleep. In Washington at four a.m. Dean again called Camille collect in Frisco. Shortly after this, as we pulled out of Washington, a cruising car overtook us with siren going and we had a speeding ticket in spite of the fact that we were going about thirty. It was the California licence plate that did it. 'You guys think you can rush through here as fast as you want just because you come from California?' said the cop.

I went with Dean to the Sergeant's desk and we tried to explain to the police that we had no money. They said Dean would have to spend the night in jail if we didn't round up the money. Of course my aunt had it, fifteen dollars; she had twenty in all, and it was going to be just fine. And in fact while we were arguing with the cops one of them went out to peek at my aunt, who sat wrapped in the back of the car. She saw him.

'Don't worry, I'm not a gun moll. If you want to come and search the car, go right ahead. I'm going home with my nephew, and this furniture isn't stolen; it's my niece's, she just had a baby and she's moving to her new house.' This flabbergasted Sherlock and he went back in the station house. My aunt had to pay the fine for Dean or we'd be stuck in Washington; I had no licence. He promised to pay it back, and he actually did, exactly a year and a half later and to my aunt's pleased surprise. My aunt – a respectable woman hung-up in this sad world, and well she knew the world. She told us about the cop. 'He was hiding behind the tree, trying to see what I looked like. I told him – I told him to search the car if he wanted. I've nothing to be ashamed of.' She knew Dean had something to be ashamed of, and me too, by virtue of my being with Dean, and Dean and I accepted this sadly.

My aunt once said the world would never find peace until men fell at their women's feet and asked for forgiveness. But

Dean knew this; he'd mentioned it many times. 'I've pleaded and pleaded with Marylou for a peaceful sweet understanding of pure love between us forever with all hassles thrown out – she understands; her mind is bent on something else – she's after me; she won't understand how much I love her, she's knittting my doom.'

'The truth of the matter is we don't understand our women; we blame on them and it's all our fault,' I said.

'But it isn't as simple as that,' warned Dean. 'Peace will come suddenly, we won't understand when it does – see, man?' Doggedly, bleakly, he pushed the car through New Jersey; at dawn I drove into Paterson as he slept in the back. We arrived at the house at eight in the morning to find Marylou and Ed Dunkel sitting around smoking butts from the ashtrays; they hadn't eaten since Dean and I left. My aunt bought groceries and cooked up a tremendous breakfast.

4

NOW it was time for the Western threesome to find new living quarters in Manhattan proper. Carlo had a pad on York Avenue; they were moving in that evening. We slept all day, Dean and I, and woke up as a great snowstorm ushered in New Year's Eve, 1948. Ed Dunkel was sitting in my easy chair, telling about the previous New Year's. 'I was in Chicago. I was broke. I was sitting at the window of my hotel room on North Clark Street and the most delicious smell rose to my nostrils from the bakery downstairs. I didn't have a dime but I went down and talked to the girl. She gave me bread and coffee cakes free. I went back to my room and ate them. I stayed in my room all night. In Farmington, Utah, once, where I went to work with Ed Wall – you know Ed Wall, the rancher's son in Denver – I was in my bed and all of a sudden I saw my dead mother standing in the corner with light all around her. I said, "Mother!" She disappeared. I have visions all the time,' said Ed Dunkel, nodding his head.

'What are you going to do about Galatea?'

'Oh, we'll see. When we get to New Orleans. Don't you think so, huh?' He was starting to turn to me as well for advice; one Dean wasn't enough for him. But he was already in love with Galatea, pondering it.

'What are you going to do with yourself, Ed?' I asked.

'I don't know,' he said. 'I just go along. I dig life.' He repeated it, following Dean's line. He had no direction. He sat reminiscing about that night in Chicago and the hot coffee cakes in the lonely room.

The snow whirled outside. A big party was on hand in New York; we were all going. Dean packed his broken trunk, put it in the car, and we all took off for the big night. My aunt was happy with the thought that my brother would be visiting her the following week; she sat with her paper and waited for the midnight New Year's Eve broadcast from Times Square. We roared into New York, swerving on ice. I was never scared when Dean drove; he could handle a car under any circumstances. The radio had been fixed and now he had wild bop to urge us along the night. I didn't know where all this was leading; I didn't care.

Just about that time a strange thing began to haunt me. It was this: I had forgotten something. There was a decision that I was about to make before Dean showed up, and now it was driven clear out of my mind but still hung on the tip of my mind's tongue. I kept snapping my fingers, trying to remember it. I even mentioned it. And I couldn't even tell if it was a real decision or just a thought I had forgotten. It haunted and flabbergasted me, made me sad. It had to do somewhat with the Shrouded Traveller. Carlo Marx and I once sat down together, knee to knee, in two chairs, facing, and I told him a dream I had about a strange Arabian figure that was pursuing me across the desert; that I tried to avoid; that finally overtook me just before I reached the Protective City. 'Who is this?' said Carlo. We pondered it. I proposed it was myself, wearing a shroud. That wasn't it. Something, someone, some spirit was pursuing all of us across the desert of life and was bound to catch us before we reached heaven. Naturally, now that I look back on it, this is only death: death will overtake us before heaven. The one thing that we yearn for in our living days, that makes us sigh and groan and undergo sweet nauseas of all kinds, is the remembrance of some lost bliss that was probably experienced in the womb and can only be reproduced (though we hate to admit it) in death. But who wants to die? In the rush of events I kept thinking about this in the back of my mind. I told it to Dean and he instantly recognized it as the mere simple longing for pure death; and because we're all of us never in life again, he, rightly, would have nothing to do with it, and I agreed with him then.

We went looking for my New York gang of friends. The crazy flowers bloom there too. We went to Tom Saybrook's first. Tom is a sad, handsome fellow, sweet, generous, and amenable; only once in a while he suddenly has fits of depression and rushes off without saying a word to anyone. This night he was overjoyed. 'Sal, where did you find these absolutely wonderful people? I've never seen anyone like them.'

'I found them in the West.'

Dean was having his kicks; he put on a jazz record, grabbed Marylou, held her tight, and bounced against her with the beat of the music. She bounced right back. It was a real love dance. Ian MacArthur came in with a huge gang. The New Year's weekend began, and lasted three days and three nights. Great gangs got in the Hudson and swerved in the snowy New York streets from party to party. I brought Lucille and her sister to the biggest party. When Lucille saw me with Dean and Marylou her face darkened – she sensed the madness they put in me.

'I don't like you when you're with them.'

'Ah, it's all right, it's just kicks. We only live once. We're having a good time.'

'No, it's sad and I don't like it.'

Then Marylou began making love to me; she said Dean was going to stay with Camille and she wanted me to go with her. 'Come back to San Francisco with us. We'll live together. I'll be a good girl for you.' But I knew Dean loved Marylou, and I also knew Marylou was doing this to make Lucille jealous, and I wanted nothing of it. Still and all, I licked my lips for the luscious blonde. When Lucille saw Marylou pushing me into the corners and giving me the word and forcing kisses on me she accepted Dean's invitation to go out in the car; but they just talked and drank some of the Southern moonshine I left in the compartment. Everything was being mixed up, and all was falling. I knew my affair with Lucille wouldn't last much longer. She wanted me to be *her way*. She was married to a longshoreman who treated her badly. I was willing to marry her and take her baby daughter and all if she divorced the husband; but there wasn't even enough money to get a divorce and the whole thing was hopeless, besides which Lucille would never understand me because I like too many things and get all confused and hung-up running from one falling star to another till I drop. This is the night, what it does to you. I had nothing to offer anybody except my own confusion.

The parties were enormous; there were at least a hundred people at a basement apartment in the West Nineties. People overflowed into the cellar compartments near the furnace. Something was going on in every corner, on every bed and couch – not an orgy but just a New Year's party with frantic screaming and wild radio music. There was even a Chinese girl. Dean ran like Groucho Marx from group to group, digging everybody. Periodically we rushed out to the car to pick up more people. Damion came. Damion is the hero of my New York gang, as Dean is the chief hero of the Western. They immediately took a dislike to each other. Damion's girl suddenly socked Damion on the jaw with a roundhouse right. He stood reeling. She carried him home. Some of our mad newspaper friends came in from the office with bottles. There was a tremendous and wonderful snowstorm going on outside. Ed Dunkel met Lucille's sister and disappeared with her; I forgot to say that Ed Dunkel is a very smooth man with the women. He's six foot four, mild, affable, agreeable, bland, and delightful. He helps women on with their coats. That's the way to do things. At five o'clock in the morning we were all rushing through the backyard of a tenement and climbing in through a window of an apartment where a huge party was going on. At dawn we were back at Tom Saybrook's. People were drawing pictures and drinking stale beer. I slept on a couch with a girl called Mona in my arms. Great groups filed in from the old Columbia Campus bar. Everything in life, all the faces of life, were piling into the same dank room. At Ian MacArthur's the party went on. Ian MacArthur is a wonderful sweet fellow who wears glasses and peers out of them with delight. He began to learn 'Yes!' to everything, just like Dean at this time, and hasn't stopped since. To the wild sounds of Dexter Gordon and Wardell Gray blowing 'The Hunt', Dean and I played catch with Marylou over the couch; she was no small doll either. Dean went around with no undershirt, just his pants, barefoot, till it was time to hit the car and fetch more people. Everything happened. We found the wild, ecstatic Rollo Greb and spent a night at his house on Long Island. Rollo lives in a nice house with his aunt; when she dies the house is all his. Meanwhile she refuses to comply with any of his wishes and hates his friends. He brought this ragged gang of Dean, Marylou, Ed, and me, and began a roaring party. The woman prowled upstairs; she threatened to call the police. 'Oh, shut up, you old bag!' yelled Greb. I wondered how he could live with her like this. He had more books than I've ever seen in all my life – two libraries, two rooms loaded from floor to ceiling around all four walls, and such books as the Apocryphal Something-or-Other in ten volumes. He played Verdi operas and pantomimed them in his pyjamas with a great rip down the back. He didn't give a damn about anything. He is a great scholar who goes reeling down the New York waterfront with original seventeenth-century musical manuscripts under his arm, shouting. He crawls like a big spider through the streets. His excitement blew out of his eyes in stabs of fiendish light. He rolled his neck in spastic ecstasy. He lisped, he writhed, he flopped, he moaned, he howled, he fell back in despair. He could hardly get a word out, he was so excited with life. Dean stood before him with head bowed, repeating over and over again, 'Yes ... Yes ... Yes.' He took me into a corner. 'That Rollo Greb is the greatest, most wonderful of all. That's what I was trying to tell you – that's what I want to be. I want to be like him. He's never hung-up, he goes every direction, he lets it all out, he knows time, he has nothing to do but rock back and forth. Man, he's the end! You see, if you go like him all the time you'll finally get it.'

'Get what?'

'IT! IT! I'll tell you – now no time, we have no time now.'
Dean rushed back to watch Rollo Greb some more.

George Shearing, the great jazz pianist, Dean said, was exactly like Rollo Greb. Dean and I went to see Shearing at Birdland in the midst of the long, mad weekend. The place was
deserted, we were the first customers, ten o'clock. Shearing
came out, blind, led by the hand to his keyboard. He was a
distinguished-looking Englishman with a stiff white collar,
slightly beefy, blond, with a delicate English-summer's-night
air about him that came out in the first rippling sweet number
he played as the bass-player leaned to him reverently and
thrummed the beat. The drummer, Denzil Best, sat motionless
except for his wrists snapping the brushes. And Shearing began to rock; a smile broke over his ecstatic face; he began to
rock in the piano seat, back and forth, slowly at first, then the
beat went up, and he began rocking fast, his left foot jumped
up with every beat, his neck began to rock crookedly, he
brought his face down to the keys, he pushed his hair back,
his combed hair dissolved, he began to sweat. The music picked
up. The bass-player hunched over and socked it in, faster and
faster, it seemed faster and faster, that's all. Shearing began to
play his chords; they rolled out of the piano in great rich
showers, you'd think the man wouldn't have time to line them
up. They rolled and rolled like the sea. Folks yelled for him to
'Go!' Dean was sweating; the sweat poured down his collar.
'There he is! That's him! Old God! Old God Shearing! Yes!
Yes! Yes!' And Shearing was conscious of the madman behind
him, he could hear every one of Dean's gasps and imprecations,
he could sense it though he couldn't see. 'That's right!' Dean
said. 'Yes!' Shearing smiled; he rocked. Shearing rose from the
piano, dripping with sweat; these were his great 1949 days
before he became cool and commercial. When he was gone
Dean pointed to the empty piano seat. 'God's empty chair,' he
said. On the piano a horn sat; its golden shadow made a strange
reflection along the desert caravan painted on the wall behind
the drums. God was gone; it was the silence of his departure.
It was a rainy night. It was the myth of the rainy night. Dean
was popeyed with awe. This madness would lead nowhere. I
didn't know what was happening to me, and I suddenly realized

it was only the tea that we were smoking; Dean had bought some in New York. It made me think that everything was about to arrive – the moment when you know all and everything is decided forever.

5

I LEFT everybody and went home to rest. My aunt said I was wasting my time hanging around with Dean and his gang. I knew that was wrong, too. Life is life, and kind is kind. What I wanted was to take one more magnificent trip to the West Coast and get back in time for the spring semester in school. And what a trip it turned out to be! I only went along for the ride, and to see what else Dean was going to do, and finally, also, knowing Dean would go back to Camille in Frisco, I wanted to have an affair with Marylou. We got ready to cross the groaning continent again. I drew my GI check and gave Dean eighteen dollars to mail to his wife; she was waiting for him to come home and she was broke. What was on Marylou's mind I don't know. Ed Dunkel, as ever, just followed.

There were long, funny days spent in Carlo's apartment before we left. He went around in his bathrobe and made semi-ironical speeches: 'Now I'm not trying to take your hincty sweets from you, but it seems to me the time has come to decide what you are and what you're going to do.' Carlo was working as typist in an office. 'I want to know what all this sitting around the house all day is intended to mean. What all this talk is and what you propose to do. Dean, why did you leave Camille and pick up Marylou?' No answer – giggles. 'Marylou, why are you travelling around the country like this and what are your womanly intentions concerning the shroud?' Same answer. 'Ed Dunkel, why did you abandon your new wife in Tucson and what are you doing here sitting on your big fat ass? Where's your home? What's your job?' Ed Dunkel bowed his head in genuine befuddlement. 'Sal – how comes it you've fallen on such sloppy days and what have you done with Lucille?' He adjusted his bathrobe and sat facing us all. 'The days of wrath are yet to come. The balloon won't sustain you much longer. And not only that, but it's an abstract balloon. You'll all go flying to the West Coast and come staggering back in search of your stone.'

In these days Carlo had developed a tone of voice which he hoped sounded like what he called The Voice of Rock; the whole idea was to stun people into the realization of the rock. 'You pin a dragon to your hats,' he warned us; 'you're up in the attic with the bats.' His mad eyes glittered at us. Since the Dakar Doldrums he had gone through a terrible period which he called the Holy Doldrums, or Harlem Doldrums, when he lived in Harlem in midsummer and at night woke up in his lonely room and heard 'the great machine' descending from the sky; and when he walked on 125th Street 'under water' with all the other fish. It was a riot of radiant ideas that had come to enlighten his brain. He made Marylou sit on his lap and commanded her to subside. He told Dean, 'Why don't you just sit down and relax? Why do you jump around so much?' Dean ran around, putting sugar in his coffee and saying, 'Yes! Yes! Yes!' At night Ed Dunkel slept on the floor on cushions, Dean and Marylou pushed Carlo out of bed, and Carlo sat up in the kitchen over his kidney stew, mumbling the predictions of the rock. I came in days and watched everything.

Ed Dunkel said to me, 'Last night I walked clear down to Times Square and just as I arrived I suddenly realized I was a ghost – it was my ghost walking on the sidewalk.' He said these things to me without comment, nodding his head emphatically. Ten hours later, in the midst of someone else's conversation, Ed said, 'Yep, it was my ghost walking on the sidewalk.'

Suddenly Dean leaned to me earnestly and said, 'Sal, I have something to ask of you – very important to me – I wonder how you'll take it – we're buddies, aren't we?'

'Sure are, Dean.' He almost blushed. Finally he came out with it: he wanted me to work Marylou. I didn't ask him why because I knew he wanted to see what Marylou was like with another man. We were sitting in Ritzy's Bar when he proposed the idea; we'd spent an hour walking Times Square, looking for Hassel. Ritzy's Bar is the hoodlum bar of the streets around Times Square; it changes names every year. You walk in here and you don't see a single girl, even in the booths, just a great mob of young men dressed in all varieties of hoodlum cloth, from red shirts to zoot suits. It is also the hustlers' bar – the boys who make a living among the sad old homos of the Eighth Avenue night. Dean walked in there with his eyes slitted to see every single face. There were wild Negro queers, sullen guys with guns, shiv-packing seamen, thin, non-committal junkies, and an occasional well-dressed middle-aged detective, posing as a bookie and hanging around half for interest and half for duty. It was the typical place for Dean to put down his request. All kinds of evil plans are hatched in Ritzy's Bar – you can sense it in the air – and all kinds of mad sexual routines are initiated to go with them. The safecracker proposes not only a certain loft on 14th Street to the hoodlum, but that they sleep together. Kinsey spent a lot of time in Ritzy's Bar, interviewing some of the boys; I was there the night his assistant came, in 1945. Hassel and Carlo were interviewed.

Dean and I drove back to the pad and found Marylou in bed. Dunkel was roaming his ghost around New York. Dean told her what we had decided. She said she was pleased. I wasn't so sure myself. I had to prove that I'd go through with it. The bed had been the deathbed of a big man and sagged in the middle. Maylou lay there, with Dean and myself on each side of her, poised on the upjutting mattress-ends, not knowing what to say. I said, 'Ah hell, I can't do this.'

'Go on, man, you promised!' said Dean.

'What about Marylou?' I said. 'Come on, Marylou, what do you think?'

'Go ahead,' she said.

She embraced me and I tried to forget old Dean was there. Every time I realized he was there in the dark, listening for every sound, I couldn't do anything but laugh. It was horrible.

'We must all relax,' said Dean.

'I'm afraid I can't make it. Why don't you go in the kitchen a minute?'

Dean did so. Marylou was so lovely, but I whispered, 'Wait until we be lovers in San Francisco; my heart isn't in it.' I was right, she could tell. It was three children of the earth trying to decide something in the night and having all the weight of past centuries ballooning in the dark before them. There was a strange quiet in the apartment. I went and tapped Dean and told him to go to Marylou; and I retired to the couch. I could hear Dean, blissful and blabbering and frantically rocking. Only a guy who's spent five years in jail can go to such maniacal helpless extremes; beseeching at the portals of the soft source, mad with a completely physical realization of the origins of life-bliss; blindly seeking to return the way he came. This is the result of years looking at sexy pictures behind bars; looking at the legs and breasts of women in popular magazines; evaluating the hardness of the steel halls and the softness of the woman who is not there. Prison is where you promise yourself the right to live. Dean had never seen his mother's face. Every new girl, every new wife, every new child was an addition to his bleak impoverishment. Where was his father? – old bum Dean Moriarty the Tinsmith, riding freights, working as a scullion in railroad cookshacks, stumbling, down-crashing in wino alley nights, expiring on coal piles, dropping his yellowed teeth one by one in the gutters of the West. Dean had every right to die the sweet deaths of complete love of his Marylou. I didn't want to interfere, I just wanted to follow.

Carlo came back at dawn and put on his bathrobe. He wasn't sleeping any more those days. 'Ech!' he screamed. He was going out of his mind from the confusion of jam on the floor, pants, dresses thrown around, cigarette butts, dirty dishes, open books – it was a great forum we were having. Every day the world groaned to turn and we were making our appalling studies of the night. Marylou was black and blue from a fight with Dean about something; his face was scratched. It was time to go.

We drove to my house, a whole gang of ten, to get my bag and call Old Bull Lee in New Orleans from the phone in the bar where Dean and I had our first talk years ago when he came to my door to learn to write. We heard Bull's whining voice eighteen hundred miles away. 'Say, what do you boys expect me to do with this Galatea Dunkel? She's been here two weeks now, hiding in her room and refusing to talk to either Jane or me. Have you got this character Ed Dunkel with you? For krissakes bring him down and get rid of her. She's sleeping in our best bedroom and's run clear out of money. This ain't a hotel.' He assured Bull with whoops and cries over the phone – there was Dean, Marylou, Carlo, Dunkel, me, Ian Mac-Arthur, his wife, Tom Saybrook, God knows who else, all yelling and drinking beer over the phone at befuddled Bull, who above all things hated confusion. 'Well,' he said, 'maybe you'll make better sense when you gets down here if you gets down here.' I said good-bye to my aunt and promised to be back in two weeks and took off for California again.

6

IT WAS drizzling and mysterious at the beginning of our journey. I could see that it was all going to be one big saga of the mist. 'Whooee!' yelled Dean. 'Here we go!' And he hunched over the wheel and gunned her; he was back in his element, everybody could see that. We were all delighted, we all realized we were leaving confusion and nonsense behind and performing our one and noble function of the time, *move*. And we moved! We flashed past the mysterious white signs in the night somewhere in New Jersey that say SOUTH (with an arrow) and WEST (with an arrow) and took the south one. New Orleans! It burned in our brains. From the dirty snows of 'frosty fagtown New York', as Dean called it, all the way to the greeneries and river smells of old New Orleans at the washed-out bottom of America; then west. Ed was in the back seat; Marylou and Dean and I sat in front and had the warmest talk about the goodness and joy of life. Dean suddenly became tender. 'Now dammit, look here, all of you, we all must admit that everything is fine and there's no need in the world to worry, and in fact we should realize what it would mean to us to UNDERSTAND that we're not REALLY worried about ANYTHING. Am I right?' We all agreed. 'Here we go, we're all together ... What did we do in New York? Let's forgive.' We all had our spats back there. 'That's behind us, merely by miles and inclinations. Now we're heading down to New Orleans to dig Old Bull Lee and ain't that going to be kicks and listen will you to this old tenorman blow his top' – he shot up the radio volume till the car shuddered – 'and listen to him tell the story and put down true relaxation and knowledge.'

We all jumped to the music and agreed. The purity of the road. The white line in the middle of the highway unrolled and hugged our left front tyre as if glued to our groove. Dean hunched his muscular neck, T-shirted in the winter night, and blasted the car along. He insisted I drive through Baltimore for traffic practice; that was all right, except he and Marylou insisted on steering while they kissed and fooled around. It was crazy; the radio was on full blast. Dean beat drums on the dashboard till a great sag developed in it; I did too. The poor Hudson – the slow boat to China – was receiving her beating.

'Oh man, what kicks!' yelled Dean. 'Now, Marylou, listen really, honey, you know that I'm hotrock capable of everything at the same time and I have unlimited energy – now in San Francisco we must go on living together. I know just the place for you – at the end of the regular chain-gang run – I'll be home just a cut-hair less than every two days and for twelve hours at a stretch, and *man*, you know what we can do in twelve hours, darling. Meanwhile I'll go right on living at Camille's like nothin, see, she won't know. We can work it, we've done it before.' It was all right with Marylou, she was really out for Camille's scalp. The understanding had been that Marylou would switch to me in Frisco, but I now began to see they were going to stick and I was going to be left alone on my butt at the other end of the continent. But why think about that when all the golden land's ahead of you and all kinds of unforeseen events wait lurking to surprise you and make you glad you're alive to see?

We arrived in Washington at dawn. It was the day of Harry Truman's inauguration for his second term. Great displays of war might were lined along Pennsylvania Avenue as we rolled by in our battered boat. There were B-29s, PT boats, artillery, all kinds of war material that looked murderous in the snowy grass; the last thing was a regular small ordinary lifeboat that looked pitiful and foolish. Dean slowed down to look at it. He kept shaking his head in awe. 'What are these people up to? Harry's sleeping somewhere in this town. ... Good old Harry. ... Man from Missouri, as I am. ... That must be his own boat.'

Dean went to sleep in the back seat and Dunkel drove. We gave him specific instructions to take it easy. No sooner were we snoring than he gunned the car up to eighty, bad bearings and all, and not only that but he made a triple pass at a spot where a cop was arguing with a motorist – he was in the fourth lane of a four-lane highway, going the wrong way. Naturally the cop took after us with his siren whining. We were stopped. He told us to follow him to the station house. There was a mean cop in there who took an immediate dislike to Dean; he could smell jail all over him. He sent his cohort outdoors to question Marylou and me privately. They wanted to know how old Marylou was, they were trying to whip up a Mann Act idea. But she had her marriage certificate. Then they took me aside alone and wanted to know who was sleeping with Marylou. 'Her husband,' I said quite simply. They were curious. Something was fishy. They tried some amateur Sherlocking by asking the same questions twice, expecting us to make a slip. I said, 'Those two fellows are going back to work on the railroad in California, this is the short one's wife, and I'm a friend on a two-week vacation from college.'

The cop smiled and said, 'Yeah? Is this really your own wallet?'

Finally the mean one inside fined Dean twenty-five dollars. We told them we only had forty to go all the way to the Coast; they said that made no difference to them. When Dean protested, the mean cop threatened to take him back to Pennsylvania and slap a special charge on him.

'What charge?'

'Never mind what charge. Don't worry about *that*, wise guy.'

We had to give them the twenty-five. But first Ed Dunkel, that culprit, offered to go to jail. Dean considered it. The cop was infuriated; he said, 'If you let your partner go to jail I'm taking you back to Pennsylvania right now. You hear that?' All we wanted to do was go. 'Another speeding ticket in Virginia and you lose your car,' said the mean cop as a parting volley. Dean was red in the face. We drove off silently. It was just like an invitation to steal to take our trip-money away from us. They knew we were broke and had no relatives on the road or to wire to for money. The American police are involved in psychological warfare against those Americans who don't frighten them with imposing papers and threats. It's a Victorian police force; it peers out of musty windows and wants to inquire about everything. and can make crimes if the crimes don't exist to its satisfaction. 'Nine lines of crime, one of boredom,' said Louis-Ferdinand Céline. Dean was so mad he wanted to come back to Virginia and shoot the cop as soon as he had a gun.

'Pennsylvania!' he scoffed. 'I wish I knew what that charge was! Vag, probably; take all my money and charge me vag. Those guys have it so damn easy. They'll out and shoot you if you complain, too.' There was nothing to do but get happy with ourselves again and forget about it. When we got through Richmond we began forgetting about it, and soon everything was okay.

Now we had fifteen dollars to go all the way. We'd have to pick up hitchhikers and bum quarters off them for gas. In the Virginia wilderness suddenly we saw a man walking on the road. Dean zoomed to a stop. I looked back and said he was only a bum and probably didn't have a cent.

'We'll just pick him up for kicks!' Dean laughed. The man was a ragged, bespectacled mad type, walking along reading a paperbacked muddy book he'd found in a culvert by the road. He got in the car and went right on reading; he was incredibly filthy and covered with scabs. He said his name was Hyman Solomon and that he walked all over the USA, knocking and sometimes kicking at Jewish doors and demanding money: 'Give me money to eat, I am a Jew.'

He said it worked very well and that it was coming to him. We asked him what he was reading. He didn't know. He didn't bother to look at the title page. He was only looking at the words, as though he had found the real Torah where it belonged, in the wilderness.

'See? See? See?' cackled Dean, poking my ribs. 'I told you it was kicks. Everybody's kicks, man!' We carried Solomon all the way to Testament. My brother by now was in his new house on the other side of town. Here we were back on the long, bleak street with the railroad track running down the middle and the sad, sullen Southerners loping in front of hardware stores and five-and-tens.

Solomon said, 'I see you people need a little money to continue your journey. You wait for me and I'll go hustle up a few dollars at a Jewish home and I'll go along with you as far as Alabama.' Dean was all beside himself with happiness; he and I rushed off to buy bread and cheese spread for a lunch in the car. Marylou and Ed waited in the car. We spent two hours in Testament waiting for Hyman Solomon to show up; he was hustling for his bread somewhere in town, but we couldn't see him. The sun began to grow red and late.

Solomon never showed up so we roared out of Testament. 'Now you see, Sal, God does exist, because we keep getting hung-up with this town, no matter what we try to do, and you'll notice the strange Biblical name of it, and that strange Biblical character who made us stop here once more, and all things tied together all over like rain connecting everybody the world over by chain touch. ...' Dean rattled on like this; he was overjoyed and exuberant. He and I suddenly saw the whole country like an oyster for us to open; and the pearl was there, the pearl was there. Off we roared south. We picked up another hitchhiker. This was a sad young kid who said he had an aunt who owned a grocery store in Dunn, North Carolina, right outside Fayetteville. 'When we get there can you bum a buck off her? Right! Fine! Let's go!' We were in Dunn in an hour, at dusk. We drove to where the kid said his aunt had the grocery store. It was a sad little street that dead-ended at a factory wall. There was a grocery store but there was no aunt. We wondered what the kid was talking about. We asked him how far he was going; he didn't know. It was a big hoax; once upon a time, in some lost back-alley adventure, he had seen the grocery store in Dunn, and it was the first story that popped into his disordered, feverish mind. We bought him a hot dog, but Dean said we couldn't take him along because we needed room to sleep and room for hitchhikers who could buy a little gas. This was sad but true. We left him in Dunn at nightfall.

I drove through South Carolina and beyond Macon, Georgia, as Dean, Marylou, and Ed slept. All alone in the night I had my own thoughts and held the car to the white line in the holy road. What was I doing? Where was I going? I'd soon find out. I got dog-tired beyond Macon and woke up Dean to resume. We got out of the car for air and suddenly both of us were stoned with joy to realize that in the darkness all around us was fragrant green grass and the smell of fresh manure and warm waters. 'We're in the South! We've left the winter!' Faint daybreak illuminated green shoots by the side of the road. I took a deep breath; a locomotive howled across the darkness, Mobile-bound. So were we. I took off my shirt and exulted. Ten miles down the road Dean drove into a filling station with the motor off, noticed that the attendant was fast asleep at the desk, jumped out, quietly filled the gas tank, saw to it the bell didn't ring, and rolled off like an Arab with a five-dollar tankful of gas for our pilgrimage.

I slept and woke up to the crazy exultant sounds of music and Dean and Marylou talking and the great green land rolling by. 'Where are we?'

'Just passed the tip of Florida, man – Flomaton, it's called.' Florida! We were rolling down to the coastal plain and Mobile; up ahead were great soaring clouds of the Gulf of Mexico. It was only thirty-two hours since we'd said good-bye to every-body in the dirty snows of the North. We stopped at a gas station, and there Dean and Marylou played piggyback around the tanks and Dunkel went inside and stole three packs of cigarettes without trying. We were fresh out. Rolling into Mobile over the long tidal highway, we all took our winter clothes off and enjoyed the Southern temperature. This was when Dean started telling his life story and when, beyond Mobile, he came upon an obstruction of wrangling cars at a crossroads and instead of slipping around them just balled right through the driveway of a gas station and went right on with-out relaxing his steady continental seventy. We left gaping faces behind us. He went right on with his tale. 'I tell you it's true, I started at nine, with a girl called Milly Mayfair in back of Rod's garage on Grant Street – same street Carlo lived on in Denver. That's when my father was still working at the smithy's a bit. I remember my aunt yelling out the window, "What are you do-ing down there in back of the garage?" Oh honey Marylou, if I'd known you then! Wow! How sweet you musta been at nine.' He tittered maniacally; he stuck his finger in her mouth and licked it; he took her hand and rubbed it over himself. She just sat there, smiling serenely.

Big long Ed Dunkel sat looking out the window, talking to himself. 'Yes sir, I thought I was a ghost that night.' He was also wondering what Galatea Dunkel would say to him in New Orleans.

Dean went on. 'One time I rode a freight from New Mexico clear to LA – I was eleven years old, lost my father at a siding, we were all in a hobo jungle, I was with a man called Big Red, my father was out drunk in a boxcar – it started to roll – Big Red and I missed it – I didn't see my father for months. I rode a long freight all the way to California, really flying, first-class freight, a desert Zipper. All the way I rode over the couplings – you can imagine how dangerous, I was only a kid, I didn't know – clutching a loaf of bread under one arm and the other hooked around the brake bar. This is no story, this is true. When I got to LA I was so starved for milk and cream I got a job in a dairy and the first thing I did I drank two quarts of heavy cream and puked.'

'Poor Dean,' said Marylou, and she kissed him. He stared ahead proudly. He loved her.

We were suddenly driving along the blue waters of the Gulf, and at the same time a momentous mad thing began on the radio; it was the Chicken Jazz'n Gumbo disc-jockey show from New Orleans, all mad jazz records, coloured records, with the disc-jockey saying, 'Don't worry 'bout *nothing*!' We saw New Orleans in the night ahead of us with joy. Dean rubbed his hands over the wheel. 'Now we're going to get our kicks!' At dusk we were coming into the humming streets of New Orleans. 'Oh, smell the people!' yelled Dean with his face out the window, sniffing. 'Ah! God! Life!' He swung around a trolley. 'Yes!' He darted the car and looked in every direction for girls. 'Look at *her*!' The air was so sweet in New Orleans it seemed to come in soft bandannas; and you could smell the river and really smell the people, and mud, and molasses, and every kind of tropical exhalation with your nose suddenly removed from the dry ices of a Northern winter. We bounced in our seats. 'And dig her!' yelled Dean, pointing at another woman. 'Oh, I love, love, love women! I think women are wonderful! I love women!' He spat out the window; he groaned; he clutched his head. Great beads of sweat fell from his forehead from pure excitement and exhaustion.

We bounced the car up on the Algiers ferry and found ourselves crossing the Mississippi River by boat. 'Now we must all get out and dig the river and the people and smell the world, said Dean, bustling with his sunglasses and cigarettes and leaping out of the car like a jack-in-the-box. We followed. On rails we leaned and looked at the great brown father of waters rolling down from mid-America like the torrent of broken souls – bearing Montana logs and Dakota muds and Iowa vales and things that had drowned in Three Forks, where the secret began in ice. Smoky New Orleans receded on one side; old, sleepy Algiers with its warped woodsides bumped us on the other. Negroes were working in the hot afternoon, stoking the ferry furnaces that burned red and made our tyres smell. Dean dug them, hopping up and down in the heat. He rushed around the deck and upstairs with his baggy pants hanging halfway down his belly. Suddenly I saw him eagering on the flying bridge. I expected him to take off on wings. I heard his mad laugh all over the boat – 'Hee-hee-hee-hee-hee!' Marylou was with him. He covered everything in a jiffy, came back with the full story, jumped in the car just as everybody was tooting to go, and we slipped off, passing two or three cars in a narrow space, and found ourselves darting through Algiers.

'Where? Where?' Dean was yelling.

We decided first to clean up at a gas station and inquire for Bull's whereabouts. Little children were playing in the drowsy river sunset; girls were going by with bandannas and cotton blouses and bare legs. Dean ran up the street to see everything. He looked around; he nodded; he rubbed his belly. Big Ed sat back in the car with his hat over his eyes, smiling at Dean. I sat on the fender. Marylou was in the women's john. From bushy shores where infinitesimal men fished with sticks, and from delta sleeps that stretched up along the reddening land, the big humpbacked river with its mainstream leaping came coiling around Algiers like a snake, with a nameless rumble. Drowsy, peninsular Algiers with all her bees and shanties was like to be

134

washed away someday. The sun slanted, bugs flip-flopped, the awful waters groaned.

We went to Old Bull Lee's house outside town near the river levee. It was on a road that ran across a swampy field. The house was a dilapidated old heap with sagging porches running around and weeping willows in the yard; the grass was a yard high, old fences leaned, old barns collapsed. There was no one in sight. We pulled right into the yard and saw washtubs on the back porch. I got out and went to the screen door. Jane Lee was standing in it with her eyes cupped towards the sun. 'Jane,' I said. 'It's me. It's us.'

She knew that. 'Yes, I know. Bull isn't here now. Isn't that a fire or something over there?' We both looked towards the sun.

'You mean the sun?'

'Of course I don't mean the sun — I heard sirens that way. Don't you know a peculiar glow?' It was towards New Orleans; the clouds were strange.

'I don't see anything,' I said.

Jane snuffed down her nose. 'Same old Paradise.'

That was the way we greeted each other after four years; Jane used to live with my wife and me in New York. 'And is Galatea Dunkel here?' I asked. Jane was still looking for her fire; in those days she ate three tubes of benzedrine paper a day. Her face, once plump and Germanic and pretty, had become stony and red and gaunt. She had caught polio in New Orleans and limped a little. Sheepishly Dean and the gang came out of the car and more or less made themselves at home. Galatea Dunkel came out of her stately retirement in the back of the house to meet her tormentor. Galatea was a serious girl. She was pale and looked like tears all over. Big Ed passed his hand through his hair and said hello. She looked at him steadily.

'Where have you been? Why did you do this to me?' And she gave Dean a dirty look; she knew the score. Dean paid absolutely no attention; what he wanted now was food; he asked Jane if there was anything. The confusion began right there.

Poor Bull came home in his Texas Chevy and found his house invaded by maniacs; but he greeted me with a nice warmth I hadn't seen in him for a long time. He had bought this house in New Orleans with some money he had made growing black-eyed peas in Texas with an old college school-mate whose father, a mad paretic, had died and left a fortune. Bull himself only got fifty dollars a week from his own family, which wasn't too bad except that he spent almost that much per week on his drug habit – and his wife was also expensive, gobbling up about ten dollars' worth of benny tubes a week. Their food bill was the lowest in the country; they hardly ever ate; nor did the children – they didn't seem to care. They had two wonderful children : Dodie, eight years old; and little Ray, one year. Ray ran around stark naked in the yard, a little blond child of the rainbow. Bull called him 'the Little Beast', after W. C. Fields. Bull came driving into the yard and unrolled himself from the car bone by bone, and came over wearily, wearing glasses, felt hat, shabby suit, long, lean, strange, and laconic, saying, 'Why, Sal, you finally got here; let's go in the house and have a drink.'

It would take all night to tell about Old Bull Lee; let's just say now, he was a teacher, and it may be said that he had every right to teach because he spent all his time learning; and the things he learned were what he considered to be and called 'the facts of life', which he learned not only out of necessity but because he wanted to. He dragged his long, thin body around the entire United States and most of Europe and North Africa in his time, only to see what was going on; he married a White Russian countess in Yugoslavia to get her away from the Nazis in the thirties; there are pictures of him with the international cocaine set of the thirties – gangs with wild hair, leaning on one another; there are other pictures of him in a Panama hat, surveying the streets of Algiers; he never saw the White Russian countess again. He was an exterminator in Chicago, a bartender in New York, a summons-server in Newark. In Paris he sat at café tables, watching the sullen French faces go by. In Athens he looked up from his *ouzo* at what he called the ugliest people in the world. In Istanbul he threaded his way through crowds of opium addicts and rug-sellers, looking for the facts. In English hotels he read Spengler and the Marquis de Sade. In Chicago he planned to hold up a Turkish bath, hesitated just for two minutes too long for a drink, and wound up with two dollars and had to make a run for it. He did all these things merely for the experience. Now the final study was the drug habit. He was now in New Orleans, slipping along the streets with shady characters and haunting connection bars.

There is a strange story about his college days that illustrates something else about him: he had friends for cocktails in his well-appointed rooms one afternoon when suddenly his pet ferret rushed out and bit an elegant teacup queer on the ankle and everybody hightailed it out the door, screaming. Old Bull leaped up and grabbed his shotgun and said, 'He smells that old rat again,' and shot a hole in the wall big enough for fifty rats. On the wall hung a picture of an ugly old Cape Cod house. His friends said, 'Why do you have that ugly thing hanging there?' and Bull said, 'I like it because it's ugly.' All his life was in that line. Once I knocked on his door in the 60th Street slums of New York and he opened it wearing a derby hat, a vest with nothing underneath, and long striped sharpster pants; in his hands he had a cookpot, birdseed in the pot, and was trying to mash the seed to roll in cigarettes. He also experimented in boiling codeine cough syrup down to black mash – that didn't work too well. He spent long hours with Shakespeare – the 'Immortal Bard', he called him – on his lap. In New Orleans he had begun to spend long hours with the Mayan Codices on his lap, and, although he went on talking, the book lay open all the time. I said once, 'What's going to happen to us when we die?' and he said, 'When you die you're just dead, that's all.' He had a set of chains in his room that he said he used with his psychoanalyst; they were experimenting with narcoanalysis and found that Old Bull had seven separate personalities, each growing worse and worse on the way down, till finally he was a raving idiot and had to be restrained with chains. The top personality was an English lord, the bottom the idiot. Halfway he was an old Negro who stood in line, waiting with everyone else, and said, 'Some's bastards, some's ain't, that's the score.'

Bull had a sentimental streak about the old days in America, especially 1910, when you could get morphine in a drugstore without prescription and Chinese smoked opium in their evening windows and the country was wild and brawling and free, with abundance and any kind of freedom for everyone. His chief hate was Washington bureaucracy; second to that, liberals; then cops. He spent all his time talking and teaching others. Jane sat at his feet; so did I; so did Dean; and so had Carlo Marx. We'd all learned from him. He was a grey, non-descript-looking fellow you wouldn't notice on the street, unless you looked closer and saw his mad, bony skull with its strange youthfulness – a Kansas minister with exotic, pheno-menal fires and mysteries. He had studied medicine in Vienna; had studied anthropology, read everything; and now he was settling to his life's work, which was the study of things them-selves in the streets of life and the night. He sat in his chair; Jane brought drinks, martinis. The shades by his chair were always drawn, day and night; it was his corner of the house. On his lap were the Mayan Codices and an air gun which he occa-sionally raised to pop benzedrine tubes across the room. I kept rushing around, putting up new ones. We all took shots and meanwhile we talked. Bull was curious to know the reason for this trip. He peered at us and snuffed down his nose, *thfump*, like a sound in a dry tank.

'Now, Dean, I want you to sit quiet a minute and tell me what you're doing crossing the country like this.'

Dean could only blush and say, 'Ah well, you know how it is.'

'Sal, what are you going to the Coast for?'

'Only for a few days. I'm coming back to school.'

'What's the score with this Ed Dunkel? What kind of charac-ter is he?' At that moment Ed was making up to Galatea in the bedroom; it didn't take him long. We didn't know what to tell Bull about Ed Dunkel. Seeing that we didn't know anything about ourselves, he whipped out three sticks of tea and said to go ahead, supper'd be ready soon.

'Ain't nothing better in the world to give you an appetite. I once ate a horrible lunchcart hamburg on tea and it seemed like the most delicious thing in the world. I just got back from Houston last week, went to see Dale about our black-eyed peas. I was sleeping in a motel one morning when all of a sudden I was blasted out of bed. This damn fool had just shot his wife in the room next to mine. Everybody stood around confused, and the guy just got in his car and drove off, left the shotgun on the floor for the sheriff. They finally caught him in Houma, drunk as a lord. Man ain't safe going around this country any more without a gun.' He pulled back his coat and showed us his revolver. Then he opened the drawer and showed us the rest of his arsenal. In New York he once had a sub-machine-gun under his bed. 'I got something better than that now – a German Scheintoth gas gun; look at this beauty, only got one shell. I could knock out a hundred men with this gun and have plenty of time to make a getaway. Only thing wrong, I only got one shell.'

'I hope I'm not around when you try it,' said Jane from the kitchen. 'How do *you* know it's a gas shell?' Bull snuffed; he never paid any attention to her sallies but he heard them. His relation with his wife was one of the strangest : they talked till late at night; Bull liked to hold the floor, he went right on in his dreary monotonous voice, she tried to break in, she never could; at dawn he got tired and then Jane talked and he listened, snuffing and going *thfump* down his nose. She loved that man madly, but in a delirious way of some kind; there was never any mooching and mincing around, just talk and a very deep companionship that none of us would ever be able to fathom. Something curiously unsympathetic and cold between them was really a form of humour by which they communicated their own set of subtle vibrations. Love is all; Jane was never more than ten feet away from Bull and never missed a word he said, and he spoke in a very low voice, too.

Dean and I were yelling about a big night in New Orleans and wanted Bull to show us around. He threw a damper on this. 'New Orleans is a very dull town. It's against the law to go to the coloured section. The bars are insufferably dreary.'

I said, 'There must be some ideal bars in town.'

'The ideal bar doesn't exist in America. An ideal bar is something that's gone beyond our ken. In nineteen ten a bar was a place where men went to meet during or after work, and all there was was a long counter, brass rails, spittoons, player piano for music, a few mirrors, and barrels of whisky at ten cents a shot together with barrels of beer at five cents a mug. Now all you get is chromium, drunken women, fags, hostile bartenders, anxious owners who hover around the door, worried about their leather seats and the law; just a lot of screaming at the wrong time and deadly silence when a stranger walks in.'

We argued about bars. 'All right,' he said, 'I'll take you to New Orleans tonight and show you what I mean.' And he deliberately took us to the dullest bars. We left Jane with the children; supper was over; she was reading the want ads of the New Orleans *Times-Picayune*. I asked her if she was looking for a job; she only said it was the most interesting part of the paper. Bull rode into town with us and went right on talking. 'Take it easy, Dean, we'll get there, I hope; hup, there's the ferry, you don't have to drive us clear into the river.' He held on. Dean had gotten worse, he confided in me. 'He seems to me to be headed for his ideal fate, which is compulsive psychosis dashed with a jigger of psychopathic irresponsibility and violence.' He looked at Dean out of the corner of his eye. 'If you go to California with this madman you'll never make it. Why don't you stay in New Orleans with me? We'll play the horses over to Graetna and relax in my yard. I've got a nice set of knives and I'm building a target. Some pretty juicy dolls downtown, too, if that's in your line these days.' He snuffed. We were on the ferry and Dean had leaped out to lean over the rail. I followed, but Bull sat on in the car, snuffing, *thfump*. There was a mystic wraith of fog over the brown waters that night, together with dark driftwoods; and across the way New Orleans glowed orange-bright, with a few dark ships at her hem, ghostly fogbound Cereno ships with Spanish balconies and ornamental poops, till you got up close and saw they were just old freighters from Sweden and Panama. The ferry fires glowed in the night; the same Negroes plied the shovel and sang. Old Big Slim Hazard had once worked on the Algiers ferry as a deckhand; this made me think of Mississippi Gene too; and as the river poured down from mid-America by starlight I knew, I knew like mad that everything I had ever known and would ever know was One. Strange to say, too, that night we crossed the ferry with Bull Lee a girl committed suicide off the deck; either just before or just after us; we saw it in the paper the next day.

We hit all the dull bars in the French Quarter with Old Bull and went back home at midnight. That night Marylou took everything in the books; she took tea, goofballs, benny, liquor, and even asked Old Bull for a shot of M, which of course he didn't give her; he did give her a martini. She was so saturated with elements of all kinds that she came to a standstill and stood goofy on the porch with me. It was a wonderful porch Bull had. It ran clear around the house; by moonlight with the willows it looked like an old Southern mansion that had seen better days. In the house Jane sat reading the want ads in the living room; Bull was in the bathroom taking his fix, clutching his old black necktie in his teeth for a tourniquet and jabbing with the needle into his woesome arm with the thousand holes; Ed Dunkel was sprawled out with Galatea in the massive master bed that Old Bull and Jane never used; Dean was rolling tea; and Marylou and I imitated Southern aristocracy.

'Why, Miss Lou, you look lovely and most fetching tonight.'

'Why, thank you, Crawford, I sure do appreciate the nice things you do say.'

Doors kept opening around the crooked porch, and members of our sad drama in the American night kept popping out to find out where everybody was. Finally I took a walk alone to the levee. I wanted to sit on the muddy bank and dig the Mississippi River; instead of that I had to look at it with my nose against a wire fence. When you start separating the people from their rivers what have you got? 'Bureaucracy!' says Old Bull; he sits with Kafka on his lap, the lamp burns above him, he snuffs, *thfump*. His old house creaks. And the Montana log rolls by in the big black river of the night. ' 'Tain't nothin but bureaucracy. And unions! Especially unions!' But dark laughter would come again.

7

IT WAS there in the morning when I got up bright and early and found Old Bull and Dean in the back yard. Dean was wearing his gas-station coveralls and helping Bull. Bull had found a great big piece of thick rotten wood and was desperately yanking with a hammerhook at little nails embedded in it. We stared at the nails; there were millions of them; they were like worms.

'When I get all these nails out of this I'm going to build me a shelf that'll last a *thousand years!*' said Bull, every bone shuddering with boyish excitement. 'Why, Sal, do you realize the shelves they build these days crack under the weight of knick-knacks after six months or generally collapse? Same with houses, same with clothes. These bastards have invented plastics by which they could make houses that last *forever*. And tyres. Americans are killing themselves by the millions every year with defective rubber tyres that get hot on the road and blow up. They could make tyres that never blow up. Same with tooth powder. There's a certain gum they've invented and they won't show it to anybody that if you chew it as a kid you'll never get a cavity for the rest of your born days. Same with clothes. They can make clothes that last forever. They prefer making cheap goods so's everybody'll have to go on working and punching timeclocks and organizing themselves in sullen unions and floundering around while the big grab goes on in Washington and Moscow.' He raised his big piece of rotten wood. 'Don't you think this'll make a splendid shelf?'

It was early in the morning; his energy was at its peak. The poor fellow took so much junk into his system he could only weather the greater proportion of his day in that chair with the lamp burning at noon, but in the morning he was magnificent. We began throwing knives at the target. He said he'd seen an Arab in Tunis who could stick a man's eye from forty feet. This got him going on his aunt, who went to the Casbah in the thirties. 'She was with a party of tourists led by a guide. She had a diamond ring on her little finger. She leaned on a wall to rest a minute and an Ay-rab rushed up and appropriated her ring finger before she could let out a cry, my dear. She suddenly realized she had no little finger. Hi-hi-hi-hi-hi!' When he laughed and compressed his lips together and made it come out from his belly, from far away, and doubled up to lean on his knees. He laughed a long time. 'Hey Jane!' he yelled gleefully. 'I was just telling Dean and Sal about my aunt in the Casbah!'

'I heard you,' she said across the lovely warm Gulf morning from the kitchen door. Great beautiful clouds floated overhead, valley clouds that made you feel the vastness of old tumbledown holy America from mouth to mouth and tip to tip. All pep and juices was Bull. 'Say, did I ever tell you about Dale's father? He was the funniest old man you ever saw in your life. He had paresis, which eats away the forepart of your brain and you get so's you're not responsible for anything that comes into your mind. He had a house in Texas and had carpenters working twenty-four hours a day putting on new wings. He'd leap up in the middle of the night and say, 'I don't want that goddam wing; put it over there.' The carpenters had to take everything down and start all over again. Come dawn you'd see them hammering away at the new wing. Then the old man'd get bored with that and say, 'Goddammit, I wanta go to Maine!' And he'd get into his car and drive off a hundred miles an hour – great showers of chicken feathers followed his track for hundreds of miles. He'd stop his car in the middle of a Texas town just to get out and buy some whisky. Traffic would honk all around him and he'd come rushing out of the store, yelling, "Thet your goddam noith, you bunth of bathats!" He lisped; when you have paresis you lips, I mean you lisps. One night he came to my house in Cincinnati and tooted the horn and said, "Come on out and let's go to Texas to see Dale." He was going back from Maine. He claimed he bought a house – oh, we wrote a story about him at college, where you see this horrible shipwreck and people in the water clutching at the sides of the lifeboat, and the old man is there with a machete, hackin' at their fingers. "Get away, ya bunth a bathats, thith my cottham boath!" Oh, he was horrible. I could tell you stories about him all day. Say, ain't this a nice day?'

And it sure was. The softest breezes blew in from the levee; it was worth the whole trip. We went into the house after Bull to measure the wall for a shelf. He showed us the dining-room table he built. It was made of wood six inches thick. 'This is a table that'll last a thousand years!' said Bull, leaning his long thin face at us maniacally. He banged on it.

In the evenings he sat at this table, picking at his food and throwing the bones to the cats. He had seven cats. 'I love cats. I especially like the ones that squeal when I hold 'em over the bathtub.' He insisted on demonstrating; someone was in the bathroom. 'Well,' he said, 'we can't do that now. Say, I been having a fight with the neighbours next door.' He told us about the neighbours; they were a vast crew with sassy children who threw stones over the rickety fence at Dodie and Ray and sometimes at Old Bull. He told them to cut it out; the old man rushed out and yelled something in Portuguese. Bull went in the house and came back with his shotgun, upon which he leaned demurely; the incredible simper on his face beneath the long hatbrim, his whole body writhing coyly and snakily as he waited, a grotesque, lank, lonely clown beneath the clouds. The sight of him the Portuguese must have thought something out of an old evil dream.

We scoured the yard for things to do. There was a tremendous fence Bull had been working on to separate him from the obnoxious neighbours; it would never be finished, the task was too much. He rocked it back and forth to show how solid it was. Suddenly he grew tired and quiet and went in the house and disappeared in the bathroom for his pre-lunch fix. He came out glassy-eyed and calm, and sat down under his burning lamp. The sunlight poked feebly behind the drawn shade. 'Say, why don't you fellows try my orgone accumulator? Put some juice in your bones. I always rush up and take off ninety miles an hour for the nearest whorehouse, hor-hor-hor!' This was his 'laugh' laugh – when he wasn't really laughing. The orgone accumulator is an ordinary box big enough for a man to sit inside on a chair: a layer of wood, a layer of metal, and another layer of wood gather in orgones from the atmosphere and hold them captive long enough for the human body to absorb more than a usual share. According to Reich, orgones are vibratory atmospheric atoms of the life-principle. People get cancer because they run out of orgones. Old Bull thought his orgone accumulator would be improved if the wood he used was as organic as possible, so he tied bush bayou leaves and twigs to his mystical outhouse. It stood there in the hot, flat yard, an exfoliate machine clustered and bedecked with maniacal contrivances. Old Bull slipped off his clothes and went in to sit and moon over his navel. 'Say, Sal, after lunch let's you and me go play the horses over to the bookie joint in Graetna.' He was magnificent. He took a nap after lunch in his chair, the air gun on his lap and little Ray curled around his neck, sleeping. It was a pretty sight, father and son, a father who would certainly never bore his son when it came to finding things to do and talk about. He woke up with a start and stared at me. It took him a minute to recognize who I was. 'What are you going to the Coast for, Sal?' he asked, and went back to sleep in a moment.

In the afternoon we went to Graetna, just Bull and me. We drove in his old Chevy. Dean's Hudson was low and sleek; Bull's Chevy was high and rattly. It was just like 1910. The bookie joint was located near the waterfront in a big chromium-leather bar that opened up in the back to a tremendous hall where entries and numbers were posted on the wall. Louisiana characters lounged around with *Racing Forms*. Bull and I had a beer, and casually Bull went over to the slot machine and threw a half-dollar piece in. The counters clicked 'Jackpot' – 'Jackpot' – 'Jackpot' – and the last 'Jackpot' hung for just a moment and slipped back to 'Cherry'. He had lost a hundred dollars or more just by a hair. 'Damn!' yelled Bull. 'They got these things adjusted. You could see it right then. I had the jackpot and the mechanism clicked it back. Well, what you gonna do.' We examined the *Racing Form*. I hadn't played the horses in years and was bemused with all the new names. There was one horse called Big Pop that sent me into a temporary trance thinking of my father, who used to play the horses with me. I was just about to mention it to Old Bull when he said, 'Well I think I'll try this Ebony Corsair here.'

Then I finally said it. 'Big Pop reminds me of my father.'

He mused for just a second, his clear blue eyes fixed on mine hypnotically so that I couldn't tell what he was thinking or where he was. Then he went over and bet on Ebony Corsair. Big Pop won and paid fifty to one.

'Damn!' said Bull. 'I should have known better, I've had experience with this before. Oh, when will we ever learn?'

'What do you mean?'

'Big Pop is what I mean. You had a vision, boy, a *vision*. Only damn fools pay no attention to visions. How do you know your father, who was an old horseplayer, just didn't momentarily communicate to you that Big Pop was going to win the race? The name brought the feeling up in you, he took ad-

vantage of the name to communicate. That's what I was thinking about when you mentioned it. My cousin in Missouri once
bet on a horse that had a name that reminded him of his
mother, and it won and paid a big price. The same thing happened this afternoon.' He shook his head. 'Ah, let's go. This is
the last time I'll ever play the horses with you around; all these
visions drive me to distraction.' In the car as we drove back
to his old house he said, 'Mankind will someday realize that we
are actually in contact with the dead and with the other world,
whatever it is; right now we could predict, if we only exerted
enough mental will, what is going to happen within the next
hundred years and be able to take steps to avoid all kinds of
catastrophes. When a man dies he undergoes a mutation in his
brain that we know nothing about now but which will be very
clear someday if scientists get on the ball. The bastards right
now are only interested in seeing if they can blow up the
world.'

We told Jane about it. She sniffed. 'It sounds silly to me.'
She plied the broom around the kitchen. Bull went in the bathroom for his afternoon fix.

Out on the road Dean and Ed Dunkel were playing basketball with Dodie's ball and a bucket nailed on a lamp-post. I
joined in. Then we turned to feats of athletic prowess. Dean
completely amazed me. He had Ed and me hold a bar of iron up
to our waists, and just standing there he popped right over it,
holding his heels. 'Go ahead, raise it.' We kept raising it till it
was chest-high. Still he jumped over it with ease. Then he tried
the running broad jump and did at least twenty feet and more.
Then I raced him down the road. I can do the hundred in 10:5.
He passed me like the wind. As we ran I had a mad vision of
Dean running through all of life just like that – his bony face
out-thrust to life, his arms pumping, his brow sweating, his
legs twinkling like Groucho Marx, yelling, 'Yes! Yes, man, you
sure can go!' But nobody could go as fast as he could, and that's
the truth. Then Bull came out with a couple of knives and
started showing us how to disarm a would-be shivver in a dark
alley. I for my part showed him a very good trick, which is
falling on the ground in front of your adversary and gripping
him with your ankles and flipping him over on his hands and

grabbing his wrists in full nelson. He said it was pretty good. He demonstrated some jujitsu. Little Dodie called her mother to the porch and said, 'Look at the silly men.' She was such a cute sassy little thing that Dean couldn't take his eyes off her.

'Wow. Wait till *she* grows up! Can you see *her* cuttin down Canal Street with her cute eyes. Ah! Oh!' He hissed through his teeth.

We spent a mad day in downtown New Orleans walking around with the Dunkels. Dean was out of his mind that day. When he saw the T & NO freight trains in the yard he wanted to show me everything at once. 'You'll be brakeman 'fore I'm through with ya!' He and I and Ed Dunkel ran across the tracks and hopped a freight at three individual points; Marylou and Galatea were waiting in the car. We rode the train a half-mile into the piers, waving at switchmen and flagmen. They showed me the proper way to get off a moving car; the back foot first and let the train go away from you and come around and place the other foot down. They showed me the refrigerator cars, the ice compartments, good for a ride on any winter night in a string of empties. 'Remember what I told you about New Mexico to LA?' cried Dean. 'This was the way I hung on . . .'

We got back to the girls an hour late and of course they were mad. Ed and Galatea had decided to get a room in New Orleans and stay there and work. This was okay with Bull, who was getting sick and tired of the whole mob. The invitation, originally, was for me to come alone. In the front room, where Dean and Marylou slept, there were jam and coffee stains and empty benny tubes all over the floor; what's more it was Bull's workroom and he couldn't get on with his shelves. Poor Jane was driven to distraction by the continual jumping and running around on the part of Dean. We were waiting for my next GI cheque to come through; my aunt was forwarding it. Then we were off, the three of us – Dean, Marylou, me. When the cheque came I realized I hated to leave Bull's wonderful house so suddenly, but Dean was all energies and ready to do.

In a sad red dusk we were finally seated in the car and Jane, Dodie, little boy Ray, Bull, Ed, and Galatea stood around in the high grass, smiling. It was good-bye. At the last moment Dean and Bull had a misunderstanding over money; Dean had wanted to borrow; Bull said it was out of the question. The feeling reached back to Texas days. Con-man Dean was antagonizing people away from him by degrees. He giggled maniacally and didn't care; he rubbed his fly, stuck his finger in Marylou's dress, slurped up her knee, frothed at the mouth, and said, 'Darling, you know and I know that everything is straight between us at least beyond the furthest abstract definition in metaphysical terms or any terms you want to specify or sweetly impose or harken back ...' and so on, and zoom went the car and we were off again for California.

8

WHAT is that feeling when you're driving away from people and they recede on the plain till you see their specks dispersing? – it's the too-huge world vaulting us, and it's good-bye. But we lean forward to the next crazy venture beneath the skies.

We wheeled through the sultry old light of Algiers, back on the ferry, back towards the mud-splashed, crabbed old ships across the river, back on Canal, and out; on a two-lane highway to Baton Rouge in purple darkness; swung west there, crossed the Mississippi at a place called Port Allen. Port Allen – where the river's all rain and roses in a misty pinpoint darkness and where we swung around a circular drive in yellow foglight and suddenly saw the great black body below a bridge and crossed eternity again. What is the Mississippi River? – a washed clod in the rainy night, a soft plopping from drooping Missouri banks, a dissolving, a riding of the tide down the eternal waterbed, a contribution to brown foams, a voyaging past endless vales and trees and levees, down along, down along, by Memphis, Greenville, Eudora, Vicksburg, Natchez, Port Allen, and Port Orleans and Port of the Deltas, by Potash, Venice, and the Night's Great Gulf, and out.

With the radio on to a mystery programme, and as I looked out the window and saw a sign that said USE COOPER'S PAINT and I said, 'Okay, I will,' we rolled across the hoodwink night of the Louisiana plains – Lawtell, Eunice, Kinder, and De

Quincy, western rickety towns becoming more bayou-like as we reached the Sabine. In Old Opelousas I went into a grocery store to buy bread and cheese while Dean saw to gas and oil. It was just a shack; I could hear the family eating supper in the back. I waited a minute; they went on talking. I took bread and cheese and slipped out the door. We had barely enough money to make Frisco. Meanwhile Dean took a carton of cigarettes from the gas station and we were stocked for the voyage – gas, oil, cigarettes, and food. Crooks don't know. He pointed the car straight down the road.

Somewhere near Starks we saw a great red glow in the sky ahead; we wondered what it was; in a moment we were passing it. It was a fire beyond the trees; there were many cars parked on the highway. It must have been some kind of fish-fry, and on the other hand it might have been anything. The country turned strange and dark near Deweyville. Suddenly we were in the swamps.

'Man, do you imagine what it would be like if we found a jazzjoint in these swamps, with great big black fellas moanin guitar blues and drinkin snakejuice and makin signs at us?'

'Yes!'

There were mysteries around here. The car was going over a dirt road elevated off the swamps that dropped on both sides and drooped with vines. We passed an apparition; it was a Negro man in a white shirt walking along with his arms upspread to the inky firmament. He must have been praying or calling down a curse. We zoomed right by; I looked out the back window to see his white eyes. 'Whoo!' said Dean. 'Look out. We better not stop in this here country.' At one point we got stuck at a crossroads and stopped the car anyway. Dean turned off the headlamps. We were surrounded by a great forest of viny trees in which we could almost hear the slither of a million copperheads. The only thing we could see was the red amperc button on the Hudson dashboard. Marylou squealed with fright. We began laughing maniac laughs to scare her. We were scared too. We wanted to get out of this mansion of the snake, this mireful drooping dark, and zoom on back to familiar American ground and cowtowns. There was a smell of oil and dead water in the air. This was a manuscript of the night we couldn't read. An owl hooted. We took a chance on one of the dirt roads, and pretty soon we were crossing the evil old Sabine River that is responsible for all these swamps. With amazement we saw great structures of light ahead of us. 'Texas! It's Texas! Beaumont oil town!' Huge oil tanks and refineries loomed like cities in the oily fragrant air.

'I'm glad we got out of there,' said Marylou. 'Let's play some more mystery programmes now.'

We zoomed through Beaumont, over the Trinity River at Liberty, and straight for Houston. Now Dean got talking about his Houston days in 1947. 'Hassel! That mad Hassel! I look for him everywhere I go and I never find him. He used to get us so hung-up in Texas here. We'd drive in with Bull for groceries and Hassel'd disappear. We'd have to go looking for him in every shooting gallery in town.' We were entering Houston. 'We had to look for him in this spade part of town most of the time. Man, he'd be blasting with every mad cat he could find. One night we lost him and took a hotel room. We were supposed to bring ice back to Jane because her food was rotting. It took us two days to find Hassel. I got hung-up myself – I gunned shopping women in the afternoon, right here, downtown, supermarkets' – we flashed by in the empty night – 'and found a real gone dumb girl who was out of her mind and just wandering, trying to steal an orange. She was from Wyoming. Her beautiful body was matched only by her idiot mind. I found her babbling and took her back to the room. Bull was drunk trying to get this young Mexican kid drunk. Carlo was writing poetry on heroin. Hassel didn't show up till midnight at the jeep. We found him sleeping in the back seat. The ice was all melted. Hassel said he took about five sleeping pills. Man, if my memory could only serve me right the way my mind works I could tell you every detail of the things we did. Ah, but we know time. Everything takes care of itself. I could close my eyes and this old car would take care of itself.'

In the empty Houston streets of four o'clock in the morning a motorcycle kid suddenly roared through, all bespangled and bedecked with glittering buttons, visor, slick black jacket, a Texas poet of the night, girl gripped on his back like a papoose, hair flying, onward-going, singing, 'Houston, Austin,

Fort Worth, Dallas – and sometimes Kansas City – and sometimes old Antone, ah-haaaaa!' They pinpointed out of sight. 'Wow! Dig that gone gal on his belt! Let's all blow!' Dean tried to catch up with them. 'Now wouldn't it be fine if we could all get together and have a real going goofbang together with everybody sweet and fine and agreeable, no hassles, no infant rise of protest or body woes misconceptalized or sumpin? Ah! but we know time.' He bent to it and pushed the car.

Beyond Houston his energies, great as they were, gave out and I drove. Rain began to fall just as I took the wheel. Now we were on the great Texas plain and, as Dean said, 'You drive and drive and you're still in Texas tomorrow night.' The rain lashed down. I drove through a rickety little cowtown with a muddy main street and found myself in a dead end. 'Hey, what do I do?' They were both asleep. I turned and crawled back through town. There wasn't a soul in sight and not a single light. Suddenly a horseman in a raincoat appeared in my headlamps. It was the sheriff. He had a ten-gallon hat, drooping in the torrent. 'Which way to Austin?' He told me politely and I started off. Outside town I suddenly saw two headlamps flaring directly at me in the lashing rain. Whoops, I thought I was on the wrong side of the road; I eased right and found myself rolling in the mud; I rolled back to the road. Still the headlamps came straight for me. At the last moment I realized the other driver was on the wrong side of the road and didn't know it. I swerved at thirty into the mud; it was flat, no ditch, thank God. The offending car backed up in the downpour. Four sullen fieldworkers, snuck from their chores to brawl in drinking fields, all white shirts and dirty brown arms, sat looking at me dumbly in the night. The driver was as drunk as the lot.

He said, 'Which way t'Houston?' I pointed my thumb back. I was thunderstruck in the middle of the thought that they had done this on purpose just to ask directions, as a panhandler advances on you straight up the sidewalk to bar your way. They gazed ruefully at the floor of their car, where empty bottles rolled, and clanked away. I started the car; it was stuck in the mud a foot deep. I sighed in the rainy Texas wilderness.

'Dean,' I said, 'wake up.

'What?'

'We're stuck in the mud.'

'What happened?' I told him. He swore up and down. We put on old shoes and sweaters and barged out of the car into the driving rain. I put my back on the rear fender and lifted and heaved; Dean stuck chains under the swishing wheels. In a minute we were covered with mud. We woke up Marylou to these horrors and made her gun the car while we pushed. The tormented Hudson heaved and heaved. Suddenly it jolted out and went skidding across the road. Marylou pulled it up just in time, and we got in. That was that – the work had taken thirty minutes and we were soaked and miserable.

I fell asleep, all caked with mud; and in the morning when I woke up the mud was solidified and outside there was snow. We were near Fredericksburg, in the high plains. It was one of the worst winters in Texas and Western history, when cattle perished like flies in great blizzards and snow fell on San Francisco and LA. We were all miserable. We wished we were back in New Orleans with Ed Dunkel. Marylou was driving; Dean was sleeping. She drove with one hand on the wheel and the other reaching back to me in the back seat. She cooed promises about San Francisco. I slavered miserably over it. At ten I took the wheel – Dean was out for hours – and drove several hundred dreary miles across the bushy snows and ragged sage hills. Cowboys went by in baseball caps and ear-muffs, looking for cows. Comfortable little homes with chimneys smoking appeared along the road at intervals. I wished we could go in for buttermilk and beans in front of the fireplace.

At Sonora I again helped myself to free bread and cheese while the proprietor chatted with a big rancher on the other side of the store. Dean huzzahed when he heard it; he was hungry. We couldn't spend a cent on food. 'Yass, yass,' said Dean, watching the ranchers loping up and down Sonora main street, 'every one of them is a bloody millionaire, thousand head of cattle, workhands, buildings, money in the bank. If I lived around here I'd go be an idjit in the sagebrush, I'd be jackrabbit, I'd lick up the branches, I'd look for pretty cow-girls – hee-hee-hee-hee! Damn! Bam!' He socked himself. 'Yes! Right! Oh me!' We didn't know what he was talking about any more. He took the wheel and flew the rest of the way across the state of Texas, about five hundred miles, clear to El Paso, arriving at dusk and not stopping except once when he took all his clothes off, near Ozona, and ran yipping and leaping naked in the sage. Cars zoomed by and didn't see him. He scurried back to the car and drove on. 'Now Sal, now Marylou, I want both of you to do as I'm doing, disemburden yourselves of all that clothes – now what's the sense of clothes? now that's what I'm sayin – and sun your pretty bellies with me. Come on!' We were driving west into the sun; it fell in through the windshield. 'Open your belly as we drive into it.' Marylou complied; unfuddyduddied, so did I. We sat in the front seat, all three. Marylou took out cold cream and applied it to us for kicks. Every now and then a big truck zoomed by; the driver in high cab caught a glimpse of a golden beauty sitting naked with two naked men : you could see them swerve a moment as they vanished in our rear-view window. Great sage plains, snowless now, rolled on. Soon we were in the orange-rocked Pecos Canyon country. Blue distances opened up in the sky. We got out of the car to examine an old Indian ruin. Dean did so stark naked. Marylou and I put on our overcoats. We wandered among the old stones, hooting and howling. Certain tourists caught sight of Dean naked in the plain but they could not believe their eyes and wobbled on.

Dean and Marylou parked the car near Van Horn and made love while I went to sleep. I woke up just as we were rolling down the tremendous Rio Grande Valley through Clint and Ysleta to El Paso. Marylou jumped to the back seat, I jumped to the front seat, and we rolled along. To our left across the vast Rio Grande spaces were the moorish-red mounts of the Mexican border, the land of the Tarahumare; soft dusk played on the peaks. Straight ahead lay the distant lights of El Paso and Juárez, sown in a tremendous valley so big that you could see several railroads puffing at the same time in every direction, as though it was the Valley of the World. We descended into it.

'Clint, Texas!' said Dean. He had the radio on to the Clint station. Every fifteen minutes they played a record; the rest of the time it was commercials about a high-school correspondence course. 'This programme is beamed all over the West,' cried Dean excitedly. 'Man, I used to listen to it day and night in reform school and prison. All of us used to write in. You get a high-school diploma by mail, facsimile thereof, if you pass the test. All the young wranglers in the West, I don't care who, at one time or another write in for this; it's all they hear; you tune the radio in Sterling, Colorado, Lusk, Wyoming, I don't care where, you get Clint, Texas, Clint, Texas. And the music is always cowboy hillbilly and Mexican, absolutely the worst programme in the entire history of the country and nobody can do anything about it. They have a tremendous beam; they've got the whole land hogtied.' We saw the high antenna beyond the shacks of Clint. 'Oh, man, the things I could tell you!' cried Dean, almost weeping. Eyes bent on Frisco and the Coast, we came into El Paso as it got dark, broke. We absolutely had to get some money for gas or we'd never make it.

We tried everything. We buzzed the travel bureau, but no one was going west that night. The travel bureau is where you go for share-the-gas rides, legal in the West. Shifty characters wait with battered suitcases. We went to the Greyhound bus station to try to persuade somebody to give us the money instead of taking a bus for the Coast. We were too bashful to approach anyone. We wandered around sadly. It was cold outside. A college boy was sweating at the sight of luscious Marylou and trying to look unconcerned. Dean and I consulted but decided we weren't pimps. Suddenly a crazy dumb young kid, fresh out of reform school, attached himself to us, and he and Dean rushed out for a beer. 'Come on, man, let's go mash somebody on the head and get his money.'

'I dig you, man!' yelled Dean. They dashed off. For a moment I was worried; but Dean only wanted to dig the streets of El Paso with the kid and get his kicks. Marylou and I waited in the car. She put her arms around me.

I said, 'Dammit, Lou, wait till we get to Frisco.'

'I don't care. Dean's going to leave me anyway.'

'When are you going back to Denver?'

'I don't know. I don't care what I'm doing. Can I go back east with you?'

'We'll have to get some money in Frisco.'

'I know where you can get a job in a lunchcart behind the counter, and I'll be a waitress. I know a hotel where we can stay on credit. We'll stick together. Gee, I'm sad.'

'What are you sad about, kid?'

'I'm sad about everything. Oh damn, I wish Dean wasn't so crazy now.' Dean came twinkling back, giggling, and jumped in the car.

'What a crazy cat that was, whoo! Did I dig him! I used to know thousands of guys like that, they're all the same, their minds work in uniform clockwork, oh, the infinite ramifications, no time, no time ...' And he shot up the car, hunched over the wheel, and roared out of El Paso. 'We'll just have to pick up hitchhikers. I'm positive we'll find some. Hup! hup! here we go. Look out!' he yelled at a motorist, and swung around him, and dodged a truck and bounced over the city limits. Across the river were the jewel lights of Juárez and the sad dry land and the jewel stars of Chihuahua. Marylou was watching Dean as she had watched him clear across the country and back, out of the corner of her eye – with a sullen, sad air, as though she wanted to cut off his head and hide it in her closet, an envious and rueful love of him so amazingly himself, all raging and sniffy and crazy-wayed, a smile of tender dotage but also sinister envy that frightened me about her, a love she knew would never bear fruit because when she looked at his hangjawed bony face with its male self-containment and absentmindedness she knew he was too mad. Dean was convinced Marylou was a whore; he confided in me that she was a pathological liar. But when she watched him like this it was love too; and when Dean noticed he always turned with his big false flirtatious smile, with the eyelashes fluttering and the teeth pearly white, while a moment ago he was only dreaming in his eternity. Then Marylou and I both laughed – and Dean gave no sign of discomfiture, just a goofy glad grin that said to us, Ain't we gettin our kicks anyway? And that was it.

Outside El Paso, in the darkness, we saw a small huddled figure with thumb stuck out. It was our promised hitchhiker. We pulled up and backed to his side. 'How much money you got, kid?' The kid had no money; he was about seventeen, pale, strange, with one undeveloped crippled hand and no suitcase. 'Ain't he sweet?' said Dean, turning to me with a serious awe. 'Come on in, fella, we'll take you out –' The kid saw his advantage. He said he had an aunt in Tulare, California, who owned a grocery store and as soon as we got there he'd have some money for us. Dean rolled on the floor laughing, it was so much like the kid in North Carolina. 'Yes! Yes!' he yelled. 'We've *all* got aunts; well, let's go, let's see the aunts and the uncles and the grocery stores all the way ALONG that road!!' And we had a new passenger, and a fine little guy he turned out to be, too. He didn't say a word, he listened to us. After a minute of Dean's talk he was probably convinced he had joined a car of madmen. He said he was hitchhiking from Alabama to Oregon, where his home was. We asked him what he was doing in Alabama.

'I went to visit my uncle; he said he'd have a job for me in a lumber mill. The job fell through, so I'm comin back home.'

'Goin home,' said Dean, 'goin home, yes, I know, we'll take you home, far as Frisco anyhow.' But we didn't have any money. Then it occurred to me I could borrow five dollars from my old friend Hal Hingham in Tucson, Arizona. Immediately Dean said it was all settled and we were going to Tucson. And we did.

We passed Las Cruces, New Mexico, in the night and arrived in Arizona at dawn. I woke up from a deep sleep to find everybody sleeping like lambs and the car parked God knows where, because I couldn't see out the steamy windows. I got out of the car. We were in the mountains : there was a heaven of sunrise, cool purple airs, red mountainsides, emerald pastures in valleys, dew, and transmuting clouds of gold; on the ground gopher holes, cactus, mesquite. It was time for me to drive on. I pushed Dean and the kid over and went down the mountain with the clutch in and the motor off to save gas. In this manner I rolled into Benson, Arizona. It occurred to me that I had a pocket watch Rocco had just given me for a birthday present, a four-dollar watch. At the gas station I asked the man if he knew a pawnshop in Benson. It was right next door to the station. I knocked, someone got up out of bed, and in a minute I had a dollar for the watch. It went into the tank.

Now we had enough gas for Tucson. But suddenly a big pistol-packing trooper appeared, just as I was ready to pull out, and asked to see my driver's licence. 'The fella in the back seat has the licence,' I said. Dean and Marylou were sleeping together under the blanket. The cop told Dean to come out. Suddenly he whipped out his gun and yelled, 'Keep your hands up!'

'Offisah,' I heard Dean say in the most unctious and ridiculous tones, 'offisah, I was only buttoning my flah.' Even the cop almost smiled. Dean came out, muddy, ragged, T-shirted, rubbing his belly, cursing, looking everywhere for his licence and his car papers. The cop rummaged through our back trunk. All the papers were straight.

'Only checking up,' he said with a broad smile. 'You can go on now. Benson ain't a bad town actually; you might enjoy it if you had breakfast here.'

'Yes yes yes,' said Dean, paying absolutely no attention to him, and drove off. We all sighed with relief. The police are suspicious when gangs of youngsters come by in new cars without a cent in their pockets and have to pawn watches. 'Oh, they're always interfering,' said Dean, 'but he was a much better cop than that rat in Virginia. They try to make head-line arrests; they think every car going by is some big Chicago gang. They ain't got nothin else to do.' We drove on to Tucson.

Tucson is situated in beautiful mesquite riverbed country, overlooked by the snowy Catalina range. The city was one big construction job; the people transient, wild, ambitious, busy, gay; washlines, trailers; bustling downtown streets with banners; altogether very Californian. Fort Lowell Road, out where Hingham lived, wound along lovely riverbed trees in the flat desert. We saw Hingham himself brooding in the yard. He was a writer; he had come to Arizona to work on his book in peace. He was a tall, gangly, shy satirist who mumbled to you with his head turned away and always said funny things. His wife and baby were with him in the dobe house, a small one that his Indian stepfather had built. His mother lived across the yard in her own house. She was an excited American woman who loved pottery, beads, and books. Hingham had heard of Dean through letters from New York. We came down on him like a cloud, every one of us hungry, even Alfred, the crippled hitchhiker. Hingham was wearing an old sweater and smoking a pipe in the keen desert air. His mother came out and invited us into her kitchen to eat. We cooked noodles in a great pot.

Then we all drove to a crossroads liquor store, where Hingham cashed a check for five dollars and handed me the money.

There was a brief good-bye. 'It certainly was pleasant,' said Hingham, looking away. Beyond some trees, across the sand, a great neon sign of a roadhouse glowed red. Hingham always went there for a beer when he was tired of writing. He was very lonely, he wanted to get back to New York. It was sad to see his tall figure receding in the dark as we drove away, just like the other figures in New York and New Orleans: they stand uncertainly underneath immense skies, and everything about them is drowned. Where go? what do? what for? – sleep. But this foolish gang was bending onward.

9

OUTSIDE Tucson we saw another hitchhiker in the dark road. This was an Okie from Bakersfield, California, who put down his story. '*Hot* damn, I left Bakersfield with the travel-bureau car and left my gui-tar in the trunk of another one and they never showed up – gui-tar and cowboy duds; you see, I'm a moo-sician, I was headed for Arizona to play with Johnny Mackaw's Sagebrush Boys. Well, hell, here I am in Arizona, broke, and m'gui-tar's been stoled. You boys drive me back to Bakersfield and I'll get the money from my brother. How much you want?' We wanted just enough gas to make Frisco from Bakersfield, about three dollars. Now we were five in the car. 'Evenin, ma'am,' he said, tipping his hat to Marylou, and we were off.

In the middle of the night we overtopped the lights of Palm Springs from a mountain road. At dawn, in snowy passes, we laboured towards the town of Mojave, which was the entryway to the great Tehachapi Pass. The Okie woke up and told funny stories; sweet little Alfred sat smiling. Okie told us he knew a man who forgave his wife for shooting him and got her out of prison, only to be shot a second time. We were passing the women's prison when he told it. Up ahead we saw Tehachapi Pass starting up. Dean took the wheel and carried us clear to the top of the world. We passed a great shroudy cement factory in the canyon. Then we started down. Dean cut off the gas, threw in the clutch, and negotiated every hairpin turn and passed cars and did everything in the books without the benefit of accelerator. I held on tight. Sometimes the road went up again briefly; he merely passed cars without a sound, on pure momentum. He knew every rhythm and every kick of a first-class pass. When it was time to U-turn left around a low stone wall that overlooked the bottom of the world, he just leaned far over to his left, hands on the wheel, stiff-armed, and carried it that way; and when the turn snaked to the right again, this time with a cliff on our left, he leaned far to the right, making Marylou and me lean with him. In this way we floated and flapped down to the San Joaquin Valley. It lay spread a mile below, virtually the floor of California, green and wondrous from our aerial shelf. We made thirty miles without using gas.

Suddenly we were all excited. Dean wanted to tell me everything he knew about Bakersfield as we reached the city limits. He showed me rooming houses where he stayed, railroad hotels, poolhalls, diners, sidings where he jumped off the engine for grapes, Chinese restaurants where he ate, park benches where he met girls, and certain places where he'd done nothing but sit and wait around. Dean's California – wild, sweaty, important, the land of lonely and exiled and eccentric lovers come to foregather like birds, and the land where everybody somehow looked like broken-down, handsome, decadent movie actors. 'Man, I spent hours on that very chair in front of that drugstore!' He remembered all – every pinochle game, every woman, every sad night. And suddenly we were passing the place in the railyards where Terry and I had sat under the moon, drinking wine, on those bum crates, in October 1947, and I tried to tell him. But he was too excited. 'This is where Dunkel and I spent a whole morning drinking beer, trying to make a real gone little waitress from Watsonville – no, Tracy, yes, Tracy – and her name was Esmeralda – oh, man, something like that.' Marylou was planning what to do the moment she arrived in Frisco. Alfred said his aunt would give him plenty of money up in Tulare. The Okie directed us to his brother in the flats outside town.

We pulled up at noon in front of a little rose-covered shack, and the Okie went in and talked with some women. We waited fifteen minutes. 'I'm beginning to think this guy has no more money than I have,' said Dean. 'We get more hung-up! There's probably nobody in the family that'll give him a cent after that fool escapade.' The Okie came out sheepishly and directed us to town.

'*Hot* damn, I wisht I could find my brother.' He made inquiries. He probably felt he was our prisoner. Finally we went to a big bread bakery, and the Okie came out with his brother, who was wearing overalls and was apparently the truck mechanic inside. He talked with his brother a few minutes. We waited in the car. Okie was telling all his relatives his adventures and about the loss of his guitar. But he got the money, and he gave it to us, and we were all set for Frisco. We thanked him and took off.

Next stop was Tulare. Up the valley we roared. I lay in the back seat, exhausted, giving up completely, and sometime in the afternoon, while I dozed, the muddy Hudson zoomed by the tents outside Sabinal where I had lived and loved and worked in the spectral past. Dean was bent rigidly over the wheel, pounding the rods. I was sleeping when we finally arrived in Tulare; I woke up to hear the insane details. 'Sal, wake up! Alfred found his aunt's grocery store, but do you know what happened? His aunt shot her husband and went to jail. The store's closed down. We didn't get a cent. Think of it! The things that happen; the Okie told us the same likewise story, the trou-bles on all sides, the complications of events – whee, damn!' Alfred was biting his fingernails. We were turning off the Oregon road at Madera, and there we made our farewell with little Alfred. We wished him luck and Godspeed to Oregon. He said it was the best ride he ever had.

It seemed like a matter of minutes when we began rolling in the foothills before Oakland and suddenly reached a height and saw stretched out ahead of us the fabulous white city of San Francisco on her eleven mystic hills with the blue Pacific and its advancing wall of potato-patch fog beyond, and smoke and goldenness in the late afternoon of time. 'There she blows!' yelled Dean. 'Wow! Made it! Just enough gas! Give me water! No more land! We can't go any farther 'cause there ain't no more land! Now Marylou, darling, you and Sal go immediately to a hotel and wait for me to contact you in the morning as soon as I have definite arrangements made with Camille and call up Frenchman about my railroad watch and you and Sal buy the first thing hit town a paper for the want ads and work-plans.' And he drove into the Oakland Bay Bridge and it carried us in. The downtown office buildings were just sparkling on their lights; it made you think of Sam Spade. When we staggered out of the car on O'Farrell Street and sniffed and stretched, it was like getting on shore after a long voyage at sea; the slopy street reeled under our feet; secret chop sueys from Frisco Chinatown floated in the air. We took all our things out of the car and piled them on the sidewalk.

Suddenly Dean was saying good-bye. He was bursting to see Camille and find out what had happened. Marylou and I stood dumbly in the street and watched him drive away. 'You see what a bastard he is?' said Marylou. 'Dean will leave you out in the cold any time it's in his interest.'

'I know,' I said, and I looked back east and sighed. We had no money. Dean hadn't mentioned money. 'Where are we going to stay?' We wandered around, carrying our bundles of rags in the narrow romantic streets. Everybody looked like a broken-down movie extra, a withered starlet; disenchanted stunt-men, midget auto-racers, poignant California characters with their end-of-the-continent sadness, handsome, decadent, Casanova-ish men, puffy-eyed motel blondes, hustlers, pimps, whores, masseurs, bellhops – a lemon lot, and how's a man going to make a living with a gang like that?

10

NEVERTHELESS Marylou had been around these people – not far from the Tenderloin – and a grey-faced hotel clerk let us have a room on credit. That was the first step. Then we had to eat, and didn't do so till midnight, when we found a nightclub singer in her hotel room who turned an iron upside down on a coathanger in the wastebasket and warmed up a can of pork and beans. I looked out the window at the winking neons and said to myself, Where is Dean and why isn't he concerned about our welfare? I lost faith in him that year. I stayed in San Francisco a week and had the beatest time of my life. Marylou and I walked around for miles, looking for food-money. We even visited some drunken seamen in a flophouse on Mission Street that she knew; they offered us whisky.

In the hotel we lived together two days. I realized that, now Dean was out of the picture, Marylou had no real interest in me; she was trying to reach Dean through me, his buddy. We had arguments in the room. We also spent entire nights in bed and I told her my dreams. I told her about the big snake of the world that was coiled in the earth like a worm in an apple and would someday nudge up a hill to be thereafter known as Snake Hill and fold out upon the plain, a hundred miles long and devouring as it went along. I told her this snake was Satan. 'What's going to happen?' she squealed; meanwhile she held me tight.

'A saint called Doctor Sax will destroy it with secret herbs which he is at this very moment cooking up in his underground shack somewhere in America. It may also be disclosed that the snake is just a husk of doves; when the snake dies great clouds of seminal-grey doves will flutter out and bring tidings of peace around the world.' I was out of my mind with hunger and bitterness.

One night Marylou disappeared with a nightclub owner. I was waiting for her by appointment in a doorway across the street, at Larkin and Geary, hungry, when she suddenly stepped out of the foyer of the fancy apartment house with her girl friend, the nightclub owner, and a greasy old man with a roll. Originally she'd just gone in to see her girl friend. I saw what a whore she was. She was afraid to give me the sign, though she saw me in that doorway. She walked on little feet and got in the Cadillac and off they went. Now I had nobody, nothing.

I walked around, picking butts from the street. I passed a fish-'n-chips joint on Market Street, and suddenly the woman in there gave me a terrified look as I passed; she was the proprietress, she apparently thought I was coming in there with a gun to hold up the joint. I walked on a few feet. It suddenly occurred to me this was my mother of about two hundred years ago in England, and that I was her footpad son, returning from gaol to haunt her honest labours in the hashery. I stopped, frozen with ecstasy on the sidewalk. I looked down Market Street. I didn't know whether it was that or Canal Street in New Orleans: it led to water, ambiguous, universal water, just as 42nd Street, New York, leads to water, and you never know where you are. I thought of Ed Dunkel's ghost on Times Square. I was delirious. I wanted to go back and leer at my strange Dickensian mother in the hash joint. I tingled all over from head to foot. It seemed I had a whole host of memories leading back to 1750 in England and that I was in San Francisco now only in another life and in another body. 'No,' that woman seemed to say with that terrified glance, 'don't come back and plague your honest, hard-working mother. You are no longer like a son to me – and like your father, my first husband. 'Ere this kindly Greek took pity on me.' (The proprietor was a Greek with hairy arms.) 'You are no good, inclined to drunkenness and routs and final disgraceful robbery of the fruits of my 'umble labours in the hashery. O son! did you not ever go on your knees and pray for deliverance for all your sins and scoundrel's acts? Lost boy! Depart! Do not haunt my soul; I have done well forgetting you. Reopen no old wounds, be as if you had never returned and looked in to me – to see my labouring humilities, my few scrubbed pennies – hungry to grab, quick to deprive, sullen, unloved, mean-minded son of my flesh. Son! Son!' It made me think of the Big Pop vision in Graetna with Old Bull. And for just a moment I had reached the point of ecstasy that I always wanted to reach, which was the complete step across chronological time into timeless shadows, and wonderment in the bleakness of the mortal realm, and the sensation of death kicking at my heels to move on, with a phantom dogging its own heels, and myself hurrying to a plank where all the angels dove off and flew into the holy void of uncreated emptiness, the potent and inconceivable radiancies shining in bright Mind Essence, innumerable lotus-lands falling open in the magic mothswarm of heaven. I could hear an indescribable seething roar which wasn't in my ear but everywhere and had nothing to do with sounds. I realized that I had died and been reborn numberless times but just didn't remember especially because the transitions from life to death and back to life are so ghostly easy, a magical action for naught, like falling asleep and waking up again a million times, the utter casualness and deep ignorance of it. I realized it was only because of the stability of the intrinsic Mind that these ripples of birth and death took place, like the action of wind on a sheet of pure, serene, mirror-like water. I felt sweet, swinging bliss, like a big shot of heroin in the mainline vein; like a gulp of wine late in the afternoon and it makes you shudder; my feet tingled. I thought I was going to die the very next moment. But I didn't die, and walked four miles and picked up ten long butts and took them back to Marylou's hotel room and poured their tobacco in my old pipe and lit up. I was too young to know what had happened. In the window I smelled all the food of San Francisco. There were seafood places out there where the buns were hot, and the baskets were good enough to eat too; where the menus themselves were soft with foody esculence as though dipped in hot broths and roasted dry and good enough to eat too. Just show me the bluefish spangle on a seafood menu and I'd eat it; let me smell the drawn butter and lobster claws. There were places where they specialized in thick red roast beef *au jus*, or roast chicken basted in wine. There were places where hamburgs sizzled on grills and the coffee was only a nickel. And oh, that pan-fried chow mein flavoured air that blew into my room from Chinatown, vying with the spaghetti sauces of North Beach, the soft-shell crab of Fisherman's Wharf – nay, the ribs of Fillmore turning on spits! Throw in the Market Street chili beans, redhot, and french-fried potatoes of the Embarcadero wino night, and steamed clams from Sausalito across the bay, and that's my ah-dream of San Francisco. Add fog, hunger-making raw fog, and the throb of neons in the soft night, the clack of high-heeled beauties, white doves in a Chinese grocery window ...

II

THAT was the way Dean found me when he finally decided I was worth saving. He took me home to Camille's house. 'Where's Marylou, man?'

'The whore ran off.' Camille was a relief after Marylou; a well-bred, polite young woman, and she was aware of the fact that the eighteen dollars Dean had sent her was mine. But O where went thou, sweet Marylou? I relaxed a few days in Camille's house. From her living-room window in the wooden tenement on Liberty Street you could see all of San Francisco burning green and red in the rainy night. Dean did the most ridiculous thing of his career the few days I was there. He got a job demonstrating a new kind of pressure cooker in the kitchens of homes. The salesman gave him piles of samples and pamphlets. The first day Dean was a hurricane of energy. I drove all over town with him as he made appointments. The idea was to get invited socially to a dinner party and then leap up and start demonstrating the pressure cooker. 'Man,' cried Dean excitedly, 'this is even crazier than the time I worked for Sinah. Sinah sold encyclopedias in Oakland. Nobody could turn him down. He made long speeches, he jumped up and down, he laughed, he cried. One time we broke into an Okie house where everybody was getting ready to go to a funeral. Sinah got down on his knees and prayed for the deliverance of the deceased soul. All the Okies started crying. He sold a complete set of encyclopedias. He was the maddest guy in the world. I wonder where he is. We used to get next to pretty young daughters and feel them up in the kitchen. This afternoon I had the gonest housewife in her little kitchen – arm around her, demonstrating. Ah! Hmm! Wow!'

'Keep it up, Dean,' I said. 'Maybe someday you'll be mayor of San Francisco.' He had the whole cookpot spiel worked out; he practised on Camille and me in the evenings.

One morning he stood naked, looking at all San Francisco out the window as the sun came up. He looked like someday he'd be the pagan mayor of San Francisco. But his energies ran out. One rainy afternoon the salesman came around to find out what Dean was doing. Dean was sprawled on the couch. 'Have you been trying to sell these?'

'No,' said Dean, 'I have another job coming up.'

'Well, what are you going to do about all these samples?'

'I don't know.' In a dead silence the salesman gathered up his sad pots and left. I was sick and tired of everything and so was Dean.

But one night we suddenly went mad together again; we went to see Slim Gaillard in a little Frisco nightclub. Slim Gaillard is a tall, thin Negro with big sad eyes who's always saying, 'Right-orooni' and 'How 'bout a little bourbon-orooni.' In Frisco great eager crowds of young semi-intellectuals sat at his feet and listened to him on the piano, guitar, and bongo drums. When he gets warmed up he takes off his shirt and undershirt and really goes. He does and says anything that comes into his head. He'll sing 'Cement Mixer, Put-ti Put-ti' and suddenly slow down the beat and brood over his bongos with fingertips barely tapping the skin as everybody leans forward breathlessly to hear; you think he'll do this for a minute or so, but he goes right on, for as long as an hour, making an imperceptible little noise with the tips of his fingernails, smaller and smaller all the time till you can't hear it any more and sounds of traffic come in the open door. Then he slowly gets up and takes the mike and says, very slowly, 'Great-orooni ... fine-ovauti ... hello-orooni ... bourbon-orooni ... all-orooni ... how are the boys in the front row making out with their girls-orooni ... orooni ... vauti ... oroonirooni ...' He keeps this up for fifteen minutes, his voice getting softer and softer till you can't hear. His great sad eyes scan the audience.

Dean stands in the back, saying, 'God! Yes!' – and clasping

his hands in prayer and sweating. 'Sal, Slim knows time, he knows time.' Slim sits down at the piano and hits two notes, two Cs, then two more, then one, then two, and suddenly the big burly bass-player wakes up from a reverie and realizes Slim is playing 'C-Jam Blues' and he slugs in his big forefinger on the string and the big booming beat begins and everybody starts rocking and Slim looks just as sad as ever, and they blow jazz for half an hour, and the Slim goes mad and grabs the bongos and plays tremendous rapid Cubana beats and yells crazy things in Spanish, in Arabic, in Peruvian dialect, in Egyptian, in every language he knows, and he knows innumerable languages. Finally the set is over; each set takes two hours. Slim Gaillard goes and stands against a post, looking sadly over everybody's head as people come to talk to him. A bourbon is slipped into his hand. 'Bourbon-orooni – thank-you-ovauti ...' Nobody knows where Slim Gaillard is. Dean once had a dream that he was having a baby and his belly was all bloated up blue as he lay on the grass of a California hospital. Under a tree, with a group of coloured men, sat Slim Gaillard. Dean turned despairing eyes of a mother to him. Slim said, 'There you go-orooni.' Now Dean approached him, he approached his God; he thought Slim was God; he shuffled and bowed in front of him and asked him to join us. 'Right-orooni,' says Slim; he'll join anybody but he won't guarantee to be there with you in spirit. Dean got a table, bought drinks, and sat stiffly in front of Slim. Slim dreamed over his head. Every time Slim said, 'Orooni,' Dean said, 'Yes!' I sat there with these two madmen. Nothing happened. To Slim Gaillard the whole world was just one big orooni.

That same night I dug Lampshade on Fillmore and Geary. Lampshade is a big coloured guy who comes into musical Frisco saloons with coat, hat, and scarf and jumps on the bandstand and starts singing; the veins pop in his forehead; he heaves back and blows a big forlorn blues out of every muscle in his soul. He yells at people while he's singing : *'Don't die to go to heaven, start in on Doctor Pepper and end up on whisky!'* His voice booms over everything. He grimaces, he writhes, he does everything. He came over to our table and leaned over to us and said, 'Yes!' And then he staggered out to the street to hit another saloon. Then there's Connie Jordan, a madman who sings and flips his arms and ends up splashing sweat on everybody and kicking over the mike and screaming like a woman; and you see him late at night, exhausted, listening to wild jazz sessions at Jamson's Nook with big round eyes and limp shoulders, a big gooky stare into space, and a drink in front of him. I never saw such crazy musicians. Everybody in Frisco blew. It was the end of the continent; they didn't give a damn. Dean and I goofed around San Francisco in this manner until I got my next GI check and got ready to go back home.

What I accomplished by coming to Frisco I don't know. Camille wanted me to leave; Dean didn't care one way or the other. I bought a loaf of bread and meats and made myself ten sandwiches to cross the country with again; they were all going to go rotten on me by the time I got to Dakota. The last night Dean went mad and found Marylou somewhere downtown and we got in the car and drove all over Richmond across the bay, hitting Negro jazz shacks in the oil flats. Marylou went to sit down and a coloured guy pulled the chair out from under her. The gals approached her in the john with propositions. I was approached too. Dean was sweating around. It was the end; I wanted to get out.

At dawn I got my New York bus and said good-bye to Dean and Marylou. They wanted some of my sandwiches. I told them no. It was a sullen moment. We were all thinking we'd never see one another again and we didn't care.

PART THREE

I

IN the spring of 1949 I had a few dollars saved from GI education cheques and I went to Denver, thinking of settling down there. I saw myself in Middle America, a patriarch. I was lonesome. Nobody was there – no Babe Rawlins, Ray Rawlins, Tim Gray, Betty Gray, Roland Major, Dean Moriarty, Carlo Marx, Ed Dunkel, Roy Johnson, Tommy Snark, nobody. I wandered around Curtis Street and Larimer Street, worked awhile in the wholesale fruit market where I almost got hired in 1947 – the hardest job of my life; at one point the Japanese kids and I had to move a whole boxcar a hundred feet down the rail by hand with a jack-gadget that made it move a quarter-inch with each yank. I lugged watermelon crates over the ice floor of reefers into the blazing sun, sneezing. In God's name and under the stars, what for?

At dusk I walked. I felt like a speck on the surface of the sad red earth. I passed the Windsor Hotel, where Dean Moriarty had lived with his father in the depression thirties, and as of yore I looked everywhere for the sad and fabled tinsmith of my mind. Either you find someone who looks like your father in places like Montana or you look for a friend's father where he is no more.

At lilac evening I walked with every muscle aching among the lights of 27th and Welton in the Denver coloured section, wishing I were a Negro, feeling that the best the white world had offered was not enough ecstasy for me, not enough life, joy, kicks, darkness, music, not enough night. I stopped at a little shack where a man sold hot red chili in paper containers; I bought some and ate it, strolling in the dark mysterious streets. I wished I were a Denver Mexican, or even a poor overworked Jap, anything but what I was so drearily, a 'white man' disillusioned. All my life I'd had white ambitions; that was why I'd abandoned a good woman like Terry in the San Joaquin Valley. I passed the dark porches of Mexican and Negro homes; soft voices were there, occasionally the dusky knee of some mysterious sensual gal; and dark faces of the men behind rose arbours. Little children sat like sages in ancient rocking chairs. A gang of coloured women came by, and one of the young ones detached herself from motherlike elders and came to me fast – 'Hello Joe!' – and suddenly saw it wasn't Joe, and ran back, blushing. I wished I were Joe. I was only myself, Sal Paradise, sad, strolling in this violet dark, this unbearably sweet night, wishing I could exchange worlds with the happy, true-hearted, ecstatic Negroes of America. The raggedy neighbour-hoods reminded me of Dean and Marylou, who knew these streets so well from childhood. How I wished I could find them.

Down at 23rd and Welton a softball game was going on under floodlights which also illuminated the gas tank. A great eager crowd roared at every play. The strange young heroes of all kinds, white, coloured, Mexican, pure Indian, were on the field, performing with heart-breaking seriousness. Just sand-lot kids in uniform. Never in my life as an athlete had I ever permitted myself to perform like this in front of families and girl friends and kids of the neighbourhood, at night, under lights; always it had been college, big-time, sober-faced; no boyish, human joy like this. Now it was too late. Near me sat an old Negro who apparently watched the games every night. Next to him was an old white bum; then a Mexican family, then some girls, some boys – all humanity, the lot. Oh, the sadness of the lights that night! The young pitcher looked just like Dean. A pretty blonde in the seats looked just like Marylou. It was the Denver Night; all I did was die.

Down in Denver, down in Denver
All I did was die

Across the street Negro families sat on their front steps, talk-ing and looking up at the starry night through the trees and just relaxing in the softness and sometimes watching the game. Many cars passed in the street meanwhile, and stopped at the corner when the light turned red. There was excitement and the air was filled with the vibration of really joyous life that knows nothing of disappointment and 'white sorrows' and all that. The old Negro man had a can of beer in his coat pocket, which he proceeded to open; and the old white man enviously eyed the can and groped in his pocket to see if *he* could buy a can too. How I died! I walked away from there.

I went to see a rich girl I knew. In the morning she pulled a hundred-dollar bill out of her silk stocking and said, 'You've been talking of a trip to Frisco; that being the case, take this and go and have your fun.' So all my problems were solved and I got a travel-bureau car for eleven dollars' gas-fare to Frisco and zoomed over the land.

Two fellows were driving this car; they said they were pimps. Two other fellows were passengers with me. We sat tight and bent our minds to the goal. We went over Berthoud Pass, down to the great plateau, Tabernash, Troublesome, Kremmling; down Rabbit Ears Pass to Steamboat Springs, and out; fifty miles of dusty detour; then Craig and the Great American Desert. As we crossed the Colorado-Utah border I saw God in the sky in the form of huge gold sunburning clouds above the desert that seemed to point a finger at me and say, 'Pass here and go on, you're on the road to heaven.' Ah well, alackaday, I was more interested in some old rotted covered wagons and pool tables sitting in the Nevada desert near a Coca-Cola stand and where there were huts with the weatherbeaten signs still flapping in the haunted shrouded desert wind, saying, 'Rattlesnake Bill lived here' or 'Brokenmouth Annie holed up here for years'. Yes, zoom! In Salt Lake City the pimps checked on their girls and we drove on. Before I knew it, once again I was seeing the fabled city of San Francisco stretched on the bay in the middle of the night. I ran immediately to Dean. He had a little house now. I was burning to know what was on his mind and what would happen now, for there was nothing behind me any more, all my bridges were gone and I didn't give a damn about anything at all. I knocked on his door at two o'clock in the morning.

2

HE came to the door stark naked and it might have been the President knocking for all he cared. He received the world in the raw. 'Sal!' he said with genuine awe. 'I didn't think you'd actually do it. You've finally come to *me*.'

'Yep,' I said. 'Everything fell apart in me. How are things with you?'

'Not so good, not so good. But we've got a million things to talk about. Sal, the time has *fi-nally* come for us to talk and get with it.' We agreed it was about time and went in. My arrival was somewhat like the coming of the strange most evil angel in the home of the snow-white fleece, as Dean and I began talking excitedly in the kitchen downstairs, which brought forth sobs from upstairs. Everything I said to Dean was answered with a wild, whispering, shuddering *'Yes!'* Camille knew what was going to happen. Apparently Dean had been quiet for a few months; now the angel had arrived and he was going mad again. 'What's the matter with her?' I whispered.

He said, 'She's getting worse and worse, man, she cries and makes tantrums, won't let me out to see Slim Gaillard, gets mad every time I'm late, then when I stay home she won't talk to me and says I'm an utter beast.' He ran upstairs to soothe her. I heard Camille yell, *'You're a liar, you're a liar, you're a liar!'* I took the opportunity to examine the very wonderful house they had. It was a two-storey crooked, rickety wooden cottage in the middle of tenements, right on top of Russian Hill with a view of the bay; it had four rooms, three upstairs and one immense sort of basement kitchen downstairs. The kitchen door opened on to a grassy court where washlines were. In back of the kitchen was a storage room where Dean's old shoes still were caked an inch thick with Texas mud from the night the Hudson got stuck on the Brazos River. Of course the Hudson was gone; Dean hadn't been able to make further payments on it. He had no car at all now. Their second baby was accidentally coming. It was horrible to hear Camille sobbing so. We couldn't stand it and went out to buy beer and brought it back to the kitchen. Camille finally went to sleep or spent the night staring blankly at the dark. I had no idea what was really wrong, except perhaps Dean had driven her mad after all.

After my last leaving of Frisco he had gone crazy over Marylou again and spent months haunting her apartment on Divisadero, where every night she had a different sailor in and he peeked down through her mail-slot and could see her bed. There he saw Marylou sprawled in the mornings with a boy. He trailed her around town He wanted absolute proof that she was a whore. He loved her, he sweated over her. Finally he got hold of some bad green, as it's called in the trade – green, uncured marijuana – quite by mistake, and smoked too much of it.

'The first day,' he said, 'I lay rigid as a board in bed and couldn't move or say a word; I just looked straight up with my eyes open wide. I could hear buzzing in my head and saw all kinds of wonderful technicolour visions and felt wonderful. The second day everything came to me, EVERYTHING I'd ever done or known or read or heard of or conjectured came back to me and rearranged itself in my mind in a brand-new logical way and because I could think of nothing else in the interior concerns of holding and catering to the amazement and gratitude I felt, I kept saying, "Yes, yes, yes, yes." Not loud. Just "Yes", real quiet, and these green tea visions lasted until the third day. I had understood everything by then, my whole life was decided, I knew I loved Marylou, I knew I had to find my father wherever he is and save him, I knew you were my buddy et cetera, I knew how great Carlo is. I knew a thousand things about everybody everywhere. Then the third day I began having a terrible series of waking nightmares, and they were so absolutely horrible and grisly and green that I just lay there doubled up with my hands around my knees, saying, "Oh, oh, oh, ah, oh ..." The neighbours heard me and sent for a doctor. Camille was away with the baby, visiting her folks. The whole neighbourhood was concerned. They came in and found me lying on the bed with my arms stretched out forever. Sal, I ran to Marylou with some of that tea. And do you know that the same thing happened to that dumb little box? – the same visions, the same logic, the same final decision about everything, the view of all truths in one painful lump leading to nightmares and pain – ack! Then I knew I loved her so much I wanted to kill her. I ran home and beat my head on the wall. I ran to Ed Dunkel; he's back in Frisco with Galatea; I asked him about a guy we know has a gun, I went to the guy, I got the gun, I ran to Marylou, I looked down the mail-slot, she was sleeping with a guy, had to retreat and hesitate, came back in an hour, I barged in, she was alone – and I gave her the gun and told her to kill me. She held the gun in her hand the longest time. I asked her for a sweet dead pact. She didn't want. I said one of us had to die. She said no. I beat my head on the wall. Man, I was out of my mind. She'll tell you, she talked me out of it.'

'Then what happened?'

'That was months ago – after you left. She finally married a used-car dealer, dumb bastit has promised to kill me if he finds me, if necessary I shall have to defend myself and kill him and I'll go to San Quentin, 'cause, Sal, one more rap of *any* kind and I go to San Quentin for life – that's the end of me. Bad hand and all.' He showed me his hand. I hadn't noticed in the excitement that he had suffered a terrible accident to his hand. 'I hit Marylou on the brow on February twenty-sixth at six o'clock in the evening – in fact six-ten, because I remember I had to make my hotshot freight in an hour and twenty minutes – the last time we met and the last time we decided everything, and now listen to this: my thumb only deflected off her brow and she didn't even have a bruise and in fact laughed, but my thumb broke above the wrist and a horrible doctor made a setting of the bones that was difficult and took three separate castings, twenty-three combined hours of sitting on hard benches waiting, et cetera, and the final cast had a traction pin stuck through the tip of my thumb, so in April when they took off the cast the pin infected my bone and I developed osteomyelitis which has become chronic, and after an operation which failed amd a month in a cast the result was the amputation of a wee bare piece off the tip-ass end.'

174

He unwrapped the bandages and showed me. The flesh, about half an inch, was missing under the nail.

'It got from worse to worse. I had to support Camille and Amy and had to work as fast as I could at Firestone as mould man, curing recapped tyres and later hauling big hunnerd-fifty-pound tyres from the floor to the top of the cars – could only use my good hand and kept banging the bad – broke it again, had it reset again, and it's getting all infected and swoled again. So now I take care of baby while Camille works. You see? Heeby-jeebies, I'm classification three-A, jazz-hounded Moriarty has a sore butt, his wife gives him daily injections of peni-cillin for his thumb, which produces hives, for he's allergic. He must take sixty thousand units of Fleming's juice within a month. He must take one tablet every four hours for this month to combat allergy produced from his juice. He must take codeine aspirin to relieve the pain in his thumb. He must have surgery on his leg for an inflamed cyst. He must rise next Monday at six a.m. to get his teeth cleaned. He must see a foot doctor twice a week for treatment. He must take cough syrup each night. He must blow and snort constantly to clear his nose, which has collapsed just under the bridge where an operation some years ago weakened it. He lost his thumb on his throwing arm. Greatest seventy-yard passer in the history of New Mexico State Reformatory. And yet – and yet, I've never felt better and finer and happier with the world and to see little lovely children playing in the sun and I am so glad to see you, my fine gone wonderful Sal, and I know, I *know* everything will be all right. You'll see her tomorrow, my ter-rific darling beautiful daughter can now stand alone for thirty seconds at a time, she weighs twenty-two pounds, is twenty-nine inches long. I've just figured out she is thirty-one-and-a-quarter-per-cent English, twenty-seven-and-a-half-per-cent Irish, twenty-five-per-cent German, eight-and-three-quarters-per-cent Dutch, seven-and-a-half-per-cent Scotch, one-hundred-per-cent wonderful.' He fondly congratulated me for the book I had finished, which was now accepted by the publishers. 'We know life, Sal, we're growing older, each of us, little by little, and are coming to know things. What you tell me about your life I understand well, I've always dug your feelings, and now in fact you're ready to hook up with a real great girl if you can only find her and cultivate her and make her mind your soul as I have tried so hard with these damned women of mine. Shit! shit! shit!' he yelled.

And in the morning Camille threw both of us out, baggage and all. It began when we called Roy Johnson, old Denver Roy, and had him come over for beer, while Dean minded the baby and did the dishes and the wash in the backyard but did a sloppy job of it in his excitement. Johnson agreed to drive us to Mill City to look for Remi Boncœur. Camille came in from work at the doctor's office and gave us all the sad look of a harassed woman's life. I tried to show this haunted woman that I had no mean intentions concerning her home life by saying hello to her and talking as warmly as I could, but she knew it was a con and maybe one I'd learned from Dean, and only gave a brief smile. In the morning there was a terrible scene : she lay on the bed sobbing, and in the midst of this I suddenly had the need to go to the bathroom, and the only way I could get there was through her room. 'Dean, Dean,' I cried, 'where's the nearest bar?'

'Bar?' he said, surprised; he was washing his hands in the kitchen sink downstairs. He thought I wanted to get drunk. I told him my dilemma and he said, 'Go right ahead, she does that all the time.' No, I couldn't do that. I rushed out to look for a bar; I walked uphill and downhill in a vicinity of four blocks on Russian Hill and found nothing but laundromats, cleaners, soda fountains, beauty parlours. I came back to the crooked little house. They were yelling at each other as I slipped through with a feeble smile and locked myself in the bathroom. A few moments later Camille was throwing Dean's things on the living-room floor and telling him to pack. To my amazement I saw a full-length oil painting of Galatea Dunkel over the sofa. I suddenly realized that all these women were spending months of loneliness and womanliness together, chatting about the madness of the men. I heard Dean's maniacal giggle across the house, together with the wails of his baby. The next thing I knew he was gliding around the house like Groucho Marx, with his broken thumb wrapped in a huge white bandage sticking up like a beacon that stands motionless above the frenzy of the waves. Once again I saw his pitiful huge battered trunk with socks and dirty underwear sticking out; he bent over it, throwing in everything he could find. Then he got his suitcase, the beatest suitcase in the USA. It was made of paper with designs on it to make it look like leather, and hinges of some kind pasted on. A great rip ran down the top; Dean lashed on a rope. Then he grabbed his seabag and threw things into that. I got my bag, stuffed it, and as Camille lay in bed saying, 'Liar! Liar! Liar!' we leaped out of the house and struggled down the street to the nearest cable car – a mass of men and suitcases with that enormous bandaged thumb sticking up in the air.

That thumb became the symbol of Dean's final development. He no longer cared about anything (as before) but now he also *cared about everything in principle*; that is to say, it was all the same to him and he belonged to the world and there was nothing he could do about it. He stopped me in the middle of the street.

'Now, man, I know you're probably real bugged; you just got to town and we get thrown out the first day and you're wondering what I've done to deserve this and so on – together with all horrible appurtenances – hee-hee-hee! – but look at me. Please, Sal, look at me.'

I looked at him. He was wearing a T-shirt, torn pants hanging down his belly, tattered shoes; he had not shaved, his hair was wild and bushy, his eyes bloodshot, and that tremendous bandaged thumb stood supported in midair at heart-level (he had to hold it up that way), and on his face was the goofiest grin I ever saw. He stumbled around in a circle and looked everywhere.

'What do my eyeballs see? Ah – the blue sky. Long-fellow!' He swayed and blinked. He rubbed his eyes. 'Together with windows – have you ever dug windows? Now let's talk about windows. I have seen some really crazy windows that made faces at me, and some of them had shades drawn and so they winked.' Out of his seabag he fished a copy of Eugene Sue's *Mysteries of Paris* and, adjusting the front of his T-shirt, began reading on the street corner with a pedantic air. 'Now really, Sal, let's dig everything as we go along ...' He forgot about that in an instant and looked around blankly. I was glad I had come, he needed me now.

'Why did Camille throw you out? What are you going to do?'

'Eh?' he said. 'Eh? Eh?' We racked our brains for where to go and what to do. I realized it was up to me. Poor, poor Dean – the devil himself had never fallen farther; in idiocy, with infected thumb, surrounded by the battered suitcases of his motherless feverish life across America and back numberless times, an undone bird. 'Let's walk to New York,' he said, 'and as we do so let's take stock of everything along the way – yass.' I took out my money and counted it; I showed it to him.

'I have here,' I said, 'the sum of eighty-three dollars and change, and if you come with me let's go to New York – and after that let's go to Italy.'

'Italy?' he said. His eyes lit up. 'Italy, yass – how shall we get there, dear Sal?'

I pondered this. 'I'll make some money, I'll get a thousand dollars from the publishers. We'll go dig all the crazy women in Rome, Paris, all those places; we'll sit at sidewalk cafés; we'll live in whorehouses. Why not go to Italy?'

'Why yass,' said Dean, and then realized I was serious and looked at me out of the corner of his eye for the first time, for I'd never committed myself before with regard to his burdensome existence, and that was the look of a man weighing his chances at the last moment before the bet. There were triumph and insolence in his eyes, a devilish look, and he never took his eyes off mine for a long time. I looked back at him and blushed.

I said, 'What's the matter?' I felt wretched when I asked it. He made no answer but continued looking at me with the same wary insolent side-eye.

I tried to remember everything he'd done in his life and if there wasn't something back there to make him suspicious of something now. Resolutely and firmly I repeated what I said – 'Come to New York with me; I've got the money.' I looked at him; my eyes were watering with embarrassment and tears. Still he stared at me. Now his eyes were blank and looking through me. It was probably the pivotal point of our friend-

ship when he realized I had actually spent some hours thinking about him and his troubles, and he was trying to place that
in his tremendously involved and tormented mental categories.
Something clicked in both of us. In me it was suddenly concern for a man who was years younger than I, five years, and
whose fate was wound with mine across the passage of the recent years; in him it was a matter that I can ascertain only
from what he did afterward. He became extremely joyful and
said everything was settled. 'What was that look?' I asked. He
was pained to hear me say that. He frowned. It was rarely that
Dean frowned. We both felt perplexed and uncertain of something. We were standing on top of a hill on a beautiful sunny
day in San Francisco; our shadows fell across the sidewalk.
Out of the tenement next to Camille's house filed eleven Greek
men and women who instantly lined themselves up on the
sunny pavement while another backed up across the narrow
street and smiled at them over a camera. We gaped at these
ancient people who were having a wedding party for one of
their daughters, probably the thousandth in an unbroken dark
generation of smiling in the sun. They were well dressed, and
they were strange. Dean and I might have been in Cyprus for
all of that. Gulls flew overhead in the sparkling air.

'Well,' said Dean in a very shy and sweet voice, 'shall we
go?'

'Yes,' I said, 'let's go to Italy.' And so we picked up our
bags, he the trunk with his one good arm and I the rest, and
staggered to the cable-car stop; in a moment rolled down the
hill with our legs dangling to the sidewalk from the jiggling
shelf, two broken-down heroes of the Western night.

3

FIRST thing, we went to a bar down on Market Street and decided everything – that we would stick together and be buddies
till we died. Dean was very quiet and preoccupied, looking
at the old bums in the saloon that reminded him of his father.
'I think he's in Denver – this time we must absolutely find him,

179

he may be in County Jail, he may be around Larimer Street again, but he's to be found. Agreed?'

Yes, it was agreed; we were going to do everything we'd never done and had been too silly to do in the past. Then we promised ourselves two days of kicks in San Francisco before starting off, and of course the agreement was to go by travel bureau in share-the-gas cars and save as much money as possible. Dean claimed he no longer needed Marylou though he still loved her. We both agreed he would make out in New York.

Dean put on his pin-stripe suit with a sports shirt, we stashed our gear in a Greyhound bus locker for ten cents, and we took off to meet Roy Johnson who was going to be our chauffeur for two-day Frisco kicks. Roy agreed over the phone to do so. He arrived at the corner of Market and Third shortly thereafter and picked us up. Roy was now living in Frisco, working as a clerk and married to a pretty little blonde called Dorothy. Dean confided that her nose was too long – this was his big point of contention about her, for some strange reason – but her nose wasn't too long at all. Roy Johnson is a thin, dark, handsome kid with a pin-sharp face and combed hair that he keeps shoving back from the sides of his head. He had an extremely earnest approach and a big smile. Evidently his wife, Dorothy, had wrangled with him over the chauffeuring idea – and, determined to make a stand as the man of the house (they lived in a little room), he nevertheless stuck by his promise to us, but with consequences; his mental dilemma resolved itself in a bitter silence. He drove Dean and me all over Frisco at all hours of day and night and never said a word; all he did was go through red lights and make sharp turns on two wheels, and this was telling us the shifts to which we'd put him. He was midway between the challenge of his new wife and the challenge of his old Denver poolhall gang leader. Dean was pleased, and of course unperturbed by the driving. We paid absolutely no attention to Roy and sat in the back and yakked.

The next thing was to go to Mill City to see if we could find Remi Boncœur. I noticed with some wonder that the old ship *Admiral Freebee* was no longer in the bay; and then of course Remi was no longer in the second-to-last compartment of the shack in the canyon. A beautiful coloured girl opened the door instead; Dean and I talked to her a great deal. Roy Johnson waited in the car, reading Eugene Sue's *Mysteries of Paris*. I took one last look at Mill City and knew there was no sense trying to dig up the involved past; instead we decided to go see Galatea Dunkel about sleeping accommodations. Ed had left her again, was in Denver, and damned if she still didn't plot to get him back. We found her sitting crosslegged on the Oriental-type rug of her four-room tenement flat on upper Mission with a deck of fortune cards. Good girl. I saw sad signs that Ed Dunkel had lived here awhile and then left out of stupors and disinclinations only.

'He'll come back,' said Galatea. 'That guy can't take care of himself without me.' She gave a furious look at Dean and Roy Johnson. 'It was Tommy Snark who did it this time. All the time before he came Ed was perfectly happy and worked and we went out and had wonderful times. Dean, you know that. Then they'd sit in the bathroom for hours, Ed in the bathtub and Snarky on the seat, and talk and talk and talk – such silly things.'

Dean laughed. For years he had been chief prophet of that gang and now they were learning his technique. Tommy Snark had grown a beard and his big sorrowful blue eyes had come looking for Ed Dunkel in Frisco; what happened (actually and no lie), Tommy had his small finger amputated in a Denver mishap and collected a good sum of money. For no reason under the sun they decided to give Galatea the slip and go to Portland, Maine, where apparently Snark had an aunt. So they were now either in Denver, going through, or already in Portland.

'When Tom's money runs out Ed'll be back,' said Galatea, looking at her cards. 'Damn fool – he doesn't know anything and never did. All he has to do is know that I love him.'

Galatea looked like the daughter of the Greeks with the sunny camera as she sat there on the rug, her long hair streaming to the floor, plying the fortune-telling cards. I got to like her. We even decided to go out that night and hear jazz, and

Dean would take a six-foot blonde who lived down the street, Marie.

That night Galatea, Dean, and I went to get Marie. This girl had a basement apartment, a little daughter, and an old car that barely ran and which Dean and I had to push down the street as the girls jammed at the starter. We went to Galatea's, and there everybody sat around – Marie, her daughter, Galatea, Roy Johnson, Dorothy his wife – all sullen in the overstuffed furniture as I stood in a corner, neutral in Frisco problems, and Dean stood in the middle of the room with his balloon-thumb in the air breast-high, giggling. 'Gawd damn,' he said, 'we're all losing our fingers – hawr-hawr-hawr.'

'Dean, why do you act so foolish?' said Galatea. 'Camille called and said you left her. Don't you realize you have a daughter?'

'He didn't leave her, she kicked him out!' I said, breaking my neutrality. They all gave me dirty looks; Dean grinned. 'And with that thumb, what do you expect the poor guy to do?' I added. They all looked at me; particularly Dorothy Johnson lowered a mean gaze on me. It wasn't anything but a sewing circle, and the centre of it was the culprit, Dean – responsible, perhaps, for everything that was wrong. I looked out the window at the buzzing night-street of Mission; I wanted to get going and hear the great jazz of Frisco – and remember, this was only my second night in town.

'I think Marylou was very, very wise leaving you, Dean,' said Galatea. 'For years now you haven't had any sense of responsibility for anyone. You've done so many awful things I don't know what to say to you.'

And in fact that was the point, and they all sat around looking at Dean with lowered and hating eyes, and he stood on the carpet in the middle of them and giggled – he just giggled. He made a little dance. His bandage was getting dirtier all the time; it began to flop and unroll. I suddenly realized that Dean, by virtue of his enormous series of sins, was becoming the Idiot, the Imbecile, the Saint of the lot.

'You have absolutely no regard for anybody but yourself and your damned kicks. All you think about is what's hanging between your legs and how much money or fun you can get out of people and then you just throw them aside. Not only that but you're silly about it. It never occurs to you that life is serious and there are people trying to make something decent out of it instead of just goofing all the time.'

That's what Dean was, the HOLY GOOF.

'Camille is crying her heart out tonight but don't think for a minute she wants you back, she said she never wanted to see you again and she said it was to be final this time. Yet you stand here and make silly faces, and I don't think there's a care in your heart.'

This was not true; I knew better and I could have told them all. I didn't see any sense in trying it. I longed to go and put my arm around Dean and say, Now look here, all of you, remember just one thing: this guy has his troubles too, and another thing, he never complains and he's given all of you a damned good time just being himself, and if that isn't enough for you then send him to the firing squad, that's apparently what you're itching to do anyway . . .

Nevertheless Galatea Dunkel was the only one in the gang who wasn't afraid of Dean and could sit there calmly, with her face hanging out, telling him off in front of everybody. There were earlier days in Denver when Dean had everybody sit in the dark with the girls and just talked, and talked, and talked, with a voice that was once hypnotic and strange and was said to make the girls come across by sheer force of persuasion and the content of what he said. This was when he was fifteen, sixteen. Now his disciples were married and the wives of his disciples had him on the carpet for the sexuality and the life he had helped bring into being. I listened further.

'Now you're going East with Sal,' Galatea said, 'and what do you think you're going to accomplish by that? Camille has to stay home and mind the baby now you're gone – how can she keep her job? – and she never wants to see you again and I don't blame her. If you see Ed along the road you tell him to come back to me or I'll kill him.'

Just as flat as that. It was the saddest night. I felt as if I was with strange brothers and sisters in a pitiful dream. Then a complete silence fell over everybody; where once Dean would have talked his way out, he now fell silent himself, but standing in front of everybody, ragged and broken and idiotic, right under the lightbulbs, his bony mad face covered with sweat and throbbing veins, saying, 'Yes, yes, yes', as though tremendous revelations were pouring into him all the time now, and I am convinced they were, and the others suspected as much and were frightened. He was BEAT – the root, the soul of Beatific. What was he knowing? He tried all in his power to tell me what he was knowing, and they envied that about me, my position at his side, defending him and drinking him in as they once tried to do. Then they looked at me. What was I, a stranger, doing on the West Coast this fair night? I recoiled from the thought.

'We're going to Italy,' I said, I washed my hands of the whole matter. Then, too, there was a strange sense of maternal satisfaction in the air, for the girls were really looking at Dean the way a mother looks at the dearest and most errant child, and he with his sad thumb and all his revelations knew it well, and that was why he was able, in tick-tocking silence, to walk out of the apartment without a word, to wait for us downstairs as soon as we'd made up our minds about *time*. This was what we sensed about the ghost on the sidewalk. I looked out the window. He was alone in the doorway, digging the street. Bitterness, recriminations, advice, morality, sadness – everything was behind him, and ahead of him was the ragged and ecstatic joy of pure being.

'Come on, Galatea, Marie, let's go hit the jazz joints and forget it. Dean will be dead someday. Then what can you say to him?'

'The sooner he's dead the better,' said Galatea, and she spoke officially for almost everyone in the room.

'Very well, then,' I said, 'but now he's alive and I'll bet you want to know what he does next and that's because he's got the secret that we're all busting to find and it's splitting his head wide open and if he goes mad don't worry, it won't be your fault but the fault of God.'

They objected to this; they said I really didn't know Dean; they said he was the worst scoundrel that ever lived and I'd find out someday to my regret. I was amused to hear them protest so much. Roy Johnson rose to the defence of the ladies and said he knew Dean better than anybody, and all Dean was, was just a very interesting and even amusing con-man. I went out to find Dean and we had a brief talk about it.

'Ah, man, don't worry, everything is perfect and fine.' He was rubbing his belly and licking his lips.

4

THE girls came down and we started out on our big night, once more pushing the car down the street. 'Wheeoo! let's go!' cried Dean, and we jumped in the back seat and clanked to the little Harlem on Folsom Street.

Out we jumped in the warm, mad night, hearing a wild tenorman bawling horn across the way, going 'EE-YAH! EE-YAH! EE-YAH!' and hands clapping to the beat and folks yelling, 'Go, go, go!' Dean was already racing across the street with his thumb in the air, yelling, 'Blow, man, blow!' A bunch of coloured men in Saturday-night suits were whooping it up in front. It was a sawdust saloon with a small bandstand on which the fellows huddled with their hats on, blowing over people's heads, a crazy place; crazy floppy women wandered around sometimes in their bathrobes, bottles clanked in alleys. In back of the joint in a dark corridor beyond the splattered toilets scores of men and women stood against the wall drinking wine-spodiodi and spitting at the stars – wine and whisky. The behatted tenorman was blowing at the peak of a wonderfully satisfactory free idea, a rising and falling riff that went from 'EE-yah!' to a crazier 'EE-de-lee-yah!' and blasted along to the rolling crash of butt-scarred drums hammered by a big brutal Negro with a bullneck who didn't give a damn about anything but punishing his busted tubs, crash, rattle-ti-boom, crash. Uproars of music and the tenorman *had it* and everybody knew he had it. Dean was clutching his head in the crowd, and it was a mad crowd. They were all urging that tenorman to hold it and keep it with cries and wild eyes, and he was raising himself from a crouch and going down again with his horn, looping it up in a clear cry above the furore. A six-foot skinny Negro woman was rolling her bones at the man's hornbell, and he just jabbed it at her, 'Ee! ee! ee!'

Everybody was rocking and roaring. Galatea and Marie with beer in their hands were standing on their chairs, shaking and jumping. Groups of coloured guys stumbled in from the street, falling over one another to get there. 'Stay with it, man!' roared a man with a foghorn voice, and let out a big groan that must have been heard clear out in Sacramento, ah-haa! 'Whoo!' said Dean. He was rubbing his chest, his belly; the sweat splashed from his face. Boom, kick, that drummer was kicking his drums down the cellar and rolling the beat upstairs with his murderous sticks, rattlety-boom! A big fat man was jumping on the platform, making it sag and creak. 'Yoo!' The pianist was only pounding the keys with spread-eagled fingers, chords, at intervals when the great tenorman was drawing his breath for another blast – Chinese chords, shuddering the piano in every timber, chink, and wire, boing! The tenorman jumped down from the platform and stood in the crowd, blowing around; his hat was over his eyes; somebody pushed it back for him. He just hauled back and stamped his foot and blew down a hoarse, baughing blast, and drew breath, and raised the horn and blew high, wide, and screaming in the air. Dean was directly in front of him with his face lowered to the bell of the horn, clapping his hands, pouring sweat on the man's keys, and the man noticed and laughed in his horn a long quivering crazy laugh, and everybody else laughed and they rocked and rocked; and finally the tenorman decided to blow his top and crouched down and held a note in high C for a long time as everybody else crashed along and the cries increased and I thought the cops would come swarming from the nearest precinct. Dean was in a trance. The tenorman's eyes were fixed straight on him; he had a madman who not only understood but cared and wanted to understand more and much more than there was, and they began duelling for this; everything came out of the horn, no more phrases, just cries, cries, 'Baugh' and down to 'Beep!' and up to 'EEEEE!' and down to clinkers and over to sideways-echoing horn-sounds. He tried everything, up, down, sideways, upside down, horizontal, thirty degrees, and finally he fell back in somebody's arms and gave up and everybody pushed around and yelled, 'Yes! Yes! He blowed that one!' Dean wiped himself with his handkerchief.

Then up stepped the tenorman on the bandstand and asked for a slow beat and looked sadly out the open door over people's heads and began singing 'Close Your Eyes'. Things quieted down a minute. The tenorman wore a tattered suede jacket, a purple shirt, cracked shoes, and zoot pants without press; he didn't care. He looked like a Negro Hassel. His big brown eyes were concerned with sadness, and the singing of songs slowly and with long, thoughtful pauses. But in the second chorus he got excited and grabbed the mike and jumped down from the bandstand and bent to it. To sing a note he had to touch his shoetops and pull it all up to blow, and he blew so much he staggered from the effect, and only recovered himself in time for the next long slow note. 'Mu-u-u-usic pla-a-a-a-a-a-ay!' He leaned back with his face to the ceiling, mike held below. He shook, he swayed. Then he leaned in, almost falling with his face against the mike. 'Ma-a-a-ake it dream-y for dan-cing' – and he looked at the street outside with his lips curled in scorn, Billie Holiday's hip sneer – 'while we go ro-man-n-n-cing' – he staggered sideways – 'Lo-o-o-ove's holi-da-a-ay' – he shook his head with disgust and weariness at the whole world – 'Will make it seem' – what would it make it seem? everybody waited; he mourned – 'O-kay'. The piano hit a chord. 'So baby come on just clo-o-o-ose your pretty little ey-y-y-y-yes' – his mouth quivered, he looked at us, Dean and me, with an expression that seemed to say, Hey now, what's this thing we're all doing in this sad brown world? – and then he came to the end of his song, and for this there had to be elaborate preparations, during which time you could send all the messages to Garcia around the world twelve times and what difference did it make to anybody? because here we were dealing with the pit and prunejuice of poor beat life itself in the god-awful streets of man, so he said it and sang it, 'Close – your –' and blew it way up to the ceiling and through to the stars and on out – 'Ey-y-y-y-y-es' – and staggered off the platform to brood. He sat in the corner with a bunch of boys and paid no attention to them. He looked down and wept. He was the greatest.

Dean and I went over to talk to him. We invited him out to the car. In the car he suddenly yelled, 'Yes! ain't nothin I like better than good kicks! Where do we go?' Dean jumped up and down in the seat, giggling maniacally. 'Later! later!' said the tenorman. 'I'll get my boy to drive us down to Jamson's Nook, I got to sing. Man, I *live* to sing. Been singin "Close Your Eyes" for two weeks – I don't want to sing nothin else. What are you boys up to?' We told him we were going to New York in two days. 'Lord, I ain't never been there and they tell me it's a real jumpin town but I ain't got no cause complainin where I am. I'm married, you know.'

'O Yes?' said Dean, lighting up. 'And where is the darling tonight?'

'What do you *mean*?' said the tenorman, looking at him out of the corner of his eye. 'I tole you I was *married* to her, didn't I?'

'Oh yes, oh yes,' said Dean. 'I was just asking. Maybe she has friends? Or sisters? A ball, you know, I'm just looking for a ball.'

'Yah, what good's a ball, life's too sad to be ballin all the time,' said the tenorman, lowering his eye to the street. 'Shh-eee-it!' he said. 'I ain't got no money and I don't care tonight.'

We went back in for more. The girls were so disgusted with Dean and me for gunning off and jumping around that they had left and gone to Jamson's Nook on foot; the car wouldn't run anyway. We saw a horrible sight in the bar : a white hipster fairy had come in wearing a Hawaiian shirt and was asking the big drummer if he could sit in. The musicians looked at him suspiciously. 'Do you blow?' He said he did, mincing. They looked at one another and said, 'Yeah, yeah, that's what the man does, shhh-ee-it!' So the fairy sat down at the tubs and they started the beat of a jump number and he began stroking the snares with soft goofy bop brushes, swaying his neck with that complacent Reichianalysed ecstasy that doesn't mean anything except too much tea and soft foods and goofy kicks on the cool order. But he didn't care. He smiled joyously into space and kept the beat, though softly, with bop subtleties, a giggling, rippling background for big solid foghorn blues the boys were blowing, unaware of him. The big Negro bullneck drummer sat waiting for his turn. 'What that man doing?' he said, 'Play the music!' he said. 'What in hell!' he said. 'Shh-ee-eet!' and looked away, disgusted.

The tenorman's boy showed up; he was a little taut Negro with a great big Cadillac. We all jumped in. He hunched over the wheel and blew the car clear across Frisco without stopping once, seventy miles an hour, right through traffic and nobody even noticed him, he was so good. Dean was in ecstasies. 'Dig this guy, man! dig the way he sits there and don't move a bone and just balls the jack and can talk all night while he's doing it, only thing is he doesn't bother with talking, ah, man, the things, the things I could — I wish — oh, yes. Let's go, let's not stop — go now! Yes!' And the boy wound around a corner and bowled us right in front of Jamson's Nook and was parked. A cab pulled up; out of it jumped a skinny, withered little Negro preacherman who threw a dollar at the cabby and yelled, 'Blow!' and ran into the club and dashed right through the downstairs bar, yelling, 'Blowblowblow!' and stumbled upstairs, almost falling on his face, and blew the door open and fell into the jazz-session room with his hands out to support him against anything he might fall on, and he fell right on Lampshade, who was working as a waiter in Jamson's Nook that season, and the music was there blasting and blasting and he stood transfixed in the open door, screaming, 'Blow for me, man, blow!' And the man was a little short Negro with an alto horn that Dean said obviously lived with his grandmother just like Tom Snark, slept all day and blew all night, and blew a hundred choruses before he was ready to jump for fair, and that's what he was doing.

'It's Carlo Marx!' screamed Dean above the fury.

And it was. This little grandmother's boy with the taped-up alto had beady, glittering eyes; small, crooked feet; spindly legs; and he hopped and flopped with his horn and threw his feet around and kept his eyes fixed on the audience (which was just people laughing at a dozen tables, the room thirty by thirty feet and low ceiling), and he never stopped. He was very simple in his ideas. What he liked was the surprise of a new simple variation of a chorus. He'd go from 'ta-tup-tader-rara . . . ta-tup-tader-rara', repeating and hopping to it and

189

kissing and smiling into his horn, to 'ta-tup-EE-da-de-dera-RUP! ta-tup-EE-da-de-dera-RUP!' and it was all great moments of laughter and understanding for him and everyone else who heard. His tone was clear as a bell, high, pure, and blew straight in our faces from two feet away. Dean stood in front of him, oblivious to everything else in the world, with his head bowed, his hands socking in together, his whole body jumping on his heels and the sweat, always the sweat, pouring and splashing down his tormented collar to lie actually in a pool at his feet. Galatea and Marie were there, and it took us five minutes to realize it. Whoo, Frisco nights, the end of the continent and the end of doubt, all dull doubt and tomfoolery, good-bye. Lampshade was roaring around with his trays of beer; everything he did was in rhythm; he yelled at the waitress with the beat; 'Hey now, babybaby, make a way, make a way, it's Lampshade comin your way,' and he hurled by her with the beers in the air and roared through the swinging doors into the kitchen and danced with the cooks and came sweating back. The hornman sat absolutely motionless at a corner table with an untouched drink in front of him, staring gook-eyed into space, his hands hanging at his sides till they almost touched the floor, his feet outspread like lolling tongues, his body shrivelled into absolute weariness and entranced sorrow and what-all was on his mind: a man who knocked himself out every evening and let the others put the quietus to him in the night. Everything swirled around him like a cloud. And that little grandmother's alto, that little Carlo Marx, hopped and monkeydanced with his magic horn and blew two hundred choruses of blues, each one more frantic than the other, and no signs of failing energy or willingness to call anything a day. The whole room shivered.

On the corner of Fourth and Folsom an hour later I stood with Ed Fournier, a San Francisco alto man who waited with me while Dean made a phone call in a saloon to have Roy Johnson pick us up. It wasn't anything much, we were just talking, except that suddenly we saw a very strange and insane sight. It was Dean. He wanted to give Roy Johnson the address of the bar, so he told him to hold the phone a minute and ran out to see, and to do this he had to rush pellmell through a long bar of brawling drinkers in white shirtsleeves, go to the middle of the street, and look at the post signs. He did this, crouched low to the ground like Groucho Marx, his feet carrying him with amazing swiftness out of the bar, like an apparition, with his balloon thumb stuck up in the night, and came to a whirling stop in the middle of the road, looking everywhere above him for the signs. They were hard to see in the dark, and he spun a dozen times in the road, thumb upheld, in a wild, anxious silence, a wild-haired person with a balloon-ing thumb held up like a great goose of the sky, spinning and spinning in the dark, the other hand distractedly inside his pants. Ed Fournier was saying, 'I blow a sweet tone wherever I go and if people don't like it it ain't nothin I can do about it. Say, man, that buddy of yours is a crazy cat, looka him over there' – and we looked. There was a big silence everywhere as Dean saw the signs and rushed back in the bar, practically going under someone's legs as they came out and gliding so fast through the bar that everybody had to do a double take to see him. A moment later Roy Johnson showed up, and with the same amazing swiftness. Dean glided across the street and into the car, without a sound. We were off again.

'Now, Roy, I know you're all hung-up with your wife about this thing but we absolutely must make Forty-sixth and Geary in the incredible time of three minutes or everything is lost. Ahem! Yes! (Cough-cough.) In the morning Sal and I are leav-ing for New York and this is absolutely our last night of kicks and I know you won't mind.'

No, Roy Johnson didn't mind; he only drove through every red light he could find and hurried us along in our foolishness. At dawn he went home to bed. Dean and I had ended up with a coloured guy called Walter who ordered drinks at the bar and had them lined up and said, 'Wine-spodiodi!' which was a shot of port wine, a shot of whisky, and a shot of port wine. 'Nice sweet jacket for all that bad whisky!' he yelled.

He invited us to his home for a bottle of beer. He lived in the tenements in back of Howard. His wife was asleep when we came in. The only light in the apartment was the bulb over her bed. We had to get up on a chair and unscrew the bulb as she lay smiling there; Dean did it, fluttering his lashes. She was about fifteen years older than Walter and the sweetest woman in the world. Then we had to plug in the extension over her bed, and smiled and smiled. She never asked Walter where he'd been, what time it was, nothing. Finally we were set in the kitchen with the extension and sat down around the humble table to drink the beer and tell the stories. Dawn. It was time to leave and move the extension back to the bed-room and screw back the bulb. Walter's wife smiled and smiled as we repeated the insane thing all over again. She never said a word.

Out on the dawn street Dean said, 'Now you see, man, there's *real* woman for you. Never a harsh word, never a com-plaint, or modified; her old man can come in any hour of the night with anybody and have talks in the kitchen and drink the beer and leave any old time. This is a man, and that's his castle.' He pointed up at the tenement. We stumbled off. The big night was over. A cruising car followed us suspiciously for a few blocks. We bought fresh doughnuts in a bakery on Third Street and ate them in the grey, ragged street. A tall, be-spectacled, well-dressed fellow came stumbling down the street with a Negro in a truck-driving cap. They were a strange pair. A big truck rolled by and the Negro pointed at it excitedly and tried to express his feeling. The tall white man furtively looked over his shoulder and counted his money. 'It's Old Bull Lee!' giggled Dean. 'Counting his money and worried about everything, and all that other boy wants to do is talk about trucks and things he knows.' We followed them awhile.

Holy flowers floating in the air, were all these tired faces in the dawn of Jazz America.

We had to sleep; Galatea Dunkel's was out of the question. Dean knew a railroad brakeman called Ernest Burke who lived with his father in a hotel room on Third Street. Originally he'd been on good terms with them, but lately not so, and the idea was for me to try persuading them to let us sleep on their floor. It was horrible. I had to call from a morning diner. The old man answered the phone suspiciously. He remembered me from what his son had told him. To our surprise he came down to the lobby and let us in. It was just a sad old brown Frisco hotel. We went upstairs and the old man was kind enough to give us the entire bed. 'I have to get up anyway,' he said and retired to the little kitchenette to brew coffee. He began telling stories about his railroading days. He reminded me of my father. I stayed up and listened to the stories. Dean, not listening, was washing his teeth and bustling around and saying, 'Yes, that's right', to everything he said. Finally we slept; and in the morning Ernest came back from a Western Division run and took the bed as Dean and I got up. Now old Mr Burke dolled himself up for a date with his middle-aged sweetheart. He put on a green tweed suit, a cloth cap, also green tweed, and stuck a flower in his lapel.

'These romantic old broken-down Frisco brakemen live sad but eager lives of their own,' I told Dean in the toilet. 'It was very kind of him to let us sleep here.'

'Yass, yass,' said Dean, not listening. He rushed out to get a travel-bureau car. My job was to hurry to Galatea Dunkel's for our bags. She was sitting on the floor with her fortune-telling cards.

'Well, good-bye, Galatea, and I hope everything works out fine.'

'When Ed gets back I'm going to take him to Jamson's Nook every night and let him get his fill of madness. Do you think that'll work, Sal? I don't know what to do.'

'What do the cards say?'

'The ace of spades is far away from him. The heart cards always surround him – the queen of hearts is never far. See this jack of spades? That's Dean, he's always around.'

'Well, we're leaving for New York in an hour.'

'Someday Dean's going to go on one of these trips and never come back.'

She let me take a shower and shave, and then I said good-bye and took the bags downstairs and hailed a Frisco taxi-jitney, which was an ordinary taxi that ran a regular route and you could hail it from any corner and ride to any corner pou want for about fifteen cents, cramped in with other passengers like on a bus, but talking and telling jokes like in a private car. Mission Street that last day in Frisco was a great riot of construction work, children playing, whooping Negroes coming home from work, dust, excitement, the great buzzing and vibrating hum of what is really America's most excited city – and overhead the pure blue sky and the joy of the foggy sea that always rolls in at night to make everybody hungry for food and further excitement. I hated to leave; my stay had lasted sixty-odd hours. With frantic Dean I was rushing through the world without a chance to see it. In the afternoon we were buzzing towards Sacramento and eastwards again.

5

THE car belonged to a tall, thin fag who was on his way home to Kansas and wore dark glasses and drove with extreme care; the car was what Dean called a 'fag Plymouth'; it had no pick-up and no real power. 'Effeminate car!' whispered Dean in my ear. There were two other passengers, a couple, typical half-way tourist who wanted to stop and sleep everywhere. The first stop would have to be Sacramento, which wasn't even the faintest beginning of the trip to Denver. Dean and I sat alone in the back seat and left it up to them and talked. 'Now, man, that alto man last night had IT – he held it once he found it; I've never seen a guy who could hold so long.' I wanted to know what 'IT' meant. 'Ah well' – Dean laughed – 'now you're asking me impon-de-rables – ahem! Here's a guy and everybody's there, right? Up to him to put down what's on everybody's mind. He starts the first chorus, then lines up his ideas, people, yeah, yeah, but get it, and then he rises to his fate and has to blow equal to it. All of a sudden somewhere in the middle of the chorus he *gets it* – everybody looks up and knows; they listen; he picks it up and carries. Time stops. He's filling empty space with the substance of our lives, confessions of his bellybottom strain, remembrance of ideas, rehashes of old blowing. He has to blow across bridges and come back and do it with such infinite feeling soul-exploratory for the tune of the moment that everybody knows it's not the tune that counts but IT –' Dean could go no further; he was sweating telling about it.

Then I began talking; I never talked so much in all my life. I told Dean that when I was a kid and rode in cars I used to imagine I held a big scythe in my hand and cut down all the trees and posts and even sliced every hill that zoomed past the window. 'Yes! Yes!' yelled Dean. 'I used to do it too only different scythe – tell you why. Driving across the West with the long stretches my scythe had to be immeasurably longer and it had to curve over distant mountains, slicing off their tops, and reach another level to get at further mountains and at the same time clip off every post along the road, regular throbbing poles. For this reason – O man, I have to tell you, NOW, I have IT – I have to tell you the time my father and I and a pisspoor bum from Larimer Street took a trip to Nebraska in the middle of the depression to sell fly-swatters. And how we made them, we bought pieces of ordinary regular old screen and pieces of wire that we twisted double and little pieces of blue and red cloth to sew around the edges and all of it for a matter of cents in a five-and-ten and made thousands of fly-swatters and got in the old bum's jalopy and went clear around Nebraska to every farmhouse and sold them for a nickel apiece – mostly for charity the nickels were given us, two bums and a boy, apple pies in the sky, and my old man in those days was always singing "Hallelujah, I'm a bum, bum again". And man, now listen to this, after two whole weeks of incredible hardship and bouncing around and hustling in the heat to sell these awful makeshift fly-swatters they started to argue about the division of the proceeds and had a big fight on the side of the road and then made up and bought wine and began drinking wine and didn't stop for five days and five nights while I huddled and cried in the background, and when they were finished every last cent was spent and we were right back where we started from, Larimer Street. And my old man was arrested and I had to plead at court to the judge to let him go cause he was my pa and I had no mother. Sal, I made great mature speeches at the age of eight in front of interested lawyers...' We were hot; we were going east; we were excited.

'Let me tell you more,' I said, 'and only as a parenthesis within what you're saying and to conclude my last thought.

As a child lying back in my father's car in the back seat I also had a vision of myself on a white horse riding alongside over every possible obstacle that presented itself: this included dodging posts, hurling around houses, sometimes jumping over when I looked too late, running over hills, across sudden squares with traffic that I had to dodge through incredibly –'

'Yes! Yes! Yes!' breathed Dean ecstatically. 'Only difference with me was, I myself ran, I had no horse. You were a Eastern kid and dreamed of horses; of course we won't assume such things as we both know they are really dross and literary ideas, but merely that I in my perhaps wilder schizophrenia actually *ran* on foot along the car and at incredible speeds sometimes ninety, making it over every bush and fence and farmhouse and sometimes taking quick dashes to the hills and back without losing a moment's ground . . .'

We were telling these things and both sweating. We had completely forgotten the people up front who had begun to wonder what was going on in the back seat. At one point the driver said, 'For God's sakes, you're rocking the boat back there.' Actually we were; the car was swaying as Dean and I both swayed to the rhythm and the IT of our final excited joy in talking and living to the blank tranced end of all innumerable riotous angelic particulars that had been lurking in our souls all our lives.

'Oh, man! man! man!' moaned Dean. 'And it's not even the beginning of it – and now here we are at last going east together, we've never gone east together, Sal, think of it, we'll dig Denver together and see what everybody's doing although that matters little to us, the point being that we know what IT is and we know TIME and we know that everything is really FINE.' Then he whispered, clutching my sleeve, sweating, 'Now you just dig them in front. They have worries, they're counting the miles, they're thinking about where to sleep tonight, how much money for gas, the weather, how they'll get there – and all the time they'll get there anyway, you see. But they need to worry and betray time with urgencies false and otherwise, purely anxious and whiny, their souls really won't be at peace unless they can latch on to an established and proven worry and having once found it they assume facial expressions to fit and go with it, which is, you see, unhappiness, and all the time it all flies by them and they know it and that *too* worries them no end. Listen! Listen! "Well now,"' he mimicked, '"I don't know — maybe we shouldn't get gas in that station. I read recently in *National Petroffious Petroleum News* that this kind of gas has a great deal of O-Octane *gook* in it and someone once told me it even had semi-official high-frequency *cock* in it, and I don't know, well I just don't feel like it anyway ..." Man, you dig all this.' He was poking me furiously in the ribs to understand. I tried my wildest best. Bing, bang, it was all Yes! Yes! Yes! in the back seat and the people up front were mopping their brows with fright and wishing they'd never picked us up at the travel bureau. It was only the beginning, too.

In Sacramento the fag slyly bought a room in a hotel and invited Dean and me to come up for a drink, while the couple went to sleep at relatives', and in the hotel room Dean tried everything in the book to get money from the fag. It was insane. The fag began by saying he was very glad we had come along because he liked young men like us, and would we believe it, but he really didn't like girls and had recently concluded an affair with a man in Frisco in which he had taken the male role and the man the female role. Dean plied him with businesslike questions and nodded eagerly. The fag said he would like nothing better than to know what Dean thought about all this. Warning him first that he had once been a hustler in his youth, Dean asked him how much money he had. I was in the bathroom. The fag became extremely sullen and I think suspicious of Dean's final motives, turned over no money, and made vague promises for Denver. He kept counting his money and checking on his wallet. Dean threw up his hands and gave up. 'You see, man, it's better not to bother. Offer them what they secretly want and they of course immediately become panic-stricken.' But he had sufficiently conquered the owner of the Plymouth to take over the wheel without remonstrance, and now we really travelled.

We left Sacramento at dawn and were crossing the Nevada

desert by noon, after a hurling passage of the Sierras that made the fag and the tourists cling to each other in the back seat. We were in front, we took over. Dean was happy again. All he needed was a wheel in his hand and four on the road. He talked about how bad a driver Old Bull Lee was and to demonstrate – 'Whenever a huge big truck like that one coming loomed into sight it would take Bull infinite time to spot it, 'cause he couldn't see, man, he can't *see*.' He rubbed his eyes furiously to show. 'And I'd say, "Whoop, look out, Bull, a truck", and he'd say, "Eh? what's that you say, Dean?" "Truck! truck!" and at the *very* last *moment* he would go right up to the truck like this –' And Dean hurled the Plymouth head-on at the truck roaring our way, wobbled and hovered in front of it a moment, the truckdriver's face growing grey before our eyes, the people in the back seat subsiding in gasps of horror, and swung away at the last moment. 'Like that, you see, exactly like that, how bad he was.' I wasn't scared at all; I knew Dean. The people in the back seat were speechless. In fact they were afraid to complain : God knew what Dean would do, they thought, if they should ever complain. He balled right across the desert in this manner, demonstrating various ways of how not to drive, how his father used to drive jalopies, how great drivers made curves, how bad drivers hove over too far in the beginning and had to scramble at the curve's end, and so on. It was a hot, sunny afternoon. Reno, Battle Mountain, Elko, all the towns along the Nevada road, shot by one after another, and at dusk we were in the Salt Lake flats with the lights of Salt Lake City infinitesimally glimmering almost a hundred miles across the mirage of the flats, twice showing, above and below the curve of the earth, one clear, one dim. I told Dean that the thing that bound us all together in this world was invisible, and to prove it pointed to long lines of telephone poles that curved off out of sight over the bend of a hundred miles of salt. His floppy bandage, all dirty now, shuddered in the air, his face was a light. 'Oh yes, man, dear God, yes, yes!' Suddenly he stopped the car and collapsed. I turned and saw him huddled in the corner of the seat, sleeping. His face was down on his good hand, and the bandaged hand automatically and dutifully remained in the air.

The people in the back seat sighed with relief. I heard them whispering mutiny. 'We can't let him drive any more, he's absolutely crazy, they must have let him out of an asylum or something.'

I rose to Dean's defence and leaned back to talk to them. 'He's not crazy, he'll be all right, and don't worry about his driving, he's the best in the world.'

'I just can't stand it,' said the girl in a suppressed, hysterical whisper. I sat back and enjoyed nightfall on the desert and waited for poorchild Angel Dean to wake up again. We were on a hill overlooking Salt Lake City's neat patterns of light and he opened his eyes to the place in this spectral world where he was born, unnamed and bedraggled, years ago.

'Sal, Sal, look, this is where I was born, think of it! People change, they eat meals year after year and change with every meal. EE! Look!' He was so excited it made me cry. Where would it all lead? The tourists insisted on driving the car the rest of the way to Denver. Okay, we didn't care. We sat in the back and talked. But they got too tired in the morning and Dean took the wheel in the eastern Colorado desert at Craig. We had spent almost the entire night crawling cautiously over Strawberry Pass in Utah and lost a lot of time. They went to sleep. Dean headed pellmell for the mighty wall of Berthoud Pass that stood a hundred miles ahead on the roof of the world, a tremendous Gibraltarian door shrouded in clouds. He took Berthoud Pass like a June bug – same as at Tehachapi, cutting off the motor and floating it, passing everybody and never halting the rhythmic advance that the mountains themselves intended, till we overlooked the great hot plain of Denver again – and Dean was home.

It was with a great deal of silly relief that these people let us off the car at the corner of 27th and Federal. Our battered suitcases were piled on the sidewalk again; we had longer ways to go. But no matter, the road is life.

6

NOW we had a number of circumstances to deal with in Denver, and they were of an entirely different order from those of 1947. We could either get another travel-bureau car at once or stay a few days for kicks and look for his father.

We were both exhausted and dirty. In the john of a restaurant I was at a urinal blocking Dean's way to the sink and I stepped out before I was finished and resumed at another urinal, and said to Dean, 'Dig this trick.'

'Yes, man,' he said, washing his hands at the sink, 'it's a very good trick but awful on your kidneys and because you're getting a little older now every time you do this eventually it's years of misery in your old age, awful kidney miseries for the days when you sit in parks.'

It made me mad. 'Who's old? I'm not much older than you are!'

'I wasn't saying that, man!'

'Ah,' I said, 'you're always making cracks about my age. I'm no old fag like that fag, you don't have to warn me about *my* kidneys.' We went back to the booth and just as the waitress set down the hot-roast-beef sandwiches – and ordinarily Dean would have leaped to wolf the food at once – I said to cap my anger, 'And I don't want to hear any more of it.' And suddenly Dean's eyes grew tearful and he got up and left his food steaming there and walked out of the restaurant. I wondered if he was just wandering off forever. I didn't care, I was so mad – I had flipped momentarily and turned it down on Dean. But the sight of his uneaten food made me sadder than anything in years. I shouldn't have said that ... he likes to eat so much ... He's never left his food like this ... What the hell. That's showing him, anyway.

Dean stood outside the restaurant for exactly five minutes and then came back and sat down. 'Well,' I said, 'what were you doing out there, knotting up your fists? Cursing me, thinking up new gags about my kidneys?'

Dean mutely shook his head. 'No, man, no, man, you're all completely wrong. If you want to know, well –'

'Go ahead, tell me.' I said all this and never looked up from my food. I felt like a beast.

'I was crying,' said Dean.

'Ah hell, you never cry.'

'You say that? Why do you think I don't cry?'

'You don't die enough to cry.' Every one of these things I said was a knife at myself. Everything I had ever secretly held against my brother was coming out: how ugly I was and what filth I was discovering in the depths of my own impure psychologies.

Dean was shaking his head. 'No, man, I was crying.'

'Go on, I bet you were so mad you had to leave.'

'Believe me, Sal, really do believe me if you've ever believed anything about me.' I knew he was telling the truth and yet I didn't want to bother with the truth and when I looked up at him I think I was cockeyed from cracked intestinal twistings in my awful belly. Then I knew I was wrong.

'Ah, man, Dean, I'm sorry, I never acted this way before with you. Well, now you know me. You know I don't have close relationships with anybody any more – I don't know what to do with these things. I hold things in my hand like pieces of crap and don't know where to put it down. Let's forget it.' The holy con-man began to eat. 'It's not my fault! it's not my fault!' I told him. 'Nothing in this lousy world is my fault, don't you see that? I don't want it to be and it can't be and it *won't* be.'

'Yes, man, yes, man. But please harken back and believe me.'

'I do believe you, I do.' This was the sad story of that afternoon. All kinds of tremendous complications arose that night when Dean and I went to stay with the Okie family.

These had been neighbours of mine in my Denver solitude of two weeks before. The mother was a wonderful woman in jeans who drove coal trucks in winter mountains to support her kids, four in all, her husband having left her years before when they were travelling around the country in a trailer. They had rolled all the way from Indiana to LA in that trailer.

After many a good time and a big Sunday-afternoon drunk in crossroads bars and laughter and guitar-playing in the night, the big lout had suddenly walked off across the dark field and never returned. Her children were wonderful. The eldest was a boy, who wasn't around that summer but in a camp in the mountains; next was a lovely thirteen-year-old daughter who wrote poetry and picked flowers in the fields and wanted to grow up and be an actress in Hollywood, Janet by name; then came the little ones, little Jimmy who sat around the campfire at night and cried for his 'pee-tater' before it was half roasted, and little Lucy who made pets of worms, horny toads, beetles, and anything that crawled, and gave them names and places to live. They had four dogs. They lived their ragged and joyous lives on the little new-settlement street and were the butt of the neighbours' semi-respectable sense of propriety only because the poor woman's husband had left her and because they littered up the yard. At night all the lights of Denver lay like a great wheel on the plain below, for the house was in that part of the West where the mountains roll down foothilling to the plain and where in primeval times soft waves must have washed from sea-like Mississippi to make such round and perfect stools for the island-peaks like Evans and Pike and Longs. Dean went there and of course he was all sweats and joy at the sight of them, especially Janet, but I warned him not to touch her, and probably didn't have to. The woman was a great man's woman and took to Dean right away but she was bashful and he was bashful. She said Dean reminded her of the husband gone. 'Just like him – oh, he was a crazy one, I tell ya!'

The result was uproarious beer-drinking in the littered living room, shouting suppers, and booming Lone Ranger radio. The complications rose like clouds of butterflies: the woman – Frankie, everyone called her – was finally about to buy a jalopy as she had been threatening to do for years, and had recently come into a few bucks towards one. Dean immediately took over the responsibility of selecting and naming the price of the car, because of course he wanted to use it himself so as of yore he could pick up girls coming out of high school in the afternoons and drive them up to the mountains. Poor innocent

Frankie was always agreeable to anything. But she was afraid to part with her money when they got to the car lot and stood before the salesman. Dean sat right down in the dust of Alameda Boulevard and beat his fists on his head. 'For a hunnerd you *can't* get anything better!' He swore he'd never talk to her again, he cursed till his face was purple, he was about to jump in the car and drive it away anyway. 'Oh these dumb dumb dumb Okies, they'll never change, how com-pletely and how unbelievably dumb, the moment it comes time to act, this paralysis, scared, hysterical, nothing frightens 'em more than what they *want* – it's *my father my father my father* all over again!'

Dean was very excited that night because his cousin Sam Brady was meeting us at a bar. He was wearing a clean T-shirt and beaming all over. 'Now listen, Sal, I must tell you about Sam – he's my cousin.'

'By the way, have you looked for your father?'

'This afternoon, man, I went down to Jiggs' Buffet where he used to pour draught beer in tender befuddlement and get hell from the boss and go staggering out – no – and I went to the old barbershop next to the Windsor – no, not there – old fella told me he thought he was – imagine! – working in a railroad gandy-dancing cookshack or sumpin for the *Boston and Maine* in New England! But I don't believe him, they make up fractious stories for a dime. Now listen to hear. In my childhood Sam Brady my close cousin was my absolute hero. He used to bootleg whisky from the mountains and one time he had a tremendous fist fight with his brother that lasted two hours in the yard and had the women screaming and terrified. We used to sleep together. The one man in the family who took tender concern for me. And tonight I'm going to see him again for the first time in seven years, he just got back from Missouri.'

'And what's the pitch?'

'No pitch, man, I only want to know what's been happening in the family – I have a family, remember – and most particularly, Sal, I want him to tell me things that I've forgotten in my childhood. I want to remember, remember, I do!' I never saw Dean so glad and excited. While we waited for his cousin in the bar he talked to a lot of younger downtown hipsters and hustlers and checked on new gangs and goings-on. Then he made inquiries after Marylou, since she'd been in Denver recently. 'Sal, in my young days when I used to come to this corner to steal change off the newsstand for bowery beef stew, that rough-looking cat you see out there standing had nothing but murder in his heart, got into one horrible fight after another, I remember his scars even, till now years and y-e-a-r-s of standing on the corner have finally softened him and chastened him ragely, here completely he's become sweet and willing and patient with everybody, he's become a *fixture* on the corner, you see how things happen?'

Then Sam arrived, a wiry, curly-haired man of thirty-five with work-gnarled hands. Dean stood in awe before him. 'No,' said Sam Brady, 'I don't drink any more.'

'See? See?' whispered Dean in my ear. 'He doesn't drink any more and he used to be the biggest whiskyleg in town; he's got religion now, he told me over the phone, dig him, dig the change in a man – my hero has become so strange.' Sam Brady was suspicious of his young cousin. He took us out for a spin in his old rattly coupe and immediately he made his position clear in regard to Dean.

'Now look, Dean, I don't believe you any more or anything you're going to try to tell me. I came to see you tonight because there's a paper I want you to sign for the family. Your father is no longer mentioned among us and we want absolutely nothing to do with him, and, I'm sorry to say, with you either, any more.' I looked at Dean. His face dropped and darkened.

'Yass, yass,' he said. The cousin continued to drive us around and even bought us ice-cream pops. Nevertheless Dean plied him with innumerable questions about the past and the cousin supplied the answers and for a moment Dean almost began to sweat again with excitement. Oh, where was his raggedy father that night? The cousin dropped us off at the sad lights of a carnival on Alameda Boulevard at Federal. He made an appointment with Dean for the paper-signing next afternoon and left. I told Dean I was sorry he had nobody in the world to believe in him.

'Remember that I believe in you. I'm infinitely sorry for the foolish grievance I held against you yesterday afternoon.'

'All right, man, it's agreed,' said Dean. We dug the carnival together. There were merry-go-rounds, Ferris wheels, popcorn, roulette wheels, sawdust, and hundreds of young Denver kids in jeans wandering around. Dust rose to the stars together with every sad music on earth. Dean was wearing washed-out tight levis and a T-shirt and looked suddenly like a real Denver character again. There were motorcycle kids with visors and moustaches and beaded jackets hanging around the shrouds in back of the tents with pretty girls in levis and rose shirts. There were a lot of Mexican girls too, and one amazing little girl about three feet high, a midget, with the most beautiful and tender face in the world, who turned to her companion and said, 'Man, let's call up Gomez and cut out.' Dean stopped dead in his tracks at the sight of her. A great knife stabbed him from the darkness of the night. 'Man, I love her, oh, *love* her . . .' We had to follow her around for a long time. She finally went across the highway to make a phone call in a motel booth and Dean pretended to be looking through the pages of the directory but was really all wound tight watching her. I tried to open up a conversation with the lovey-doll's friends but they paid no attention to us. Gomez arrived in a rattly truck and took the girls off. Dean stood in the road, clutching his breast. 'Oh, man, I almost died . . .'

'Why the hell didn't you talk to her?'

'I can't, I couldn't . . .' We decided to buy some beer and go up to Okie Frankie's and play records. We hitched on the road with a bag of beer cans. Little Janet, Frankie's thirteen-year-old daughter, was the prettiest girl in the world and was about to grow up into a gone woman. Best of all were her long, tapering, sensitive fingers that she used to talk with, like a Cleopatra Nile dance. Dean sat in the farthest corner of the room, watching her with slitted eyes and saying, 'Yes, yes, yes.' Janet was already aware of him; she turned to me for protection. Previous months of that summer I had spent a lot of time with her, talking about books and little things she was interested in.

7

NOTHING happened that night; we went to sleep. Everything happened the next day. In the afternoon Dean and I went to downtown Denver for our various chores and to see the travel bureau for a car to New York. On the way home in the late afternoon we started out for Okie Frankie's, up Broadway, where Dean suddenly sauntered into a sports-goods store, calmly picked up a softball on the counter, and came out, popping it up and down in his palm. Nobody noticed; nobody ever notices such things. It was a drowsy, hot afternoon. We played catch as we went along. 'We'll get a travel-bureau car for sure tomorrow.'

A woman friend had given me a big quart of Old Grand-dad bourbon. We started drinking it at Frankie's house. Across the cornfield in back lived a beautiful young chick that Dean had been trying to make ever since he arrived. Trouble was brewing. He threw too many pebbles in her window and frightened her. As we drank the bourbon in the littered living room with all its dogs and scattered toys and sad talk, Dean kept running out the back kitchen door and crossing the cornfield to throw pebbles and whistle. Once in a while Janet went out to peek. Suddenly Dean came back pale. 'Trouble, m'boy. That gal's mother is after me with a shotgun and she got a gang of high-school kids to beat me up from down the road.'

'What's this? Where are they?'

'Across the cornfield, m'boy.' Dean was drunk and didn't care. We went out together and crossed the cornfield in the moonlight. I saw groups of people on the dark dirt road.

'Here they come!' I heard.

'Wait a minute,' I said. 'What's the matter, please?'

The mother lurked in the background with a big shotgun across her arm. 'That damn friend of yours been annoying us long enough. I'm not the kind to call the law. If he comes back here once more I'm gonna shoot and shoot to kill.' The high-school boys were clustered with their fists knotted. I was so drunk I didn't care either, but I soothed everybody some.

I said, 'He won't do it again. I'll watch him; he's my brother and listens to me. Please put your gun away and don't bother about anything.'

'Just one more time!' she said firmly and grimly across the dark. 'When my husband gets home I'm sending him after you.'

'You don't have to do that; he won't bother you any more, understand. Now be calm and it's okay.' Behind me Dean was cursing under his breath. The girl was peeking from her bedroom window. I knew these people from before and they trusted me enough to quiet down a bit. I took Dean by the arm and back we went over the moony cornrows.

'Woo-hee!' he yelled. 'I'm gonna git drunk tonight.' We went back to Frankie and the kids. Suddenly Dean got mad at a record little Janet was playing and broke it over his knee: it was a hillbilly record. There was an early Dizzy Gillespie there that he valued – 'Congo Blues', with Max West on drums. I'd given it to Janet before, and I told her as she wept to take it and break it over Dean's head. She went over and did so. Dean gaped dumbly, sensing everything. We all laughed. Everything was all right. Then Frankie-Maw wanted to go out and drink beer in the roadhouse saloons. 'Lessgo!' yelled Dean. 'Now dammit, if you'd bought that car I showed you Tuesday we wouldn't have to walk.'

'I didn't like that damn car!' yelled Frankie. Yang, yang, the kids started to cry. Dense, mothlike eternity brooded in the crazy brown parlour with the sad wallpaper, the pink lamp, the excited faces. Little Jimmy was frightened; I put him to sleep on the couch and trussed the dog on him. Frankie drunkenly called a cab and suddenly while we were waiting for it a phone call came for me from my woman friend. She had a middle-aged cousin who hated my guts, and earlier that afternoon I had written a letter to Old Bull Lee, who was now in Mexico City, relating the adventures of Dean and myself and under what circumstances we were staying in Denver. I wrote: 'I have a woman friend who gives me whisky and money and big suppers.'

I foolishly gave this letter to her middle-aged cousin to mail, right after a fried-chicken supper. He opened it, read it, and took it at once to her to prove to her that I was a con-man. Now she was calling me tearfully and saying she never wanted to see me again. Then the triumphant cousin got on the phone and began calling me a bastard. As the cab honked outside and the kids cried and the dogs barked and Dean danced with Frankie I yelled every conceivable curse I could think over that phone and added all kinds of new ones, and in my drunken frenzy I told everybody over the phone to go to hell and slammed it down and went out to get drunk.

We stumbled over one another to get out of the cab at the roadhouse, a hillbilly roadhouse near the hills, and went in and ordered beers. Everything was collapsing, and to make things inconceivably more frantic there was an ecstatic spastic fellow in the bar who threw his arms around Dean and moaned in his face, and Dean went mad again with sweats and insanity, and to add still more to the unbearable confusion Dean rushed out the next moment and stole a car right from the driveway and took a dash to downtown Denver and came back with a newer, better one. Suddenly in the bar I looked up and saw cops and people were milling around the driveway in the headlights of cruisers, talking about the stolen car. 'Somebody's been stealing cars left and right here!' the cop was saying. Dean stood right in back of him, listening and saying, 'Ah yass, ah yass.' The cops went off to check. Dean came into the bar and rocked back and forth with the poor spastic kid who had just gotten married that day and was having a tremendous drunk while his bride waited somewhere. 'Oh, man, this guy is the greatest in the world!' yelled Dean. 'Sal, Frankie, I'm going out and get a real good car this time and we'll all go and with Tony too' (the spastic saint) 'and have a big drive in the mountains.' And he rushed out. Simultaneously a cop rushed in and said a car stolen from downtown Denver was parked in the driveway. People discussed it in knots. From the window I saw Dean jump into the nearest car and roar off, and not a soul noticed him. A few minutes later he was back in an entirely different car, a brand-new convertible. 'This one is a beaut!' he whispered in my ear. 'The other one coughed too much — I left it at the crossroads, saw that lovely parked in front of a farmhouse. Took a spin in Denver. Come on, man, let's *all* go riding.' All the bitterness and madness of his entire Denver life was blasting out of his system like daggers. His face was red and sweaty and mean.

'No, I ain't gonna have nothing to do with stolen cars.'

'Aw, come on, man! Tony'll come with me, won't you, amazing darling Tony?' And Tony – a thin, dark-haired, holy-eyed moaning foaming lost soul – leaned on Dean and groaned and groaned, for he was sick suddenly and then for some odd intuitive reason he became terrified of Dean and threw up his hands and drew away with terror writhing in his face. Dean bowed his head and sweated. He ran out and drove away. Frankie and I found a cab in the driveway and decided to go home. As the cabby drove us up the infinitely dark Alameda Boulevard along which I had walked many and many a lost night the previous months of the summer, singing and moaning and eating the stars and dropping the juices of my heart drop by drop on the hot tar, Dean suddenly hove up behind us in the stolen convertible and began tooting and tooting and crowding us over and screaming. The cabby's face grew white.

'Just a friend of mine,' I said. Dean got disgusted with us and suddenly shot ahead at ninety miles an hour, throwing spectral dust across the exhaust. Then he turned in at Frankie's road and pulled up in front of the house; just as suddenly he took off again, U-turned, and went back towards town as we got out of the cab and paid the fare. A few moments later as we waited anxiously in the dark yard, he returned with still another car, a battered coupe, stopped it in a cloud of dust in front of the house, and just staggered out and went straight into the bedroom and flopped dead drunk on the bed. And there we were with a stolen car right on our doorstep.

I had to wake him up; I couldn't get the car started to dump it somewhere far off. He stumbled out of bed, wearing just his jockey shorts, and we got in the car together, while the kids giggled from the windows, and went bouncing and flying straight over the hard alfalfa-rows at the end of the road whomp-ti-whomp till finally the car couldn't take any more and stopped dead under an old cottonwood near the old mill. 'Can't go any farther,' said Dean simply and got out and started walking back over the cornfield, about half a mile, in his shorts in the moonlight. We got back to the house and he went to sleep. Everything was in a horrible mess, all of Denver, my woman friend, cars, children, poor Frankie, the living-room splattered with beer cans, and I tried to sleep. A cricket kept me awake for some time. At night in this part of the West the stars, as I had seen them in Wyoming, are big as roman candles and as lonely as the Prince of the Dharma who's lost his ancestral grove and journeys across the spaces between points in the handle of the Big Dipper, trying to find it again. So they slowly wheeled the night, and then long before actual sunrise the great red light appeared far over the dun bleak land towards West Kansas and the birds took up their trill above Denver.

8

HORRIBLE nauseas possessed us in the morning. First thing Dean did was go out across the cornfield to see if the car would carry us East. I told him no, but he went anyway. He came back pale. 'Man, that's a detective's car and every precinct in town knows my fingerprints from the year that I stole five hundred cars. You see what I do with them, I just wanta ride, man! I gotta go! Listen, we're going to wind up in jail if we don't get out of here this very instant.'

'You're damned right,' I said, and we began packing as fast as our hands could go. Dangling neckties and shirttails, we said quick good-byes to our sweet little family and stumbled off towards the protective road where nobody would know us. Little Janet was crying to see us, or me, or whatever it was, go – and Frankie was courteous, and I kissed her and apologized.

'He sure is a crazy one,' she said. 'Sure reminds me of my husband that run away. Just exactly the same guy. I sure hope my Mickey don't grow up that way, they all do now.'

And I said good-bye to little Lucy, who had her pet beetle in her hand, and little Jimmy was asleep. All this in the space of seconds, in a lovely Sunday morning dawn, as we stumbled off with our wretched baggage. We hurried. Every minute we expected a cruising car to appear from around a country bend and come sloping for us.

'If that woman with the shotgun ever finds out, we're cooked,' said Dean. 'We *must* get a cab. Then we're safe.' We were about to wake up a farm family to use their phone, but the dog drove us away. Every minute things became more dangerous; the coupe would be found wrecked in the cornfield by an early-rising country man. One lovely old lady let us use her phone finally, and we called a downtown Denver cab, but he didn't come. We stumbled on down the road. Early-morning traffic began, every car looking like a cruiser. Then we suddenly saw the cruiser coming and I knew it was the end of my life as I had known it and that it was entering a new and horrible stage of jails and iron sorrows. But the cruiser was our taxi, and from that moment on we flew east.

At the travel bureau there was a tremendous offer for someone to drive a '47 Cadillac limousine to Chicago. The owner had been driving up from Mexico with his family and got tired and put them all on a train. All he wanted was identification and for the car to get there. My papers assured him everything would come off right. I told him not to worry. I told Dean, 'And don't scrounge with this car.' Dean was jumping up and down with excitement to see it. We had to wait an hour. We lay on the grass near the church where in 1947 I had passed some time with panhandling hoboes after seeing Rita Bettencourt home, and there I fell asleep from sheer horror exhaustion with my face to the afternoon birds. In fact they were playing organ music somewhere. But Dean hustled around town. He talked up an acquaintance with a waitress in a luncheonette, made a date to take her driving in his Cadillac that afternoon, and came back to wake me with the news. Now I felt better. I rose to new complications.

When the Cadillac arrived, Dean instantly drove off with it 'to get gas', and the travel-bureau man looked at me and said, 'When's he coming back? The passengers are all ready to go.' He showed me two Irish boys from an Eastern Jesuit school waiting with their suitcases on the benches.

'He just went for gas. He'll be right back.' I cut down to the corner and watched Dean as he kept the motor running for the waitress, who had been changing in her hotel room; in fact I could see her from where I stood, in front of her mirror, primping and fixing her silk stockings, and I wished I could go along with them. She came running out and jumped in the Cadillac. I wandered back to reassure the travel-bureau boss and the passengers. From where I stood in the door I saw a faint flash of the Cadillac crossing Cleveland Place with Dean, T-shirted and joyous, fluttering his hands and talking to the girl and hunching over the wheel to go as she sat sadly and proudly beside him. They went to a parking lot in broad daylight, parked near the brick wall at the back (a lot Dean had worked in once), and there, he claims, he made it with her, in nothing flat; not only that but persuaded her to follow us east as soon as she had her pay on Friday, come by bus, and meet us at Ian MacArthur's pad on Lexington Avenue in New York. She agreed to come; her name was Beverly. Thirty minutes and Dean roared back, deposited the girl at her hotel, with kisses, farewells, promises, and zoomed right up to the travel bureau to pick up the crew.

'Well, it's about time!' said the Broadway Sam travel-bureau boss. 'I thought you'd gone off with that Cadillac.'

'It's my responsibility,' I said, 'don't worry' – and said that because Dean was in such obvious frenzy everybody could guess his madness. Dean became businesslike and assisted the Jesuit boys with their baggage. They were hardly seated, and I had hardly waved good-bye to Denver, before he was off, the big motor thrumming with immense birdlike power. Not two miles out of Denver the speedometer broke because Dean was pushing well over 110 miles an hour.

'Well, no speedometer, I won't know how fast I'm going. I'll just ball that jack to Chicago and tell by time.' It didn't seem we were even going seventy but all the cars fell from us like dead flies on the straightaway highway leading up to Greeley. 'Reason why we're going northeast is because, Sal, we must absolutely visit Ed Wall's ranch in Sterling, you've got to meet him and see his ranch and this boat cuts so fast we can make it without any time trouble and get to Chicago long before that man's train.' Okay, I was for it. It began to rain but Dean never slackened. It was a beautiful big car, the last of the old-style limousines, black, with a big elongated body and whitewall tyres and probably bulletproof windows. The Jesuit boys – St. Bonaventura – sat in the back, gleeful and glad to be underway, and they had no idea how fast we were going. They tried to talk but Dean said nothing and took off his T-shirt and drove barechested. 'Oh, that Beverly is a sweet gone little gal – she's going to join me in New York – we're going to get married as soon as I can get divorce papers from Camille – everything's jumping, Sal, and we're off. Yes!' The faster we left Denver the better I felt, and we were doing it *fast*. It grew dark when we turned off the highway at Junction and hit a dirt road that took us across dismal East Colorado plains to Ed Wall's ranch in the middle of Coyote Nowhere. But it was still raining and the mud was slippery and Dean slowed to seventy, but I told him to slow even more or we'd slide, and he said, 'Don't worry, man, you know me.'

'Not this time,' I said. 'You're really going much too fast.' And he was flying along there on that slippery mud and just as I said that we hit a complete left turn in the highway and Dean socked the wheel over to make it but the big car skidded in the grease and wobbled hugely.

'Look out!' yelled Dean, who didn't give a damn and wrestled with his Angel a moment, and we ended up backass in the ditch with the front out on the road. A great stillness fell over everything. We heard the whining wind. We were in the middle of the wild prairie. There was a farmhouse a quarter-mile up the road. I couldn't stop swearing, I was so mad and disgusted with Dean. He said nothing and went off to the farmhouse in the rain, with a coat, to look for help.

'Is he your brother?' the boys asked in the back seat. 'He's a devil with a car, isn't he – and according to his story he must be with the women.'

'He's mad,' I said, 'and yes, he's my brother.' I saw Dean coming back with the farmer in his tractor. They hooked chains on and the farmer hauled us of the ditch. The car was muddy brown, a whole fender was crushed. The farmer charged us five dollars. His daughters watched in the rain. The prettiest, shyest one hid far back in the field to watch and she had good reason because she was absolutely and finally the most beautiful girl Dean and I ever saw in all our lives. She was about sixteen, and had Plains complexion like wild roses, and the bluest eyes, the most lovely hair, and the modesty and quickness of a wild ante- lope. At every look from us she flinched. She stood there with the immense winds that blew clear down from Saskatchewan knocking her hair about her lovely head like shrouds, living curls of them. She blushed and blushed.

We finished our business with the farmer, took one last look at the prairie angel, and drove off, slower now, till dark came and Dean said Ed Wall's ranch was dead ahead. 'Oh, a girl like that scares me,' I said. 'I'd give up everything and throw myself on her mercy and if she didn't want me I'd just as simply go and throw myself off the edge of the world.' The Jesuit boys giggled. They were full of corny quips and Eastern college talk and had nothing on their bird-beans except a lot of ill-under- stood Aquinas for stuffing for their pepper. Dean and I paid absolutely no attention to them. As we crossed the muddy plains he told stories about his cowboy days, he showed us the stretch of road where he spent an entire morning riding; and where he'd done fence-mending as soon as we hit Wall's property, which was immense; and where old Wall, Ed's father, used to come clattering on the rangeland grass chasing a heifer and howling, 'Git im, git im, god-dammit!' 'He had to have a new car every six months,' said Dean. 'He just couldn't care. When a stray got away from us he'd drive right after it as far as the nearest waterhole and then get out and run after it on foot. Counted every cent he ever made and put it in a pot. A mad old Rancher. I'll show you some of his old wrecks near the bunkhouse. This is where I came on probation after my last hitch in a joint. This is where I lived when I wrote those letters you saw to Chad King.' We turned off the road and wound across a path through the winter pasture. A mournful group of whitefaced cows suddenly milled across our headlights. 'There they are! Wall's cows! We'll never be able to get through them. We'll have to get out and whoop em up! Hee-hee-hee!!'

But we didn't have to do that and only inched along through them, sometimes gently bumping as they milled and mooed like a sea around the car doors. Beyond we saw the light of Ed Wall's ranch house. Around this lonely light stretched hundreds of miles of plains.

The kind of utter darkness that falls on a prairie like that is inconceivable to an Easterner. There were no stars, no moon, no light whatever except the light of Mrs Wall's kitchen. What lay beyond the shadows of the yard was an endless view of the world that you wouldn't be able to see till dawn. After knocking on the door and calling out in the dark for Ed Wall, who was milking cows in the barn, I took a short careful walk into that darkness, about twenty feet and no more. I thought I heard coyotes. Wall said it was probably one of his father's wild horses whinnying in the distance. Ed Wall was about our age, tall, rangy, spike-toothed, laconic. He and Dean used to stand around on Curtis Street corners and whistle at girls. Now he took us graciously into his gloomy, brown, un-used parlour and fished around till he found dull lamps and lit them and said to Dean, 'What in the hell happened to yore thumb?'

'I socked Marylou and it got infected so much they had to amputate the end of it.'

'What in the hell did you go and do that for?' I could see he used to be Dean's older brother. He shook his head; the milk pail was still at his feet. 'You always been a crackbrained son-ofabitch anyhow.'

Meanwhile his young wife prepared a magnificent spread in the big ranch kitchen. She apologized for the peach ice cream: 'It ain't nothing but cream and peaches froze up together.' Of course it was the only real ice cream I ever had in my whole life. She started sparsely and ended up abundantly; as we ate, new things appeared on the table. She was a well-built blonde but like all women who live in the wide spaces she complained a little of the boredom. She enumerated the radio programmes she usually listened to at this time of night. Ed Wall sat just staring at his hands, Dean ate voraciously. He wanted me to go along with him in the fiction that I owned the Cadillac, that I was a very rich man and that he was my friend and chauffeur.

215

It made no impression on Ed Wall. Every time the stock made sounds in the barn he raised his head to listen.

'Well, I hope you boys make it to New York.' Far from believing that tale about my owning the Cadillac, he was convinced Dean had stolen it. We stayed at the ranch about an hour. Ed Wall had lost faith in Dean just like Sam Brady – he looked at him warily when he looked. There were riotous days in the past when they had stumbled around the streets of Laramie, Wyoming, arm-in-arm when the haying was over, but all this was dead and gone.

Dean hopped in his chair convulsively. 'Well yes, well yes, and now I think we'd better be cutting along because we gotta be in Chicago by tomorrow night and we've already wasted several hours.' The college boys thanked Wall graciously and we were off again. I turned to watch the kitchen light recede in the sea of night. Then I leaned ahead.

9

IN no time at all we were back on the main highway and that night I saw the entire state of Nebraska unroll before my eyes. A hundred and ten miles an hour straight through, an arrow road, sleeping towns, no traffic, and the Union Pacific streamliner falling behind us in the moonlight. I wasn't frightened at all that night; it was perfectly legitimate to go 110 and talk and have all the Nebraska towns – Ogallala, Gothenburg, Kearney, Grand Island, Columbus – unreel with dreamlike rapidity as we roared ahead and talked. It was a magnificent car; it could hold the road like a boat holds on water. Gradual curves were its singing ease. 'Ah, man, what a dreamboat,' sighed Dean. 'Think if you and I had a car like this what we could do. Do you know there's a road that goes down Mexico and all the way to Panama? – and maybe all the way to the bottom of South America where the Indians are seven feet tall and eat cocaine on the mountainside? Yes! You and I, Sal, we'd dig the whole world with a car like this because, man, the road must eventually lead to the whole world. Ain't nowhere else it can go – right? Oh, and are we going to cut around old Chi with this thing! Think of it, Sal, I've never been to Chicago in all my life, never stopped.'

'We'll come in there like gangsters in this Cadillac!'

'Yes! And girls! We can pick up girls, in fact, Sal, I've decided to make extra-special fast time so we can have an entire evening to cut around in this thing. Now you just relax and I'll ball the jack all the way.'

'Well, how fast are you going now?'

'A steady one-ten I figure — you wouldn't notice it. We've still got all Iowa in the daytime and then I'll make that old Illinois in nothing flat.' The boys fell asleep and we talked and talked all night.

It was remarkable how Dean could go mad and then suddenly continue with his soul — which I think is wrapped up in a fast car, a coast to reach, and a woman at the end of the road — calmly and sanely as though nothing had happened. 'I get like that every time in Denver now — I can't make that town any more. Gookly, gooky, Dean's a spooky. Zoom!' I told him I had been over this Nebraska road before in '47. He had too. 'Sal, when I was working for the New Era Laundry in Los Angeles, nineteen forty-four, falsifying my age, I made a trip to Indianapolis Speedway for the express purpose of seeing the Memorial Day classic hitch, hiking by day and stealing cars by night to make time. Also I had a twenty-dollar Buick back in LA, my first car, it couldn't pass the brake and light inspection so I decided I needed an out-of-state licence to operate the car without arrest so went through here to get the licence. As I was hitch-hiking through one of these very towns, with the plates concealed under my coat, a nosy sheriff who thought I was pretty young to be hitch-hiking accosted me on the main drag. He found the plates and threw me in the two-cell jail with a county delinquent who should have been in the home for the old since he couldn't feed himself (the sheriff's wife fed him) and sat through the day drooling and slobbering. After investigation, which included corny things like a fatherly quiz, then an abrupt turnabout to frighten me with threats, a comparison of my handwriting, et cetera, and after I made the most magnificent speech of my life to get out of it, concluding with the confession that I was lying about my car-stealing past and was only looking for my paw who was a farmhand hereabouts, he let me go. Of course I missed the races. The following fall I did the same thing again to see the Notre Dame–California game in South Bend, Indiana – trouble none this time and, Sal, I had just the money for the ticket and not an extra cent and didn't eat anything all up and back except for what I could panhandle from all kinds of crazy cats I met on the road and at the same time gun gals. Only guy in the United States of America that ever went to so much trouble to see a ball-game.'

I asked him the circumstances of his being in LA in 1944. 'I was arrested in Arizona, the joint absolutely the worst joint I've ever been in. I had to escape and pulled the greatest escape in my life, speaking of escapes, you see, in a general way. In the woods, you know, and crawling, and swamps – up around that mountain country. Rubber hoses and the works and accidental so-called death facing me I had to cut out of those woods along the ridge so as to keep away from trails and paths and roads. Had to get rid of my joint clothes and sneaked the neatest theft of a shirt and pants from a gas station outside Flagstaff, arriving LA two days later clad as gas attendant and walked to the first station I saw and got myself a room and changed name (Lee Buliay) and spent an exciting year in LA, including a whole gang of new friends and some really great girls, that season ending when we were all driving on Hollywood Boulevard one night and I told my buddy to steer the car while I kissed my girl – I was at the wheel, see – and *he didn't hear me* and we ran smack into a post but only going twenty and I broke my nose. You've seen before my nose – the crooked Grecian curve up here. After that I went to Denver and met Marylou in a soda fountain that spring. Oh, man, she was only fifteen and wearing jeans and just waiting for someone to pick her up. Three days three nights of talk in the Ace Hotel, third floor, southeast corner room, holy memento room and sacred scene of my days – she was so sweet then, so *young*, hmm, ahh! But hey, look down there in the night thar, hup, hup, a buncha old bums by a fire by the rail, damn me.' He almost slowed down. 'You see, I never know whether my father's there or not.' There were some figures by the tracks, reeling in front of

a woodfire. 'I never know whether to ask. He might be anywhere.' We drove on. Somewhere behind us or in front of us in
the huge night his father lay drunk under a bush, and no doubt
about it – spittle on his chin, water on his pants, molasses in his
ears, scabs on his nose, maybe blood in his hair and the moon
shining down on him.

I took Dean's arm. 'Ah, man, we're sure going home now.'
New York was going to be his permanent home for the first
time. He jiggled all over; he couldn't wait.

'And think, Sal, when we get to Pennsy we'll start hearing
that gone Eastern bop on the disc jockeys. Geeyah, roll, old
boat, roll!' The magnificent car made the wind roar; it made
the plains unfold like a roll of paper; it cast hot tar from itself
with deference – an imperial boat. I opened my eyes to a fan-
ning dawn; we were hurling up to it. Dean's rocky dogged
face as ever bent over the dashlight with a bony purpose of its
own.

'What are you thinking, Pops?'

'Ah-ha, ah-ha, same old thing, y'know – gurls gurls gurls.'

I went to sleep and woke up to the dry, hot atmosphere of
July Sunday morning in Iowa, and still Dean was driving and
driving and had not slackened his speed; he took the curvy
corndales of Iowa at a minimum of eighty and the straightaway
110 as usual, unless both-ways traffic forced him to fall in line
at a crawling and miserable sixty. When there was a chance he
shot ahead and passed cars by the half-dozen and left them behind in a cloud of dust. A mad guy in a brand-new Buick saw
all this on the road and decided to race us. When Dean was just
about to pass a passel the guy shot by us without warning and
howled and tooted his horn and flashed the tail lights for challenge. We took off after him like a big bird. 'Now wait,' laughed
Dean, 'I'm going to tease that sonofabitch for a dozen miles or
so. Watch.' He let the Buick go way ahead and then accelerated
and caught up with it most impolitely. Mad Buick went out of
his mind; he gunned up to a hundred. We had a chance to see
who he was. He seemed to be some kind of Chicago hipster
travelling with a woman old enough to be – and probably actually was – his mother. God knows if she was complaining, but
he raced. His hair was dark and wild, and Italian from old Chi;

he wore a sports shirt. Maybe there was an idea in his mind that we were a new gang from LA invading Chicago, maybe some of Mickey Cohen's men, because the limousine looked every bit the part and the licence plates were California. Mainly it was just road kicks. He took terrible chances to stay ahead of us; he passed cars on curves and barely got back in line as a truck wobbled into view and loomed up huge. Eighty miles of Iowa we unreeled in this fashion, and the race was so interesting that I had no opportunity to be frightened. Then the mad guy gave up, pulled up at a gas station, probably on orders from the old lady, and as we roared by he waved gleefully. On we sped, Dean barechested, I with my feet on the dashboard, and the college boys sleeping in the back. We stopped to eat breakfast at a diner run by a white-haired lady who gave us extra-large portions of potatoes as church-bells rang in the nearby town. Then off again.

'Dean, don't drive so fast in the daytime.'

'Don't worry, man, I know what I'm doing.' I began to flinch. Dean came up on lines of cars like the Angel of Terror. He almost rammed them along as he looked for an opening. He teased their bumpers, he eased and pushed and craned around to see the curve, then the huge car leaped to his touch and passed, and always by a hair we made it back to our side as other lines filed by in the opposite direction and I shuddered. I couldn't take it any more. It is only seldom that you find a long Nebraskan straightaway in Iowa, and when we finally hit one Dean made his usual 110 and I saw flashing by outside several scenes that I remembered from 1947 – a long stretch where Eddie and I had been stranded two hours. All that old road of the past unreeling dizzily as if the cup of life had been overturned and everything gone mad. My eyes ached in nightmare day.

'Ah hell, Dean, I'm going in the back seat, I can't stand it any more, I can't look.'

'Hee-hee-hee!' tittered Dean and he passed a car on a narrow bridge and swerved in dust and roared on. I jumped in the back seat and curled up to sleep. One of the boys jumped in front for the fun. Great horrors that we were going to crash this very morning took hold of me and I got down on the floor and closed my eyes and tried to go to sleep. As a seaman I used to think of the waves rushing beneath the shell of the ship and the bottomless deeps thereunder – now I could feel the road some twenty inches beneath me, unfurling and flying and hissing at incredible speeds across the groaning continent with that mad Ahab at the wheel. When I closed my eyes all I could see was the road unwinding into me. When I opened them I saw flashing shadows of trees vibrating on the floor of the car. There was no escaping it. I resigned myself to all. And still Dean drove, he had no thought of sleeping till we got to Chicago. In the afternoon we crossed old Des Moines again. Here of course we got snarled in traffic and had to go slow and I got back in the front seat. A strange pathetic accident took place. A fat coloured man was driving with his entire family in a sedan in front of us; on the rear bumper hung one of those canvas desert waterbags they sell tourists in the desert. He pulled up sharp, Dean was talking to the boys in the back and didn't notice, and we rammed him at five miles an hour smack on the waterbag, which burst like a boil and squirted water in the air. No other damage except a bent bumper. Dean and I got out to talk to him. The upshot of it was an exchange of addresses and some talk, and Dean not taking his eyes off the man's wife whose beautiful brown breasts were barely concealed inside a floppy cotton blouse. 'Yass, yass.' We gave him the address of our Chicago baron and went on.

The other side of Des Moines a cruising car came after us with the siren growling, with orders to pull over. 'Now what?'

The cop came out. 'Were you in an accident coming in?'

'Accident? We broke a guy's waterbag at the junction.'

'He says he was hit and run by a bunch in a stolen car.' This was one of the few instances Dean and I knew of a Negro's acting like a suspicious old fool. It so surprised us we laughed. We had to follow the patrolman to the station and there spent an hour waiting in the grass while they telephoned Chicago to get the owner of the Cadillac and verify our position as hired drivers. Mr Baron said, according to the cop, 'Yes, that is my car but I can't vouch for anything else those boys might have done.'

'They were in a minor accident in Des Moines.'

'Yes, you've already told me that – what I meant was, I can't vouch for anything they might have done in the past.'

Everything was straightened out and we roared on. Newton, Iowa, it was, where I'd taken that dawn walk in 1947. In the afternoon we crossed drowsy old Davenport again and the low-lying Mississippi in her sawdust bed; then Rock Island, a few minutes of traffic, the sun reddening, and sudden sights of lovely little tributary rivers flowing softly among the magic trees and greeneries of mid-American Illinois. It was beginning to look like the soft sweet East again; the great dry West was accomplished and done. The state of Illinois unfolded before my eyes in one vast movement that lasted a matter of hours as Dean balled straight across at the same speed. In his tiredness he was taking greater chances than ever. At a narrow bridge that crossed one of those lovely little rivers he shot precipi-tately into an almost impossible situation. Two slow cars ahead of us were bumping over the bridge; coming the other way was a huge truck-trailer with a driver who was making a close esti-mate of how long it would take the slow cars to negotiate the bridge, and his estimate was that by the time he got there they'd be over. There was absolutely no room on the bridge for the truck and any cars going the other direction. Behind the truck cars pulled out and peeked for a chance to get by it. In front of the slow cars other slow cars were pushing along. The road was crowded and everyone exploding to pass. Dean came down on all this at 110 miles an hour and never hesitated. He passed the slow cars, swerved, and almost hit the left rail of the bridge, went head-on into the shadow of the unslowing truck, cut right sharply, just missed the truck's left front wheel, almost hit the first slow car, pulled out to pass, and then had to cut back in line when another car came out from behind the truck to look, all in a matter of two seconds, flashing by and leaving nothing more than a cloud of dust instead of a horrible five-way crash with cars lurching in every direction and the great truck humping its back in the fatal red afternoon of Illinois with its dreaming fields. I couldn't get it out of my mind, also, that a famous bop clarinettist had died in an Illinois car-crash recently, probably on a day like this. I went to the back seat again.

The boys stayed in the back too now. Dean was bent on Chicago before nightfall. At a road-rail junction we picked up two hobos who rounded up a half-buck between them for gas. A moment before sitting around piles of railroad ties, polishing off the last of some wine, now they found themselves in a muddy but unbowed and splendid Cadillac limousine headed for Chicago in precipitous haste. In fact the old boy up front who sat next to Dean never took his eyes off the road and prayed his poor bum prayers, I tell you. 'Well,' they said, 'we never knew we'd get to Chicago so fast.' As we swept drowsy Illinois towns where the people are so conscious of Chicago gangs that pass like this in limousines every day, we were a strange sight; all of us unshaven, the driver barechested, two bums, myself in the back seat, holding on to a strap and my head leaned back on the cushion looking at the countryside with an imperious eye – just like a new California gang come to contest the spoils of Chicago, a band of desperadoes escaped from the prisons of the Utah moon. When we stopped for Cokes and gas at a small-town station people came out to stare at us but they never said a word and I think made mental notes of our descriptions and heights in case of future need. To transact business with the girl who ran the gas-pump Dean merely threw on his T-shirt like a scarf and was curt and abrupt as usual and got back in the car and off we roared again. Pretty soon the redness turned purple, the last of the enchanted rivers flashed by, and we saw distant smokes of Chicago beyond the drive. We had come from Denver to Chicago via Ed Wall's ranch, 1,180 miles, in exactly seventeen hours, not counting the two hours in the ditch and three at the ranch and two with the police in Newton, Iowa, for a mean average of seventy miles per hour across the land, with one driver. Which is a kind of crazy record.

10

GREAT Chicago glowed red before our eyes. We were suddenly on Madison Street among hordes of hobos, some of them sprawled out on the street with their feet on the curb, hundreds of others milling in the doorways of saloons and alleys. 'Wup! wup! look sharp for old Dean Moriarty there, he may be in Chicago by accident this year.' We let out the hobos on this street and proceeded to downtown Chicago. Screeching trolleys, newsboys, gals cutting by, the smell of fried food and beer in the air, neons winking – 'We're in the big town, Sal! Whooee!' First thing to do was park the Cadillac in a good dark spot and wash up and dress for the night. Across the street from the YMCA we found a red-brick alley between buildings, where we stashed the Cadillac with her snout pointed to the street and ready to go, then followed the college boys up to the Y, where they got a room and allowed us to use their facilities for an hour. Dean and I shaved and showered, I dropped my wallet in the hall, Dean found it and was about to sneak it in his shirt when he realized it was ours and was right disappointed. Then we said good-bye to those boys, who were glad they'd made it in one piece, and took off to eat in a cafeteria. Old brown Chicago with the strange semi-Eastern, semi-Western types going to work and spitting. Dean stood in the cafeteria rubbing his belly and taking it all in. He wanted to talk to a strange middle-aged coloured woman who had come into the cafeteria with a story about how she had no money but she had buns with her and would they give her butter. She came in flapping her hips, was turned down, and went out flipping her butt. 'Whoo!' said Dean. 'Let's follow her down the street, let's take her to the ole Cadillac in the alley. We'll have a ball.' But we forgot that and headed straight for North Clark Street, after a spin in the Loop, to see the hootchy-kootchy joints and hear the bop. And what a night it was. 'Oh, man,' said Dean to me as we stood in front of a bar, 'dig the street of life, the Chinamen that cut by in Chicago. What a weird town – wow, and that woman in that window up there, just looking down with her big breasts hanging from her nightgown, big wide eyes. Whee. Sal, we gotta go and never stop going till we get there.'

'Where we going, man?'

'I don't know but we gotta go.' Then here came a gang of young bop musicians carrying their instruments out of cars. They piled right into a saloon and we followed them. They set themselves up and started blowing. There we were! The leader was a slender, drooping, curly-haired, pursy-mouthed tenorman, thin of shoulder, draped loose in a sports shirt, cool in the warm night, self-indulgence written in his eyes, who picked up his horn and frowned in it and blew cool and complex and was dainty stamping his foot to catch ideas, and ducked to miss others – and said, 'Blow', very quietly when the other boys took solos. Then there was Prez, a husky, handsome blond like a freckled boxer, meticulously wrapped inside his sharkskin plaid suit with the long drape and the collar falling back and the tie undone for exact sharpness and casualness, sweating and hitching up his horn and writhing into it, and a tone just like Lester Young himself. 'You see, man, Prez has the technical anxieties of a money-making musician, he's the only one who's well dressed, see him grow worried when he blows a clinker, but the leader, that cool cat, tells him not to worry and just blow and blow – the mere sound and serious exuberance of the music is all *he* cares about. He's an artist. He's teaching young Prez the boxer. Now the others dig!!' The third sax was an alto, eighteen-year-old cool, contemplative young Charlie-Parker-type Negro from high school, with a broadgash mouth, taller than the rest, grave. He raised his horn and blew into it quietly and thoughtfully and elicited birdlike phrases and architectural Miles Davis logics. These were the children of the great bop innovators.

Once there was Louis Armstrong blowing his beautiful top in the muds of New Orleans; before him the mad musicians who had paraded on official days and broke up their Sousa marches into ragtime. Then there was swing, and Roy Eldridge, vigorous and virile, blasting the horn for everything it had in waves of power and logic and subtlety – leaning to it with glittering eyes and a lovely smile and sending it out broadcast to rock the jazz world. Then had come Charlie Parker, a kid in his mother's woodshed in Kansas City, blowing his taped-up alto among the logs, practising on rainy days, coming out to watch the old swinging Basie and Benny Moten band that had Hot Lips Page and the rest – Charlie Parker leaving home and coming to Harlem, and meeting mad Thelonius Monk and madder Gillespie – Charlie Parker in his early days when he was flipped and walked around in a circle while playing. Somewhat younger than Lester Young, also from KC, that gloomy, saintly goof in whom the history of jazz was wrapped; for when he held his horn high and horizontal from his mouth he blew the greatest; and as his hair grew longer and he got lazier and stretched-out, his horn came down halfway; till it finally fell all the way and today as he wears his thick-soled shoes so that he can't feel the sidewalks of life his horn is held weakly against his chest, and he blows cool and easy getout phrases. Here were the children of the American bop night.

Strange flowers yet – for as the Negro alto mused over everyone's head with dignity, the young, tall, slender, blond kid from Curtis Street, Denver, jeans and studded belt, sucked on his mouthpiece while waiting for the others to finish; and when they did he started, and you had to look around to see where the solo was coming from, for it came from angelical smiling lips upon the mouthpiece and it was a soft, sweet, fairy-tale solo on an alto. Lonely as America, a throatpierced sound in the night.

What of the others and all the soundmaking? There was the bass-player, wiry redhead with wild eyes, jabbing his hips at the fiddle with every driving slap, at hot moments his mouth hanging open trancelike. 'Man, there's a cat who can really *bend* his girl!' The sad drummer, like our white hipster in Frisco Folsom Street, completely goofed, staring into space, chewing gum, wide-eyed, rocking the neck with Reich kick and complacent ecstasy. The piano – a big husky Italian truck-driving kid with meaty hands, a burly and thoughtful joy. They played an hour. Nobody was listening. Old North Clark bums lolled at the bar, whores screeched in anger. Secret Chinamen went by. Noises of hootchy-kootchy interfered. They went right on. Out on the sidewalk came an apparition – a sixteen-year-old kid with a goatee and a trombone case. Thin as rickets, mad-faced, he

wanted to join this group and blow with them. They knew him
and didn't want to bother with him. He crept into the bar and
surreptitiously undid his trombone and raised it to his lips. No
opening. Nobody looked at him. They finished, packed up, and
left for another bar. He wanted to jump, skinny Chicago kid.
He slapped on his dark glasses, raised the trombone to his lips
alone in the bar, and went 'Baugh!' Then he rushed out after
them. They wouldn't let him play with them, just like the sand-
lot football team in back of the gas tank. 'All these guys live
with their grandmothers just like Tom Snark and our Carlo
Marx alto,' said Dean. We rushed after the whole gang.
They went into Anita O'Day's club and there unpacked and
played till nine o'clock in the morning. Dean and I were there
with beers.

At intermissions we rushed out in the Cadillac and tried to
pick up girls all up and down Chicago. They were frightened of
our big, scarred, prophetic car. In his mad frenzy Dean backed
up smack on hydrants and tittered maniacally. By nine o'clock
the car was an utter wreck; the brakes weren't working any
more; the fenders were stove in; the rods were rattling. Dean
couldn't stop it at red lights, it kept kicking convulsively over
the roadway. It had paid the price of the night. It was a muddy
boot and no longer a shiny limousine. 'Whee!' The boys were
still blowing at Neets'.

Suddenly Dean stared into the darkness of a corner beyond
the bandstand and said, 'Sal, God has arrived.'

I looked. *George Shearing.* And as always he leaned his blind
head on his pale hand, all ears opened like the ears of an ele-
phant, listening to the American sounds and mastering them for
his own English summer's night use. Then they urged him to get
up and play. He did. He played innumerable choruses with
amazing chords that mounted higher and higher till the sweat
splashed all over the piano and everybody listened in awe and
fright. They led him off the stand after an hour. He went back
to his dark corner, old God Shearing, and the boys said, 'There
ain't nothin left after that.'

But the slender leader frowned. 'Let's blow anyway.'

Something would come of it yet. There's always more, a little
further – it never ends. They sought to find new phrases after

Shearing's explorations; they tried hard. They writhed and twisted and blew. Every now and then a clear harmonic cry gave new suggestions of a tune that would someday be the only tune in the world and would raise men's souls to joy. They found it, they lost, they wrestled for it, they found it again, they laughed, they moaned – and Dean sweated at the table and told them to go, go, go. At nine o'clock in the morning everybody – musicians, girls in slacks, bartenders, and the one little skinny, unhappy trombonist – staggered out of the club into the great roar of Chicago day to sleep until the wild bop night again.

Dean and I shuddered in the raggedness. It was now time to return the Cadillac to the owner, who lived out on Lake Shore Drive in a swank apartment with an enormous garage underneath managed by oil-scarred Negroes. We drove out there and swung the muddy heap into its berth. The mechanic did not recognize the Cadillac. We handed the papers over. He scratched his head at the sight of it. We had to get out fast. We did. We took a bus back to downtown Chicago and that was that. And we never heard a word from our Chicago baron about the condition of his car, in spite of the fact that he had our addresses and could have complained.

11

IT was time for us to move on. We took a bus to Detroit. Our money was now running quite low. We lugged our wretched baggage through the station. By now Dean's thumb bandage was almost as black as coal and all unrolled. We were both as miserable-looking as anybody could be after all the things we'd done. Exhausted, Dean fell asleep in the bus that roared across the state of Michigan. I took up a conversation with a gorgeous country girl wearing a low-cut cotton blouse that displayed the beautiful sun-tan on her breast tops. She was dull. She spoke of evenings in the country making popcorn on the porch. Once this would have gladdened my heart but because her heart was not glad when she said it I knew there was nothing in it but the idea of what one should do. 'And what else do you do for fun?' I tried to bring up boy friends and sex. Her great dark eyes surveyed me with emptiness and a kind of chagrin that reached back generations and generations in her blood from not having done what was crying to be done – whatever it was, and everybody knows what it was. 'What do you want out of life?' I wanted to take her and wring it out of her. She didn't have the slightest idea what she wanted. She mumbled of jobs, movies, going to her grandmother's for the summer, wishing she could go to New York and visit the Roxy, what kind of outfit she would wear – something like the one she wore last Easter, white bonnet, roses, rose pumps, and lavender gabardine coat. 'What do you do on Sunday afternoons?' I asked. She sat on her porch. The boys went by on bicycles and stopped to chat. She read the funny papers, she reclined on the hammock. 'What do you do on a warm summer's night?' She sat on the porch, she watched the cars in the road. She and her mother made popcorn. 'What does your father do on a summer's night?' He works, he has an all-night shift at the boiler factory, he's spent his whole life supporting a woman and her outpoppings and no credit or adoration. 'What does your brother do on a summer's night?' He rides around on his bicycle, he hangs out in front of the soda fountain. 'What is he aching to do? What are we all aching to do? What do we want?' She didn't know. She yawned. She was sleepy. It was too much. Nobody could tell. Nobody would ever tell. It was all over. She was eighteen and most lovely, and lost.

And Dean and I, ragged and dirty as if we had lived off locust, stumbled out of the bus in Detroit. We decided to stay up in all-night movies on Skid Row. It was too cold for parks. Hassel had been here on Detroit Skid Row, he had dug every shooting gallery and all-night movie and every brawling bar with his dark eyes many a time. His ghost haunted us. We'd never find him on Times Square again. We thought maybe by accident Old Dean Moriarty was here too – but he was not. For thirty-five cents each we went into the beat-up old movie and sat down in the balcony till morning, when we were shooed downstairs. The people who were in that all-night movie were the end. Beat Negroes who'd come up from Alabama to work in car factories on a rumour; old white bums; young long-haired hipsters who'd reached the end of the road and were drinking wine; whores, ordinary couples, and housewives with nothing to do, nowhere to go, nobody to believe in. If you sifted all Detroit in a wire basket the beater solid core of dregs couldn't be better gathered. The picture was Singing Cowboy Eddie Dean and his gallant white horse Bloop, that was number one; number two double-feature film was George Raft, Sidney Greenstreet, and Peter Lorre in a picture about Istanbul. We saw both of these things six times each during the night. We saw them waking, we heard them sleeping, we sensed them dreaming, we were permeated completely with the strange Grey Myth of the West and the weird dark Myth of the East when morning came. All my actions since then have been dictated automatically to my subconscious by this horrible osmotic experience. I heard big Greenstreet sneer a hundred times; I heard Peter Lorre make his sinister come-on; I was with George Raft in his paranoiac fears; I rode and sang with Eddie Dean and shot up the rustlers innumerable times. People slugged out of bottles and turned around and looked everywhere in the dark theatre for something to do, somebody to talk to. In the head everybody was guiltily quiet, nobody talked. In the grey dawn that puffed ghostlike about the windows of the theatre and hugged its eaves I was sleeping with my head on the wooden arm of a seat as six attendants of the theatre converged with their night's total of swept-up rubbish and created a huge dusty pile that reached to my nose as I snored head down – till they almost swept me away too. This was reported to me by Dean, who was watching from ten seats behind. All the cigarette butts, the bottles, the matchbooks, the come and the gone were swept up in this pile. Had they taken me with it, Dean would never have seen me again. He would have had to roam the entire United States and look in every garbage pail from coast to coast before he found me embryonically convoluted among the rubbishes of my life, his life, and the life of everybody concerned and not concerned. What would I have said to him from my rubbish womb? 'Don't bother me, man, I'm happy where I am. You lost me one night in Detroit in August nineteen forty-nine. What right have you to come and disturb my reverie in this pukish can?' In 1942 I was the star in one of the filthiest dramas of all time. I was a seaman, and went to the Imperial Café on Scollay Square in Boston to drink; I drank sixty glasses of beer and retired to the toilet, where I wrapped myself around the toilet bowl and went to sleep. During the night at least a hundred seamen and assorted civilians came in and cast their sentient debouchments on me till I was unrecognizably caked. What difference does it make after all? – anonymity in the world of men is better than fame in heaven, for what's heaven? what's earth? All in the mind.

Gibberishly Dean and I stumbled out of this horror-hole at dawn and went to find our travel-bureau car. After spending a good part of the morning in Negro bars and chasing gals and listening to jazz records on jukeboxes, we struggled five miles in local buses with all our crazy gear and got to the home of a man who was going to charge us four dollars apiece for the ride to New York. He was a middle-aged blond fellow with glasses, with a wife and kid and a good home. We waited in the yard while he got ready. His lovely wife in cotton kitchen dress offered us coffee but we were too busy talking. By this time Dean was so exhausted and out of his mind that everything he saw delighted him. He was reaching another pious frenzy. He sweated and sweated. The moment we were in the new Chrysler and off to New York the poor man realized he had contracted a ride with two maniacs, but he made the best of it and in fact got used to us just as we passed Briggs Stadium and talked about next year's Detroit Tigers.

In the misty night we crossed Toledo and went onward across old Ohio. I realized I was beginning to cross and recross towns in America as though I were a travelling salesman – raggedy travellings, bad stock, rotten beans in the bottom of my bag of tricks, nobody buying. The man got tired near Pennsylvania and Dean took the wheel and drove clear the rest of the way to New York, and we began to hear the Symphony Sid show on the radio with all the latest bop, and now we were entering the great and final city of America. We got there in early morning. Times Square was being torn up, for New

York never rests. We looked for Hassel automatically as we passed.

In an hour Dean and I were out at my aunt's new flat in Long Island, and she herself was busily engaged with painters who were friends of the family, and arguing with them about the price as we stumbled up the stairs from San Francisco. 'Sal,' said my aunt, 'Dean can stay here a few days and after that he has to get out, do you understand me?' The trip was over. Dean and I took a walk that night among the gas tanks and railroad bridges and fog lamps of Long Island. I remember him standing under a streetlamp.

'Just as we passed that other lamp I was going to tell you a further thing, Sal, but now I am parenthetically continuing with a new thought and by the time we reach the next I'll return to the original subject, agreed?' I certainly agreed. We were so used to travelling we had to walk all over Long Island, but there was no more land, just the Atlantic Ocean, and we could only go so far. We clasped hands and agreed to be friends forever.

Not five nights later we went to a party in New York and I saw a girl called Inez and told her I had a friend with me that she ought to meet sometime. I was drunk and told her he was a cowboy. 'Oh, I've always wanted to meet a cowboy.'

'Dean?' I yelled across the party – which included Angel Luz García, the poet; Walter Evans; Victor Villanueva, the Venezuelan poet; Jinny Jones, a former love of mine; Carlo Marx; Gene Dexter; and innumerable others – 'Come over here, man.' Dean came bashfully over. An hour later, in the drunkenness and chichiness of the party ('It's in honour of the end of the summer, of course'), he was kneeling on the floor with his chin on her belly and telling her and promising her everything and sweating. She was a big, sexy brunette – as García said, 'Something straight out of Degas', and generally like a beautiful Parisian coquette. In a matter of days they were dickering with Camille in San Francisco by long-distance telephone for the necessary divorce papers so they could get married. Not only that, but a few months later Camille gave birth to Dean's second baby, the result of a few nights' rapport early in the year. And another matter of months and Inez had a baby. With one illegitimate child in the West somewhere, Dean then had four little ones and not a cent, and was all troubles and ecstasy and speed as ever. So we didn't go to Italy.

PART FOUR

I

I CAME into some money from selling my book. I straightened out my aunt with rent for the rest of the year. Whenever spring comes to New York I can't stand the suggestions of the land that come blowing over the river from New Jersey and I've got to go. So I went. For the first time in our lives I said good-bye to Dean in New York and left him there. He worked in a parking lot on Madison and 40th. As ever he rushed around in his ragged shoes and T-shirt and belly-hanging pants all by himself, straightening out immense noontime rushes of cars.

When usually I came to visit him at dusk there was nothing to do. He stood in the shack, counting tickets and rubbing his belly. The radio was always on. 'Man, have you dug that mad Marty Glickman announcing basketball games – up-to-midcourt-bounce-fake-set-shot, swish, two points. Absolutely the greatest announcer I ever heard.' He was reduced to simple pleasures like these. He lived with Inez in a coldwater flat in the East Eighties. When he came home at night he took off all his clothes and put on a hip-length Chinese silk jacket and sat in his easy chair to smoke a waterpipe loaded with tea. These were his coming-home pleasures, together with a deck of dirty cards. 'Lately I've been concentrating on this deuce of diamonds. Have you noticed where her other hand is? I'll bet you can't tell. Look long and try to see.' He wanted to lend me the deuce of diamonds, which depicted a tall, mournful fellow and a lascivious, sad whore on a bed trying a position. 'Go ahead, man, I've used it many times!' Inez cooked in the kitchen and looked in with a wry smile. Everything was all right with her. 'Dig her? Dig her, man? That's Inez. See, that's all she does, she pokes her head in the door and smiles. Oh, I've talked with her and we've got everything straightened out most beautifully. We're going to go and live on a farm in Pennsylvania this summer – station wagon for me to cut back to New York for kicks, nice big house, and have a lot of kids in the next few years. Ahem! Harrumph! Egad!' He leaped out of the chair and put on a Willie Jackson record, 'Gator Tail'. He stood before it, socking his palms and rocking and pumping his knees to the beat. 'Whoo! That sonumbitch! First time I heard him I thought he'd die the next night, but he's still alive.'

This was exactly what he had been doing with Camille in Frisco on the other side of the continent. The same battered trunk stuck out from under the bed, ready to fly. Inez called up Camille on the phone repeatedly and had long talks with her; they even talked about his joint, or so Dean claimed. They exchanged letters about Dean's eccentricities. Of course he had to send Camille part of his pay every month for support or he'd wind up in the workhouse for six months. To make up lost money he pulled tricks in the lot, a change artist of the first order. I saw him wish a well-to-do man Merry Christmas so volubly a five-spot in change for twenty was never missed. We went out and spent it in Birdland, the bop joint. Lester Young was on the stand, eternity on his huge eyelids.

One night we talked on the corner of 47th Street and Madison at three in the morning. 'Well, Sal, damn, I wish you weren't going, I really do, it'll be my first time in New York without my old buddy.' And he said, 'New York, I stop over in it, Frisco's my hometown. All the time I've been here I haven't had any girl but Inez – this only happens to me in New York! Damn! But the mere thought of crossing that awful continent again – Sal, we haven't talked straight in a long time.' In New York we were always jumping around frantically with crowds of friends at drunken parties. It somehow didn't seem to fit Dean. He looked more like himself huddling in the cold, misty spray of the rain on empty Madison Avenue at night. 'Inez loves me; she's told me and promised me I can do anything I want and there'll be a minimum of trouble. You see, man, you get older and troubles pile up. Someday you and me'll be coming down an alley together at sundown and looking in the cans to see.'

'You mean we'll end up old bums?'

'Why not, man? Of course we will if we want to, and all that. There's no harm ending that way. You spend a whole life of non-interference with the wishes of others, including politicians and the rich, and nobody bothers you and you cut along and make it your own way.' I agreed with him. He was reaching his Tao decisions in the simplest direct way. 'What's your road, man? – holyboy road, madman road, rainbow road, guppy road, any road. It's an anywhere road for anybody anyhow. Where body how?' We nodded in the rain. 'Sheeit, and you've got to look out for your boy. He ain't a man 'less he's a jumpin man – do what the doctor say. I'll tell you, Sal, straight, no matter where I live, my trunk's always sticking out from under the bed, I'm ready to leave or get thrown out. I've decided to leave everything out of my hands. You've seen me try and break my ass to make it and you know that it doesn't matter and we know time – how to slow it up and walk and dig and just old-fashioned spade kicks, what other kicks are there? We know.' We sighed in the rain. It was falling all up and down the Hudson Valley that night. The great world piers of the sea-wide river were drenched in it, old steamboat landings at Poughkeepsie were drenched in it, old Split Rock Pond of sources was drenched in it, Vanderwhacker Mount was drenched in it.

'So,' said Dean, 'I'm cutting along in my life as it leads me. You know I recently wrote my old man in jail in Seattle – I got the first letter in years from him the other day.'

'Did you?'

'Yass, yass. He said he wants to see the "babby" spelt with two b's when he can get to Frisco. I found a thirteen-a-month coldwater pad on East Fortieth; if I can send him the money he'll come and live in New York – if he gets here. I never told you much about my sister but you know I have a sweet little kid sister; I'd like to get her to come and live with me too.'

'Where is she?'

'Well, that's just it, I don't know – he's going to try to find her, the old man, but you know what he'll really do.'

'So he went to Seattle?'

'And straight to messy jail.'

'Where was he?'

'Texas, Texas – so you see, man, my soul, the state of things, my position – you notice I get quieter.'

'Yes, that's true.' Dean had grown quiet in New York. He wanted to talk. We were freezing to death in the cold rain. We made a date to meet at my aunt's house before I left.

He came the following Sunday afternoon. I had a television set. We played one ballgame on the TV, another on the radio, and kept switching to a third and kept track of all that was happening every moment. 'Remember, Sal, Hodges is on second in Brooklyn so while the relief pitcher is coming in for the Phillies we'll switch to Giants–Boston and at the same time notice there DiMaggio has three balls count and the pitcher is fiddling with the resin bag, so we quickly find out what happened to Bobby Thomson when we left him thirty seconds ago with a man on third. Yes!'

Later in the afternoon we went out and played baseball with the kids in the sooty field by the Long Island railyard. We also played basketball so frantically the younger boys said, 'Take it easy, you don't have to kill yourself.' They bounced smoothly all around us and beat us with ease. Dean and I were sweating. At one point Dean fell flat on his face on the concrete court. We huffed and puffed to get the ball away from the boys; they turned and flipped it away. Others darted in and smoothly shot over our heads. We jumped at the basket like maniacs, and the younger boys just reached up and grabbed the ball from our sweating hands and dribbled away. We were like hotrock blackbelly tenorman *Mad* of American back-alley go-music trying to play basketball against Stan Getz and Cool Charlie. They thought we were crazy. Dean and I went back home playing catch from each sidewalk of the street. We tried extra-special catches, diving over bushes and barely missing posts. When a car came by I ran alongside and flipped the ball to Dean just barely behind the vanishing bumper. He darted and caught it and rolled in the grass, and flipped it back for me to catch on the other side of a parked bread truck. I just made it with my meat hand and threw it back so Dean had to whirl and back up and fall on his back across the hedges. Back in the house Dean took his wallet, harrumphed, and handed my aunt the fifteen dollars he owed her from the time we got a speeding ticket in Washington. She was completely surprised and pleased. We had a big supper. 'Well, Dean,' said my aunt, 'I hope you'll be able to take care of your new baby that's coming and stay married this time.'

'Yes, yass, yes.'

'You can't go all over the country having babies like that. Those poor little things'll grow up helpless. You've got to offer them a chance to live.' He looked at his feet and nodded. In the raw red dusk we said good-bye, on a bridge over a superhighway.

'I hope you'll be in New York when I get back,' I told him. 'All I hope, Dean, is someday we'll be able to live on the same street with our families and get to be a couple of oldtimers together.'

'That's right, man – you know that I pray for it completely mindful of the troubles we both had and the troubles coming, as your aunt knows and reminds me. I didn't want the new baby, Inez insisted, and we had a fight. Did you know Marylou got married to a used-car dealer in Frisco and she's having a baby?'

'Yes. We're all getting in there now.' Ripples in the upside-down lake of the void, is what I should have said. The bottom of the world is gold and the world is upside down. He took out a snapshot of Camille in Frisco with the new baby girl. The shadow of a man crossed the child on the sunny pavement, two long trouser legs in the sadness. 'Who's that?'

'That's only Ed Dunkel. He came back to Galatea, they're gone to Denver now. They spent a day taking pictures.'

Ed Dunkel, his compassion unnoticed like the compassion of saints. Dean took out other pictures. I realized these were all the snapshots which our children would look at someday with wonder, thinking their parents had lived smooth, well-ordered, stabilized-within-the-photo lives and got up in the morning to walk proudly on the sidewalks of life, never dreaming the raggedy madness and riot of our actual lives, our actual night, the hell of it, the senseless nightmare road. All of it inside endless and beginningless emptiness. Pitiful forms of ignorance. 'Good-bye, good-bye.' Dean walked off in the long red dusk. Locomotives smoked and reeled above him. His shadow followed him, it aped his walk and thoughts and very being. He turned and waved coyly, bashfully. He gave me the boomer's highball, he jumped up and down, he yelled something I didn't catch. He ran around in a circle. All the time he came closer to the concrete corner of the railroad overpass. He made one last signal. I waved back. Suddenly he bent to his life and walked quickly out of sight. I gaped into the bleakness of my own days. I had an awful long way to go too.

2

THE following midnight, singing this little song,

> Home in Missoula,
> Home in Truckee,
> Home in Opelousas,
> Ain't no home for me.
> Home in old Medora,
> Home in Wounded Knee,
> Home in Ogallala,
> Home I'll never be,

I took the Washington bus; wasted some time there wandering around; went out of my way to see the Blue Ridge, heard the bird of Shenandoah and visited Stonewall Jackson's grave; at dusk stood expectorating in the Kanawha River and walked the hillbilly night of Charleston, West Virginia; at midnight Ashland, Kentucky, and a lonely girl under the marquee of a closed-up show. The dark and mysterious Ohio, and Cincinnati at dawn. Then Indiana fields again, and St Louis as ever in its great valley clouds of afternoon. The muddy cobbles and the Montana logs, the broken steamboats, the ancient signs, the grass and the ropes by the river. The endless poem. By night Missouri, Kansas fields, Kansas night-cows in the secret wides, crackerbox towns with a sea for the end of every street; dawn in Abilene. East Kansas grasses become West Kansas rangelands that climb up to the hill of the Western night.

Henry Glass was riding the bus with me. He had got on at Terre Haute, Indiana, and now he said to me, 'I've told you why I hate this suit I'm wearing, it's lousy – but ain't all.' He showed me papers. He had just been released from Terre Haute federal pen; the rap was for stealing and selling cars in Cincinnati. A young, curly-haired kid of twenty. 'Soon's I get to Denver I'm selling this suit in a pawnshop and getting me jeans. Do you know what they did to me in that prison? Solitary confinement with a Bible; I used it to sit on the stone floor; when they seed I was doing that they took the Bible away and brought back a leetle pocket-size one so big. Couldn't sit on it so I read the whole Bible and Testament. Hey-hey –' he poked me, munching his candy, he was always eating candy because his stomach had been ruined in the pen and couldn't stand anything else – 'you know they's some real hot things in that Bi-ble.' He told me what it was to 'signify'. 'Anybody that's leaving jail soon and starts talking about his release date is "signifying" to the other fellas that have to stay. We take him by the neck and say, "Don't signify with *me!*" Bad thing, to signify – y'hear me?'

'I won't signify, Henry.'

'Anybody signify with me, my nose opens up, I get mad enough to kill. You know why I been in jail all my life? Because I lost my temper when I was thirteen years old. I was in a movie with a boy and he made a crack about my mother – you know that dirty word – and I took out my jackknife and cut up his throat and woulda killed him if they hadn't drug me off. Judge said, "Did you know what you were doing when you attacked your friend?" "Yessir, Your Honour, I did, I wanted to kill the sonofabitch and still do." So I didn't get no parole and went straight to reform school. I got piles too from sitting in solitary. Don't ever go to a federal pen, they're worstest. Sheet, I could talk all night it's ben so long since I talked to somebody. You don't know how *good* I feel coming out. You just sitting in that bus when I got on – riding through Terre Haute – what was you thinking?'

'I was just sitting there riding.'

'Me, I was singing. I sat down next to you 'cause I was

afraid to set down next to any gals for fear I go crazy and reach under their dress. I gotta wait awhile.'

'Another hitch in prison and you'll be put away for life. You better take it easy from now.'

'That's what I intend to do, only trouble is m'nose opens up and I can't tell what I'm doing.'

He was on his way to live with his brother and sister-in-law; they had a job for him in Colorado. His ticket was bought by the feds, his destination the parole. Here was a young kid like Dean had been; his blood boiled too much for him to bear; his nose opened up; but no native strange saintliness to save him from the iron fate.

'Be a buddy and watch m'nose don't open up in Denver, will you, Sal? Mebbe I can get to my brother's safe.'

When we arrived in Denver I took him by the arm to Larimer Street to pawn the penitentiary suit. The old Jew immediately sensed what it was before it was half unwrapped. 'I don't want that damn thing here; I get them every day from the Canyon City boys.'

All of Larimer Street was overrun with ex-cons trying to sell their prison-spun suits. Henry ended up with the thing under his arm in a paper bag and walked around in brand-new jeans and sports shirt. We went to Dean's old Glenarm bar – on the way Henry threw the suit in an ashcan – and called up Tim Gray. It was evening now.

'You?' chuckled Tim Gray. 'Be right over.'

In ten minutes he came loping into the bar with Stan Shephard. They'd both had a trip to France and were tremendously disappointed with their Denver lives. They loved Henry and bought him beers. He began spending all his penitentiary money left and right. Again I was back in the soft, dark Denver night with its holy alleys and crazy houses. We started hitting all the bars in town, roadhouses out on West Colfax, Five Points Negro bars, the works.

Stan Shephard had been waiting to meet me for years and now for the first time we were suspended together in front of a venture. 'Sal, ever since I came back from France I ain't had any idea what to do with myself. Is it true you're going to Mexico? Hot damn, I could go with you? I can get a hundred bucks and once I get there sign up for GI Bill in Mexico City College.'

Okay, it was agreed, Stan was coming with me. He was a rangy, bashful, shock-haired Denver boy with a big con-man smile and slow, easy-going Gary Cooper movements. 'Hot damn!' he said and stuck his thumbs on his belt and ambled down the street, swaying from side to side but slowly. His grandfather was having it out with him. He had been opposed to France and now he was opposed to the idea of going to Mexico. Stan was wandering around Denver like a bum because of his fight with his grandfather. That night after we'd done all our drinking and restrained Henry from getting his nose opened up in the Hot Shoppe on Colfax, Stan scraggled off to sleep in Henry's hotel room on Glenarm. 'I can't even come home late – my grandfather starts fighting with me, then he turns on my mother. I tell you, Sal, I got to get out of Denver quick or I'll go crazy.'

Well, I stayed at Tim Gray's and then later Babe Rawlins fixed up a neat little basement room for me and we all ended up there with parties every night for a week. Henry vanished off to his brother's and we never saw him again and never will know if anybody's signified with him since and if they've put him away in an iron hall or if he busts his gaskets in the night free.

Tim Gray, Stan, Babe, and I spent an entire week of afternoons in lovely Denver bars where the waitresses wear slacks and cut around with bashful, loving eyes, not hardened waitresses but waitresses that fall in love with the clientele and have explosive affairs and huff and sweat and suffer from one bar to another; and we spent the same week in nights at Five Points listening to jazz, drinking booze in crazy Negro saloons and gabbing till five o'clock in the morn in my basement. Noon usually found us reclined in Babe's back yard among the little Denver kids who played cowboys and Indians and dropped on us from cherry trees in bloom. I was having a wonderful time and the whole world opened up before me because I had no dreams. Stan and I plotted to make Tim Gray come with us, but Tim was stuck to his Denver life.

I was getting ready to go to Mexico when suddenly Denver

Doll called me one night and said, 'Well, Sal, guess who's coming to Denver?' I had no idea. 'He's on his way already, I got this news from my grapevine. Dean bought a car and is coming out to join you.' Suddenly I had a vision of Dean, a burning shuddering frightful Angel, palpitating towards me across the road, approaching like a cloud, with enormous speed, pursuing me like the Shrouded Traveller on the plain, bearing down on me. I saw his huge face over the plains with the mad, bony purpose and the gleaming eyes; I saw his wings; I saw his old jalopy chariot with thousands of sparking flames shooting out from it; I saw the path it burned over the road; it even made its own road and went over the corn, through cities, destroying bridges, drying rivers. It came like wrath to the West. I knew Dean had gone mad again. There was no chance to send money to either wife if he took all his savings out of the bank and bought a car. Everything was up, the jig and all. Behind him charred ruins smoked. He rushed westward over the groaning and awful continent again, and soon he would arrive. We made hasty preparations for Dean. News was that he was going to drive me to Mexico.

'Do you think he'll let me come along?' asked Stan in awe.

'I'll talk to him,' I said grimly. We didn't know what to expect. 'Where will he sleep? What's he going to eat? Are there any girls for him?' It was like the imminent arrival of Gargantua; preparations had to be made to widen the gutters of Denver and foreshorten certain laws to fit his suffering bulk and bursting ecstasies.

3

IT was like an old-fashioned movie when Dean arrived. I was in Babe's house in a golden afternoon. A word about the house. Her mother was away in Europe. The chaperon aunt was called Charity; she was seventy-five years old and spry as a chicken. In the Rawlins family, which stretched all over the West, she was continually shuttling from one house to another and making herself generally useful. At one time she'd had dozens of sons. They were all gone; they'd all abandoned her. She was old but she was interested in everything we did and said. She shook her head sadly when we took slugs of whisky in the living-room. 'Now you might go out in the yard for that, young man.' Upstairs – it was a kind of boarding house that summer – lived a guy called Tom who was hopelessly in love with Babe. He came from Vermont, from a rich family, they said, and had a career waiting for him there and everything, but he preferred being where Babe was. In the evenings he sat in the living-room with his face burning behind a newspaper and every time one of us said anything he heard but made no sign. He particularly burned when Babe said something. When we forced him to put down the paper he looked at us with incalculable boredom and suffering. 'Eh? Oh yes, I suppose so.' He usually said just that.

Charity sat in her corner, knitting, watching us all with her birdy eyes. It was her job to chaperon, it was up to her to see nobody swore. Babe sat giggling on the couch. Tim Gray, Stan Shephard, and I sprawled around in chairs. Poor Tom suffered the tortures. He got up, yawned, and said, 'Well, another day another dollar, good night,' and disappeared upstairs. Babe had no use whatever for him as a lover. She was in love with Tim Gray; he wriggled like an eel out of her grasp. We were sitting around like this on a sunny afternoon toward supper-time when Dean pulled up in front in his jalopy and jumped out in a tweed suit with vest and watch chain.

'Hup! hup!' I heard out on the street. He was with Roy Johnson, who'd just returned from Frisco with his wife Doro-thy and was living in Denver again. So were Dunkel and Gala-tea Dunkel, and Tom Snark. Everybody was in Denver again. I went out on the porch. 'Well, m'boy,' said Dean, sticking out his big hand, 'I see everything is all right on this end of the stick. Hello hello hello,' he said to everybody. 'Oh yes, Tim Gray, Stan Shephard, howd'y'do!' We introduced him to Charity. 'Oh yass, howd'y'do. This is m'friend Roy Johnson here, was so kind as to accompany me, harrumph! egad! kaff! kaff! Major Hoople, sir,' he said, sticking out his hand to Tom, who stared at him. 'Yass, yass. Well, Sal old man, what's the story, when do we take off for Mexico? Tomorrow afternoon?

Fine, fine. Ahem! And now, Sal, I have exactly sixteen minutes to make it to Ed Dunkel's house, where I am about to recover my old railroad watch which I can pawn on Larimer Street before closing time, meanwhile buzzing very quickly and as thoroughly as time allows to see if my old man by chance may be in Jiggs' Buffet or some of the other bars and then I have an appointment with the barber Doll always told me to patronize and I have not myself changed over the years and continue with that policy – kaff! kaff! At six o'clock *sharp!* – sharp, hear me? – I want you to be right here where I'll come buzzing by to get you for one quick run to Roy Johnson's house, play Gillespie and assorted bop records, an hour of relaxation prior to any kind of further evening you and Tim and Stan and Babe may have planned for tonight irrespective of my arrival which incidentally was exactly forty-five minutes ago in my old thirty-seven Ford which you see parked out there, I made it together with a long pause in Kansas City seeing my cousin, not Sam Brady but the younger one . . .' And saying all these things, he was busily changing from his suit coat to T-shirt in the living-room alcove just out of sight of everyone and transferring his watch to another pair of pants that he got out of the same old battered trunk.

'And Inez?' I said. 'What happened in New York?'

'Officially, Sal, this trip is to get a Mexican divorce, cheaper and quicker than any kind. I've Camille's agreement at last and everything is straight, everything is fine, everything is lovely and we know that we are now not worried about a single thing, don't we, Sal?'

Well, okay, I'm always ready to follow Dean, so we all bustled to the new set of plans and arranged a big night, and it was an unforgettable night. There was a party at Ed Dunkel's brother's house. Two of his other brothers are bus-drivers. They sat there in awe of everything that went on. There was a lovely spread on the table, cake and drinks. Ed Dunkel looked happy and prosperous. 'Well, are you all set with Galatea now?'

'Yessir,' said Ed, 'I sure am. I'm about to go to Denver U, you know, me and Roy.'

'What are you going to take up?'

'Oh, sociology and all that field, you know. Say, Dean gets crazier every year, don't he?'

'He sure does.'

Galatea Dunkel was there. She was trying to talk to somebody, but Dean held the whole floor. He stood and performed before Shephard, Tim, Babe, and myself, who all sat side by side in kitchen chairs along the wall. Ed Dunkel hovered nervously behind him. His poor brother was thrust into the background. 'Hup! hup!' Dean was saying, tugging at his shirt, rubbing his belly, jumping up and down. 'Yass, well – we're all together now and the years have rolled severally behind us and yet you see none of us have really changed, that's what's so amazing, the dura – the dura – bility – in fact to prove that I have here a deck of cards with which I can tell very accurate fortunes of all sorts.' It was the dirty deck. Dorothy Johnson and Roy Johnson sat stiffly in a corner. It was a mournful party. Then Dean suddenly grew quiet and sat in a kitchen chair between Stan and me and stared straight ahead with rocky doglike wonder and paid no attention to anybody. He simply disappeared for a moment to gather up more energy. If you touched him he would sway like a boulder suspended on a pebble on the precipice of a cliff. He might come crashing down or just sway rocklike. Then the boulder exploded into a flower and his face lit up with a lovely smile and he looked around like a man waking up and said, 'Ah, look at all the nice people that are sitting here with me. Isn't it nice! Sal, why, like I was tellin Min just t'other day, why, urp, ah, yes!' He got up and went across the room, hand outstretched to one of the bus-drivers in the party. 'Howd'y'do. My name is Dean Moriarty. Yes, I remember you well. Is everything all right? Well, well. Look at the lovely cake. Oh, can I have some? Just me? Miserable me?' Ed's sister said yes. 'Oh, how wonderful. People are so nice. Cakes and pretty things set out on a table and all for the sake of wonderful little joys and delights. Hmm, ah, yes, excellent, splendid, harrumph, egad!' And he stood swaying in the middle of the room, eating his cake and looking at everyone with awe. He turned and looked around behind him. Everything amazed him, everything he saw. People talked in groups all around the room, and he said,

'Yes! That's right!' A picture on the wall made him stiffen to attention. He went up and looked closer, he backed up, he stooped, he jumped up, he wanted to see from all possible levels and angles, he tore at his T-shirt in exclamation, 'Damn!' He had no idea of the impression he was making and cared less. People were now beginning to look at Dean with maternal and paternal affection glowing in their faces. He was finally an Angel, as I always knew he would become; but like any Angel he still had rages and furies, and that night when we all left the party and repaired to the Windsor bar in one vast brawling gang, Dean became frantically and demoniacally and seraphically drunk.

Remember that the Windsor, once Denver's great Gold Rush hotel and in many respects a point of interest – in the big saloon downstairs bullet holes are still in the walls – had once been Dean's home. He'd lived here with his father in one of the rooms upstairs. He was no tourist. He drank in this saloon like the ghost of his father; he slopped down wine, beer, and whisky like water. His face got red and sweaty and he bellowed and hollered at the bar and staggered across the dancefloor where honkytonkers of the West danced with girls and tried to play the piano, and he threw his arms around ex-cons and shouted with them in the uproar. Meanwhile everybody in our party sat around two immense tables stuck together. There were Denver D. Doll, Dorothy and Roy Johnson, a girl from Buffalo, Wyoming, who was Dorothy's friend, Stan, Tim Gray, Babe, me, Ed Dunkel, Tom Snark, and several others, thirteen in all. Doll was having a great time : he took a peanut machine and set it on the table before him and poured pennies in it and ate peanuts. He suggested we all write something on a penny postcard and mail it to Carlo Marx in New York. We wrote crazy things. The fiddle music whanged in the Larimer Street night. 'Isn't it fun?' yelled Doll. In the men's room Dean and I punched the door and tried to break it but it was an inch thick. I cracked a bone in my middle finger and didn't even realize it till the next day. We were fumingly drunk. Fifty glasses of beer sat on our tables at one time. All you had to do was rush around and sip from each one. Canyon City ex-cons reeled and gabbled with us. In the foyer outside the saloon old former prospectors sat dreaming over their canes under the tocking old clock. This fury had been known by them in greater days. Everything swirled. There were scattered parties everywhere. There was even a party in a castle to which we all drove – except Dean, who ran off elsewhere – and in this castle we sat at a great table in the hall and shouted. There were a swimming pool and grottoes outside. I had finally found the castle where the great snake of the world was about to rise up.

Then in the late night it was just Dean and I and Stan Shephard and Tim Gray and Ed Dunkel and Tommy Snark in one car and everything ahead of us. We went to Mexican town, we went to Five Points, we reeled around. Stan Shephard was out of his mind with joy. He kept yelling, 'Sonofa*bitch! Hot damn!*' in a high squealing voice and slapping his knees. Dean was mad about him. He repeated everything Stan said and phewed and wiped the sweat off his face. 'Are we gonna get our kicks, Sal, travellin down to Mexico with this cat Stan! Yes!' It was our last night in holy Denver, we made it big and wild. It all ended up with wine in the basement by candle-light, and Charity creeping around upstairs in her nightgown with a flashlight. We had a coloured guy with us now, called himself Gomez. He floated around Five Points and didn't give a damn. When we saw him, Tommy Snark called out, 'Hey, is your name Johnny?'

Gomez just backed up and passed us once more and said, 'Now will you repeat what you said?'

'I said are you the guy they call Johnny?'

Gomez floated back and tried again. 'Does this look a little more like him? Because I'm tryin my best to be Johnny but I just can't find the way.'

'Well, *man*, come on with us!' cried Dean, and Gomez jumped in and we were off. We whispered frantically in the basement so as not to create disturbance with the neighbours. At nine o'clock in the morning everybody had left except Dean and Shephard, who were still yakking like maniacs. People got up to make breakfast and heard strange subterranean voices saying, 'Yes! Yes!' Babe cooked a big breakfast. The time was coming to scat off to Mexico.

Dean took the car to the nearest station and had everything shipshape. It was a '37 Ford sedan with the right-side door unhinged and tied on the frame. The right-side front seat was also broken, and you sat there leaning back with your face to the tattered roof. 'Just like Min 'n' Bill,' said Dean. 'We'll go coughing and bouncing down to Mexico; it'll take us days and days.' I looked over the map: a total of over a thousand miles, mostly Texas, to the border at Laredo, and then another 767 miles through all Mexico to the great city near the cracked Isthmus and Oaxacan heights. I couldn't imagine this trip. It was the most fabulous of all. It was no longer east-west, but magic *south*. We saw a vision of the entire Western Hemisphere rockribbing clear down to Tierra del Fuego and us flying down the curve of the world into other tropics and other worlds. 'Man, this will finally take us to IT!' said Dean with definite faith. He tapped my arm. 'Just wait and see. Hoo! Whee!'

I went with Shephard to conclude the last of his Denver business, and met his poor grandfather, who stood in the door of the house, saying, 'Stan – Stan – Stan.'

'What is it, Granpaw?'

'Don't go.'

'Oh, it's settled, I *have* to go now; why do you have to do that?' The old man had grey hair and large almond eyes and a tense, mad neck.

'Stan,' he simply said, 'don't go. Don't make your old grandfather cry. Don't leave me alone again.' It broke my heart to see all this.

'Dean,' said the old man, addressing me, 'don't take my Stan away from me. I used to take him to the park when he was a little boy and explain the swans to him. Then his little sister drowned in the same pond. I don't want you to take my boy away.'

'No,' said Stan, 'we're leaving now. Good-bye.' He struggled with his grips.

His grandfather took him by the arm. 'Stan, Stan, Stan, don't go, don't go, don't go.'

We fled with our heads bowed, and the old man still stood in the doorway of his Denver side-street cottage with the beads hanging in the doors and the overstuffed furniture in the parlour. He was as white as a sheet. He was still calling Stan. There was something paralysed about his movements, and he did nothing about leaving the doorway, but just stood in it, muttering, 'Stan,' and 'Don't go,' and looking after us anxiously as we rounded the corner.

'God, Shep, I don't know what to say.'

'Never mind!' Stan moaned. 'He's always been like that.'

We met Stan's mother at the bank, where she was drawing money for him. She was a lovely white-haired woman, still very young in appearance. She and her son stood on the marble floor of the bank, whispering. Stan was wearing a levi outfit, jacket and all, and looked like a man going to Mexico sure enough. This was his tender existence in Denver, and he was going off with the flaming tyro Dean. Dean came popping around the corner and met us just on time. Mrs Shephard insisted on buying us all a cup of coffee.

'Take care of my Stan,' she said. 'No telling what things might happen in that country.'

'We'll all watch over each other,' I said. Stan and his mother strolled on ahead, and I walked in back with crazy Dean; he was telling me about the inscriptions carved on toilet walls in the East and in the West.

'They're entirely different; in the East they make cracks and corny jokes and obvious references, scatological bits of data and drawings; in the West they just write their names, Red O'Hara, Blufftown Montana, came by here, date, real solemn, like, say, Ed Dunkel, the reason being the enormous loneliness that differs just a shade and cut hair as you move across the Mississippi.' Well, there was a lonely guy in front of us, for Shephard's mother was a lovely mother and she hated to see her son go but knew he had to go. I saw he was fleeing his grandfather. Here were the three of us – Dean looking for his father, mine dead, Stan fleeing his old one, and going off into the night together. He kissed his mother in the rushing crowds of 17th and she got in a cab and waved at us. Good-bye, good-bye.

We got in the car at Babe's and said good-bye to her. Tim was riding with us to his house outside town. Babe was beautiful that day; her hair was long and blond and Swedish, her freckles showed in the sun. She looked exactly like the little girl she had been. There was a mist in her eyes. She might join us later with Tim – but she didn't. Good-bye, good-bye.

We roared off. We left Tim in his yard on the Plains outside town and I looked back to watch Tim Gray recede on the plain. That strange guy stood there for a full two minutes watching us go away and thinking God knows what sorrowful thoughts. He grew smaller and smaller, and still he stood motionless with one hand on a washline, like a captain, and I was twisted around to see more of Tim Gray till there was nothing but a growing absence in space, and the space was the eastward view towards Kansas that led all the way back to my home in Atlantis.

Now we pointed our rattly snout south and headed for Castle Rock, Colorado, as the sun turned red and the rock of the mountains to the west looked like a Brooklyn brewery in November dusks. Far up in the purple shades of the rock there was someone walking, walking, but we could not see; maybe that old man with the white hair I had sensed years ago up in the peaks. Zacatecan Jack. But he was coming closer to me, if only ever just behind. And Denver receded back of us like the city of salt, her smokes breaking up in the air and dissolving to our sight.

4

IT was May. And how can homely afternoons in Colorado with its farms and irrigation ditches and shady dells – the places where little boys go swimming – produce a bug like the bug that bit Stan Shephard? He had his arm draped over the broken door and was riding along and talking happily when suddenly a bug flew into his arm and embedded a long stinger in it that made him howl. It had come out of an American afternoon. He yanked and slapped at his arm and dug out the stinger, and in a few minutes his arm had begun to swell and hurt. Dean and I couldn't figure what it was. The thing was to wait and see if the swelling went down. Here we were, heading for unknown southern lands, and barely three miles out of hometown, poor old hometown of childhood, a strange feverish exotic bug rose from secret corruptions and sent fear into our hearts. 'What is it?'

'I've never known of a bug around here that can make a swelling like that.'

'Damn!' It made the trip seem sinister and doomed. We drove on. Stan's arm got worse. We'd stop at the first hospital and have him get a shot of penicillin. We passed Castle Rock, came to Colorado Springs at dark. The great shadow of Pike's Peak loomed to our right. We bowled down the Pueblo highway. 'I've hitched thousands and thousands of time on this road,' said Dean. 'I hid behind that exact wire fence there one night when I suddenly took fright for no reason whatever.'

We all decided to tell our stories, but one by one, and Stan was first. 'We've got a long way to go,' preambled Dean, 'and so you must take every indulgence and deal with every single detail you can bring to mind – and still it won't all be told. Easy, easy,' he cautioned Stan, who began telling his story, 'you've got to relax too.' Stan swung into his life story as we shot across the dark. He started with his experiences in France but to round out ever-growing difficulties he came back and started at the beginning with his boyhood in Denver. He and Dean compared times they'd seen each other zooming around on bicycles. 'One time you've forgotten, I know – Arapahoe Garage? Recall? I bounced a ball at you on the corner and you knocked it back to me with your fist and it went in the sewer. Grammar days. Now recall?' Stan was nervous and feverish. He wanted to tell Dean everything. Dean was now arbiter, old man, judge, listener, approver, nodder. 'Yes, yes, go on please.' We passed Walsenburg; suddenly we passed Trinidad, where Chad King was somewhere off the road in front of a campfire with perhaps a handful of anthropologists and as of yore he too was telling his life story and never dreamed we were passing at that exact moment on the highway, headed for Mexico, telling our own stories. O sad American night! Then we were in New Mexico and passed the rounded rocks of Raton and stopped at a diner, ravingly hungry for hamburgers, some of which we wrapped in a napkin to eat over the border below. 'The whole vertical state of Texas lies before us, Sal,' said Dean. 'Before we made it horizontal. Every bit as long. We'll be in Texas in a few minutes and won't be out till tomorrow this time and won't stop driving. Think of it.'

We drove on. Across the immense plain of night lay the first Texas town, Dalhart, which I'd crossed in 1947. It lay glimmering on the dark floor of the earth, fifty miles away. The land by moonlight was all mesquite and wastes. On the horizon was the moon. She fattened, she grew huge and rusty, she mellowed and rolled, till the morning star contended and dews began to blow in our windows – and still we rolled. After Dalhart – empty crackerbox town – we bowled for Amarillo, and reached it in the morning among windy panhandle grasses that only a few years ago waved around a collection of buffalo tents. Now there were gas stations and new 1950 jukeboxes with immense ornate snouts and ten-cent slots and awful songs. All the way from Amarillo to Childress, Dean and I pounded plot after plot of books we'd read into Stan, who asked for it because he wanted to know. At Childress in the hot sun we turned directly south on a lesser road and highballed across abysmal wastes to Paducah, Guthrie, and Abilene, Texas. Now Dean had to sleep, and Stan and I sat in the front seat and drove. The old car burned and bopped and struggled on. Great clouds of gritty wind blew at us from shimmering spaces. Stan rolled right along with stories about Monte Carlo and Cagnes-sur-Mer and the blue places near Menton where dark-faced people wandered among white walls.

Texas is undeniable: we burned slowly into Abilene and all woke up to look at it. 'Imagine living in this town a thousand miles from cities. Whoop, whoop, over there by the tracks, old town Abilene where they shipped the cows and shot it up for gumshoes and drank red-eye. Look out there!' yelled Dean out the window with his mouth contorted like W. C. Fields. He didn't care about Texas or any place. Red-faced Texans paid him no mind and hurried along the burning sidewalks. We stopped to eat on the highway south of town. Nightfall seemed like a million miles away as we resumed for Coleman and Brady – the heart of Texas, only wildernesses of brush with an occasional house near a thirsty creek and a fifty-mile dirt road detour and endless heat. 'Old dobe Mexico's a long way away,' said Dean sleepily from the back seat, 'so keep her rolling, boys, and we'll be kissing señoritas b'dawn 'cause this old Ford can roll if y'know how to talk to her and ease her along – except the back end's about to fall but don't worry about it till we get there.' And he went to sleep.

I took the wheel and drove to Fredericksburg, and here again I was crisscrossing the old map again, same place Marylou and I had held hands on a snowy morning in 1949, and where was Marylou now? 'Blow!' yelled Dean in a dream and I guess he was dreaming of Frisco jazz and maybe Mexican mambo to come. Stan talked and talked; Dean had wound him up the night before and now he was never going to stop. He was in England by now, relating adventures hitchhiking on the English road, London to Liverpool, with his hair long and his pants ragged, and strange British truck-drivers giving him lifts in glooms of the Europe void. We were all red-eyed from the continual mistral-winds of old Tex-ass. There was a rock in each of our bellies and we knew we were getting there, if slowly. The car pushed forty with shuddering effort. From Fredericksburg we descended the great western high plains. Moths began smashing our windshield. 'Getting down into the hot country now, boys, the desert rats and the tequila. And this is my first time this far south in Texas,' added Dean with wonder. 'Gawd-damn! this is where my old man comes in the wintertime, sly old bum.'

Suddenly we were in absolutely tropical heat at the bottom of a five-mile-long hill, and up ahead we saw the lights of old San Antonio. You had the feeling all this used to be Mexican territory indeed. Houses by the side of the road were different, gas stations beater, fewer lamps. Dean delightedly took the wheel to roll us into San Antonio. We entered town in a wilderness of Mexican rickety southern shacks without cellars and with old rocking chairs on the porch. We stopped at a mad gas station to get a grease job. Mexicans were standing around in the hot light of the overhead bulbs that were blackened by valley summerbugs, reaching down into a soft-drink box and pulling out beer bottles and throwing the money to the attendant. Whole families lingered around doing this. All around there were shacks and drooping trees and a wild cinnamon smell in the air. Frantic teenage Mexican girls came by with boys. 'Hoo!' yelled Dean. '*Si! Mañana!*' Music was coming from all sides, and all kinds of music. Stan and I drank several bottles of beer and got high. We were already almost out of America and yet definitely in it and in the middle of where it's maddest. Hotrods blew by. San Antonio, ah-haa!

'Now, men, listen to me – we might as well goof a coupla hours in San Antone and so we will go and find a hospital clinic for Stan's arm and you and I, Sal, will cut around and get these streets dug – look at those houses across the street, you can see right into the front room and all the purty daughters layin around with *True Love* magazines, whee! Come, let's go!'

We drove around aimlessly awhile and asked people for the nearest hospital clinic. It was near downtown, where things looked more sleek and American, several semi-skyscrapers and many neons and chain drugstores, yet with cars crashing through from the dark around town as if there were no traffic laws. We parked the car in the hospital driveway and I went with Stan to see an intern while Dean stayed in the car and changed. The hall of the hospital was full of poor Mexican women, some of them pregnant, some of them sick or bringing their little sick kiddies. It was sad. I thought of poor Terry and wondered what she was doing now. Stan had to wait an entire hour till an intern came along and looked at his swollen arm. There was a name for the infection he had, but none of us bothered to pronounce it. They gave him a shot of penicillin.

Meanwhile Dean and I went out to dig the streets of Mexican San Antonio. It was fragrant and soft – the softest air I'd ever known – and dark, and mysterious, and buzzing. Sudden figures of girls in white bandannas appeared in the humming dark. Dean crept along and said not a word. 'Oh, this is too wonderful to do anything!' he whispered. 'Let's just creep along and see everything. Look! Look! A crazy San Antonio pool shack.' We went in. A dozen boys were shooting pool at three tables, all Mexicans. Dean and I bought Cokes and shoved nickels in the jukebox and played Wynonie Blues Harris and

Lionel Hampton and Lucky Millinder and jumped. Meanwhile Dean warned me to watch.

'Dig, now, out of the corner of your eye and as we listen to Wynonie blow about his baby's pudding and as we also smell the soft air as you say – dig the kid, the crippled kid shooting pool at table one, the butt of the joint's jokes, y'see, he's been the butt all his life. The other fellows are merciless but they love him.'

The crippled kid was some kind of malformed midget with a great big beautiful face, much too large, in which enormous brown eyes moistly gleamed. 'Don't you see, Sal, a San Antonio Mex Tom Snark, the same story the world over. See, they hit him on the ass with a cue? Ha-ha-ha! hear them laugh. You see, he wants to win the game, he's bet four bits. Watch! Watch!' We watched as the angelic young midget aimed for a bank shot. He missed. The other fellows roared. 'Ah, man,' said Dean, 'and now watch.' They had the little boy by the scruff of the neck and were mauling him around, playful. He squealed. He stalked out in the night but not without a backward bashful, sweet glance. 'Ah, man, I'd love to know that gone little cat and what he thinks and what kind of girls he has – oh, man, I'm high on this air!' We wandered out and negotiated several dark, mysterious blocks. Innumerable houses hid behind verdant, almost jungle-like yards; we saw glimpses of girls in front rooms, girls on porches, girls in the bushes with boys. 'I never knew this mad San Antonio! Think what Mexico'll be like! Lessgo! Lessgo!' We rushed back to the hospital. Stan was ready and said he felt much better. We put our arms around him and told him everything we'd done.

And now we were ready for the last hundred and fifty miles to the magic border. We leaped into the car and off. I was so exhausted by now I slept all the way through Dilley and Encinal to Laredo and didn't wake up till they were parking the car in front of a lunchroom at two o'clock in the morning. 'Ah,' sighed Dean, 'the end of Texas, the end of America, we don't know no more.' It was tremendously hot: we were all sweating buckets. There was no night dew, not a breath of air, nothing except billions of moths smashing at bulbs everywhere and the low, rank smell of a hot river in the night near by – the Rio Grande, that begins in cool Rocky Mountain dales and ends up fashioning world-valleys to mingle its heats with the Mississippi muds in the great Gulf.

Laredo was a sinister town that morning. All kinds of cab-drivers and border rats wandered around, looking for opportunities. There weren't many; it was too late. It was the bottom and dregs of America where all the heavy villains sink, where disoriented people have to go to be near a specific elsewhere they can slip into unnoticed. Contraband brooded in the heavy syrup air. Cops were red-faced and sullen and sweaty, no swagger. Waitresses were dirty and disgusted. Just beyond, you could feel the enormous presence of whole great Mexico and almost smell the billion tortillas frying and smoking in the night. We had no idea what Mexico would really be like. We were at sea level again, and when we tried to eat a snack we could hardly swallow it. I wrapped it up in napkins for the trip anyway. We felt awful and sad. But everything changed when we crossed the mysterious bridge over the river and our wheels rolled on official Mexican soil, though it wasn't anything but carway for border inspection. Just across the street Mexico began. We looked with wonder. To our amazement, it looked exactly like Mexico. It was three in the morning, and fellows in straw hats and white pants were lounging by the dozen against battered pocky storefronts.

'Look – at – those – cats!' whispered Dean, 'Oo,' he breathed softly, 'wait, wait.' The Mexican officials came out, grinning, and asked please if we would take out our baggage. We did. We couldn't take our eyes from across the street. We were longing to rush right up there and get lost in those mysterious Spanish streets. It was only Nuevo Laredo but it looked like Holy Lhasa to us. 'Man, those guys are up all night,' whispered Dean. We hurried to get our papers straightened. We were warned not to drink tapwater now we were over the border. The Mexicans looked at our baggage in a desultory way. They weren't like officials at all. They were lazy and tender. Dean couldn't stop staring at them. He turned to me. 'See how the *cops* are in this country. I can't believe it!' He rubbed his eyes. 'I'm dreaming.' Then it was time to change our money. We saw great stacks of pesos on a table and learned that eight of them made an American buck, or thereabouts. We changed most of our money and stuffed the big rolls in our pockets with delight.

5

THEN we turned our faces to Mexico with bashfulness and wonder as those dozens of Mexican cats watched us from under their secret hatbrims in the night. Beyond were music and all-night restaurants with smoke pouring out of the door. 'Whee,' whispered Dean very softly.

'Thassall!' A Mexican official grinned. 'You boys all set. Go ahead. Welcome Mehico. Have good time. Watch you money. Watch you driving. I say this to you personal, I'm Red, everybody call me Red. Ask for Red. Eat good. Don't worry. Everything fine. Is not hard enjoin yourself in Mehico.'

'*Yes!*' shuddered Dean and off we went across the street into Mexico on soft feet. We left the car parked, and all three of us abreast went down the Spanish street into the middle of the dull brown lights. Old men sat on chairs in the night and looked like Oriental junkies and oracles. No one was actually looking at us, yet everybody was aware of everything we did. We turned sharp left into the smoky lunchroom and went in to music of campo guitars on an American 'thirties jukebox. Shirt-sleeved Mexican cabdrivers and straw-hatted Mexican hipsters sat at stools, devouring shapeless messes of tortillas, beans, tacos, whatnot. We bought three bottles of cold beer – *cerveza* was the name of beer – for about thirty Mexican cents or ten American cents each. We bought packs of Mexican cigarettes for six cents each. We gazed and gazed at our wonderful Mexican money that went so far, and played with it and looked around and smiled at everyone. Behind us lay the whole of America and everything Dean and I had previously known about life, and life on the road. We had finally found the magic land at the end of the road and we never dreamed the extent of the magic. '*Think* of these cats staying up all hours of the night,' whispered Dean. 'And think of this big continent ahead of us with those enormous Sierra Madre mountains we saw in the movies, and the jungles all the way down and a whole desert plateau as big as ours and reaching clear down to Guatemala and God knows where, whoo! What'll we do? What'll we do? Let's move!' We got out and went back to the car. One last glimpse of America across the hot lights of the Rio Grande bridge, and we turned our back and fender to it and roared off.

Instantly we were out in the desert and there wasn't a light or a car for fifty miles across the flats. And just then dawn was coming over the Gulf of Mexico and we began to see the ghostly shapes of yucca cactus and organpipe on all sides. 'What a wild country!' I yelped. Dean and I were completely awake. In Laredo we'd been half dead. Stan, who'd been to foreign countries before, just calmly slept in the back seat. Dean and I had the whole of Mexico before us.

'Now, Sal, we're leaving everything behind us and entering a new and unknown phase of things. All the years and troubles and kicks – and now *this!* so that we can safely think of nothing else and just go on ahead with our faces stuck out like this, you see, and *understand* the world as, really and genuinely speaking, other Americans haven't done before us – they were here, weren't they? The Mexican war. Cutting across here with cannon.'

'This road,' I told him, 'is also the route of old American outlaws who used to skip over the border and go down to old Monterrey, so if you'll look out on that greying desert and picture the ghost of an old Tombstone hellcat making his lonely exile gallop into the unknown, you'll see farther . . .'

'It's the world,' said Dean. 'My God!' he cried, slapping the wheel. 'It's the world! We can go right on to South America if the road goes. Think of it! Son-of-a-*bitch!* Gawd-*damn!*' We rushed on. The dawn spread immediately and we began to see the white sand of the desert and occasional huts in the distance of the road. Dean slowed down to peer at them. 'Real beat huts, man, the kind you only find in Death Valley and much worse. These people don't *bother* with appearances.' The first town ahead that had any consequence on the map was called Sabinas Hidalgo. We looked forward to it eagerly. 'And the road don't look any different than the American road,' cried Dean, 'except one mad thing and if you'll notice, right here, the mile-posts are written in kilometres and they click off the distance to Mexico City. See, it's the only city in the entire land, everything points to it.' There were only 767 more miles to that metropolis; in kilometres the figure was over a thousand. 'Damn! I gotta go!' cried Dean. For a while I closed my eyes in utter exhaustion and kept hearing Dean pound the wheel with his fists and say, 'Damn,' and 'What kicks!' and 'Oh, what a land!' and, 'Yes!' We arrived at Sabinas Hidalgo, across the desert, at about seven o'clock in the morning. We slowed down completely to see this. We woke up Stan in the back seat. We sat up straight to dig. The main street was muddy and full of holes. On each side were dirty broken-down adobe fronts. Burros walked in the street with packs. Barefoot women watched us from dark doorways. The street was completely crowded with people on foot beginning a new day in the Mexican countryside. Old men with handlebar moustaches stared at us. The sight of three bearded, bedraggled American youths instead of the usual well-dressed tourists was of unusual interest to them. We bounced along over Main Street at ten miles an hour, taking everything in. A group of girls walked directly in front of us. As we bounced by, one of them said, 'Where you going, man?'

I turned to Dean, amazed. 'Did you hear what she said?'

Dean was so astounded he kept on driving slowly and saying, 'Yes, I heard what she said, I certainly damn well did, oh me, oh my, I don't know what to do I'm so excited and sweetened in this morning world. We've finally got to heaven. It couldn't be cooler, it couldn't be grander, it couldn't be any*thing.*'

'Well, let's go back and pick em up!' I said.

'Yes,' said Dean and drove right on at five miles an hour. He was knocked out, he didn't have to do the usual things he would have done in America. 'There's millions of them all along the road!' he said. Nevertheless he U-turned and came by the girls again. They were headed for work in the fields; they smiled at us. Dean stared at them with rocky eyes. 'Damn,' he said under his breath. '*Oh!* This is too great to be true. Gurls, gurls. And particularly right now in my stage and condition, Sal, I am digging the interiors of these homes as we pass them – these gone doorways and you look inside and see beds of straw and little brown kids sleeping and stirring to wake, their thoughts congealing from the empty mind of sleep, their selves rising, and the mothers cooking up breakfast in iron pots, and dig them shutters they have for windows and the old men, the *old men* are so cool and grand and not bothered by anything. There's no *suspicion* here, nothing like that. Everybody's cool, everybody looks at you with such straight brown eyes and they don't say anything, just *look*, and in that look all of the human qualities are soft and subdued and still there. Dig all the foolish stories you read about Mexico and the sleeping gringo and all that crap – and crap about greasers and so on – and all it is, people here are straight and kind and don't put down any bull. I'm so amazed by this.' Schooled in the raw road night, Dean was come into the world to see it. He bent over the wheel and looked both ways and rolled along slowly. We stopped for gas the other side of Sabinas Hidalgo. Here a congregation of local straw-hatted ranchers with handlebar moustaches growled and joked in front of antique gas-pumps. Across the fields an old man plodded with a burro in front of his switch stick. The sun rose pure on pure and ancient activities of human life.

Now we resumed the road to Monterrey. The great mountains rose snow-capped before us; we bowled right for them. A gap widened and wound up a pass and we went with it. In a matter of minutes we were out of the mesquite desert and climbing among cool airs in a road with a stone wall along the precipice side and great whitewashed names of presidents on the cliffsides – ALEMAN! We met nobody on this high road. It wound among the clouds and took us to the great plateau on top. Across this plateau the big manufacturing town of Monterrey sent smoke to the blue skies with their enormous Gulf clouds written across the bowl of day like fleece. Entering Monterrey was like entering Detroit, among great long walls of factories, except for the burros that sunned in the grass before them and the sight of thick city adobe neighbourhoods with thousands of shifty hipsters hanging around doorways and whores looking out of windows and strange shops that might have sold anything and narrow sidewalks crowded with Hong-kong-like humanity. 'Yow!' yelled Dean. 'And all in that sun. Have you dug this Mexican sun, Sal? It makes you high. Whoo!

I want to get on and on – this road drives *me!!*' We mentioned stopping in the excitements of Monterrey, but Dean wanted to make extra-special time to get to Mexico City, and besides he knew the road would get more interesting, especially ahead, always ahead. He drove like a fiend and never rested. Stan and I were completely bushed and gave it up and had to sleep. I looked up outside Monterrey and saw enormous weird twin peaks beyond Old Monterrey, beyond where the outlaws went.

Montemorelos was ahead, a descent again to hotter altitudes. It grew exceedingly hot and strange. Dean absolutely had to wake me up to see this. 'Look, Sal, you *must* not miss.' I looked. We were going through swamps and alongside the road at ragged intervals strange Mexicans in tattered rags walked along with machetes hanging from their rope belts, and some of them cut at the bushes. They all stopped to watch us without expression. Through the tangled bush we occasionally saw thatched huts with African-like bamboo walls, just stick huts. Strange young girls, dark as the moon, stared from mysterious verdant doorways. 'Oh, man, I want to stop and twiddle thumbs with the little darlings,' cried Dean, 'but notice the old lady or the old man is always somewhere around – in the back usually, sometimes a hundred yards, gathering twigs and wood or tending animals. They're never alone. Nobody's ever alone in this country. While you've been sleeping I've been digging this road and this country, and if I could only tell you all the thoughts I've had, man!' He was sweating. His eyes were red-streaked and mad and also subdued and tender – he had found people like himself. We bowled right through the endless swamp country at a steady forty-five. 'Sal, I think the country won't change for a long time. If you'll drive, I'll sleep now.'

I took the wheel and drove among reveries of my own, through Linares, through hot, flat swamp country, across the steaming Rio Soto la Marina near Hidalgo, and on. A great verdant jungle valley with long fields of green crops opened before me. Groups of men watched us pass from a narrow old-fashioned bridge. The hot river flowed. Then we rose in altitude till a kind of desert country began reappearing. The city of Gregoria was ahead. The boys were sleeping, and I was alone in my eternity at the wheel, and the road ran straight as an arrow. Not like driving across Carolina, or Texas, or Arizona, or Illinois; but like driving across the world and into the places where we would finally learn ourselves among the Fellahin Indians of the world, the essential strain of the basic primitive, wailing humanity that stretches in a belt around the equatorial belly of the world from Malaya (the long fingernail of China) to India the great subcontinent to Arabia to Morocco to the self-same deserts and jungles of Mexico and over the waves to Polynesia to mystic Siam of the Yellow Robe and on around, on around, so that you hear the same mournful wail by the rotted walls of Cádiz, Spain, that you hear 12,000 miles around in the depths of Benares the Capital of the World. These people were unmistakably Indians and were not at all like the Pedros and Panchos of silly civilized American lore – they had high cheekbones, and slanted eyes, and soft ways; they were not fools, they were not clowns; they were great, grave Indians and they were the source of mankind and the fathers of it. The waves are Chinese, but the earth is an Indian thing. As essential as rocks in the desert are they in the desert of 'history'. And they knew this when we passed, ostensibly self-important moneybag Americans on a lark in their land; they knew who was the father and who was the son of antique life on earth, and made no comment. For when destruction comes to the world of 'history' and the Apocalypse of the Fellahin returns once more as so many times before, people will still stare with the same eyes from the caves of Mexico as well as from the caves of Bali, where it all began and where Adam was suckled and taught to know. These were my growing thoughts as I drove the car into the hot, sun-baked town of Gregoria.

Earlier, back at San Antonio, I had promised Dean, as a joke, that I would get him a girl. It was a bet and a challenge. As I pulled up the car at the gas station near sunny Gregoria a kid came across the road on tattered feet, carrying an enormous windshield-shade, and wanted to know if I'd buy. 'You like? Sixty peso. *Habla Español? Sesenta peso.* My name Victor.'

'Nah,' I said jokingly, 'buy señorita.'

'Sure, sure!' he cried excitedly. 'I get you gurls, onnytime. Too hot now,' he added with distaste. 'No good gurls when hot day. Wait tonight. You like shade?'

I didn't want the shade but I wanted the girls. I woke up Dean. 'Hey, man, I told you in Texas I'd get you a girl – all right, stretch your bones and wake up, boy; we've got girls waiting for us.'

'What? what?' he cried, leaping up, haggard. 'Where? where?'

'This boy Victor's going to show us where.'

'Well, lessgo, lessgo!' Dean leaped out of the car and clasped Victor's hand. There was a group of other boys hanging around the station and grinning, half of them barefoot, all wearing floppy straw hats. 'Man,' said Dean to me, 'ain't this a nice way to spend an afternoon. It's so much *cooler* than Denver poolhalls. Victor, you got gurls? Where? *A donde?*' he cried in Spanish. 'Dig that, Sal, I'm speaking Spanish.'

'Ask him if we can get any tea. Hey kid, you got ma-ree-wa-na?'

The kid nodded gravely. 'Sho, onnytime, mon. Come with me.'

'Hee! Whee! Hoo!' yelled Dean. He was wide awake and jumping up and down in that drowsy Mexican street. 'Let's all go!' I was passing Lucky Strikes to the other boys. They were getting great pleasure out of us and especially Dean. They turned to one another with cupped hands and rattled off comments about the mad American cat. 'Dig them, Sal, talking about us and digging. Oh my goodness, what a world!' Victor got in the car with us, and we lurched off. Stan Shephard had been sleeping soundly and woke up to this madness.

We drove way out to the desert the other side of town and turned on a rutty dirt road that made the car bounce as never before. Up ahead was Victor's house. It sat on the edge of cactus flats overtopped by a few trees, just an adobe crackerbox, with a few men lounging around in the yard. 'Who that?' cried Dean, all excited.

'Those my brothers. My mother there too. My sistair too. That my family. I married, I live downtown.'

'What about your mother?' Dean flinched. 'What she say about marijuana.'

'Oh, she get it for me.' And as we waited in the car Victor got out and loped over to the house and said a few words to an old lady, who promptly turned and went to the garden in back and began gathering dry fronds of marijuana that had been pulled off the plants and left to dry in the desert sun. Meanwhile Victor's brothers grinned from under a tree. They were coming over to meet us but it would take a while for them to get up and walk over. Victor came back, grinning sweetly.

'Man,' said Dean, 'that Victor is the sweetest, gonest, franticest little bangtail cat I've ever in all my life met. Just look at him, look at his cool slow walk. There's no need to hurry around here.' A steady, insistent desert breeze blew into the car. It was very hot.

'You see how hot?' said Victor, sitting down with Dean in the front seat and pointing up at the burning roof of the Ford. 'You have ma-ree-gwana and it no hot no more. You wait.'

'Yes,' said Dean, adjusting his dark glasses, 'I wait. For sure, Victor m'boy.'

Presently Victor's tall brother came ambling along with some weed piled on a page of newspaper. He dumped it on Victor's lap and leaned casually on the door of the car to nod and smile at us and say, 'Hallo.' Dean nodded and smiled pleasantly at *him*. Nobody talked; it was fine. Victor proceeded to roll the biggest bomber anybody ever saw. He rolled (using brown bag paper) what amounted to a tremendous Corona cigar of tea. It was huge. Dean stared at it, popeyed. Victor casually lit it and passed it around. To drag on this thing was like leaning over a chimney and inhaling. It blew into your throat in one great blast of heat. We held our breaths and all let out just about simultaneously. Instantly we were all high. The sweat froze on our foreheads and it was suddenly like the beach at Acapulco. I looked out the back window of the car, and another and the strangest of Victor's brothers – a tall Peruvian of an Indian with a sash over his shoulder – leaned grinning on a post, too bashful to come up and shake hands. It seemed the car was surrounded by brothers, for another one appeared on Dean's side. Then the strangest thing happened. Everybody became so high that usual formalities were dispensed with and things of immediate interest were concentrated on, and now it was the strangeness of Americans and Mexicans blasting together on the desert and, more than that, the strangeness of seeing in close proximity the

266

faces and pores of skins and calluses of fingers and general abashed cheekbones of another world. So the Indian brothers began talking about us in low voices and commenting; you saw them look, and size, and compare mutualities of impression, or correct and modify, 'Yeh, yeh'; while Dean and Stan and I commented on them in English.

'Will you d-i-g that weird brother in the back that hasn't moved from that post and hasn't by one cut hair diminished the intensity of the glad *funny* bashfulness of his smile? And the one to my left here, older, more sure of himself but sad, like hung-up, like a bum even maybe, in town, while Victor is respectably married – he's like a gawddam Egyptian king, that you see. These guys are real *cats*. Ain't never seen anything like it. And they're talking and wondering about us, like see? Just like we are but with a difference of their own, their interest probably resolving around how we're dressed – same as ours, really – but the strangeness of the things we have in the car and the strange ways that we laugh so different from them, and maybe even the way we smell compared to them. Nevertheless I'd give my eye-teeth to know what they're saying about us.' And Dean tried. 'Hey Victor, man – what you brother say just then?'

Victor turned mournful high brown eyes on Dean. 'Yeah, yeah.'

'No, you didn't understand my question. What you boys talking about?'

'Oh,' said Victor with great perturbation, 'you no like this mar-gwana?'

'Oh, yeah, yes fine! What you *talk* about?'

'Talk? Yes, we talk. How you like Mexico?' It was hard to come around without a common language. And everybody grew quiet and cool and high again and just enjoyed the breeze from the desert and mused separate national and racial and personal high-eternity thoughts.

It was time for the girls. The brothers eased back to their station under the tree, the mother watched from her sunny doorway, and we slowly bounced back to town.

But now the bouncing was no longer unpleasant; it was the

most pleasant and graceful billowy trip in the world, as over a blue sea, and Dean's face was suffused with an unnatural glow that was like gold as he told us to understand the springs of the car now for the first time and dig the ride. Up and down we bounced, and even Victor understood and laughed. Then he pointed left to show which way to go for the girls, and Dean, looking left with indescribable delight and leaning that way, pulled the wheel around and rolled us smoothly and surely to the goal, meanwhile listening to Victor's attempt to speak and saying grandly and magniloquently 'Yes, of course! There's not a doubt in my mind! Decidedly, man! Oh, indeed! Why, pish, posh, you say the dearest things to me! Of course! Yes! Please go on!' To this Victor talked gravely and with magnificent Spanish eloquence. For a mad moment I thought Dean was understanding everything he said by sheer wild insight and sudden revelatory genius inconceivably inspired by his glowing happiness. In that moment, too, he looked so exactly like Franklin Delano Roosevelt – some delusion in my flaming eyes and floating brain – that I drew up in my seat and gasped with amazement. In myriad pricklings of heavenly radiation I had to struggle to see Dean's figure, and he looked like God. I was so high I had to lean my head back on the seat; the bouncing of the car sent shivers of ecstasy through me. The mere thought of looking out the window at Mexico – which was now something else in my mind – was like recoiling from some gloriously riddled glittering treasure-box that you're afraid to look at because of your eyes, they bend inward, the riches and the treasures are too much to take all at once. I gulped. I saw streams of gold pouring through the sky and right across the tattered roof of the poor old car, right across my eyeballs and indeed right inside them; it was everywhere. I looked out the window at the hot, sunny streets and saw a woman in a doorway and I thought she was listening to every word we said and nodding to herself – routine paranoiac visions due to tea. But the stream of gold continued. For a long time I lost consciousness in my lower mind of what we were doing and only came around sometime later when I looked up from fire and silence like waking from sleep to the world, or waking from void to a dream, and they told me we were parked outside Victor's house and he was already at the door of the car with his little baby son in his arms, showing him to us.

'You see my baby? Hees name Pérez, he six month age.'

'Why,' said Dean, his face still transfigured into a shower of supreme pleasure and even bliss, 'he is the prettiest child I have ever seen. Look at those eyes. Now, Sal and Stan,' he said, turning to us with a serious and tender air, 'I want you par-ti-cu-lar-ly to see the eyes of this little Mexican boy who is the son of our wonderful friend Victor, and notice how he will come to manhood with his own particular soul bespeaking itself through the windows which are his eyes, and such lovely eyes surely do prophesy and indicate the loveliest of souls.' It was a beautiful speech. And it was a beautiful baby. Victor mournfully looked down at his angel. We all wished we had a little son like that. So great was our intensity over the child's soul that he sensed something and began a grimace which led to bitter tears and some unknown sorrow that we had no means to soothe because it reached too far back into innumerable mysteries and time. We tried everything; Victor smothered him in his neck and rocked, Dean cooed, I reached over and stroked the baby's little arms. His bawls grew louder. 'Ah,' said Dean, 'I'm awfully sorry, Victor, that we've made him sad.'

'He is not sad, baby cry.' In the doorway in back of Victor, too bashful to come out, was his little barefoot wife, with anxious tenderness waiting for the babe to be put back in her arms so brown and soft. Victor, having shown us his child, climbed back into the car and proudly pointed to the right.

'Yes,' said Dean, and swung the car over and directed it through narrow Algerian streets with faces on all sides watching us with gentle wonder. We came to the whorehouse. It was a magnificent establishment of stucco in the golden sun. In the street, and leaning on the windowsills that opened into the whorehouse, were two cops, saggy-trousered, drowsy, bored, who gave us brief interested looks as we walked in, and stayed there the entire three hours that we cavorted under their noses, until we came out at dusk and at Victor's bidding gave them the equivalent of twenty-four cents each, just for the sake of form.

And in there we found the girls. Some of them were reclining on couches across the dance floor, some of them were boozing at the long bar to the right. In the centre an arch led into small cubicle shacks that looked like the places where you put on your bathing suit at public municipal beaches. These shacks were in the sun of the court. Behind the bar was the proprietor, a young fellow who instantly ran out when we told him we wanted to hear mambo music and came back with a stack of records, mostly by Pérez Prado, and put them on over the loudspeaker. In an instant all the city of Gregoria could hear the good times going on at the Sala de Baile. In the hall itself the din of the music – for this is the real way to play a jukebox and what it was originally for – was so tremendous that it shattered Dean and Stan and me for a moment in the realization that we had never dared to play music as loud as we wanted, and this was how loud we wanted. It blew and shuddered directly at us. In a few minutes half that portion of town was at the windows, watching the *Americanos* dance with the gals. They all stood, side by side with the cops, on the dirt sidewalk, leaning in with indifference and casualness. 'More Mambo Jambo', 'Chattanooga de Mambo', 'Mambo Numero Ocho' – all these tremendous numbers resounded and flared in the golden, mysterious after-noon like the sounds you expect to hear on the last day of the world and the Second Coming. The trumpets seemed so loud I thought they could hear them clear out in the desert, where the trumpets had originated anyway. The drums were mad. The mambo beat is the conga beat from Congo, the river of Africa and the world; it's really the world beat. Oom-*ta*, ta-poo-*poom* – oom-*ta*, ta-poo-*poom*. The piano montunos showered down on us from the speaker. The cries of the leader were like great gasps in the air. The final trumpet choruses that came with drum climaxes on conga and bongo drums, on the great mad Chatta-nooga record, froze Dean in his tracks for a moment till he shuddered and sweated; then when the trumpets bit the drowsy air with their quivering echoes, like a cavern's or a cave's, his eyes grew large and round as though seeing the devil, and he closed them tight. I myself was shaken like a puppet by it; I heard the trumpets flail the light I had seen and trembled in my boots.

On the fast 'Mambo Jambo' we danced frantically with the girls. Through our deliriums we began to discern their varying personalities. They were great girls. Strangely the wildest one was half Indian, half white, and came from Venezuela, and only eighteen. She looked as if she came from a good family. What she was doing whoring in Mexico at that age and with that tender cheek and fair aspect, God knows. Some awful grief had driven her to it. She drank beyond all bounds. She threw down drinks when it seemed she was about to chuck up the last. She overturned glasses continually, the idea also being to make us spend as much money as possible. Wearing her flimsy housecoat in broad afternoon, she frantically danced with Dean and clung about his neck and begged and begged for everything. Dean was so stoned he didn't know what to start with, girls or mambo. They ran off to the lockers. I was set upon by a fat and uninteresting girl with a puppy dog, who got sore at me when I took a dislike to the dog because it kept trying to bite me. She compromised by putting it away in the back, but by the time she returned I had been hooked by another girl, better looking but not the best, who clung to my neck like a leech. I was trying to break loose to get at a sixteen-year-old coloured girl who sat gloomily inspecting her navel through an opening in her short shirty dress across the hall. I couldn't do it. Stan had a fifteen-year-old girl with an almond-coloured skin and a dress that was buttoned halfway down and halfway up. It was mad. A good twenty men leaned in that window, watching.

At one point the mother of the little coloured girl – not coloured, but dark – came in to hold a brief and mournful convocation with her daughter. When I saw that, I was too ashamed to try for the one I really wanted. I let the leech take me off to the back, where, as in a dream, to the din and roar of more loudspeakers inside, we made the bed bounce a half-hour. It was just a square room with wooden slats and no ceiling, ikon in a corner, a washbasin in another. All up and down the dark hall the girls were calling, '*Agua, agua caliente!*' which means 'hot water'. Stan and Dean were also out of sight. My girl charged thirty pesos, or about three dollars and a half, and begged for an extra ten pesos and gave a long story about something. I didn't know the value of Mexican money; for all I knew I had a million pesos. I threw money at her. We rushed back to dance. A greater crowd was gathered in the street. The cops looked as bored as usual. Dean's pretty Venezuelan dragged me through a door and into another strange bar that apparently belonged to the whorehouse. Here a young bartender was talking and wiping glasses and an old man with handlebar moustache sat discussing something earnestly. And here too the mambo roared over another loudspeaker. It seemed the whole world was turned on. Venezuela clung about my neck and begged for drinks. The bartender wouldn't give her one. She begged and begged, and when he gave it to her she spilled it and this time not on purpose, for I saw the chagrin in her poor sunken lost eyes. 'Take it easy, baby,' I told her. I had to support her on the stool; she kept slipping off. I've never seen a drunker woman, and only eighteen. I bought her another drink; she was tugging at my pants for mercy. She gulped it up. I didn't have the heart to try her. My own girl was about thirty and took care of herself better. With Venezuela writhing and suffering in my arms, I had a longing to take her in the back and undress her and only talk to her – this I told myself. I was delirious with want of her and the other little dark girl.

Poor Victor, all this time he stood on the brass rail of the bar with his back to the counter and jumped up and down gladly to see his three American friends cavort. We bought him drinks. His eyes gleamed for a woman but he wouldn't accept any, being faithful to his wife. Dean thrust money at him. In this welter of madness I had an opportunity to see what Dean was up to. He was so out of his mind he didn't know who I was when I peered at his face. 'Yeah, yeah!' is all he said. It seemed it would never end. It was like a long, spectral Arabian dream in the afternoon in another life – Ali Baba and the alleys and the courtesans. Again I rushed off with my girl to her room; Dean and Stan switched the girls they'd had before; and we were out of sight a moment, and the spectators had to wait for the show to go on. The afternoon grew long and cool.

Soon it would be mysterious night in old gone Gregoria. The mambo never let up for a moment, it frenzied on like an endless journey in the jungle. I couldn't take my eyes off the little dark girl and the way, like a queen, she walked around and was even reduced by the sullen bartender to menial tasks such as bringing us drinks and sweeping the back. Of all the girls in there she needed the money most; maybe her mother had come to get money from her for her little infant sisters and brothers. Mexicans are poor. It never, never occurred to me just to approach her and give her some money. I have a feeling she would have taken it with a degree of scorn, and scorn from the likes of her made me flinch. In my madness I was actually in love with her for the few hours it all lasted; it was the same unmistakable ache and stab across the mind, the same sighs, the same pain, and above all the same reluctance and fear to approach. Strange that Dean and Stan also failed to approach her; her unimpeachable dignity was the thing that made her poor in a wild old whorehouse, and think of that. At one point I saw Dean leaning like a statue towards her, ready to fly, and befuddlement cross his face as she glanced coolly and imperiously his way and he stopped rubbing his belly and gaped and finally bowed his head. For she was the queen.

Now Victor suddenly clutched at our arms in the furore and made frantic signs.

'What's the matter?' He tried everything to make us understand. Then he ran to the bar and grabbed the cheque from the bartender, who scowled at him, and took it to us to see. The bill was over three hundred pesos, or thirty-six American dollars, which is a lot of money in any whorehouse. Still we couldn't sober up and didn't want to leave, and though we were all run out we still wanted to hang around with our lovely girls in this strange Arabian paradise we had finally found at the end of the hard, hard road. But night was coming and we had to get on to the end; and Dean saw that, and began frowning and thinking and trying to straighten himself out, and finally I broached the idea of leaving once and for all. 'So much ahead of us, man, it won't make any difference.'

'That's right!' cried Dean, glassy-eyed, and turned to his Venezuelan. She had finally passed out and lay on a wooden bench with her white legs protruding from the silk. The gallery in the window took advantage of the show; behind them red shadows were beginning to creep, and somewhere I heard a baby wail in a sudden lull, remembering I was in Mexico after all and not in a pornographic hasheesh daydream in heaven.

We staggered out; we had forgotten Stan; we ran back in to

get him and found him charmingly bowing to the new evening whores, who had just come in for night shift. He wanted to start all over again. When he is drunk he lumbers like a man ten feet tall and when he is drunk he can't be dragged away from women. Moreover women cling to him like ivy. He insisted on staying and trying some of the newer, stranger, more proficient señoritas. Dean and I pounded him on the back and dragged him out. He waved profuse good-byes to everybody – the girls, the cops, the crowds, the children in the street outside; he blew kisses in all directions to ovations of Gregoria and staggered proudly among the gangs and tried to speak to them and communicate his joy and love of everything this fine afternoon of life. Everybody laughed; some slapped him on the back. Dean rushed over and paid the policemen the four pesos and shook hands and grinned and bowed with them.' Then he jumped in the car, and the girls we had known, even Venezuela, who was wakened for the farewell, gathered around the car, huddling in their flimsy duds, and chattered good-byes and kissed us, and Venezuela even began to weep – though not for us, we knew, not altogether for us, yet enough and good enough. My dusky darling love had disappeared in the shadows inside. It was all over. We pulled out and left joys and celebrations over hundreds of pesos behind us, and it didn't seem like a bad day's work. The haunting mambo followed us a few blocks. It was all over. 'Good-bye, Gregoria!' cried Dean, blowing it a kiss.

Victor was proud of us and proud of himself. 'Now you like bath?' he asked. Yes, we all wanted wonderful bath.

And he directed us to the strangest thing in the world : it was an ordinary American-type bathhouse one mile out of town on the highway, full of kids splashing in a pool and showers inside a stone building for a few centavos a crack, with soap and towel from the attendant. Besides this, it was also a sad kiddy park with swings and a broken-down merry-go-round, and in the fading red sun it seemed so strange and beautiful. Stan and I got towels and jumped right into ice-cold showers inside and came out refreshed and new. Dean didn't bother with a shower, and we saw him far across the sad park, strolling arm in arm with good Victor and chatting volubly and pleasantly and even

274

leaning excitedly towards him to make a point, and pounding his fist. Then they resumed the arm-in-arm position and strolled. The time was coming to say good-bye to Victor, so Dean was taking the opportunity to have moments alone with him and to inspect the park and get his views on things in general and in all dig him as only Dean could do.

Victor was very sad now that we had to go. 'You come back Gregoria, see me?'

'Sure, man!' said Dean. He even promised to take Victor back to the States if he so wished it. Victor said he would have to mull this over.

'I got wife and kid – ain't got a money – I see.' His sweet polite smile glowed in the redness as we waved to him from the car. Behind him were the sad park and the children.

6

IMMEDIATELY outside Gregoria the road began to drop, great trees arose on each side, and in the trees as it grew dark we heard the great roar of billions of insects that sounded like one continuous high-screeching cry. 'Whoo!' said Dean, and he turned on his headlights and they weren't working. 'What! what! damn now what?' And he punched and fumed at his dashboard. 'Oh, my, we'll have to drive through the jungle without lights, think of the horror of that, the only time I'll see is when another car comes by and there just *aren't* any cars! And of course no lights? Oh, what'll we do, dammit?'

'Let's just drive. Maybe we ought to go back, though?'

'No, never-never! Let's go on. I can barely see the road. We'll make it.' And now we shot in inky darkness through the scream of insects, and the great, rank, almost rotten smell descended, and we remembered and realized that the map indicated just after Gregoria the beginning of the Tropic of Cancer. 'We're in a new tropic! No wonder the smell! Smell it!' I stuck my head out of the window; bugs smashed at my face; a great screech rose the moment I cocked my ear to the wind. Suddenly our lights were working again and they poked ahead, illuminating the lonely road that ran between solid walls of drooping, snaky trees as high as a hundred feet.

'Son-of-a-*bitch!*' yelled Stan in the back. 'Hot *damn!*' He was still so high. We suddenly realized he was still high and the jungle and troubles made no difference to his happy soul. We began laughing, all of us.

'To hell with it! We'll just throw ourselves on the gawddamn jungle, we'll sleep in it tonight, let's go!' yelled Dean. 'Ole Stan is right. Ole Stan don't care! He's so high on those women and that tea and that crazy out-of-this-world impossible-to-absorb mambo blasting so loud that my eardrums still beat to it – whee! he's so high he knows what he's doing!' We took off our T-shirts and roared through the jungle, bare-chested. No towns, nothing, lost jungle, miles and miles, and down-going, getting hotter, the insects screaming louder, the vegetation growing higher, the smell ranker and hotter until we began to get used to it and like it. 'I'd just like to get naked and roll and roll in that jungle,' said Dean. 'No, hell, man, that's what I'm going to do soon's I find a good spot.' And suddenly Limòn appeared before us, a jungle town, a few brown lights, dark shadows, enormous skies overhead, and a cluster of men in front of a jumble of woodshacks – tropical crossroads.

We stopped in the unimaginable softness. It was as hot as the inside of a baker's oven on a June night in New Orleans. All up and down the street whole families were sitting around in the dark, chatting; occasional girls came by, but extremely young and only curious to see what we looked like. They were barefoot and dirty. We leaned on the wooden porch of a brokendown general store with sacks of flour an fresh pineapple rotting with flies on the counter. There was one oil lamp in here, and outside a few more brown lights, and the rest all black, black, black. Now of course we were so tired we had to sleep at once and moved the car a few yards down a dirt road to the backside of town. It was so incredibly hot it was impossible to sleep. So Dean took a blanket and laid it out on the soft, hot sand in the road and flopped out. Stan was stretched on the front seat of the Ford with both doors open for a draught, but there wasn't even the faintest puff of a wind. I, in the back seat, suffered in a pool of sweat. I got out of the car and stood swaying in the blackness. The whole town had instantly gone to bed; the only noise now was barking dogs. How could I ever sleep? Thousands of mosquitoes had already bitten all of us on chest and arms and ankles. Then a bright idea came to me: I jumped up on the steel roof of the car and stretched out flat on my back. Still there was no breeze, but the steel had an element of coolness in it and dried my back of sweat, clotting up thousands of dead bugs into cakes on my skin, and I realized the jungle takes you over and you become it. Lying on the top of the car with my face to the black sky was like lying in a closed trunk on a summer night. For the first time in my life the weather was not something that touched me, that caressed me, froze or sweated me, but became me. The atmosphere and I became the same. Soft infinitesimal showers of microscopic bugs fanned down on my face as I slept, and they were extremely pleasant and soothing. The sky was starless, utterly unseen and heavy. I could lie there all night long with my face exposed to the heavens, and it would do me no more harm than a velvet drape drawn over me. The dead bugs mingled with my blood; the live mosquitoes exchanged further portions; I began to tingle all over and to smell of the rank, hot, and rotten jungle, all over from hair and face to feet and toes. Of course I was barefoot. To minimize the sweat I put on my bug-smeared T-shirt and lay back again. A huddle of darkness on the blacker road showed where Dean was sleeping. I could hear him snoring. Stan was snoring too.

Occasionally a dim light flashed in town, and this was the sheriff making his rounds with a weak flashlight and mumbling to himself in the jungle night. Then I saw his light jiggling towards us and heard his footfalls coming soft on the mats of sand and vegetation. He stopped and flashed the car. I sat up and looked at him. In a quivering, almost querulous, and extremely tender voice he said, 'Dormiendo?' indicating Dean in the road. I knew this meant 'sleep'.

'Sí, dormiendo.'

'Bueno, bueno,' he said to himself and with reluctance and sadness turned away and went back to his lonely rounds. Such lovely policemen God hath never wrought in America. No suspicions, no fuss, no bother: he was the guardian of the sleeping town, period.

I went back to my bed of steel and stretched out with my arms spread. I didn't even know if branches or open sky were directly above me, and it made no difference. I opened my mouth to it and drew deep breaths of jungle atmosphere. It was not air, never air, but the palpable and living emanation of trees and swamp. I stayed awake. Roosters began to crow the dawn across the brakes somewhere. Still no air, no breeze, no dew, but the same Tropic of Cancer heaviness held us all pinned to earth, where we belonged and tingled. There was no sign of dawn in the skies. Suddenly I heard the dogs barking furiously across the dark, and then I heard the faint clip-clop of a horse's hooves. It came closer and closer. What kind of mad rider in the night would this be? Then I saw an apparition: a wild horse, white as a ghost, came trotting down the road directly towards Dean. Behind him the dogs yammered and contended. I couldn't see them, they were dirty old jungle dogs, but the horse was white as snow and immense and almost phosphorescent and easy to see. I felt no panic for Dean. The horse saw him and trotted right by his head, passed the car like a ship, whinnied softly, and continued on through town, bedevilled by the dogs, and clip-clopped back to the jungle on the other side, and all I heard was the faint hoofbeat fading away in the woods. The dogs subsided and sat to lick themselves. What was this horse? What myth and ghost, what spirit? I told Dean about it when he woke up. He thought I'd been dreaming. Then he recalled faintly dreaming of a white horse, and I told him it had been no dream. Stan Shephard slowly woke up. The faintest movements, and we were sweating profusely again. It was still pitch dark. 'Let's start the car and blow some air!' I cried. 'I'm dying of heat.'

'Right!' We roared out of town and continued along the mad highway with our hair flying. Dawn came rapidly in a grey haze, revealing dense swamps sunk on both sides, with tall, forlorn, viny trees leaning and bowing over tangled bottoms. We bowled right along the railroad tracks for a while. The strange radio-station antenna of Ciudad Mante appeared ahead, as if we were in Nebraska. We found a gas station and loaded the tank just as the last of the jungle-night bugs hurled themselves in a black mass against the bulbs and fell fluttering at our feet in huge wriggly groups, some of them with wings a good four inches long, others frightful dragonflies big enough to eat a bird, and thousands of immense yangling mosquitoes and unnamable spidery insects of all sorts. I hopped up and down on the pavement for fear of them; I finally ended up in the car with my feet in my hands, looking fearfully at the ground where they swarmed around our wheels. 'Lessgo!' I yelled. Dean and Stan weren't perturbed at all by the bugs; they calmly drank a couple of bottles of Mission Orange and kicked them away from the water cooler. Their shirts and pants, like mine, were soaked in the blood and black of thousands of dead bugs. We smelled our clothes deeply.

'You know, I'm beginning to like this smell,' said Stan. 'I can't smell myself any more.'

'It's a strange, good smell,' said Dean. 'I'm not going to change my shirt till Mexico City, I want to take it all in and remember it.' So off we roared again, creating air for our hot, caked faces.

Then the mountains loomed ahead, all green. After this climb we would be on the great central plateau again and ready to roll ahead to Mexico City. In no time at all we soared to an elevation of five thousand feet among misty passes that overlooked steaming yellow rivers a mile below. It was the great River Moctezuma. The Indians along the road began to be extremely weird. They were a nation in themselves, mountain Indians, shut off from everything else but the Pan-American Highway. They were short and squat and dark, with bad teeth; they carried immense loads on their backs. Across enormous vegetated ravines we saw patchworks of agriculture on steep slopes. They walked up and down those slopes and worked the crops. Dean drove the car five miles an hour to see. 'Whooee, this I never thought existed!' High on the highest peak, as great as any Rocky Mountain peak, we saw bananas growing. Dean got out of the car to point, to stand around rubbing his belly. We were on a ledge where a little thatched hut suspended itself over the precipice of the world. The sun created golden hazes that obscured the Moctezuma, now more than a mile below.

In the yard in front of the hut a little three-year-old Indian girl stood with her finger in her mouth, watching us with big brown eyes. 'She's probably never seen anybody parked here before in her entire life!' breathed Dean. 'Hel-lo, little girl. How are you? Do you like us?' The little girl looked away bashfully and pouted. We began to talk and she again examined us with finger in mouth. 'Gee, I wish there was something I could give her! *Think of it*, being born and living on this ledge – this ledge representing all you know of life. Her father is probably groping down the ravine with a rope and getting his pineapples out of a cave and hacking wood at an eighty-degree angle with all the bottom below. She'll never, never leave here and know anything about the outside world. It's a nation. Think of the wild chief they must have! They probably, off the road, over that bluff, miles back, must be even wilder and stranger, yeah, because the Pan-American Highway partially civilizes this nation on this road. Notice the beads of sweat on her brow,' Dean pointed out with a grimace of pain. 'It's not the kind of sweat we have, it's oily and it's *always there* because it's *always* hot the year round and she knows nothing of non-sweat, she was born with sweat and dies with sweat.' The sweat on her little brow was heavy, sluggish; it didn't run; it just stood there and gleamed like a fine olive oil. 'What that must do to their souls! How different they must be in their private concerns and evaluations and wishes!' Dean drove on with his mouth hanging in awe, ten miles an hour, desirous to see every possible human being on the road. We climbed and climbed.

As we climbed, the air grew cooler and the Indian girls on the road wore shawls over their heads and shoulders. They hailed us desperately; we stopped to see. They wanted to sell us little pieces of rock crystal. Their great brown, innocent eyes looked into ours with such soulful intensity that not one of us had the slightest sexual thought about them; moreover they were very young, some of them eleven and looking almost thirty. 'Look at those eyes!' breathed Dean. They were like the eyes of the Virgin Mother when she was a child. We saw in them the tender and forgiving gaze of Jesus. And they stared unflinching into ours. We rubbed our nervous blue eyes and looked again. Still they penetrated us with sorrowful and hypnotic gleam.

When they talked they suddenly became frantic and almost silly. In their silence they were themselves. 'They've only *recently* learned to sell these crystals, since the highway was built about ten years back – up until that time this entire nation must have been *silent*!'

The girls yammered around the car. One particularly soulful child gripped at Dean's sweaty arm. She yammered in Indian. 'Ah yes, ah yes, dear one,' said Dean tenderly and almost sadly. He got out of the car and went fishing around in the battered trunk in the back – the same old tortured American trunk – and pulled out a wristwatch. He showed it to the child. She whimpered with glee. The others crowded around with amazement. Then Dean poked in the little girl's hand for 'the sweetest and purest and smallest crystal she has personally picked from the mountain for me'. He found one no bigger than a berry. And he handed her the wristwatch dangling. Their mouths rounded like the mouths of chorister children. The lucky little girl squeezed it to her ragged breastrobes. They stroked Dean and thanked him. He stood among them with his ragged face to the sky, looking for the next and highest and final pass, and seemed like the Prophet that had come to them. He got back in the car. They hated to see us go. For the longest time, as we mounted a straight pass, they waved and ran after us. We made a turn and never saw them again, and they were still running after us. 'Ah, this breaks my heart!' cried Dean, punching his chest. 'How far do they carry out these loyalties and wonders? What's going to happen to them? Would they try to follow the car all the way to Mexico City if we drove slow enough?'

'Yes,' I said, for I knew.

We came into the dizzying heights of the Sierra Madre Oriental. The banana trees gleamed golden in the haze. Great fogs yawned beyond stone walls along the precipice. Below, the Moctezuma was a thin golden thread in a green jungle mat. Strange crossroad towns on top of the world rolled by, with shawled Indians watching us from under hatbrims and *rebezos*. Life was dense, dark, ancient. They watched Dean, serious and insane at his raving wheel, with eyes of hawks. All had their hands outstretched. They had come down from the back mountains and higher places to hold forth their hands for something they thought civilization could offer, and they never dreamed the sadness and the poor broken delusion of it. They didn't know that a bomb had come that could crack all our bridges and roads and reduce them to jumbles, and we would be as poor as they someday, and stretching out our hands in the same, same way. Our broken Ford, old thirties upgoing American Ford, rattled through them and vanished in dust.

We had reached the approaches of the last plateau. Now the sun was golden, the air keen blue, and the desert with its occasional rivers a riot of sandy, hot space and sudden Biblical tree shade. Now Dean was sleeping and Stan driving. The shepherds appeared, dressed as in first times, in long flowing robes, the woman carrying golden bundles of flax, the men staves. Under great trees on the shimmering desert the shepherds sat and convened, and the sheep moiled in the sun and raised dust beyond. 'Man, man,' I yelled to Dean, 'wake up and see the shepherds, wake up and see the golden world that Jesus came from, with your own eyes you can tell!'

He shot his head up from the seat, saw one glimpse of it all in the fading red sun, and dropped back to sleep. When he woke up he described it to me in detail and said, 'Yes, man, I'm glad you told me to look. Oh, Lord, what shall I do? Where will I go?' He rubbed his belly, he looked to heaven with red eyes, he almost wept.

The end of our journey impended. Great fields stretched on both sides of us; a noble wind blew across the occasional immense tree groves and over old missions turning salmon pink in the late sun. The clouds were close and huge and rose. 'Mexico City by dusk!' We'd made it, a total of nineteen hundred miles from the afternoon yards of Denver to these vast and Biblical areas of the world, and now we were about to reach the end of the road.

'Shall we change our insect T-shirts?'

'Naw, let's wear them into town, hell's bells.' And we drove into Mexico City.

A brief mountain pass took us suddenly to a height from which we saw all of Mexico City stretched out in its volcanic crater below and spewing city smokes and early dusklights. Down to it we zoomed, down Insurgentes Boulevard, straight towards the heart of town at Reforma. Kids played soccer in enormous sad fields and threw up dust. Taxi-drivers overtook us and wanted to know if we wanted girls. No, we didn't want girls now. Long, ragged adobe slums stretched out on the plain; we saw lonely figures in the dimming alleys. Soon night would come. Then the city roared in and suddenly we were passing crowded cafés and theatres and many lights. Newsboys yelled at us. Mechanics slouched by, barefoot, with wrenches and rags. Mad barefoot Indian drivers cut across us and surrounded us and tooted and made frantic traffic. The noise was incredible. No mufflers are used on Mexican cars. Horns are batted with glee continual. 'Whee!' yelled Dean. 'Look out!' He staggered the car through the traffic and played with everybody. He drove like an Indian. He got on a circular glorietta drive on Reforma Boulevard and rolled around it with its eight spokes shooting cars at us from all directions, left, right, *izquierda*, dead ahead, and yelled and jumped with joy. 'This is traffic I've always dreamed of! Everybody *goes!*' An ambulance came balling through. American ambulances dart and weave through traffic with siren blowing; the great world-wide Fellahin Indian ambulances merely come through at eighty miles an hour in the city streets, and everybody just has to get out of the way and they don't pause for anybody or any circumstances and fly straight through. We saw it reeling out of sight on skittering wheels in the breaking-up moil of dense downtown traffic. The drivers were Indians. People, even old ladies, ran for buses that never stopped. Young Mexico City businessmen made bets and ran by squads for buses and athletically jumped them. The bus-drivers were barefoot, sneering and insane, and sat low and squat in T-shirts at the low, enormous wheels. Ikons burned over them. The lights in the buses were brown and greenish, and dark faces were lined on wooden benches.

In downtown Mexico City thousands of hipsters in floppy straw hats and long-lapelled jackets over bare chests padded along the main drag, some of them selling crucifixes and weed in the alleys, some of them kneeling in beat chapels next to Mexican burlesque shows in sheds. Some alleys were rubble, with open sewers, and little doors led to closet-size bars stuck in adobe walls. You had to jump over a ditch to get your drink, and in the bottom of the ditch was the ancient lake of the Aztec. You came out of the bar with your back to the wall and edged back to the street. They served coffee mixed with rum and nutmeg. Mambo blared from everywhere. Hundreds of whores lined themselves along the dark and narrow streets and their sorrowful eyes gleamed at us in the night. We wandered in a frenzy and a dream. We ate beautiful steaks for forty-eight cents in a strange tiled Mexican cafeteria with generations of marimba musicians standing at one immense marimba – also wandering singing guitarists, and old men on corners blowing trumpets. You went by the sour stink of pulque saloons; they gave you a water glass of cactus juice in there, two cents. Nothing stopped; the streets were alive all night. Beggars slept wrapped in advertising posters torn off fences. Whole families of them sat on the sidewalk, playing little flutes and chuckling in the night. Their bare feet stuck out, their dim candles burned, all Mexico was one vast Bohemian camp. On corners old women cut up the boiled heads of cows and wrapped morsels in tortillas and served them with hot sauce on newspaper napkins. This was the great and final wild uninhibited Fellahin-childlike city that we knew we would find at the end of the road. Dean walked through with his arms hanging zombie-like at his sides, his mouth open, his eyes gleaming, and conducted a ragged and holy tour that lasted till dawn in a field with a boy in a straw hat who laughed and chatted with us and wanted to play catch, for nothing ever ended.

Then I got fever and became delirious and unconscious. Dysentery. I looked up out of the dark swirl of my mind and I knew I was on a bed eight thousand feet above sea level, on a roof of the world, and I knew that I had lived a whole life and many others in the poor atomistic husk of my flesh, and I had all the dreams. And I saw Dean bending over the kitchen table. It was several nights later and he was leaving Mexico City already. 'What you doin, man?' I moaned.

'Poor Sal, poor Sal, got sick. Stan'll take care of you. Now listen to hear if you can in your sickness : I got my divorce from Camille down here and I'm driving back to Inez in New York tonight if the car holds out.'

'All that again?' I cried.

'All that again, good buddy. Gotta get back to my life. Wish I could stay with you. Pray I can come back.' I grabbed the cramps in my belly and groaned. When I looked up again bold noble Dean was standing with his old broken trunk and looking down at me. I didn't know who he was any more, and he knew this, and sympathized, and pulled the blankets over my shoulders. 'Yes, yes, yes, I've got to go now. Old fever Sal, Good-bye.' And he was gone. Twelve hours later in my sorrowful fever I finally came to understand that he was gone. By that time he was driving back alone through those banana mountains, this time at night.

When I got better I realized what a rat he was, but then I had to understand the impossible complexity of his life, how he had to leave me there, sick, to get on with his wives and woes. 'Okay, old Dean, I'll say nothing.'

PART FIVE

DEAN drove from Mexico City and saw Victor again in Gregoria and pushed that old car all the way to Lake Charles, Louisiana, before the rear end finally dropped on the road as he had always known it would. So he wired Inez for airplane fare and flew the rest of the way. When he arrived in New York with the divorce papers in his hands, he and Inez immediately went to Newark and got married; and that night, telling her everything was all right and not to worry, and making logics where there was nothing but inestimable sorrowful sweats, he jumped on a bus and roared off again across the awful continent to San Francisco to rejoin Camille and the two baby girls. So now he was three times married, twice divorced, and living with his second wife.

In the fall I myself started back home from Mexico City and one night just over Laredo border in Dilley, Texas, I was standing on the hot road underneath an arc-lamp with the summer moths smashing into it when I heard the sound of footsteps from the darkness beyond, and lo, a tall old man with flowing white hair came clomping by with a pack on his back, and when he saw me as he passed, he said, 'Go moan for man', and clomped on back to his dark. Did this mean that I should at last go on my pilgrimage on foot on the dark roads around America? I struggled and hurried to New York, and one night I was standing in a dark street in Manhattan and called up to the window of a loft where I thought my friends were having a party. But a pretty girl stuck her head out the window and said, 'Yes? Who is it?'

'Sal Paradise,' I said, and heard my name resound in the sad and empty street.

'Come on up,' she called. 'I'm making hot chocolate.' So I

went up and there she was, the girl with the pure and innocent dear eyes that I had always searched for and for so long. We agreed to love each other madly. In the winter we planned to migrate to San Francisco, bringing all our beat furniture and broken belongings with us in a jalopy panel truck. I wrote to Dean and told him. He wrote back a huge letter eighteen thousand words long, all about his young years in Denver, and said he was coming to get me and personally select the old truck himself and drive us home. We had six weeks to save up the money for the truck and began working and counting every cent. And suddenly Dean arrived anyway, five and a half weeks in advance, and nobody had any money to go through with the plan.

I was taking a walk in the middle of the night and came back to my girl to tell her what I thought about during my walk. She stood in the dark little pad with a strange smile. I told her a number of things and suddenly I noticed the hush in the room and looked around and saw a battered book on the radio. I knew it was Dean's high-eternity-in-the-afternoon Proust. As in a dream I saw him tiptoe in from the dark hall in his stocking feet. He couldn't talk any more. He hopped and laughed, he stuttered and fluttered his hands and said, 'Ah – ah – you must listen to hear.' We listened, all ears. But he forgot what he wanted to say. 'Really listen – ahem. Look, dear Sal – sweet Laura – I've come – I'm gone – but wait – ah yes.' And he stared with rocky sorrow into his hands. 'Can't talk no more – do you understand that it is – or might be – But listen!' We all listened. He was listening to sounds in the night.'Yes!' he whispered with awe. 'But you see – no need to talk any more – and further.'

'But why did you come so soon, Dean?'

'Ah,' he said, looking at me as if for the first time, 'so soon, yes. We – we'll know – that is, I don't know. I came on the railroad pass – cabooses – old hard-bench coaches – Texas – played flute and wooden sweet potato all the way.' He took out his new wooden flute. He played a few squeaky notes on it and jumped up and down in his stocking feet. 'See?' he said. 'But of course, Sal, I can talk as soon as ever and have many things to say to you in fact with my own little bangtail mind I've

288

been reading and reading this gone Proust all the way across the country and digging a great number of things I'll never have TIME to tell you about and we STILL haven't talked of Mexico and our parting there in fever – but no need to talk. Absolutely, now, yes?'

'All right, we won't talk.' And he started telling the story of what he did in LA on the way over in every possible detail, how he visited a family, had dinner, talked to the father, the sons, the sisters – what they looked like, what they ate, their furnishings, their thoughts, their interests, their very souls; it took him three hours of detailed elucidation, and having concluded this he said, 'Ah, but you see what I wanted to REALLY tell you – much later – Arkansas, crossing on train, – playing flute – play cards with boys, my dirty deck – won money, blew sweet-potato solo – for sailors. Long long awful trip five days and five nights just to SEE you, Sal.'

'What about Camille?'

'Gave permission of course – waiting for me. Camille and I all straight forever-and-ever ...'

'And Inez?'

'I – I – I want her to come back to Frisco with me live other side of town – don't you think? Don't know why I came.' Later he said in a sudden moment of gaping wonder, 'Well and yes, of course, I wanted to see your sweet girl and you – glad of you – love you as ever.' He stayed in New York three days and hastily made preparations to get back on the train with his rail-road passes and again recross the continent, five days and five nights in dusty coaches and hard-bench crummies, and of course we had no money for a truck and couldn't go back with him. With Inez he spent one night explaining and sweating and fighting, and she threw him out. A letter came for him, care of me. I saw it. It was from Camille. 'My heart broke when I saw you go across the tracks with your bag. I pray and pray you get back safe. ... I do want Sal and his friend to come and live on the same street. ... I know you'll make it but I can't help worrying – now that we've decided everything. ... Dear Dean, it's the end of the first half of the century. Welcome with love and kisses to spend the other half with us. We all wait for you. [Signed] Camille, Amy, and Little Joanie.' So Dean's life was settled with his most constant, most embittered, and best-knowing wife Camille, and I thanked God for him.

The last time I saw him it was under sad and strange circumstances. Remi Boncœur had arrived in New York after having gone around the world several times in ships. I wanted him to meet and know Dean. They did meet, but Dean couldn't talk any more and said nothing, and Remi turned away. Remi had gotten tickets for the Duke Ellington concert at the Metropolitan Opera and insisted Laura and I come with him and his girl. Remi was fat and sad now but still the eager and formal gentleman, and he wanted to do things the *right* way, as he emphasized. So he got his bookie to drive us to the concert in a Cadillac. It was a cold winter night. The Cadillac was parked and ready to go. Dean stood outside the windows with his bag, ready to go to Penn Station and on across the land.

'Good-bye, Dean,' I said. 'I sure wish I didn't have to go to the concert.'

'D'you think I can ride to Fortieth Street with you?' he whispered. 'Want to be with you as much as possible, m'boy, and besides it's so durned cold in this here New Yawk ...' I whispered to Remi. No, he wouldn't have it, he liked me but he didn't like my idiot friends. I was going to start all over again ruining his planned evenings as I had done at Alfred's in San Francisco in 1947 with Roland Major.

'Absolutely out of the question, Sal!' Poor Remi, he had a special necktie made for this evening; on it was painted a replica of the concert tickets, and the names Sal and Laura and Remi and Vicki, the girl, together with a series of sad jokes and some of his favourite sayings such as 'You can't teach the old maestro a new tune'.

So Dean couldn't ride uptown with us and the only thing I could do was sit in the back of the Cadillac and wave at him. The bookie at the wheel also wanted nothing to do with Dean. Dean, ragged in a motheaten overcoat he brought specially for the freezing temperatures of the East, walked off alone, and the last I saw of him he rounded the corner of Seventh Avenue, eyes on the street ahead, and bent to it again. Poor little Laura, my baby, to whom I'd told everything about Dean, began almost to cry.

'Oh, we shouldn't let him go like this. What'll we do?'

Old Dean's gone, I thought, and out loud I said, 'He'll be all right.' And off we went to the sad and disinclined concert for which I had no stomach whatever and all the time I was thinking of Dean and how he got back on the train and rode over three thousand miles over that awful land and never knew why he had come anyway, except to see me.

So in America when the sun goes down and I sit on the old broken-down river pier watching the long, long skies over New Jersey and sense all that raw land that rolls in one unbelievable huge bulge over to the West Coast, and all that road going, all the people dreaming in the immensity of it, and in Iowa I know by now the children must be crying in the land where they let the children cry, and tonight the stars'll be out, and don't you know that God is Pooh Bear? the evening star must be drooping and shedding her sparkler dims on the prairie, which is just before the coming of complete night that blesses the earth, darkens all rivers, cups the peaks and folds the final shore in, and nobody, nobody knows what's going to happen to anybody besides the forlorn rags of growing old, I think of Dean Moriarty, I even think of Old Dean Moriarty the father we never found, I think of Dean Moriarty.

MORE ABOUT PENGUINS

Penguinews, which appears every month, contains details of all the new books issued by Penguins as they are published. From time to time it is supplemented by *Penguins in Print*, which is a complete list of all available books published by Penguins. (There are well over three thousand of these.)

A specimen copy of *Penguinews* will be sent to you free on request, and you can become a subscriber for the price of the postage. For a year's issues (including the complete lists) please send 30p if you live in the United Kingdom, or 60p if you live elsewhere. Just write to Dept EP, Penguin Books Ltd, Harmondsworth, Middlesex, enclosing a cheque or postal order, and your name will be added to the mailing list.

Note: *Penguinews* and *Penguins in Print* are not available in the U.S.A. or Canada